SECRETS

RAY ALLISON

Tellwell Talent
www.tellwell.ca

ISBN
978-0-2288-6476-9 (Paperback)
978-0-2288-6477-6 (eBook)

PROLOGUE

"*W*ill you pick up more bread on your way home? And can you go by the local farm to pick up a dozen fresh eggs? And I hope you remember to collect the dry cleaning that you forgot yesterday. And by the way, have you seen my reading glasses anywhere?"

Isabel had slipped her shoes on and was opening the front door for a quick escape. Heavens above! Would this torture ever cease?

Biting her lip, she turned around briefly to answer, "Yes!" to every query except the last one. "Try looking in the living room, Doug. You were watching TV last night."

She gave the door a yank, grabbed her briefcase and began running down the garden path before he could ask her anything else. As she unlocked the car door, out of the corner of her eye she could see Doug on the doorstep, motioning for her to wait. She ignored him, backed her car out of the driveway and sped away.

'Why did I ever invite him to move in with me? I guess I was sorry for him when his wife died last year, barely a month after he'd retired from his job at the local newspaper. Even if he were lonely in their apartment, I should have let him fall

on his own feet. But no, I had to invite my older brother to share my house. I never realized that he'd changed so much over the years.'

As she drove through the morning traffic she continued fretting over her problem, wondering if she had been too selfish in wanting someone to look after the house while she was travelling to give her lectures. It seemed a good idea to have someone else living at home. It especially made sense for both of them to share the costs of the house.

Such worrying thoughts were interrupted by the need to concentrate on driving into the correct lane to exit the highway, but when she was safely on the quiet road that led to her workplace the familiarity of her surroundings gave her time to continue her self-doubting.

'I should have remembered how over-protective he was while we were growing up. In his eyes I'm still his little sister. But his constant questioning and worrying are driving me crazy! I can't stand it! How am I going to get out of this? My life is stressful enough without Doug adding to the mix. But I can't ask him to leave since he's the only family I have now. No, I'm well and truly stuck with him.'

With this sense of helplessness, she turned into her own parking place at the Boston National Institute of Robotics, ready to start the workday and leave all her troubles behind.

CHAPTER 1

$\mathcal{P}$assing Security, Isabel took the elevator to her second floor office with its adjoining laboratories. It always felt good to be back on her own familiar territory. That morning she was interviewing an up-and-coming scientist. Her home worries faded as she began to read his credentials.

"Hmm," she muttered as she read, "If you believe everything that's written here, this Vincente Da Cosa seems to be a genius. He took Top Honors in his degree programs and has accolades from his professors for being a brilliant, innovative, and knowledgeable researcher. He even has a degree in psychology. Sounds too good to be true!"

She checked his C.V. and noticed that there was no account for the past four years. *'Strange error! Wonder what he's been doing?'* Isabel replaced the typewritten sheets in a folder to make her way to the interview room. But although she was early, the aspiring scientist was already sitting in the chair opposite the desk. Isabel was not pleased. She made a mental note to find out which staff-member had let him in.

He rose to greet her with a firm handshake and a broad smile. He didn't seem nervous and that was always a good sign. She motioned him to sit down and as Isabel went through the ritual of interviewing, she was watching him closely. He was certainly very self-assured, answering every question confidently and in great detail. Vincente Da Cosa seemed to have a wealth of knowledge about the new advances being made in their mutual fields of computer science, artificial intelligence and robotics.

"So, what do you know about deep-learning and neural networks?"

"These are presently being used but I see the need for a master algorithm to unite the future progress of artificial intelligence," Vincente replied.

He had touched on a favorite topic for computer scientists. Both of them became animated, discussing that elusive master algorithm with its prospect of being able to hold unbelievably vast quantities of data that was especially important for robotics. Isabel almost forgot that this was only a preliminary interview.

'He's certainly an interesting person', she thought as she sat back to consider him. 'Very personable, with those dark eyes and black hair that he ruffles with his fingers while he's talking. Quite charming, the way he shrugs when he's animated. He must be well into his thirties now, after finishing all his degrees. Seems mature enough and knows a great deal about artificial intelligence. Very impressive indeed!'

Their exchange of ideas flowed freely. With a master algorithm, it would be possible to select any individual and compile all that person's habits and characteristics, beliefs and thought processes. It could store information of whom and what the person cared about, as well as indicating how that individual would behave in various situations. In effect, it would be able to store intelligence data that totally personified a particular individual. It would be possible to create an 'alter ego' of the original subject. A robot that was the exact replica of a person. Fascinating!

She forgot to ask him about those missing four years of his background.

CHAPTER 2

A sharp knock on the door of the interview room startled Isabel. She jumped up from her seat to confront the man who was entering.

"Yes? What do you want?" she asked irritably, "You're interrupting an interview."

"But I have an appointment for an interview with you. I've come at the specified time," he said amiably. "You are Dr. Lindsay?"

Isabel glanced at her timetable. "What's your name?" she asked.

"My name is Vincente Da Cosa."

She turned her head to look at the person sitting opposite her, "Then who are you?" she demanded.

"I'm Vincente Da Cosa too," came his reply.

She was stunned. After a brief pause to collect her thoughts, she said, "You look like identical twins. Are you trying to trick me? Do you both want a job here? Is that it? If so, this is not the way to go about it."

The person who had entered the room replied reasonably, "No, we can't be twins with the same name."

Isabel was beginning to get angry, "Then what's going on here? Why are you both trying to confuse me?"

She was about to call Security when the newest arrival closed the office door firmly behind him, saying, "Can't you tell that one of us is a robot? You, of all people, should be able to tell a robot from a real person."

In response to this discourteous statement, she started scrutinizing both of them. They were as alike as two peas in a pod, and they were both watching her intently with that same charming smile on their similarly alert faces. Then, as if in unison, they both ruffled their black hair and smiled at her.

Isabel shuddered and backed into her chair, her mind racing.

'One of them is a robot? Really? That's hard to believe! More likely they're identical twins having fun at my expense. But, why? What could these two men possibly hope to achieve by this charade?'

She cleared her throat. "And what if I say that I don't believe that one of you is a robot? What proof can you offer me?"

She continued, "So far, I have only your word for something that's totally improbable."

The man who had just entered, drew a chair up to her desk. Now there were two identical faces in front of her. She pushed her chair further away.

"If we demonstrate the fact, would you consider that to be worthy of a post in your department?" asked the man she had been interviewing.

Isabel bristled at this temerity. "No, I will not be a party to your blackmail tactics. Show me proof that one of you is a robot, or leave!"

"Please give me one moment and I will put my companion to sleep," requested the newcomer. He drew a small device from his coat pocket and pressed some buttons. The man she had been interviewing froze in his chair.

Isabel could feel her face beginning to burn. She gritted her teeth, realizing that she had been exchanging ideas with a robot. Vincente was watching her closely to see how she would react. She was frowning and did not look pleased. He hurried to fill in the awkward silence.

"I'm sorry if you think that I was trying to trick you," he began, "But I thought that this was the quickest way to gain your attention for my discovery. For the last four years with the help of other scientists, I have been creating my own alter ego as you can see."

"Why?" Isabel asked shortly, still smarting from being tricked by this stranger.

"Because I wanted to test what I think will be a master algorithm that can store huge amounts of data. Like scientists the world over, I decided to be my own guinea pig and store all the facets of what I am as a person in a robot's database. I wanted to create a humanoid that could act and think as I do. And here it is. It is so like me that even you thought it was real."

Isabel squirmed in her chair at this true statement, but he certainly had managed to capture her full attention.

"You mean that this robot 'clone' can think and behave exactly like you do?"

"That is correct. In every way."

"But why?" she asked again, determined not to show how excited she was by this new technical development unfolding in front of her. '*What a find for her department!*'

Vincente leaned forward, "Because I can trust it to do the jobs that I'm too busy to do or don't want to do."

"Such as?"

"If I have to give a talk when I don't want to travel or I am too busy, I can insert the lecture information into my robot's database and send him instead. I know that he will do as good a job as I would do if I were there in person."

In spite of her annoyance, Isabel had a sudden appreciation of how useful that option could be in her own crowded life.

"What about the questions that come up after a talk?" she asked.

"We both know that some questions are predictable, so I can program those answers in beforehand. And I would add a concluding statement that there was no more question time left, in order to end the session."

"Don't you think that you would be defrauding the public?" Isabel persisted.

"No. I would ask the organizers beforehand if they want to announce that a robot will be giving the talk. Or we could come to some agreement to inform the audience about the robot either before or after the lecture. Everything would be above board, one way or another."

"And what do you think the audience reaction would be?"

"I'm sure that most of the audience will be delighted to have had a lecture from a humanoid robot that looks like the lecturer who was supposed to give the talk. You'll always have a few who might disagree of course." He shrugged as if those were negligible.

Isabel was aware that the scientist was watching for her reaction as she thought, '*This Vincente da Cosa seems to have an answer for everything. But maybe he's just a little too glib to be credible.*'

"You know that I can't accept your word for all this?" she asked, looking at him over her dark-rimmed reading glasses.

Vincente became excited. "Yes, of course! We are both scientists. So, I am inviting you to attend my first experimental lecture. Tomorrow evening at Boston University, at seven. Will you come?"

Isabel had the uncomfortable feeling that she was being very skillfully manipulated by this enthusiastic scientist who was looking at her so intently. But she had to admit that she was also intrigued by this totally astounding and novel situation that had arrived out of the blue.

She stood up abruptly, nearly knocking over her chair. "Leave all the details and I will let you know," she answered gruffly.

Looking at his application, she continued, "I have your phone number so I will call you to let you know if I can attend."

Vincente da Cosa had also risen to his feet and now he shook her hand firmly. Bowing slightly, he said, "Until we meet again, Dr. Lindsay."

Activating his look-alike robot, he walked out of her office.

As Isabel watched them go, too distracted to even wonder how both of them could get past the front door Security, she sank back into her chair.

Her hands were trembling slightly as she thought about the bizarre interview that had just taken place. If she hadn't witnessed it herself, she would think it were some fantasy, thought up by a wishful scientist.

"A robot that's the spitting image of yourself and can behave exactly how you behave and can think freely too! Now that was something to only dream about until now!" she muttered. "I could think of ways in which that could be very useful. Hmm, needs more thinking about."

Still musing, turning over in her mind more emerging ideas, she gathered up her papers and went in search of a very strong coffee.

CHAPTER 3

The next evening, Isabel was seated near the front of the Boston University lecture hall. From her vantage point, she had an unimpeded view of the lectern on the stage, where the robot would be giving Vincente's talk to the students. She could watch its every movement.

An excited buzz of talk came from the restless student body around her. She looked at their fresh young faces and thought back some twenty or more years to when she was a student as enthusiastic as they seemed to be.

'*How naïve I was then!*' she thought, '*I had no idea where it would lead when I chose to study Computer Science, no idea that the rapid pace of modern technology would alter everyone's world. No idea of the burgeoning discoveries and information that everyone tries to keep up with nowadays.*'

Isabel opened her large leather purse to extract a notebook and her pen. After being at a computer all day long, she felt the welcome relief of using these simpler materials, though she noted that the youngsters beside her were well equipped with I-phones and I-pads. Leaning back comfortably, she waited for the talk to begin. When would the announcement be made that the lecture was to be delivered by a robot? It would be interesting to see how these students reacted.

As if in answer to her unspoken question, the robot strode on to the stage and began to shuffle papers at the lectern while a professor welcomed Vincente da Cosa to the university. There was no other announcement to the audience, only that there would be a brief mid-lecture break to allow students who were due at other classes to leave, while others just finished their classes could enter.

'Bit unusual,' Isabel thought, *'but probably a good idea to have a seventh innings stretch to allow people to renew their concentration. Artificial Intelligence isn't easy to understand.'*

The lecture began. After a few minutes, she was mentally praising the robot as it looked and acted completely human and natural, even walking across the stage to engage the audience's attention while informing everyone of what could be achieved with modern technology. Isabel was so intrigued that she forgot to make notes and was quite sorry when the mid-talk break came. The robot walked off the stage.

'I guess it's not primed to answer questions at this point,' she thought.

When the second half of the talk was finished and questions were satisfactorily answered, the students gave Vincente a standing ovation. There could be no doubt that the lecture had been a complete success. The professor reappeared to give the usual vote of thanks but instead, he said, "I have a question for the audience now. Who knows who gave the lecture?"

There was a buzz of puzzlement from the audience. What did he mean?

A student shouted out, "Dr. Vincente Da Cosa of course. You already told us that at the beginning."

Instead of replying, the professor beckoned off stage and the other Vincente walked up to him. The students were now faced with two beings looking exactly alike.

"One of these is the real Vincente and the other is his look-alike humanoid robot. So, I ask you again, which one gave the lecture?" the professor persisted.

Those students who were about to collect their belongings stopped short to listen and some of them began to hazard guesses, until Vincente himself stepped forward to say that he had given the first half of the lecture and the robot had delivered the second half.

There was a moment of silence as the audience digested that new information. Then someone called out the question that Isabel herself had previously asked, "But we don't know if you're the real Vincente da Cosa. Perhaps you're the robot."

The audience erupted into good-natured laughter. Isabel began to smile at the absurdity of the situation.

When the scientist demonstrated how he controlled the robot, more spontaneous applause broke out. After being thanked for the lecture, Vincente and the robot both bowed and were shepherded off the stage by the professor.

She turned to go, joining the students as they exited the hall. As she tucked away her pen and notepad, she couldn't help overhearing what some of the crowd were saying.

"Can you believe we were actually listening to a robot?"

"Best lecture I've heard so far this term." "Fantastic though, when you come to think about it!"

Isabel hid a smile as one wit said, "I wonder how many of our university teachers are really robots."

In the laughter that followed this remark, she observed busy thumbs at work and realized that the evening's unusual lecture was about to hit the social media.

CHAPTER 4

$\mathcal{O}$utside the university, the summer sky was beginning to fade from a rosy hue into a hazy twilight. Isabel checked her watch. It was only nine o'clock. The lecture had kept to schedule. As she watched the cheerful crowd of students dispersing in different directions, no doubt heading to some favorite eating or drinking place, she felt a strong sense of loss for her own carefree student days. Where had her young sense of adventure gone since then? Lost, somewhere in the depths of computer science?

Vincente's lecture had strangely disturbed her. She fastened the clasp of the seatbelt in her car, thinking, *'I don't feel like going home to talk to Doug. I don't even want to talk to Vincente yet, though he's probably too busy at the moment, explaining his research to the university faculty.'*

Isabel stared out into the gloom and noticed the strands of lights shining across Boston Bridge. She could see students walking there, high above the Charles River, chatting amongst themselves.

"Well, nothing else to do," she decided, "I might as well go back over the bridge too." Isabel started the car and drove back to her office.

Once inside, in the quietness of the workday's end and next to strangely silent labs, she sat at her desk toying with papers, trying to identify what was causing her present dissatisfaction.

Was she jealous of Vincente's tremendous achievements in the robotic field? Or was she discontent with the unfolding of her own career? Where had her ambition gone? Did she really want to spend the rest of her life interviewing candidates and progressing up the government ladder instead of doing her own research?

Scientists like Vincente were surging ahead, breaking boundaries and making their names famous, while she sat imprisoned behind a desk. Unable to sit still, Isabel went to make some coffee though she knew it would keep her awake that night. But then, so would her present discomfort if she didn't find some way to solve it.

It was much later that she reached home at the same time as Doug. She had forgotten that this was his weekly evening out at the pub with his former newspaper colleagues. Unfortunately, he wanted to talk, even if she didn't.

"You'll never guess what we were discussing tonight," he began as they hung up their coats in the little glassed-in porch full of potted plants.

Isabel tossed off her shoes. "No, what?" she responded shortly.

He followed her into the kitchen. "Robots!" he said.

She half-listened as she filled a glass with water from the filter tap but she perked up as he continued, "The guys were watching some scientist give a lecture at Boston University on the TV. But it turned out that it was a robot giving the lecture and not a real person. What do you think of that? Robots are taking over the world!"

"But I was at there tonight," Isabel corrected him. "The robot didn't give the whole lecture. Besides, I didn't know it was being televised. I didn't see any cameras."

"Well, must have been hidden cameras then, because we saw it on TV," her brother answered cheerfully, "And we all had a good laugh at the joke being played on the students. They're all supposed to be studying computer science so they should have known the difference between a real person and a robot. These young people nowadays! Absolutely clueless! But the guys agreed it makes good newspaper copy."

She was going to inform him of how that lecture came about-before he got going about the shortcomings of modern youth-but shut her lips firmly. Opening them just long enough to wish Doug, 'Goodnight,' she escaped to her bedroom to think over everything that had happened that evening.

CHAPTER 5

True to her premonition, she endured a restless night and red-eyed, was late appearing in the kitchen next morning. Doug was already up, whistling while cooking omelets. He slipped her breakfast in front of her and she automatically began eating. The fluffy eggs were cooked to perfection and the filling of ham, cheese and spinach seasoned so skillfully, that she had to admit that her brother was an excellent cook. She praised his skill.

"Had to learn while Mary was ill as she couldn't do anything by the end. I think I have a flair for cooking. Here's your toast and marmalade."

He sat down and began eating his own breakfast, "Hmm. Not bad, even if I do say so myself. I think I've found another interest in life, Isabel. Cooking is like science. Creative too. I like that."

Isabel asked if he needed any groceries that day, but he said that he intended to go out himself, so she was soon in her car driving to work, unencumbered by having to remember what to pick up on the way home. Her car ride to the NIR was when she indulged in her mind-monologues and it wasn't long before her thoughts were keeping pace with the traffic.

'After last night and all the media publicity, Vincente will be becoming very well known. I wonder if he still wants a job with the NIR? There must be lots of businesses that would count him an asset. I can think of two corporations in Boston that would welcome his creativity for their robot manufacturing. They might offer to pay him a big salary. Will the NIR be able to afford him?'

Turning off the highway, she muttered, "I was going to recommend him to my superiors for a post with us. I've already thought of some useful research he can do. But there are still things I need to know about him. What was he doing for those missing four years on his application? Why does he want to work for the government? What is he not telling me?"

Isabel parked her car at the Institute and went inside, curious to see what revelations this day would bring.

As she passed security, one of the guards informed her that there was a man waiting for her by the front door.

She turned to see Vincente sitting there. As she went over to greet him, she wondered what he had done with his 'alter ego' robot. It was nowhere to be seen. Or was this the robot again with an absent human being? She straightened her shoulders, determined to be on her guard this time.

Vincente jumped up as he saw her coming towards him. He looked very excited. Isabel noticed that his dark hair was tousled and his shirt askew as if he had just got out of bed and haphazardly thrown on his clothes. Unconsciously, she patted her own hair to see if she had combed it properly.

He came up to her to take her hand and holding it over his heart, he said, "I have such good news to tell you. I came here as fast as I could."

Isabel's face flushed as she snatched her hand away. "Then you had better come up to my office after you've passed security. I'll go on ahead."

She walked into the elevator wondering why this man always managed to fluster her. She waited at her desk hands firmly folded.

Her office door was thrown open wide and Vincente rushed towards her. "Quick, Dr. Lindsay, turn on your television."

Taken aback, she faltered, "It's in the next room."

"Come quickly! There's a new robot being introduced at a news conference. By a colleague of mine. You'll find this interesting."

He had continued barging through to the adjoining room and had found the TV station by the time she reached him. Without preamble, he began explaining by pointing to the screen.

"This is Dr. Stanley, a colleague of mine. Today, he and his team are revealing a humanoid robot called Andrew. It looks like any young man you might meet on the street, but it can move and talk, think, solve problems and assess situations faster than any human being can. It has a superior computer memory and even recognizes people it has met before. Let's watch Stanley demonstrate what it can do."

After looking for a while, Isabel became restless. Her foot started tapping on the floor.

"A few more minutes, please, Dr. Lindsay. I want you to see Stanley's team. Ah! Here they come."

Three more scientists appeared on screen and were introduced as Dr. Dorothy Hardy from England, Dr. Susie Mitzumi from Japan, and a Mexican named Dr. José Rivera.

Vincente was beaming, "Look, a perfect international team of scientists."

"Yes, yes," Isabel agreed. "They're making a breakthrough into the commercial world, but your own robot is much more advanced, being an exact copy of a particular person. This one looks like any other human being."

Vincente, looking a little crestfallen, turned off the television.

"I wanted you to see the team I've been working with for the last four years," he explained. "Dr. Stanley allowed me to share his private laboratory facilities in New Mexico while I was creating my own robot. We helped one another solve many problems. Their goal is to make more robots like Andrew, to provide help for people who can't do things for themselves."

"My robot only helps me," he added, sounding almost regretful.

As they moved back into the main office, Isabel realized that he had now skillfully accounted for the missing years on his application. Once more behind her desk, she addressed the question of those missing years.

"Why didn't you write those years into your CV? Why leave that time space blank?"

Pushing his unruly mop of dark hair out of his eyes, he sat down facing her.

Spreading his arms wide, he said, "I had to wait until they unveiled Andrew. Their rich benefactor wanted their work to be kept secret until the robot was finished and tested in public. The team has had one previous disappointment, so he didn't want the same thing to happen again. They asked me to join them because they needed more up-to-date robot-control technology. We shared our resources working on both our robots."

He laid his hand over his heart, his dark eyes warmly regarding her, "For which I will be forever grateful."

Isabel hid a smile at this dramatic gesture, thinking, *'Really, this Dr. Da Cosa is too much!'*

Without warning, her visitor changed the subject. "But, Dr. Lindsay, how did you enjoy the lecture last evening? I saw you sitting near the front, but you had gone by the time I was free to leave."

He leaned forward attentively, his eyes shining. Isabel unconsciously backed her chair away. Her mind seemed sluggish compared to her visitor's lightning switches of conversation. She tried to gather her thoughts, still distracted by his new revelations of working with an international team of experts in a secret laboratory in New Mexico.

That team of scientists had managed to create not one, but two different robots. She knew that they were well ahead of what was presently happening in the Boston NIR labs.

Again, she wondered why Vincente wanted to work for the government in a National Institute when he had access to well-funded labs in New Mexico. He was the most infuriatingly secretive individual she had ever met.

"I was very impressed by your evening lecture," Isabel began carefully, "The students seemed to enjoy its novelty too. I wasn't aware that it was being televised but with that and the students texting to various social medias, I wouldn't be surprised if you have become an overnight celebrity."

Vincente's face lit up at her praise. "But you are right, Dr. Lindsay, I was awakened very early this morning by phone calls from people I've never even met. It seems that everyone knows how to get my phone number and they all want to talk to me."

He turned the full force of his charming smile on Isabel. That only resulted in her becoming irritated at seeing him bask so obviously in his own glory. This man was certainly no shrinking violet.

"No doubt you will be receiving other job offers now?" she queried. "May I ask why you want to work at the NIR when you can do research in New Mexico with your international team?"

Her visitor looked at her in astonishment.

"But of course, I would much rather accept a research post here. After all, the NIR is world famous and it's backed by the U.S. government."

He paused, drew a deep breath and added darkly, "And I may need government protection in the future."

"Protection?" Isabel echoed incredulously, "What do you mean?"

Vincente leaned over her desk towards her and lowering his voice, whispered, "There are people in the world who would like nothing better than to have a robot exactly like themselves. And not always for good or lawful purposes."

Isabel drew closer to him in order to hear him more clearly.

"Who, for instance?" she demanded.

"Why, criminals in the Mafia who want to be in two places at once or foreign dictators who fear assassination attempts. Think how useful it would be for them to have a robot that acts exactly like they do. They could send out the robot to do what has to be done while safely staying at home themselves!"

Her fair hair and his dark head were now close together as Isabel digested this new twist in the potential use of 'alter ego' robots. Realizing their proximity, she hastily pulled back.

She asked incredulously, "And do you really think our government can protect you from those people?"

Vincente sat up in his chair. "If foreign powers want to have my research or have me create a robot for them, then I want the government to make that decision. I will do whatever it decides. I do not want to be personally responsible for providing look-alike robots to criminals and dictators. But if I am an employee here, higher authorities will have to make the decision. Not I. I think that would be so, is it not?"

To Isabel, it was a novel idea that the Institute she worked for could offer its employees protection against criminals. But then, she had never met anyone like Vincente, with such a quick mind for benefitting himself. Was there no end to his ingenuity?

Watching him shrug as if to suggest that this was a totally understandable situation, she squared her own shoulders.

"If you're expecting the NIR to protect you, you might have a long wait. Should I set in motion the paperwork recommending you for the present vacancy here, you must realize that by the time it has moved through all the channels of the upper echelon, it could be many months before you hear from the Institute. In the meantime, you will be on your own."

Her fellow scientist jumped to his feet.

"But, Dr. Lindsay, I cannot wait that long! Can't you speed up the process?"

He paced up and down before rounding on her. "I don't want to be hounded by evil people who want me to make robot copies of themselves."

She studied him quietly before replying.

"Why don't you go back to New Mexico to work with your other scientific colleagues? Once they sell Andrew, there'll be a demand for more robots like that. Maybe they would welcome your help again."

"But now everyone knows about me here, I need to continue to be in the public eye, not hidden in New Mexico," he objected. "People forget easily."

"You can always leave your robot-self here, to do performances and you can be working in another place. Isn't that what you programmed it to do for you?" she suggested sweetly.

Vincente sat down slowly. "Dr. Lindsay, you have a point. But I have the feeling that you have more to say on this topic?"

"Yes, I have. I've given much thought to your application and I feel that you would be a good candidate for our vacant post, so I would be ready to recommend you. On one condition."

"And that is?"

He waited impatiently until she continued slowly, "If you agree, I think we can arrange something to fill your spare time until you hear the outcome of your application to the NIR. However, it will mean that you will have to return to those labs in New Mexico, as it would be a secret assignment. Would you like to hear about it?"

Now intrigued, he nodded and drew his chair closer to her desk.

Soon their two heads were together again as Isabel carefully outlined her plan. After asking many questions and ironing out the logistics of the project, Vincente agreed that he could do what she proposed, providing that she could find the funds to pay for the venture.

They would have to set up a secure communications mechanism so he could have questions answered immediately. The internet was not always reliable, so it was agreed that they each purchase a disposable cellphone and keep those solely for their project communications.

Later when he left her office, he was thinking that this lady was almost as clever as he was. He was intrigued by her proposed project. He thought that he might even make a profit on the deal as he had materials on hand from his own robot, Vincente Two. She didn't know about those, but he could still charge her for them.

He smiled to himself. Ah, a clever lady, but not clever enough.

CHAPTER 6

*I*sabel sat in her office turning over in her mind various strategies to fund the venture she had asked Vincente to undertake. It was an expensive proposition and there was no way that she could pay for it herself. She sat writing down options for obtaining the money but ended up by scrapping all of them.

It was evident that there was only one place that had enough money in its budget for this type of venture. But that meant interesting the NIR officials in how it might be to the Institute's benefit to fund it. She needed more advice. After a while, she put in a call to Gwen, her superior officer, and arranged to meet with her that afternoon.

In the meantime, she did as she had promised and sent Vincente's job application on its steep climb up the management ladder of the NIR. Hopefully, it would advance to the pertinent government agency that would eventually decide on the scientist's fate.

'If they are interested in him, Vincente will have to return for more interviews. I hope he won't try to be too clever and send his robot instead. He's so unpredictable.'

She rolled her eyes thinking about what he might do.

The subject of her misgivings was busy making arrangements to keep his rented rooms for a longer period of time. He intended to leave his robot inside his apartment where nobody would disturb it and where it could be programmed from his personal computer. If anyone saw it enter or leave, they would think it was the scientist himself. He felt quite at ease with this arrangement.

That settled, his active mind began reliving his recent visit to the NIR. He was getting more and more interested in Dr. Lindsay's project, looking at it from many angles. *'It seems simple enough but now I think about it, I might just add a few ideas of my own. Yes, there's always space for more sophistication and she would never need to know.'*

Then switching to his travel arrangements, *'But first, I should get in touch with Stanley to see if I can use the facilities in New Mexico while his team is here in Boston.'*

He managed to reach Stanley by phone and was greeted excitedly, "Oh, Vincente! We've already had some offers to buy our robot, Andrew. We didn't think it would happen so fast but evidently there's a great deal of interest in using robots for people who need extra care."

Vincente was about to reply but his colleague rambled on.

"Our sponsor is handling all the finances and he's extremely pleased with his negotiations. It's good to know that his faith in our research has finally paid off. He says that he's intending to expand our buildings in New Mexico to give us all bigger labs so that we can make more robots."

Stanley sounded gleeful. "We might even hire more scientists. Would you be interested in joining us?"

Vincente laughed. "I'm glad for your well-deserved success, Stanley. Your sponsor must be making a great deal of money with your humanoid robot, to be able to plough some of it back into better facilities for you and the team. Thanks for your job offer but I'm about to start a new project myself."

His fellow scientist was instantly curious.

"I hear that you were an overnight sensation after your lecture featuring your look-alike robot. How are you going to follow that triumph? What are you intending to work on next?"

Vincente smiled. "You know how secretive we scientists are about our research, so I can't tell you at the moment. But I do have a question for you! May I continue to work at the New Mexico complex until I finish this new project? Or will there be construction going on?"

"No problem! We are all busy here in town at present and the plans for the new labs haven't been drawn up yet. So, feel free to use what lab facilities you need. You know where everything is. But if you want to use the main computer, you'll need our new passwords. We change them frequently. I prefer to give you the passwords privately. Can you come by our hotel before we leave Boston?"

Vincente agreed to meet him within the hour and after a final check with Isabel to say that their project was feasible, he packed his bags and set out for the Castle Hotel, where he met Stanley at the front desk.

"I need to tell you some other things you should know about our labs in New Mexico. Have you time for lunch?" Stanley asked.

Seated across from one another in the hotel's sunny cafeteria with their sandwiches in front of them and a light breeze coming through an open window, stirring the leaves of the indoor dwarf palm trees, the two scientists got down to business. Stanley exchanged the relevant passwords with Vincente, also giving him a personal cellphone number where he could be reached at all times.

Stanley leaned over the table towards his companion, "A word in your ear. You need to be aware of some adverse reaction from the townspeople to our lab."

Vincente looked puzzled as this was news to him.

Stanley continued, "For some reason, some of the locals look on the lab complex with some suspicion that we are doing unlawful things there."

"What sort of illegal things?"

"Well, in the past, we had a visit from the local sheriff who wanted to know if we were harboring illegal women. Of-course it was all nonsense, but you should be on your guard if the sheriff comes around again. I know you won't be inviting strange women to the complex, but you need to know that every move you make will be watched."

His fellow scientist was intrigued, his quick mind racing with many possibilities of why the strange suspicion had started.

"If anyone from the town saw that first robot you made, could they have mistaken it for a human female? What was your robot called again? Oh, yes! Andrea. Did they ever see it?"

To Stanley's discomfort, Vincente asked, "Whatever happened to it? You never told me."

Stanley regarded him with astonishment. "I had no idea that your mind worked so deviously, Vincente. Andrea was another matter altogether. They might have seen it, but that's nothing to do what I'm saying. I'm just warning you to be aware of 'small town' reactions while you're there. Be on your guard."

After Vincente had left, the scientist sat toying with a spoon, while his tea cooled rapidly in front of him. He was uncomfortable about how fast and adeptly his fellow scientist had put his finger on the crux of the problem that they had had with Andrea. Yes, she had appeared to be human to other people, like the townsfolk. Furthermore, the robot had developed independent ways of thinking that took her out of their control. But on the positive side and learning from their mistakes, they had made sure that Andrew, their newly introduced robot, was controllable and traceable.

Stanley's dismay had increased when his companion had asked what had happened to Andrea. He hoped that Vincente wouldn't try to find out. There was no knowing how his fellow scientist's mind worked or what he might do if he did discover the truth about Andrea.

Stanley gestured to the waitress for the bill. By the time he walked out of the cafeteria, he was gnawing on his lip.

'Am I being too helpful, giving him the passwords to the big computer in the lab? Did anyone leave information on it about where Andrea is now? If they did, Vincente is sure to find it. Norma would know what was left on the computer. I'll check with her. I can't have Vincente nosing around.'

As he was riding the elevator to his room, he was turning the problem over and over in his troubled mind.

'I've only known Vincente since he came to work with us on his own robot. But former colleagues vouched for him then and he was very co-operative with the team, sometimes even giving us advice. We were all working on humanoid robots. He seemed responsible enough then.'

Stanley unlocked the door of his room but once inside, came to a firm decision that was quite unlike his usual kindly, trusting self.

"No help for it!" he muttered aloud. "I can't be worrying all the time about what Vincente may be doing in the labs. I'm going to have to change the password for the main computer. If Vincente wants to use it, he'll have to ask my permission. Then I could ask him what he wants to use it for."

After changing the password on his main computer, he felt much more at ease with the situation and began to concentrate on their next port of call with their new robot, Andrew.

Stanley began thinking about New York City.

CHAPTER 7

*A*t the NIR, Isabel was seated in front of Gwen's desk. Gwen was not only her immediate superior in the management hierarchy but also a good friend, who often accompanied her to musical concerts. Both of them being classical music lovers, a Mahler concert was their idea of a wonderful evening. Their favorite outing was attending the traditional Boston Pops.

Isabel was hoping that Gwen would have a similar affinity to the project that she was nervously about to outline to her.

"Well, Isabel, did you want to see me about some trouble you're dealing with?"

"Not really, Gwen. Just the opposite in fact. I wanted to tell you about a scientist who has applied for that vacant post in our labs. I'm sure that you will want to know about him. In my opinion, he's quite unique."

Gwen's curiosity was aroused. She leaned back comfortably in her chair, giving her full attention to her colleague's explanation of why this man was so special.

Isabel took a deep breath and began by telling her how Vincente Da Cosa had presented himself and his look-alike robot when he had arrived at her office to be interviewed. She followed that story with her visit to Boston University to listen to his lecture to the students. Gwen perked up in her chair.

"I saw that lecture on Boston News TV. Half the lecture was given by his robot. What did you think of it?" she asked.

"It was uncanny. It was an unbelievably brilliant performance. You couldn't tell which one was the real person until it was revealed at the end. The students were very enthusiastic and gave Vincente a standing ovation. I must admit that I was very envious that we have nothing as advanced as his robot at the NIR."

Gwen sighed. "I'm afraid it will be many years before we make that much progress in the Institute. So, I gather that you are thinking of recommending him for a post here?"

Isabel nodded. "He would be a tremendous asset to our research. I've already submitted the paperwork from my office so it will be landing on your desk soon. I'm hoping that you will advance it to the next level."

Gwen swiveled in her chair to click on her computer screen. "Ah! Here it is. You have been very quick to get this on its way," she observed, giving her a searching look.

Isabel took another deep breath. "Yes, I think that after the televised lecture, many companies will try to hire him. Nobody else has his expertise for creating look-alike robots that look amazingly human."

"I'll do research into his background and let you know if I agree with your assessment. We have to be so careful nowadays that we don't hire someone who might take advantage of our own research. There will be a C.V. security check too. It's a slow process. You know that."

"Yes, I've told him that. Thanks, Gwen, but there is something else."

"That sounds ominous," Gwen smilingly commented. "Out with it!"

"Vincente is very serious about wanting to come to the NIR, but he's in a hurry to know where he stands. Obviously, he may be considering other offers. In order to keep him interested in the NIR, I had to give him a project that would keep him connected to us until we know if he'll succeed in being appointed here. He's too good to let him slip away."

"What sort of project did you suggest to him?"

Isabel took a deep breath. "The kind that he's good at, making a look-alike robot."

"Interesting. And who would the robot look like?" asked Gwen.

"Me," Isabel blurted out.

Gwen couldn't help herself. The idea was so bizarre. Much to Isabel's embarrassment, her colleague laughed so much that she nearly choked. Finally, wiping her eyes, Gwen asked the pertinent question. "And can you afford this doppelgänger robot, Isabel?"

"No," Isabel had to admit. "I was hoping that the NIR would fund it."

Gwen couldn't believe her ears. She brought her chair upright so briskly that her desk shook. "You can't really mean that! Why would the NIR want a robot that looks like you? They already have the real you. Why should they pay this scientist for another one?"

But Isabel was stubborn.

"It's the only way the Institute can get their own unique, state-of-the-art robot and be able to find out how it works. Then we could create our own without relying on Da Cosa. He isn't going to offer his own robot secrets to us for free."

"I believe you're serious!" Gwen answered. "You think this is the only way the NIR can keep up with modern competition?"

"Yes, I do. Vincente is so far ahead of us already. We have to do something drastic. Like having our own robot. It would be worth its weight in gold. It's a small price to pay for the NIR to fund its creation."

"Hmm. You have a point. And what did Da Cosa think about your proposal?" Gwen asked, "I should have thought that he would never agree."

"But he did! He thinks that I want a look-alike robot for my own purposes," Isabel answered cagily.

Gwen raised her eyebrows in query, her lips quivering again.

Isabel hesitated uncomfortably. "Like sending it to places to give my lectures while I could be free from having to travel everywhere. That's what he does. So, it was a viable excuse for me, too. He doesn't need to know that we have other ideas for the robot."

She could see that Gwen was considering her arguments. She waited.

"Well, my friend, send me your request for funding in writing. I will take it to the Director to see what he thinks about your proposal. I'll take it to him myself, rather than sending it through other departments. I think he will find it as surprising as I do. But if he agrees, he's the one who can budget the money for the robot. In the meantime, please keep this under wraps. Secrecy is our best policy."

Relieved that her submission had gone well enough, Isabel thanked Gwen profusely and walked out of her office as if floating on air.

CHAPTER 8

That summer in Boston was one of the hottest and busiest that Isabel could remember. The town was flooded with tourists and the banks of the Charles River were awash with students sunning themselves or rowing on the water. The benches along the shore were packed with visitors as they sat picnicking under the shady old trees while watching the more active people jogging by.

Although she spent a great deal of time in her air-conditioned office following her usual routine, Isabel was invited quite often to give talks at conferences in other parts of the country. It seemed to her that, without fail, all those destinations proved to be even hotter than Boston and she grew weary of travelling in the oppressive heat.

"I definitely need a holiday," she'd say to herself, "Somewhere I don't have to talk about technology. Some sandy desert island in the Pacific, being fanned by the ocean breezes and drinking coconut juice with maybe a little rum in it, would be heaven."

But having initiated her project with Vincente, she knew that far distant places were not on her itinerary for any time in the near future. She had been relieved when the NIR had finally decided to fund her look-alike robot, but now she was duty-bound to keep them up to date on its progress.

'I can't take time off in case I need to check some details for Vincente. He's forever asking me questions and expecting me to supply the answers. Good thing we bought new cellphones, or he'd be burning up the NIR communications network every day.'

She was weary of having to keep their communications secret. Going outside into the summer humidity every time he phoned, so that she wouldn't be overheard, was a necessary pain. Sometimes she wondered if she were trusting him too much to do the job since she had no way of checking its true progress. Only what little he chose to tell her.

Such fretting did nothing for her morale, but she did become expert at finding quiet places away from other people, in order to talk with him. But after a time, she began to look forward to their unusual conversations. Vincente made her so aware of the many technical details in the project he was doing for her, that she became totally fascinated.

One day he had sent Vincente-Two to the NIR for some accurate measurements he needed urgently. For a moment she'd been shocked, thinking that it was the scientist himself who was entering her office. It was only when she observed the hairless skin on its face that she knew it was the robot.

After he left, she thought, *'I don't like Vincente's sudden surprises. He's too tricky by half! I'll have to be more on my guard. Maybe having him do this project was a mistake. But it's too late now. He's started on it and when it's finished, perhaps we'll all get what we want. But it's hard to trust him entirely.'*

She shook her head, realizing that for the moment she had to be content with how things were.

The hot summer passed into a sunny Fall that lasted well into November. By then, Isabel knew that the project must be nearing its completion and began experiencing a rising excitement mixed with apprehension. Then at the end of the month, she was invited to join other members of the Institute for a final NIR interview with Vincente before the vacant post was decided.

The scientist had phoned briefly to say that he was catching a flight to Boston and would see her the next day at the NIR meeting.

"Oh, I wish there'd been time to ask him if he'd finished the project," she fumed afterwards. "Why didn't he say something about it?"

That night, Isabel couldn't sleep. She kept tossing and turning, thinking about the next day's meeting and hoping that Vincente would make a good impression. After all, she was the one who had proposed that he be given the vacant post, so she wanted him to do well.

'Surely he wouldn't be so foolish as to send his robot instead?' she tormented herself. Since it was so hard to fathom how his mind worked, that was a distinct possibility. Would he be so foolish as to do that, in order to prove his point of how useful it was to have a look-alike robot?

By dawn, Isabel decided that it was useless trying to sleep, so she dragged herself downstairs to make some coffee. The fragrant smell of the brewing beverage soon brought Doug into the kitchen that fateful day. Rubbing his eyes, he said, "My, you're up early, Sis. I thought you told me that your meeting wasn't until ten o'clock this morning."

"It is," she answered, "But I couldn't sleep for thinking about it. I've been awake for hours. I'm worried that Vincente will play one of his tricks."

"He's that 'brilliant' scientist you've been telling me about?"

"Yes, I never know how he's going to react. It keeps me on edge thinking about what he might do next."

"Hmm," her brother grunted as he poured a cup of coffee for himself and opened the fridge for the cream. "You're thinking about him a lot. Do you think it might mean you're a bit sweet on him?"

Isabel was aghast. "You can't seriously believe that!" she retorted. "Why he's at least ten years younger than I am!"

She took such a great gulp of her java that she scalded her mouth and had to reach for a glass of water.

"That don't mean much nowadays," Doug replied nonchalantly as he went to see if the newspaper was on the doorstep.

His sister took this opportunity to escape to her room to shower and get dressed. She definitely did not want to eat breakfast with Doug.

As it was, she took so long having a hot shower and selecting what she would wear, that by the time she drove on to the highway, a morning accident was causing congestion. She barely made it to the NIR on time for the meeting.

Entering the building, she could see Vincente waiting outside the boardroom. Instead of going directly to her office as she had planned, she made a beeline for him. She needed to make sure that it was really Da Cosa and not the robot.

He hurried forward and she sighed with relief when Vincente took one of her hands in both of his and gallantly kissed it. His lips were warm to the touch. It really was the scientist.

Vincente took her sigh to mean that she was happy to see him again and whispered, "Will you have lunch with me after the meeting?"

CHAPTER 9

The NIR meeting went on longer than usual as everyone had questions to ask the newcomer scientist. Isabel admired his confidence in answering them. Vincente came across as knowledgeable, competent and well versed in the field of artificial intelligence technology. A few members had witnessed his 'twin' robot in action at the lecture given at Boston University in the early summer and they expressed their appreciative admiration for his talents.

Isabel was glad that she wasn't called upon to explain why she had proposed Vincente for the vacant position, since it was apparent that he was demonstrating to everyone how valuable he would be as an addition to their research department.

The conference room in winter was always over-heated so it wasn't long before she began to feel the effects of her troubled night. Once or twice she had to catch herself from dozing off in the warmth. She was startled fully awake when she suddenly heard the Chairman say, "Dr. Da Cosa, the majority opinion is that we would like to offer you a position in our faculty."

She applauded the choice with the rest of the room and hastily shut her briefcase, glad to be able to escape to her own office.

As she reached the elevator, the triumphant scientist caught up with her.

"Dr. Lindsay! Now that we are going to be colleagues, I will repeat my invitation. Would you have lunch with me today?"

Isabel hedged. "I have to check at my office first, to see what appointments have been scheduled for me."

"I'll come with you," Vincente offered, following her into the elevator.

As they emerged, they encountered a lab secretary who looked surprised to see them. "Oh!" she greeted them with a puzzled frown. "Dr, Lindsay I didn't see you leave your office. I thought I saw you there when I left."

"You couldn't have, because I never…"

She didn't finish what she was about to say because Vincente interrupted quickly, "Eileen, you are looking very smart. That green dress is such a beautiful color. You must have a special date today?"

The secretary smiled at him. "Thank you! This is my favorite dress. No date. I'm just going downstairs to take my lunch hour."

Vincente was holding the elevator door open for her, so she waltzed inside and still smiling, pressed the button to descend. Then, he hurried to open Isabel's office door for her.

She stopped short as she stepped into her office. There was someone sitting in her chair. Isabel gasped. Vincente stepped swiftly around her to turn the swivel chair so that she could see who it was.

With a flourish, he said, "Dr. Lindsay, meet your other self."

Isabel felt a shock course through her body. "Heavens above, Vincente! Do you always have to take me by surprise?"

Unfazed by her outburst, he replied, "I wanted to see your face when you saw my creation for the first time. I can see that you're surprised, but come, how do you like your own doppelgänger? Isn't it exactly like you?"

She sank into the chair facing the robot and stared at it.

Even though she had been anticipating their project's outcome for months, Isabel was flustered at seeing her mirror image sitting at her own desk.

Taking a deep breath, she said, "You're a genius, Vincente. I don't know how you can create such realistic robots. I'm sorry if I sounded irritated but it is disconcerting to see oneself as a robot when you least expect it. Really, I can't thank you enough. The robot looks amazingly like me! It's better than I ever imagined."

As she enthused, her weariness faded away and she was about to elaborate further until she suddenly remembered that robots could record conversations into a database, so she abruptly stopped talking.

Vincente, sensing her discomfort, came to her side and dropped a small object into her hand, saying reassuringly, "There you are, Dr. Lindsay. With this, you can control your own humanoid. It is not activated now. Go ahead and get acquainted. Press the control and talk. Give it a name. I doubt that you want to call it Isabel-Two."

Isabel hesitated, feeling self-conscious having the other scientist beside her. "In a moment. I'm still trying to get used to seeing myself as a robot. It is a little disconcerting. Does that make sense?"

"Of-course it does, dear lady. Come, I'll show you how to activate it and you can converse with your alter ego."

He continued, "It's programmed to know how your mind works and knows all your likes and dislikes and how you would react in any given situation. Look on it as if it were your identical twin sister."

He showed her how to activate the robot, then said, "I'll be in your outer office in case anyone drops by unexpectantly. I will keep guard."

"Thank you," Isabel breathed, "You know that I don't want anyone to know about this, don't you??"

"Yes, indeed." He closed the door to her office as he heard the robot say, "Hello, you must be Dr. Lindsay."

He sat in the anteroom, well satisfied with the way things were going. He could hear the robot-human conversation from where he sat. He admired the speed with which Dr. Lindsay was learning the robot controls.

After a while, he stuck his head around her door to say, "Excuse me, I know that you are getting comfortable with the robot, but may I show you something else important?"

Isabel had been enjoying getting acquainted with her 'look-alike' and reluctantly gave way to Vincente.

"Would you de-activate the robot now?" he requested.

His fellow scientist obeyed, then waited to view whatever revelations were about to be unfolded.

"I've invented some modifications to the robot that I haven't yet told you about," Vincente began.

Isabel felt a sharp prick of apprehension. Modifications? How could he even think of modifying any of her robot's characteristics? Had he tinkered with the personal data that she'd provided for him? Had she trusted him too much with her own ideas and opinions and he'd had the effrontery to modify them? She shifted uncomfortably in her chair.

"Now, watch what I do," he instructed. "You must first make sure that the robot is closed down securely."

Vincente proceeded to demonstrate how to securely lock the robot.

"Do you see this tiny lever on the robot's back?" he asked as he swiveled the office chair around. Isabel nodded. "Watch what happens when I pull it down."

To her amazement, the robot began to fold its arms, then its body and finally its legs until she was a quarter of the original size. Isabel watched closely as the scientist rolled out a suitcase that he must have brought with him and fitted the robot neatly inside. Zipping up the case, he ended by locking it with a combination lock.

"Good Lord!" she cried out, "Is there no end to your surprises, Vincente? I've never seen anything like this before! Why do you think I need a suitcase for the robot?"

"This way, you can move it around securely and nobody will suspect that you have a robot in your suitcase. Even if people do wonder about the case, you work in Robotics so it's a reasonable assumption that you might be transporting one. Everyone seems to have these rolling suitcases, so it won't be unusual for you to have one too. See how easily it rolls?"

Isabel was astounded when Vincente proudly announced, "I have submitted my invention to the Patent Office already. It won't come under the auspices of the NIR as I had invented the mechanism before joining your staff." He grinned at her triumphantly.

Isabel could only manage to whisper weakly, "Then I'll need to know the combination for the lock."

"Of course, my dear lady. I will tell you what it is, over lunch. After that you can use your own numbers. I'm going to push this locked suitcase into your office closet. Don't worry your head about anyone else seeing it while we are out. It will be quite safe in there. Are you ready to go now?"

As he spoke, Isabel realized that she had waived her breakfast that morning and now that food was mentioned, she felt famished.

"Where can we go for a late lunch?" she enquired. "It's well after midday."

"I thought we would go out of town instead of staying around here," Vincente replied quickly. "In fact, I've already made reservations for us. It won't matter to this restaurant that we'll be later than I said. People stay there for very long lunch hours. Is that okay with you?"

Isabel was getting used to his audacious behavior. On one hand, she felt disgruntled that he had taken her acquiescence for granted but on the other hand, she was gratified at not having to make quick decisions herself. Besides, she was feeling too tired to challenge him.

When he mentioned the name of the restaurant, she recognized it as an upscale place on the road out of Boston. How did he know about that?

"Fine with me," she agreed, "Do you want me to drive?"

It was over a lunch of mixed baby greens, fresh warm bread, Boston scrod and lobster tails, apple and peach cream tarts, and perhaps a little too much wine, that they discussed plans for what to do next with Bella, the name Isabel had chosen for the robot.

Her companion signaled to the hovering waiter to refill their coffee cups while stating, "You will have to give the robot a trial run. It is too risky testing it at the NIR until I'm established there. Eventually, you will need someone at the lab to see how effective the robot will be when you leave it in charge. In the meantime, is there somewhere else you could test it?"

Isabel searched her mind as she stirred cream into her coffee.

"Well, I could always try it out on my brother Doug at home," she suggested tentatively. "That way, I would be keeping it inside the family, though I don't know how my brother will react to Bella. It might upset him."

Vincente drained his cup. "I'm sure that you can wave away his fears, my dear lady. You need to test it sooner or later and your own brother might be a good adviser since he knows you so well. Today is Friday, so you have all the weekend to solve the problem."

On the return drive to the NIR, they refined their plan to involve the unsuspecting Doug. Isabel would take the suitcase home that evening. Now that she knew the lock combination, she could activate the robot after she had talked with her brother and if she encountered any difficulties in operating the robot, she could phone Vincente at his apartment. It sounded quite simple.

CHAPTER 10

$\mathcal{T}$hat evening, Doug spotted the suitcase as soon as Isabel pulled it into the house. "Going away again, are you?" he enquired.

"Only for a couple of days," she answered. "I was wondering if you could look after something for me while I'm away."

"Sure thing," her brother replied cheerfully, "What is it? Come into the kitchen to talk. I'm making supper."

"Well, it is more like a 'who,'" she said as she trailed after him.

"Oh no, you haven't invited Aunt Millie to stay for the weekend, have you? You know I can't stand her for very long. She never stops talking and she keeps following me around to tell me boring stories about her friends. Besides, I meet my buddies at the pub on Saturday night and I'm certainly not going to take her there!"

"No, no!" Isabel hastened to assure him, "Not Aunt Millie. It's a robot."

"Well, in that case, there's no trouble. Put it in your bedroom and shut the door. I won't disturb it," he replied as he stirred the sauce for the poached fish.

She took a seat to watch him pottering about in the kitchen, laying out plates and cutlery. She hoped he was paying some attention to her as she tried to explain.

"It's a robot that can talk. I was hoping that you would test it out for me."

Doug paused to lower the temperature of the sauce. "You're asking me to talk to a robot? Why can't you talk to it yourself? What's so special about this robot that I have to test it out for you?"

"I can tell you more when you actually see it," Isabel replied patiently.

"Okay. Supper's nearly ready. Let's eat first and you can show me the robot when we finish."

After supper, Isabel rolled the suitcase into the living room where she proceeded to unlock it, carefully extracting her look-alike robot. When it was fully upright again, an astounded Doug turned to his sister to voice what was so apparent.

"This robot looks exactly like you, Isabel! Why?"

"I can't tell you that just at present,' she hedged, "But what I need at the moment is for someone to treat it as if it were a human being. You know, talk to her, engage her in conversation, teach her things. Be friendly."

He frowned. "What do you mean by 'teach her things'?"

Isabel explained, "Look, she's a humanoid robot equipped with artificial intelligence. She has computers that can process and do things at a faster rate than people can. She can even remember what you say to her. She is capable of learning. You can teach her household tasks, for instance. Just pretend it's a more intelligent sister that you're talking to. Can you do that for me?"

She sighed. This persuasion of Doug was wearying, especially as Doug was regarding her as if she had lost her mind.

Doug didn't say anything for a minute. Tentatively, he said, "This is very weird, Isabel, but turn the robot on and let me see what it (or 'She') can do." Isabel activated the robot.

Doug nearly jumped out of his skin when she said in his sister's familiar voice, "Hello, you must be Isabel's brother Doug."

"How does she know that?" he hissed at his sister.

"She has some basic programming already, like face recognition, from her databank of our family members," she explained.

"You mean that she would recognize Aunt Millie, too?"

He sounded incredulous as Isabel answered in the affirmative. He let that fact sink into his brain. "So, will it-she- recognize all the others in our family?"

"Only those that are on her present database but as she meets other people, she will remember them the next time she sees them."

"My God!" he exclaimed, "What is the world coming to, when robots can think like people?"

But by the time Isabel went to bed early that night, ready to sink into a deep and welcome sleep, she was feeling happier with the way her brother had taken to the robot. She drifted off with their remembered conversation echoing in her ears.

They had been talking about the Boston Red Sox' chances in future baseball games, one of Doug's favorite topics. The robot was informing him of all the statistical evidence culled from its rapid computer brain and Doug was making his human arguments for the opposite. Isabel chuckled. He would soon learn that the robot could counter any argument Doug might start.

Next morning, when she entered the kitchen, Doug and the robot were discussing whether scrambled eggs and bacon constituted a healthy human breakfast. It was the robot that was pouring hot coffee for her brother. Had they talked all night?

Doug winked at his sister, "Your robot learns fast. At this rate, she will soon learn how to cook all the meals and I'll have more time to write my newspaper columns. I'm thinking of writing a column about robots. People might be happy to know how helpful they can be, instead of viewing them as a threat to normal life."

"Oh, no you don't, Doug!" Isabel was quick to protest. "This is a strictly secret scientific experiment and you can't mention anything about this particular robot. I don't want other people knowing about Bella. Ever. So that topic is off limits."

"Just thought I'd ask," Doug replied cheekily.

Isabel drained her coffee and said, "I'm leaving now but I'll be back on Sunday. You'll remember how to control the robot and how to fold her into the suitcase? Is there anything else you need to know before I go? If you run into difficulties, you can always phone me on my cell."

"Well, you haven't told me what to call her. Has she got a name?"

"Oh, I thought I'd told you already. Her name is Bella. And Doug, when you go to the pub, please lock her up in the suitcase."

"Yes, yes," Doug replied testily, "Don't be such a fusspot, Sis. I'll remember. I'm not senile yet!"

As Isabel was closing the front door behind her, she heard Doug saying. "Now that you know how to load the dishwasher, Bella, you can put the dirty dishes inside it and clean up the kitchen while I read my newspaper in the living room."

CHAPTER 11

$\mathcal{N}$either Doug nor the robot paid much attention to the front door clicking shut after Isabel. The robot was explaining to Doug, "You don't need to read a newspaper. I can tell you all the up-to-date global news from my database."

"Is that so?" Doug queried, "Well, maybe you have a direct line to the White House? You can tell me what's going on in there?"

After Bella had informed him of the latest U.S. news, Doug laughed and said, "Okay. Now I'll go check my newspaper to see if you're right."

In the evening, the robot watched Doug making preparations for going out to meet his former newspaper colleagues at the local pub.

"I will go with you," she stated.

"Don't even think it," he replied, "My buddies are all seasoned newspaper men, used to sniffing out stories. Don't want them to guess that you're a robot, do we? If they did, my sister would roast me alive!"

"It would be impractical for Dr. Lindsay to roast you alive," Bella said, "Your oven isn't big enough. Also, it is cruel and against the law."

Doug guffawed. "You're so entertaining, Bella Robot! I'm sure the guys would get a kick out of you if they met you. But, sorry, can't be done."

"I'm not programmed to kick," the robot replied, "I am a non-aggressive robot. I have no emotions. Meeting your friends would test my ability to look and behave like a human, just like your sister. That is all."

Doug digested her idea for a minute. Maybe taking the robot with him might supply useful information for his sister on how it behaves in public. He was torn between Isabel's instructions for secrecy and his own desire to see the robot's effect on his buddies. He was sorely tempted.

The robot waited.

He finally decided. "Okay! Okay! But we have to make a plan so that you don't stay there too long. I'll tell them that you have to meet a friend in half an hour and you're only stopping by briefly. That way, you can say that you don't have time for a drink with them. The guys are sure to offer you one. Then I'll walk you out, supposedly to meet your friend and bring you home. I'll return to the pub later."

He laughed. "That's when I'll be able to find out if they believe you really are my sister. Can you remember all that?"

"Of course," Isabella said, "It was entered into my memory while you were speaking."

Doug took a deep breath. He hoped he was not about to precipitate a major domestic disaster with this plan. His sister would never forgive him if he did. On the other hand, it would be such a good joke to play on his friends.

He turned to the robot saying, "You'll have to wear one of Isabel's winter coats over your woolen dress and put on a hat and mitts. It's turned cold outside."

"I don't feel the cold like humans do."

Doug wasn't listening. He was looking at the robot's feet. "You can't go out in those flimsy shoes either. The guys would notice them straight away. I'll have to get some boots onto your feet. Sit down here on this bench."

He was thankful that the robot was flexible enough to bend and sit while he pulled off her shoes to slide on Isabel's boots. Even the robot's feet were exactly like those of his sister, so the boots fit perfectly. Doug pocketed the robot control saying, "Okay, you are now called 'Isabel' for the rest of the evening. Remember that! Now let's go to the pub."

The Black Horse Inn was on a quiet side street off the main road that ran from Boston through their little town and on to the highway two miles away. A century ago it had been a changing station for stagecoach horses. The large cobblestoned area where in the past the passengers had alighted to go into the inn for refreshments, was now a car park. The original stables had become modern apartments and condominiums.

"Watch your head when you go in at the door," cautioned Doug, "People used to be much shorter in the olden days."

Bella didn't reply because she was swiftly gathering information from her database on how to watch one's head while walking.

Finding out that it was another way of saying, 'Bend your head down,' she ducked through the low doorway and followed Doug along the narrow passageway that opened out into a large timbered bar room.

She was stopping to gain information from a huge television screen behind the bar when Doug grabbed her arm to guide her to a small cloakroom area, where he stuffed the woolen mitts into the pockets of Isabel's coat. Together with his own overcoat, he hung their clothes on hooks shaped like horses' heads.

"You can keep your hat on because you're not staying long," he instructed.

There was a loud buzz of conversation filling the crowded room. As they walked to a table in one corner near the roaring fire, Bella's eyes were photographing the highly polished oak tables and benches, the comfortable, well-worn armchairs and the red-faced customers clinking beer glasses under the low, black-beamed ceiling.

"Evening, Colin and Burt. Les not here tonight?" Doug greeted his friends.

"No, he's coming in later. Had a deadline to meet," Colin stated as both men looked curiously at Isabel. "Brought a lady tonight, have you?"

"Have you met my sister, Isabel?" Doug said, "I didn't think you'd mind if she sat with us for a while until she meets a friend. It's too damned cold for her to wait outside. Looks like it might snow later on."

Both men stood up, Burt to bring an extra chair and Colin to offer to get 'Isabel' a drink.

"No, thank you," the robot answered as she sat down on a carved wooden chair, "I don't drink."

"Oh! No hard stuff then? How about a soda or a juice instead?"

As Colin hovered waiting for a reply, Doug cut in, "She won't have time, Colin. Her friend will be coming soon. But I'll have a pint, thanks."

Doug turned to Burt. "So, what's been happening behind scenes at the paper? Anything I've been missing?"

He sat beside Bella, never suspecting that the robot was recording their animated conversation about the politics of newspaper coverage and what disasters had happened at some recent local events. It wasn't until they started discussing sports and golf, in particular, that she spoke.

"Tiger Woods is one of Sports All-time Greats."

She had the group's instant attention as she commenced to give a detailed account of the famous golfer's career on and off the golf course.

Colin, returning with the beers, looked at her in astonishment as she continued to feed them information. "He has earned millions of dollars just playing a sport that he loves."

As he put down the beers, Colin said, "It's usually Les who keeps us up to date on golf. When he comes, he'll be interested in meeting another golf aficionado, Isabel. Do you play golf yourself?"

Doug was getting hot under the collar wondering what the robot would reply to that question, so he interjected, "We both watch golf on the television. But, talking of TV, did you watch the recent Tour de France, by any chance? I don't know how those cyclists have the stamina to bike that far. It must kill their legs going up those winding mountain roads."

"Can't say that I'm all that interested in watching cycling, Doug," Colin replied as he sat down. "It's too painful seeing them struggle to avoid bumping into each other on those bikes that wobble from side to side. Makes me feel nervous looking at them. It's worse than watching trapeze artists at the circus and wondering if they're going to fall."

Burt took a long drink of his beer and with the froth still on his upper lip, offered his opinion. "Me, I used to like watching soccer but it's different from when I played, way back when. It used to be about skill, like cleverly dribbling the ball past your opponent. But all the players do nowadays, is pass the ball back to the goalkeeper when someone gets in their way-when they are not slyly kicking their opponent, that is."

'Isabel' interjected, "Kicking another player would be against the rules of the FIFA."

Once again, the men stared at her in surprise as Burt asked, "How come you know about the rules of the International Federation of Football Association?"

"I have a very good memory," the robot replied. "In soccer, if there is a violent action, such as deliberately kicking an opponent, the referee will intervene by giving the offender a yellow card. If the player continues to violate the rules, after two yellow cards, he will be shown a red card and sent off the field."

Burt raised his glass to her. "You're some knowledgeable lady!" he enthused, happy to have found someone also interested in soccer.

"I wonder what's keeping Les," Colin fretted, "I wish he would hurry up and get here to meet you, Isabel. He's our Sports Editor and he would enjoy talking sports with you. You know so much."

Doug was finding this conversation far too nerve-racking. He was on tenterhooks as to what the robot would say next. He quickly gulped down his drink, then stood up and said, "Too bad we can't continue this discussion. Sis, it's time you were going to meet your friend."

"Oh, don't go yet, Doug," Burt pleaded. "Stay a little longer. I'm sure Les would like to meet your sister. He'll be here soon."

But Doug turned a deaf ear to his friends, saying, "I'll be back shortly but Isabel has to go right now."

"Well, bring her in again with you next week," Colin said as he smiled at the robot, "We'll tell Les all about her in the meantime."

"It's been a pleasure to meet you, Isabel," Burt stated gallantly.

At that, Doug quickly shepherded Bella from the room before she could accept Colin's invitation to return. He helped her don his sister's outdoor clothing before quickly buttoning up his own overcoat and steering the robot towards the front door.

Once outside, he took a sweeping glance around the parking lot to see if Les' car was there. Reassured that there was no tall Jamaican sports editor arriving to slow them down, he hurried the robot to his car, saw that she could secure the passenger seatbelt without his help and drove off through the swirling snow.

CHAPTER 12

*O*n the way home from the Black Horse Inn, Doug's nerves gradually calmed down while his mind was giving rise to a growing curiosity.

"How did you know all that sports stuff, Bella?" he asked.

"I have only to send a word to my database and it will give me the information. I saw Tiger Woods on the television at the pub so when I queried who he is, I had access to his records. Then later, I programmed in the word, 'soccer' when it was mentioned. My database came up with the soccer, otherwise known as 'football,' rules. I can find answers to anything I search for."

Doug let that sink in for a minute before another thought, this time unwelcome, struck him. All his sister had to do was to mention the word 'pub' in Bella's hearing and the robot would spill the beans about all pubs, including the Black Horse Inn.

Doug's mind raced on, inventing more and more complications.

'Isabel is sure to ask me about my meeting with my friends, if only to find out if I'd locked up the robot before

going out. What if the robot is nearby and tells Sis the names of my pals now that she has met them? Then Isabel would want to know how Bella knows their names.'

He was still fretting when they reached his driveway.

'Life with this robot is beginning to get out of hand. Why did I ever agree to taking care of her? I can see that she's going to cause me a lot of trouble.'

After opening the front door, Doug eased off the robot's shoes, replacing them with her own footwear. Taking his sister's coat, hat and mitts, he shook off the flakes of snow before hanging the clothes up to dry in the front porch. Keeping his own overcoat on, he instructed the robot to walk upstairs.

As they reached his sister's bedroom, Doug stated emphatically, "Now Bella, listen to me. I definitely don't want you telling anyone about our visit to the pub tonight. If anyone mentions 'pub' to you, don't tell them anything."

"Very well," the robot replied, "I will put all that information into my secret storage place. It will stay there until it is opened."

"What do you mean, 'your secret storage place'?" he demanded in alarm.

"I am equipped with a 'Secret' app so that important information can be kept securely. I sense that you are surprised. Don't humans have a place in their brains where they store secrets or something they don't want to think or talk about?"

Doug ignored the question. His thoughts were flying elsewhere, to the ingenious inventor who had created the robot. *'That crafty scientist must have inserted the 'Secret' application. Why would he do that?'*

Muttering to himself, "I bet he didn't tell Isabel he was installing a 'Secret' app. The devil! I'll bet that Vincente guy uses it for finding out what the robot-and that means my sister-is keeping secret. He must know how to access those secrets for himself. Bet he hasn't told Isabel about that! I think he's spying on her, the bastard!"

Seething with suspicions, Doug turned off the robot, saw that she was folded into the suitcase and secured the lock.

Going downstairs, his dark thoughts continued to plague him.

'If he's going to open that Secret app, he'll find out that I took the robot to the pub. Then what will he do? Tell Sis?'

He paused indecisively at the bottom of the staircase, softly muttering,

"I should warn Isabel about her precious inventor. But if I do, I'll have to tell her how I know about the app. Then, I'll have to own up about going against her wishes and taking the robot to the Black Horse Inn."

He ran his fingers through his thick wiry hair, making it stand on end with static electricity. His thoughts were not pleasant as they chased each other through his inventive brain.

'On the other hand, Isabel might know about that app and the next time she opens it, she'll find out about me taking the robot to the pub. Either way, it looks like my goose is really cooked.'

"I think I'll need a strong drink tonight," he decided as he hurried to the door. He wound a thick scarf around his neck, felt in his pocket for his car keys and gladly left behind the source of his woes.

CHAPTER 13

When Doug re-entered the Black Horse Inn, he noticed that Les had joined Colin and Burt. He collected a drink as he pushed his way through the noisy crowd to their corner table. Many more people had come in out of the snow, raising the decibel level to 'High' in the bar.

Les greeted him with a hearty Jamaican greeting, "Hey, man! What's this I hear, Doug? You got a sister who knows a lot about sports? How come we haven't met her before? The guys here think she's real cool."

Doug slid his shot glass on to the polished table that now showed wet rings where previous drinks had been placed. He sank down on a chair facing Les and holding his hands out towards the fire to warm them, began to rub the circulation back into them.

"She surprises me too," he admitted. "Lost touch with my sister Isabel when my wife was so sick. Now I'm living with her for a while to help out in the house while she travels to her job in the city. She lectures in other towns and she's away a lot."

"What does she do?" Colin asked curiously, "She seems very intelligent."

"Oh, some high- powered government job. She doesn't talk much about it," Doug hedged.

Les laughed, his warm brown eyes twinkling in the firelight, "Man, she sounds like somebody I'd like to meet if she knows so much about sports. Are you going to bring her here again?"

As Doug was silently thinking, '*Over my dead body!*' his voice was saying, "I could ask her if she's interested but I know that she's very busy at the moment with a new project, so don't get your hopes up."

Then he added the words that would come to haunt him afterwards, "But she's interested in a lot of other things too, not just sports."

"What sort of things?" Burt enquired, putting down his empty glass and helping himself to some salted peanuts.

"Oh, you know, most of the stuff you find in the newspapers - politics, current affairs, art, films, general knowledge. Isabel is the brainy one in the family. She has a terrific memory. Amazes me all the time."

His friends nodded at his mention of their common workplace, the newspaper office. They knew the wide variety of subjects that were constantly covered in their daily operations.

"You're not such a duffer yourself, Doug," Colin claimed. "Don't be so hard on yourself."

"Thanks, young Colin. For that, I'll buy the next round. Another beer for everyone?" Doug asked.

He and Colin, who offered to help carry the beers, were on their way to the bar when there was a familiar noise that made them stop. There were tinkling crystal sounds coming from the direction of the bar. Someone was tapping a spoon against a glass to get everyone's attention, but it took some time for the buzz of conversation to quieten down.

Even so, the innkeeper had to raise his voice to make himself heard.

"I have an important announcement to make! Our first ever Quiz Night at the pub will be starting next Saturday at 8 o'clock. I hope that everyone who is here tonight will come back to play and join in the fun."

After this stark announcement, there was a sudden upsurge of conversation in the room until someone shouted, "Tell us more about it, Fred!"

The innkeeper was a short, rotund man with a ruddy complexion and a bulbous red nose, whether from drinking or from contact with the cold weather no one could tell. He was popular with his regular customers who treated him familiarly as 'one of the guys.'

"Stand on a chair, Fred, so we can see you," someone else called out.

Two burly men took him by the arms and hoisted him on to a chair as everyone turned to listen. The only sounds to be heard were the smooth sliding of glasses on polished tables and the crackling of the log fire.

Everyone waited patiently.

With his bald spot shining in the lights of the bar, Fred explained, "A retired teacher came into the inn last week and offered to run a Quiz Night on weekends. I'd heard about other pubs doing quizzes but never gave it a thought for the Black Horse. But I liked the enthusiastic way Henry Oxley talked about it. It sounded like something a lot of people might enjoy on a Saturday night. Especially in the wintertime."

Beside him, Colin made Doug jump by calling out loudly, "Tell us how it works, Fred. Do you have to have a university degree to join in?"

As the crowd chuckled at this, the two friends took the opportunity to push to the front of the crowd to hear the answer as well as to get nearer to the bar.

"No, you don't have to have a degree, in spite of this being a university town!" the innkeeper reassured Colin.

"There'll be all sorts of questions, about general knowledge, transport, TV, food and drink (he was interrupted by a cheer here), or music, history, art, films. About anything really. So, anyone who wants to play has a chance to answer questions about what he knows best. You don't even need a high school-leaving certificate for that!"

A tall lady in a thick red sweater held her hand up to ask a question. "You say 'he' but what about all of us intelligent women in here? Don't we have a say in this too?"

There were low murmurs of agreement from the other women in the room.

"Of course, Debra, as many women as you like can join your team."

"How many people do you need?"

"Just coming to that!" he continued, "You can form your own team, from two up to six members. We collect five dollars from each person and all the money collected is paid out at the end of the quiz. Of-course a winning team will get the most payout money from the kitty, the second a little less and the third will get the rest of what's been collected. I repeat: all the money collected is paid out the same night. We at the Black Horse just want you to have a bit of fun these coming winter nights, that's all."

"Hey, Fred! Might be good business for the pub too!" some wit shouted.

Fred laughed and his red face grew even ruddier as he answered,

"The pub and the teacher I told you about, aren't doing this for profit. Though I dare say that I'm hoping you'll all be buying drinks to make your brains work better while you're thinking of the answers to the questions!"

There was good-natured laughter following his remark. As Fred was about to climb down from his chair, he raised his voice once more to announce loudly, "Remember, our first Quiz Night will be next Saturday at eight o'clock."

A renewed buzz of excited conversation filled the room as patrons began discussing this unexpected new event.

"Bet that teacher will come in for some free drinks too," Colin remarked to his colleagues as he and Doug carefully lowered the new beers on to the table. "Well, guys, what do you think of this quiz idea?"

They all looked at one another to see who would speak first. Les took a swig of his beer before exclaiming, "Hey! We're newspapermen. Think between us we can answer a whole lot of questions, don't you? The quiz sounds good to me. It might even pay for our drinks if we win. I'm in! What about the rest of you?"

There were murmurs of agreement as the other three men decided to take part and so a team of four was quickly formed for the following Saturday evening. Les was jubilant, his wide toothy smile spreading across his face as he rubbed his hands together at the prospect of a new kind of sports competition. "Right!" he said, "I'll make a point of being here by eight o'clock next week, deadline or not!"

He raised his glass. "Cheers! Here's to our first win of the season!"

Much later, as Doug drove home along the dark streets, a sharp icy wind had sprung up and was skittering the snow across the road. The car tires kept slipping as he braked around corners. Doug drove carefully with his nose almost touching the car's windshield and sighed with relief on reaching home without the car skidding and ending up in a snowdrift.

Thinking fuzzily that he shouldn't have mixed his drinks, whisky and beers, that evening, he threw his scarf and overcoat haphazardly over a chair, then lurched his way upstairs to bed where not even bothering to undress, he fell into a deep sleep.

CHAPTER 14

The next morning Doug was jolted awake by his sister's voice. "Hel-lo! Anybody at home? Doug, are you there?"

He slowly rolled over in bed to squint at the clock on his nightstand. It was only ten o'clock. What on earth was Isabel doing here so early on a Sunday morning? And why did she have to shout so loudly? He plugged his ears with his fingers. He'd been expecting her later that afternoon.

Groggily, he looked around for his bathrobe and realized that he'd been sleeping in yesterday's shirt and pants. Taking his hands away from his ears, he heard the unmistakable sounds of his sister climbing the stairs. He froze and waited, but she opened the door to her own bedroom and went in.

A wave of relief washed over him. Isabel would find the robot safely stored in the suitcase according to her own instructions. But surely, she hadn't come home early just to check up on him to see if he'd done what she'd asked?

He gave a huge yawn. Although feeling distinctly queasy, he leaned over the bed to feel around on the floor for his slippers. Once on his feet, he managed to rescue his blue bathrobe from its hook on the door without it falling off. Doug knotted its belt tightly around his waist, hastily combed his hair with his fingers before venturing out of his bedroom.

Isabel was coming out of her own room wheeling the robot suitcase.

"Oh! So, you are at home!" she exclaimed. "I was beginning to wonder if you'd gone out somewhere. But I can see that you've just rolled out of bed."

Doug thought that his sister was too perky by half and her voice sounded far too shrill. It made his ears ring painfully.

Coming towards him on the landing, his sister peered at him closely. She said, "Hmm. Looks like you had a big party last night. I'll go make you some strong coffee. You look as if you need it."

Pulling the suitcase carefully behind her, she gently bumped her way downstairs to the kitchen. Doug watched her go and then went back to his bedroom to search for some clean clothes. On his way down the stairs to the kitchen, he cautiously put one foot in front of the other on each stair whilst gripping the side banister.

Reaching the hall, he paused to straighten up and noticed the robot suitcase, parked near the front door, was still locked. Thankful that the robot hadn't been activated yet, he walked more steadily into the kitchen where the weak winter sunlight was much too bright.

Isabel was pouring coffee into two mugs while listening to the weather forecast on the radio. He collected one coffee and adding a great deal of sugar to it, carefully sat down at the table. Cradling the mug in both hands, he brought it to his lips only spilling a little. No mean feat with Isabel watching him so intently.

"Want to tell me about last night?" she asked, bringing her own coffee to the table. She sat opposite him, giving him a searching look.

Doug shook his head and took another shot of caffeine before asking testily, "Why are you here so early, Isabel? I wasn't expecting you till later this afternoon."

"I couldn't wait! I was so curious about how you and the robot were getting along. Was everything all right? Did the robot act and think like me? Did you have any problems that I need to know about?"

Her brother grimaced, thinking, *'Problems? If she only knew!'*

"Sis, can we not talk about this now? My head feels as if it's about to burst."

"Ah!" she replied unsympathetically. "Then you shouldn't have drunk so much last night. Take an aspirin or whatever else can help. We can talk about what you think of the robot when you're feeling better."

Isabel rose to rinse out her coffee mug but continued talking in the same irritating voice that was grating on his nerves.

"Doug, I meant to ask you why my winter clothes are on the porch. Why are they there? What were you doing with them?"

Doug groaned inwardly. Surprising himself, he thought of a quick response. "I wanted to see if your clothes fit the robot. Did I forget to hang them up?"

"And did they fit?" Isabel asked curiously, turning to smile at him.

"Like a glove," he answered, taking another gulp of coffee.

"If you'd asked me beforehand, I could have saved you the bother. All the robot's measurements are exactly the same as mine. Vincente made sure of that. He's meticulous in everything he does."

Doug shifted uncomfortably in his chair at the mention of the tricky scientist, whom, though he had never met him, he had decided that he didn't like or trust. *'Poor Isabel. I'll say he's meticulous- in tricking her.'*

"Seeing as you are not feeling up to scratch at present, I think I'll take Bella back to the lab this morning to do some more programming on her. I know that Vincente will be at work and he can help me."

She looked at her brother again.

"Why did you make such a funny expression when I said that?"

"Did I?" Doug scowled, "It's probably because I've such a foul headache."

Isabel chose to disregard him.

"I think I'll wear my winter coat. The snow is melting now but it's bitterly cold outside. Doug, I'll be home this afternoon and we can talk then. I'm dying to hear all about your day with my robot."

She breezed out of the kitchen.

Doug congratulated himself for escaping the potential disaster of trying to answer Isabel's questions while feeling neither too lucid or helpful. He was shakily pouring another coffee for himself, when Isabel suddenly popped her head around the kitchen door.

"Doug, I do have another favor to ask you. A really big one. But I think we'll have to leave that until I get home this afternoon. Hope you're feeling more like yourself by then."

She left at last, leaving Doug to his own private agony. Would the robot remember not to say anything about last night when it was reactivated? And what was this 'big favor' that Isabel wanted? His sister was never satisfied.

It wasn't only the after-effects of his night at the Black Horse that made him groan as he went to look for something to ease his pain.

CHAPTER 15

That evening, Isabel waited until they had finished their light meal of vegetable frittata, green salad and avocado toast before mentioning the 'favor' that she was going to ask for and which Doug was dreading.

Putting down her glass of Pinot Grigio, she eyed her brother's glass of water and decided that he was now hydrated enough to have recovered from his hangover.

She had hardly outlined her request when Doug exploded, "You can't be serious! You're really asking me to do that?"

"Why not?" Isabel retorted. "It seems perfectly rational to me. I can't do it myself, for obvious reasons, and you are the best instructor I know. You taught me."

Doug drank more water and glared at his sister.

"Don't try to butter me up! It won't work. You're asking me to teach that robot how to drive your car? That's ridiculous! It can walk and talk. Isn't that enough? Why do you want it to be able to drive too?"

"Well, I can't go into that right now, but I do have good reasons. For my project to work, Bella needs to be able to drive my car."

"How could you even think that I would agree to something so dangerous? Even though self-propelled cars are beginning to appear downtown, it doesn't mean that I think that they're safe. And now you're asking me to teach a robot to drive and then let it loose on the roads by itself? No! I won't do it."

Her brother shook his head, abruptly getting up from his chair to begin clearing the dishes from the table to emphasize that those were his final words on the matter.

Isabel rose from her chair too and still talking, pursued him to the kitchen counter.

"Look, Doug, all I am asking is for you to take Bella out, to show her our street so that she knows where we live. Then take her along the same route that I take to work each day. Bella will enter it into her database and won't ever forget. Robots learn so fast that you'll only need to teach her once."

She could see that Doug had clenched his jaw and was wearing that stubborn expression she remembered so well from childhood, when he didn't want to do something. He was rinsing the plates in heavy silence, so she began to stack the dishes inside the dishwasher to give him time to consider what she was asking.

When he didn't say anything after taking the apple pie out of the oven and setting it on the table, she wheedled, "It won't take too much of your time, Doug. Vincente has already programmed Bella to understand how the car engine works and how to operate my particular car. So, all it needs now is for someone to show her the safety rules of the road."

At the mention of the scientist's name, Doug viciously cut the pie.

He carved it into slices and slapped two on dessert plates, passing them to Isabel. She calmly spooned whipped cream over them.

Finally, he said, "If Vincente has done so much already why doesn't he teach Bella how to drive? Why ask me?"

"Oh, Doug! He has just started his job with the NIR and if people saw him driving around with my look-alike, people would begin thinking that I was showing him too much favoritism. That wouldn't look very professional on my part. I have to treat everyone the same way in my job. Unbiased."

Isabel could see that her brother was not convinced so she persisted. "Whereas, if people saw you with whom they took to be me, they wouldn't give another glance at a brother and sister driving together."

She took a bite of her dessert and said, "Mmm! You make the best apple pie, Doug. You're a great cook! I'm glad you've come to live with me. I am so lucky!"

Her brother was not so appreciative of the choice he had made. He was thinking that each day that he lived with his super-intelligent and hyper sister was more wearing on his nerves. Why couldn't she be like normal people who did their jobs and came home to relax each night? How did he get stuck with the crazy projects she conjured up? He was already in trouble because of that robot.

Isabel didn't like how quiet he had become. It was not a good sign.

"Doug, I promise you that this is the last thing I'll ask you to do for Bella. After you teach her to drive, I can get on with my project and leave you in peace. What do you say?"

Her brother tried one last tack.

"You could take her to a driving school where they have driving simulators. Bella could learn how to drive there."

"But I can't be seen with her. Together we are too noticeable. Do you want to take her there? Wouldn't it be better to do the driving from home where it would look natural if you went out with your own sister?"

Doug closed his eyes. From past experience, he knew only too well how Isabel always got what she wanted. When she was young and being the only daughter, had given her a special status with their parents. She, being so intelligent, had made the most of being spoilt. He knew that he didn't have much chance of winning this present argument.

"Okay! Okay! I'll try to teach the robot to drive, even though I don't approve. I hope you have a very good reason for wanting something so stupid. And remember, it's your car we'll use."

As Isabel's face broke out into a big smile, he added, "But you'll have to promise that if I make any mistakes, you'll not blame me afterwards."

CHAPTER 16

*B*y the next day, the previous night's snow had melted into wet slush that splattered unpleasantly against people's legs as they walked along or crossed the streets. A bitter wind had sprung up to add to the cold and misery of the winter weather, the worst of which everyone feared was yet to come.

At the end of their workday, Isabel and Vincente had decided to escape the Institute and the dark, gloomy winter's evening, by driving to one of the remote restaurants that Vincente seemed to know so well.

He had found an Italian restaurant far away from their workplace and now Vincente and Isabel were sitting at a plain wooden table, opposite from one another, enjoying their antipasto of olives, mushrooms, artichoke hearts and marinated vegetables. Gradually the cares and concerns of their science-dominated environment were slipping away with the help of a glass of red wine.

Isabel felt very comfortable with Vincente.

"What did your brother say when you asked him to teach your robot how to drive?" her fellow scientist enquired as he speared a mushroom.

"He wasn't too happy about it and said that he wouldn't do it at first. I had quite a time persuading him that it was perfectly safe and very easy for a robot to learn how to drive. But after some initial resistance, he finally agreed," Isabel replied smugly.

Vincente raised his glass of wine to salute her. "Wise brother!" he remarked, "Not to argue with someone as resolute as you are, dear lady."

Isabel's face flushed, either from his praise or the wine, but she was saved from replying by the arrival of their cannelloni, stuffed with ricotta cheese and spinach and steaming under a covering of tomato sauce. The waiter refilled their wine glasses, wishing them, "*Buon appetito!*"

As they were eating, Vincente returned to the subject of the robot.

"Once Bella can drive herself, when will you put your plans into action?" he asked.

"That will depend on you," she answered. "I will need you to be in the lab to see that everything is going smoothly and to see to Bella, if there is any problem with the robot. You'll be able to contact me on our private cellphones if need be. So, I would like to know your availability. Do you have any out-of-town lectures planned for the next few months?"

"No. I am still getting to know the NIR systems and my personal work arrangements, so I will be staying here in town for a while. Besides which, I don't like travelling in the winter. It's much too cold and unpleasant."

"You could always send your robot instead," Isabel suggested.

Vincente grinned, "Since Vincente-Two is like me, he doesn't want to travel in the winter either."

"Well, I could argue that point about your robot, but I won't," she fired back, returning his smile.

They lapsed into companionable silence as they enjoyed their meal. When they had finally laid down their forks on empty plates, Isabel said, "I can't wait to take my first long vacation in many years. The Institute doesn't mind us taking a few days here and there during the year, but they frown on anyone taking long holidays because of our ongoing research projects."

"I see!" Vincente said gravely. "It's good that you are taking the opportunity to travel, now that Bella can cover for you. I am very glad to be in a position to help you do what you have always wanted to do. You know you can always count on me."

He was leaning across the table to take Isabel's hand when the waiter interrupted him by offering to clear their plates and by asking if they would like dessert.

Vincente sat back in his chair to look at Isabel. "I can recommend the tiramisu or the tartufo. Both are excellent here."

They both chose the tiramisu and coffee and waited to be served before renewing their conversation.

"Where will you go for this clandestine holiday?" Vincente asked, taking up his spoon.

But Isabel's mouth was full. "Mmm! This tiramisu is so delicious. How do they make it?"

By the time her companion had described the ingredients and how to make the dessert, she had deflected his question and with coffees finished, they left the restaurant.

On the drive back to the NIR to retrieve Isabel's car from the parking lot so that she could drive herself home, the two scientists talked about their research projects. Afterwards, when she had collected Bella's suitcase, from her office and was driving home along the highway, she was hoping that the topic Vincente tried to bring up would be forgotten.

'*The fewer people who know what I'm doing, the better,*' Isabel thought as she pulled into the driveway of her house. '*When the time comes, I'm not sure if I'm going to tell Doug either.*'

She rolled the robot suitcase out of the back seat of her car to steer it to the front porch where she dried the wheels before entering the house. She deposited it inside by the front door. Then, smelling something succulent and spicy like fried chicken, she went to look for Doug in the kitchen.

Her brother was busy preparing their evening meal.

Belatedly, Isabel had to confess that she had eaten already.

"You could have phoned to tell me," Doug complained.

"I'm sorry. I got caught up with science talk," she apologized. "But I did bring you a dessert. I hope you like it."

She produced a container of tiramisu. Doug looked at it thoughtfully and then at Isabel. "What do you want from me, this time?" he asked.

"This is just a thank you gift for promising to teach Bella how to drive," she protested.

Doug regulated the oven temperature before turning to his sister, saying, "Somehow I get the distinct feeling that there's something more than that going on. Want to tell me what you're really up to?"

"Why do you think that I'm up to something?" Isabel countered.

"Oh, come on, Sis! I know how you manipulate people. Watched you while you were growing up. It's no use trying to hide anything from your brother. So, I'll ask you again, what plans are you hatching now? Why is it so important that the robot is able to drive your car?"

She carefully put the tiramisu in the fridge and thinking fast, went to sit at the kitchen table. Clearing her throat ready to deflect this latest question, she said, "My plan was to ask you if I could borrow your car during the week while I leave mine with you to teach Bella. Would that be okay with you? That's all I'm planning at the moment. You needn't be quite so suspicious!"

Doug nodded his head sagely, "Ha! I knew you wanted something," he replied as he filled his plate with food, carried it to the table and began eating.

Isabel fidgeted as she watched him, wishing that she hadn't eaten quite so much at the Italian restaurant. The smell of the chicken was mouth-watering, and she couldn't help seeing how the tender, succulent meat fell apart as Doug cut into it.

"Well, what's your answer?" she finally asked.

"That's fine with me," Doug answered, wiping his hands on a paper napkin. "I'll spend three days max with that robot and if she can't drive well after that, it won't be my fault."

"Thanks, I do appreciate your help, Doug. You taught me how to drive so I know you're a very good instructor. Bella thinks like me so you shouldn't have any trouble. She probably has good road sense already. It might even just need two days of instruction."

Her brother gave her a quizzical look from under his bushy eyebrows. She quickly jumped up from her chair, saying "Goodnight," before he could say anything and snatched a chicken leg from the pan on her way upstairs.

CHAPTER 17

*M*onday morning dawned clear and bright with a sparkle of frost dusting the lawn. Doug looked out of the kitchen window as he sipped his hot coffee, knowing that his breath would steam outside in the cold like his beverage was steaming from his cup. It promised to be a chilly morning without any cloud cover.

Isabel had taken his car earlier to try to beat the morning traffic on her way to work, so when he had calculated what time the stream of traffic might have thinned out, he donned his winter jacket and boots and released Bella from her suitcase prison.

"I know you don't feel the cold, but we have to look the part," he remarked as he found an old down jacket of Isabel's and zipped it around the robot. He jammed a woolen hat on Bella's head but hesitated before putting winter boots on her feet. He decided that it would be difficult to teach the robot how to drive when her feet were weighed down by heavy footwear.

Nobody could see the robot's feet in the car, so he opted to leave her own shoes in place.

"I know a great spot where I can teach you to drive," Doug said to Bella as he backed out of the driveway. "But before that, I want you to watch how I drive on the way there. I will explain everything I'm doing."

Bella, strapped into the passenger seat, nodded obediently and watched him attentively while sending all his instructions and observations to her database.

"This is it!" Doug announced as he drove into a deserted park area at the other end of town. The grounds were adjacent to the Psychiatric Hospital and it did cross his mind that it was an appropriate spot for someone like himself, who needed his head examined for even trying to teach a robot how to drive.

He parked on a road that wound around the park to demonstrate how to start the car with the key and importantly, how to use the brakes to stop. After a few repetitions, he allowed Bella to sit in the driver's seat while he became the nervous passenger. Much to his surprise, he had no need to worry so much because Bella quickly mastered the first elements of driving.

She learned how to change the mirrors so that there was an unimpeded view of the road, how to use the dashboard instruments, the gears, the lights, the windshield wipers, and the direction signals.

"Okay," he said cautiously, "Try driving to that curve in the road and then stop slowly. If you see a hazard, brake quickly."

After checking what 'a hazard' was, Bella performed as if she were a past master of the art of driving. Doug was impressed when she stopped abruptly as a suicidal squirrel darted in front of the car.

"Of course, a robot must have quicker reflexes than we do. Now that's a comforting thought," he muttered to himself as he unclenched his hands.

Bella's ears had picked up his reactions. She answered, "I am a good driver, like Isabel. I think like her and I can adapt to any situation just as she would. Shall I drive you home now?"

But that was a little too audacious for Doug. "No, I've seen enough of your driving for today. You'll be the passenger on our way back through town. I'll point out the streets and crossings so that you'll remember them."

"But I already know them from driving here, and from last night when we drove from the Black Horse Inn."

Doug's hands froze on the steering wheel at the mention of the Black Horse Inn. He turned to Bella and snapped, "I thought I told you to keep quiet about pubs."

He glared at the unfazed robot. "Has your secret app been opened so you can now talk freely about it?"

"Nobody has unsecured my secret app," the robot reassured him. "You ordered me not to say anything if the word 'pub' was mentioned. You did not specify the name of any special one."

Doug was trying to remember exactly what he had told Bella to do, but he was too shaken to think straight. His worst fear, that of the scientist Vincente being able to access information while Isabel had no idea of what he was doing, surfaced again. Eventually he would have to tackle the problem so that it wouldn't keep bothering him all the time.

But for now, he had enough to do in teaching this robot how to drive. She was such an exact copy of his annoying sister, who always had a ready answer for everything, that he felt he had to be constantly alert, double time, to keep his wits about him. It frayed his nerves.

Aggravated by these irritating thoughts, he started the car saying gruffly to Bella, "Since you know all the streets, you can point them out to me as we drive by and you can also direct me the way to get home."

To his further annoyance, it was soon evident that the robot knew the names of every street and cross-street. She also instructed Doug about traffic signs and the speed limits and reminded him of road skills all the way into the driveway of their house. Bella had even accessed the current weather and road conditions for their town, and these were related in great detail to Doug.

By this time, his jaw was hurting from gritting his teeth. He couldn't wait to get Bella into the suitcase to have some quiet time for himself.

However, it was not to be.

No sooner had he settled Bella into her suitcase and himself into a cozy armchair with the morning newspaper and a hot drink, than his phone started ringing. It was Isabel, wanting an update on how the driving lesson had gone. On hearing that the robot had proved to be a competent student, she asked if Doug would take her out on the highway the next day. She wanted Bella to be able to drive to the NIR, Isabel's workplace, so that she would know the way there.

This suggestion was greeted with such a long silence that his sister had to repeat the question.

"I heard you the first time!" he snarled. "That's something we'll have to discuss when you come home this evening."

Before Isabel could argue, he abruptly ended the call.

Trying to remain calm, he made a beeline for a comfortable chair. He lay back against its soft headrest, but he couldn't get comfortable or even sit still, because his mind continued racing with a cacophony of disturbing thoughts that rattled around his brain.

Isabel was clearly up to something that she hadn't bothered to tell him about, but she was involving him in the training of her look-alike robot, so it was only fair that he be told what was going on.

Why did she need a facsimile of herself in the first place? Wasn't one of her enough? It was for Doug.

If Isabel wanted Bella to be able to drive to the NIR and return home, that suggested to him that his sister intended to have the robot replace her in some capacity when she, herself, was not present. Why? Where was Isabel going to be while that was happening?

Doug shook his head in puzzlement. Looking back, it was obvious to him that his sister had gone off the rails after she'd met that Vincente person. She used to be open and honest, even if she were a little too smart for her own good. How honest was it to pass off a robot as yourself at work, while you were elsewhere? Was it ethical to earn a salary when the robot was doing Isabel's work?

With these thoughts invading his peace of mind, Doug got up and began pacing, muttering distractedly to himself while he tried to make sense of his sister's behavior. He went from room to room until he reached the kitchen.

There, he steeled himself for a big showdown with Isabel that evening. He was going to insist on some straight answers from his sister.

He would refuse to budge unless she told him what exactly she was planning to do. He wanted to know the real reason Bella had to know the way to the National Institute of Robotics. If Isabel wouldn't tell him, he would refuse to take the robot out.

Having reached that momentous decision, he turned his thoughts to a calmer subject - what to prepare for dinner when his sister came home that evening.

CHAPTER 18

*A*fter he had collected the ingredients for a vegetable chili, Doug set to work slicing vegetables and mixing spices while listening to the news on the radio. His sister had a small television on a ledge near the kitchen sink, but he rarely watched it, in case he became so distracted that he might accidentally slice his fingers instead of the vegetables. The radio was not as dangerous and furthermore, it didn't demand his constant attention.

As he washed the zucchini, he listened to a news item about a Middle Eastern dictator who had avoided assassination by sending a double of himself to appear at a conference. Unfortunately for the double, he had been the victim of a shooting and had died, while the assassin had escaped during the ensuing commotion. The dictator of course, had lived.

"What is this world coming to?" Doug trumpeted as he added the now sliced zucchini to the pot on the stove.

His mind wandered to his sister and her doppelgänger robot. If that dictator had had a robot instead of a person disguised as himself, nobody would have died. He immediately started worrying again. Had Isabel been receiving threats and needed a double to protect herself?

His hand shook a little as he added more water and turned up the heat to cook the vegetables. Setting the timer, Doug began assembling cans of chopped tomatoes, black and red kidney beans and his mixed spices.

Waiting for the timer's final warning ting, he fretted over his sister and her strange requests for making the robot even more like herself than it was now, by adding skills like driving. He returned to the thorny question of why the robot needed to drive. Was Isabel going somewhere while the robot drove to the NIR and did her lab work for her? Where was his sister going? Was she ever intending to tell him?

At one time, he would have thought the idea of a robot doing human's work laughable, but after becoming more aware of what scientists could do and what was happening in the robotic field, it seemed quite feasible now.

He emptied the beans and chili spices into the pot and set it to simmer. Then he cracked open a can of beer from the fridge, to calm his misgivings.

When Isabel got home, he was going to insist on having his questions answered. No more of her hedging or wiggling out of his questions. He was going to stand his ground.

Later, when she came into the kitchen rubbing her cold hands and cheerfully exclaiming, "Hmm, something smells good in here!" she was met by her brother waving a contradictory wooden spoon at her.

"No! I smell something really bad," he stated baldly.

"Why, what's wrong? What's gone bad?" she puzzled, looking around the kitchen but not seeing anything untoward.

"It's your behavior that's giving me bad vibes," Doug said, jabbing his spoon in the air to punctuate what he was saying.

"My behavior? I've been out all day. What do you mean? What have I been supposed to be doing that's got you so worked up?" she prickled in return.

"That's what I want to know!" her brother demanded. "What exactly are you doing with this robot?"

Isabel swerved around him to avoid having her eye put out by the waving spoon, to sit down at a safer distance away.

Doug noticed that the chili was bubbling so he laid the wooden spoon across the pot and checked the temperature. He switched off the radio.

"Now listen to me, Isabel. I want the truth from you this time. Have you been receiving death threats?"

She looked at him in amazement. "Me? Death threats? Of-course not! Whatever gave you that strange idea?"

He brushed away her query by rejoining, "Then why does that robot have to be so like you that nobody can tell the difference? Why does it need to know how to drive your car to work? Are you intending to stay home doing nothing while the robot goes to the NIR?"

"No, I'll be doing something else. The NIR will be benefitting from having both of us employed, as well as Vincente showing how he will manage the robot at the labs. I will have programmed her to act exactly as I do, but he can deal with any difficulties that might arise."

Doug slid into an adjacent chair. "Then why all this cloak and dagger stuff, Isabel? Where will you be if you're not at the NIR? Will I be able to get in touch with you?"

"It's difficult to explain, Doug. I have to follow my instructions. It's a kind of experiment we are doing, so I don't know where I'll be."

"Why not? What if there's an emergency here or with you?"

"You can contact Vincente."

Doug bristled at the name. "So, you're going to tell him where you'll be, but not me, your own brother?"

"No, Vincente won't know either."

"Sis, this sounds like a disaster waiting to happen. You're telling me that you're just going to disappear for - how long?"

"Not long, as far as I know. All I can say, is for you to remember that I work for the government and the people there can trace me at any time."

"That doesn't make me feel any better. Who trusts governments nowadays?"

"I can't tell you anything more, Doug. Can we eat now?" she pleaded.

He glared at her.

"Not until I get more satisfactory answers. You're involving me in some mysterious activity, but you won't tell me what it is or why. What if I wash my hands of all this and you get somebody else to teach Bella how to drive?"

"Oh, don't say that, Doug! You're the only person I can trust at the moment."

Doug folded his arms. "In that case, tell me what you're up to."

After a lot of sighing and swallowing hard, Isabel finally said, "Okay, I'll tell you as much as you need to know. I'm only trying to protect you too. The less you know, the better."

"Talk!" he commanded unsympathetically.

"It's like this," she started, choosing her words carefully," My department wants me to do some undercover work and Bella is the perfect way to ensure that I'll not be missed. The robot has to come to the NIR every day and be seen to drive home, as I would normally do."

Doug considered this information. "And does Vincente know what this experimental project is?"

"No, he is only being asked to regulate the robot. He isn't in the loop. He thinks I'm going on holiday. My superiors are testing him also, since he is a new employee."

Then she added, "Doug, I've already told you more than I should. I appreciate you teaching Bella how to drive but I really can't tell you anything more. Please don't ask me to. I simply cannot."

Her brother regarded her steadily while he digested that information. She hadn't turned her eyes away as she usually did when telling white lies, so he finally had to accept what little information she was telling him. He rose and went to the stove, saying, "Well, I accept your explanation for now. But I'll still worry about you being in danger."

Isabel visibly relaxed, asking plaintively, "Can we eat now? I'm famished!"

She watched as Doug stirred grated bitter chocolate into the chili.

"I'm ready to serve now," he said.

CHAPTER 19

The next morning, Isabel was not yet downstairs when Doug entered the kitchen. Since she seemed to be sleeping in, he decided not to wait for her, but to take Bella out before the daily traffic congested the roads. The flow of cars would be brisk enough for the robot to get to know the reality of driving on a busy highway. He didn't need a horrendous traffic jam to gum up the driving lesson he was about to give Bella.

It was certainly going to be a messy drive that day. What snow that had not disappeared, had been reduced by passing cars to dirty water running along the street gutters. Doug didn't have much faith that the highway would be any drier, so he checked his windshield washer fluid before seating the mercifully quiet robot in the passenger seat. He wondered if he had forgotten to turn her on.

His concern was short lived as Bella began listing all the streets they were driving by on the way to the highway.

"Can't you be quiet and let me concentrate on driving?" Doug growled. "I already know you can remember all the names from yesterday. You'll have plenty of time to talk on the way home. Watch me carefully now."

The robot watched him so intently while sending information to her database, that her staring began making him feel hot under the collar.

"Don't just watch me!" he instructed tersely. "Watch the road as well. I'm going to instruct you on how to drive on a highway so that you'll be able to manage it for yourself. I'll give you a running commentary on what I'm doing, as I do it."

Bella obediently turned to look out of the window at the road while checking on what 'a running commentary' could be. Doug couldn't help thinking that it would be nice if his sister could learn some things from her own robot. Like how not to argue.

As they began to enter the highway, Doug said, "I'll demonstrate how to enter at the proper speed, how to change lanes and how to keep a safe distance from other cars. You'll have to watch the road signs for directions and for keeping to the speed limits."

With the robot watching and recording his copious instructions as they went along, Doug drove carefully, keeping to the slow lane. When the traffic began to thin out, Bella asked, "Where are you going?"

Doug started in surprise. "I thought I told you that we were going to the main building at the NIR."

"No. That data has not been recorded."

Doug caught himself before he started to apologize. *To a robot?*

"Well, you know now."

"What will I do when I get to the NIR?"

"Nothing!" Doug replied shortly. "I'll show you where and how to park. Then I'll ask you to drive back home while I direct you on the return journey."

He didn't feel good about that latter part, but it had to be done. He comforted himself with the thought that unlike being in a driverless car, it was probably safer being driven by a robot that he could watch all the time. He still had the option of taking over in case of an emergency or a mistake. He could even grab the steering wheel if necessary.

As before, probably due to his sister's expertise being housed in the robot's database, Bella made the return journey look easy, driving them home without incident. Doug gave a huge sigh of relief when at last they reached the house.

"Very good, Bella," he said. "I just wish I had your nerves of steel. That ride home made me quite jittery!"

"I don't have any nerves made of steel, Doug," Bella stated. "I have connections of super-fine optical fiber cables."

Doug groaned to himself. The robot was as pedantic as his sister.

"Never mind! It was only a joke," he said.

Then he added quickly, in case Bella provided him with a definition for 'a joke,' "Unfasten your seatbelt, get out of the car and wait for me by the porch."

He was happy when he was obeyed without further robot comments. Doug noticed that his own car had gone, so Isabel must have taken it. He had thought that she would have stayed at home, waiting for his progress report.

'*Did she say that she was going to the NIR?*' There was so much going on in his life that he couldn't remember.

He locked the car, thinking that he needed a nap but what to do with Bella? He was too tired to lock her into the suitcase again. He needed a break from all this constant activity.

Entering the porch together, he turned to the robot., "Bella, I'm going to take a nap for half an hour. When it is 11:30 am. by the kitchen clock, start making a pot of coffee and I'll get up to make my lunch. In the meantime, you sit in the kitchen and watch the clock."

Congratulating himself at solving this problem, Doug walked to the living room, sank thankfully into the soft cushions of the sofa and was soon dead to the world, both robot and human.

The smell of coffee woke him. Rubbing his eyes, he acknowledged to himself that Bella certainly had some good points. He slowly stretched to get out the kinks in his back and walked to the kitchen. A steaming mug was ready for him. But where was the robot? He had told Bella to wait in the kitchen. So why was it nowhere to be seen?

Suddenly worried by the fact that he always left his car keys on a tray at the front door, he peered out of the kitchen window to check that Isabel's car was still in the driveway. '*I wouldn't put it past this robot to go practising driving while I was asleep. After all, it is a copy of my rebellious sister.*'

To his relief, the car was parked where he had left it.

'*If the robot is still in the house, where is she and what's she doing?*'

Cursing himself for trusting a robot, Doug began an anxious search. He hurried from room to room downstairs and then began mounting the stairs two at a time until halfway up, he stopped, thinking that it was far more probable that the robot had gone down into the basement area. Their computers were in the rooms there, and the robot had a family affinity for such machines and technology.

But since he was on the way up the stairs, he swiftly climbed the remainder. He started opening the doors to the bedrooms, bathrooms and closets, searching every nook and cranny upstairs. No robot.

Doug scampered down to the lower levels of the house.

'If that robot has found the office downstairs, it better not be messing with Isabel's papers.'

He hadn't noticed that the door to the basement was slightly ajar. *'How could I have missed that when I went past?'*

Doug thundered down the flight of wooden stairs.

He saw Bella in the little basement office. In front of a computer. Looking at 'How to Drive Safely' videos. It flashed through his mind that she had found an easier way of sending information to her database than driving with him.

Relieved as he was at finding Bella, he was also livid at all the extra anxiety she had caused him that day. Quickly reaching past her, he turned off the computer and before the robot could react, quickly turned Bella off too.

'High time to put her back into the suitcase where it belongs! I'm glad Isabel wasn't home to tell me that I should've done that in the first place.'

Feeling the heavy load of responsibility slide off his shoulders, he went to rescue his now cold coffee from the kitchen. '*Peace at last!*'

But he had hardly finished reheating his drink before Isabel shattered the kitchen calm by phoning him. "How did Bella cope with highway driving today?"

"As robots go, pretty good," he answered warily.

"Any problems?" Isabel persisted.

"Only that she talks too much," Doug responded, thinking that the same could be said of his sister at times. That quiet time he had hoped for himself seemed to be rapidly disappearing. Any minute now she would ask for more favors.

"I thought you were staying home until I returned," he accused. "So where are you now?"

"I had an urgent message to meet some of my superiors at work. Sorry I had to leave so quickly that I forgot to write you a note."

Isabel seemed somewhat distracted. "I won't be home tonight, Doug. Something has come up and I have to deal with it. I'll stay at one of the university residences because I'll be working late on Bella's programming. I'll give you the phone number."

Doug detected an undercurrent of excitement in her voice but decided to be quiet and not ask what was going on. He didn't wish to push his luck by starting a long conversation that he didn't want at the moment. He wrote down the phone number.

"Do you mean that I don't have to give any more driving lessons?" he ventured hopefully.

"I'm trusting that Bella has learned enough to drive to the NIR and then return by herself in the afternoons. I know it's a bit of a rush."

"What's happening?" Doug asked, in spite of his resolve not to question her.

"Afraid I can't tell you. Sorry."

"Your secret mission?" Her brother couldn't help needling her.

"Doug! I told you not to mention that to anyone!" she scolded.

"But I was only talking to you and you know about it already."

"Bye, Doug. I'll let you know if I'll be coming home tomorrow or on Sunday to collect Bella."

Smiling as he put down the phone, he decided to eat a long, leisurely lunch, then do exactly as he pleased for the rest of the day – undisturbed by any human or robot.

It wasn't until a long while after that troubling Friday, that he wished he had taken more time to find out what Isabel was about to do, before his whole life altered.

CHAPTER 20

*I*t was the Saturday night of the first quiz game at the Black Horse Inn. There was an excited hum of anticipation coming from the patrons sipping their drinks when Doug arrived to join his colleagues, Les, Colin and Burt at their usual seat by the fireplace.

He noticed a tall thin man shuffling papers and pencils near the bar.

"Who's that?" he asked as he sat down. "Haven't seen him here before."

Burt slid a beer over the polished oak table towards Doug, saying, "That's the schoolteacher who's going to lead the quiz." He looked at his wristwatch. "It's due to start any minute now."

They turned expectantly to the stranger. He was as pale and lanky as Fred the innkeeper who was talking to him, was round and rosy. The teacher's fine black hair kept falling over his eyes as they talked together, while Fred's shiny bald head reflected the twinkling lights from the bar. One tall, one short, they made an incongruous pair.

"His name's Henry Oxley," young Colin confided, "And he runs quizzes in other pubs so he should know what he's doing tonight."

To the friends' chagrin, their young colleague started banging his beer mug on the table, shouting, "Hey! Fred! When's this quiz going to start?"

Fred glared across the room at them and called, "Hold your horses, Colin. There's a few rules to settle first." His words dissipated into the general buzz of conversation in the room.

Colin cupped his hand around one ear. "What did you say, Fred?"

They were all astonished when a deep booming voice, emanating from Henry Oxley, cut into the hubbub, effectively silencing everyone. It wasn't hard to imagine him having total control in his own classroom. A voice like that would frighten any child into submission.

"Good evening, to all! Fred and I will be running the quiz together and we have two rules. One, the quizmasters are always right. And Two, disputes are settled by referring to Rule One."

Some rueful laughter greeted this announcement. Undeterred, the teacher continued, "You'll have chosen your teams by now, so could we have a show of hands as to where you are? Then we can get an idea of how many teams are playing tonight."

Obedient hands shot up in the air and eight teams were counted.

"Fred will come around to collect your entry fees. Remember we ask you for five dollars from each member of the team and at the end of the quiz, there'll be three prizes: for the first, second and third winners. Rest assured that all the money will be paid out."

As Fred wandered through the crowd, Henry Oxley added, "Please come here to collect your papers and pencils."

He was interrupted by a woman who asked if she could use a pen.

"If you wish. But these pencils have erasers on them for when you make a mistake or change your mind about the answers. Remember to put the names of your team on the paper because after Fred and I check the answers, we'll be giving the papers back to you for verification."

There was a busy giving out of papers and a noisy shifting of places in the room, as everyone got prepared for the fun. Fred squeezed through the tables to reach the bar with his collection of prize money.

Henry Oxley had one last request - for everyone to turn off their cellphones and to please not cheat by any means that might occur to them.

Doug and his friends hunkered down over their papers, Les being designated to write the answers. Colin rubbed his hands together excitedly.

"I think we have a good chance of winning, don't you?"

The quiz began with general knowledge questions: Name three hats that start with the letter B: Name three kinds of footwear that start with 'S':

Name three animals that only have three letters in their name. The questions became more difficult as the quiz progressed, with history and geography interspersed with sports, films, television shows, art and music.

The four newspaper buddies soon realised that they didn't know all the answers from their combined work experience. They were still stewing over who played the nanny in 1) Mary Poppins 2) Mrs. Doubtfire 3) Nanny McPhee, when Fred came to collect the papers.

"Hope you enjoyed the evening," he said. "There'll be different questions every time we have a quiz. Want another drink now?"

But Burt was already on his feet, fighting his way through the deluge of customers wanting to reach the bar. Using their brains was thirsty work.

While Colin went to help carry the drinks, Les and Doug caught up with the week's happenings, Doug being careful not to mention his own driving experiences with Bella.

"When are you going to bring your sister here again?" Les asked. "She seems to be a pretty smart cookie – from what the others told me. We could have a team of five. No problem."

"I don't think you'll see her any time soon. She's busy on a special project at work at the moment."

"Oh! Where does she work?" Les asked curiously.

Doug was saved from answering by the arrival of their drinks and the booming announcement that their papers would soon to be handed back for each team to verify that they had been marked correctly.

How did they do? They found out that they had some wrong answers but on the whole, they had made a reasonably good attempt at their first quiz. After the teams had agreed on the marking done by Henry Oxley and Fred the host, the winners were announced. The newspaper team was awarded the third prize. Everyone applauded the winners and happily went back to socializing.

Only Colin was disappointed. He frowned and whispered to them, "Did you see the team that won first prize? It was those young upstarts from the Boston universities. High achievers. Now we know who we're up against."

Burt leaned back in his chair and twirled the glass in his hand.

"Could be that we need a better strategy than just thinking we know enough from our work experience. Though Colin, I have to say that I'm satisfied with third place. The prize money covers our drinks so far tonight."

He lifted his glass to salute the others.

Les rose to poke the fire, sending sparks up the chimney. He held his hands out to warm them near the roaring flames before returning to the table.

"Man, I do miss my Island sunshine at this time of year. Would be nice to have some of that Jamaican heat in my old bones in wintertime."

He rubbed his hands together to produce as much warmth as possible while saying in his soft lilting voice, "Just thinkin' what Anansi would do in our situation. Dat spider would sure think of some clever way to win."

He stretched his long legs towards the roaring blaze in the fireplace and looked pointedly at Doug, who immediately knew what he was going to suggest.

"This is no fictitious Anansi story, Les. I've already told you that my sister can't help us. She's working on some important project and she doesn't have the time nor inclination to take part in a pub quiz."

Burt snorted his disagreement. "She was quite happy to give us lots of information when she was here the last time. Why don't you mention it to her to see if she's interested? She doesn't have to come every week. We just need to show those youngsters once in a while that we oldies can win too!"

"And it would do them good to have their oversized egos deflated," Colin couldn't resist saying. "Do them good to know they're not the only bees' knees around here!"

Doug shrugged his shoulders.

"Okay! Okay! I'll ask her when I see her," he answered, knowing full well that there was a slim to no possibility that he would keep that promise.

What Doug didn't know was that Fate was soon to step in and decide.

CHAPTER 21

*I*t rained all Sunday morning, a cold, dousing rain that chilled to the bone. As Doug stirred his coffee, he could hear it drumming against the kitchen window as if trying to break through. He turned his head to watch heavy raindrops splatter the glass before transforming into thin rivulets that slowly snaked down the windowpane. Behind them, the gray sky looked dark and ominous.

He sighed, wishing that he had done his grocery shopping the day before, but he had procrastinated, wanting to avoid the Saturday crowds in the busy market. Doug savoured his hot drink, wondering if Isabel would be coming home for dinner that evening. She hadn't phoned to let him know, but in any case, whether she came or not, he needed to buy things for the supper he had planned.

Idly, he nibbled his fingernails thinking of what he should do.

Should he contact her? Not wanting to bother her at work by phoning like some over-anxious brother, maybe he could send her a text message. She might answer that straight away. He reached for his cellphone.

Doug looked at the rain again. Checking the weather report failed to ease his concern. It forecast heavy rain for the rest of the day and overnight. *'Guess I have no choice but to brave the rain squalls to get what I want.'*

Reluctantly, Doug went to look for a raincoat and hat. On leaving, he checked to see if his sister had replied to his text. No new message.

Holding an umbrella before him like a battering ram against the gusting wind, Doug made a dash for his car and slid damply into the driver's seat, tossing the folded umbrella onto the floor on the passenger side. *'What a day to have to go shopping!'*

By the time he returned home, he was cold and shivering. The key to the porch slipped to the ground as he fumbled to fit it into the lock. He had to take off his gloves to retrieve it and his wet fingers became icicles.

Once inside, he dumped the groceries on the porch floor. Then easing off his soggy shoes, he gingerly shed his raincoat and hat, hanging them on a peg where they commenced to drip. He heaved the sodden grocery bags into the warm house and thence onto the kitchen counter. He looked at his cellphone. Still no reply from Isabel.

Before he unpacked the groceries, he boiled some water to make tea into which when brewed, he poured a liberal amount of rum. He cradled his cold fingers around the cup to warm them before drinking and after a few minutes felt thawed out enough to tidy away his purchases.

He was about to go find his recipe for shepherds' pie but stopped himself. *'What am I thinking? I don't need a recipe. I've made shepherd's pie hundreds of times. Could do it in my sleep. What I really need is to find a nice, warm place to sit down and stop shivering.'*

To the tune of the rain drumming on the window, he carried his tea into the living room, where he turned on the electric fire and snuggled into a comfortable chair. That was where Isabel found him in the afternoon. She stretched out a hand to touch his shoulder, but he must have sensed a presence because he struggled to sit up.

Doug rubbed the back of his stiff neck, saying gruffly, "I must have fallen asleep." He peered at her. "Isabel, you didn't text me to tell me when you were coming home."

"I didn't get a chance. There's a lot of unexpected things happening at the NIR, Doug. I came to get Bella to take her back with me. I need to program her in case I'm required elsewhere sooner than I expected. My alter-ego robot will have to take my place."

"Is that what your bosses wanted to talk to you about? I've never heard of such nonsense, a robot taking your place!" Her brother was incensed. "And where will you be?"

"I can't tell you anything else, Doug," she answered firmly. "I don't even know what is going to happen or even when. All I know is that I can have dinner with you and then I have to take Bella back to the NIR with me tonight."

He scrambled up from the sofa, thoroughly disgruntled at the unsettling way their lives were unfolding and headed for the kitchen.

That was the beginning of Isabel's spasmodic visits to her home, though she did her best to alert her brother ahead of time if she were returning to have dinner with him or was staying overnight. She claimed to be extremely busy with some sort of project that kept being extended throughout the winter months but about which she didn't want to talk.

After a while, Doug didn't bother to question her. He reckoned that he would find out sooner or later. But that didn't stop him from worrying about what his sister was dealing with at the Institute. *'But as sure as Spring follows Winter, it'll have something to do with that two-faced Da Cosa guy who she seems to like so much.'*

CHAPTER 22

𝒜t the NIR, Isabel and Vincente were co-operating on the apps that were being inserted into Bella's programming, ready for when the robot would be taking over Isabel's work routine. Vincente was both speedy and skillful at creating this intricate software and for the most part, Isabel was so appreciative of his expertise that she could only sit back and marvel.

Her superiors had instructed her to ask for expert assistance in this task since her own skills were not in the software area. They had given her carte blanche as to whom she would consult. Not surprisingly, she had asked Vincente to assist and her enthusiastic fellow scientist had wholeheartedly taken on the task. He was making good progress, forging ahead with the designs for the robot's work programs while Isabel watched.

Whenever he took a break, she took the opportunity to thank him profusely.

"I don't know what I would do without your help, Vincente. You have such a brilliant mind for computer technology. I would be quite lost without you. I did learn some computer programming, but I can't create anything on the scale that you can. I really enjoy watching you work."

Vincente would take her hand and look into her face with his intense dark eyes. "I will do anything for you, dear lady. I would only ask in return that sometimes you have dinner with me."

So it was, that if they worked late into the evening, Isabel phoned Doug to say that she would not be home that night. Then she and Vincente would dine at one of the quiet restaurants around Boston that he seemed to know so well.

The winter months with their often cold and damp weather gave these warm, cozy dining places an extra allure while their shared project drew them closer together as they shared ideas and how to put them into action. Isabel felt very comfortable with the younger scientist. It was quite evident that he enjoyed her company despite their age difference.

Their scientific discussions did not stop him from trying to find out where she planned to go on her illicit vacation. One day, he made a startling proposal that Isabel had not anticipated.

"Dear lady, I have a wonderful idea. I can program Vincente-Two to do my lab work at the same time as Bella is covering for you. Then I can holiday with you on that tropical island that you have talked about before. You must have selected it by now. Where did you say it was?"

Isabel had to laugh at his audacity and imaginative thinking.

"You know that won't work, Vincente. I need you at the lab while I'm away in case something goes wrong with

Bella. You're the only one who knows about my secret vacation and also, you're the only one who knows how my robot's technology works."

Vincente looked crestfallen until she added," But I do want to thank you for all the work you have done on Bella. I can't tell you that enough times, but I can say--"

"Yes? Yes?" her colleague interrupted eagerly.

"I can say that I will pay for our dinners all this week. I know that we both usually pay our own way, but I hope you will take up my offer?"

Her fellow scientist looked disappointed but somewhat mollified. After a moment's hesitation, he graciously accepted, much to Isabel's relief. The conversation turned to what restaurants they should try.

Doug also had to accept his sister's new and erratic schedule even though he didn't like it. As he was alone in the house for most of the time now, with his only commitment being to write a weekly column for his former newspaper, he decided to do something entirely different. Attracted by a course called, "From Cook to Chef,' he enrolled at the local cooking school as a part-time student.

"This will be my new hobby. It'll be good for my morale to have experts teach me the best way to cook and bake, though I'm not bad as it is.

I'm even allowed to eat what I cook at the school. And won't Sis be surprised by a gourmet menu when she comes home!"

The following weeks flew by. There were a few snowstorms, but they could not dampen Doug's enthusiasm for his new educational field. At the cooking school, he wore his hat and apron with aplomb and looked forward to each day's new learning. Little by little his expertise grew as he also learned the best places to shop for fresh ingredients and which farms and natural product stores were reliable for quality foods. He especially enjoyed his visits to the harbour to buy fresh fish.

"Isabel doesn't know what super meals she's going to be eating when her project is over."

This kept his spirits high until the day that he had been dreading arrived.

It was a Monday afternoon, one of the days he didn't go to the school. It being a cold, damp day, Doug had decided to start his own recipe book, by copying some of the school's recipes for meals into a hardbacked notebook that would be handy to have in the kitchen. He had so many student information papers that he was in danger of losing track of all of them.

He was muttering to himself as he concentrated on which ones to select.

"I like the idea of putting them into complete meals, like the menus we write at the cooking school. I could do this on the computer, but it's more fun and more impressive to have a hand-written recipe book."

Doug was whistling a happy tune when he heard familiar footsteps approaching across the hall. He paused and raised his eyes to see Isabel coming into the room. He took his reading glasses off to greet her in a brotherly fashion.

"Isabel! Why didn't you phone to tell me that you were coming home for dinner tonight?"

"I am Bella," corrected the robot.

Doug sat up straighter, his heart pounding. "Bella? Why are you here? Where's my sister?"

"She's gone."

For an instant he felt as if he had been stabbed in the heart. Those were the same words the doctor had used last year, when he had verified that Doug's wife had died. The same sharp sense of desolation, and now added dread, swept over him again. His throat was so dry that it hurt to speak. He whispered hoarsely, "How did it happen?"

The robot could sense his uneasiness but not the cause of it.

She explained. "After upgrading my databank, Isabel packed her bag and instructed me that I was to act in her place while she was gone. Dr. Da Cosa would help if there were any difficulties. Then she went away and now everyone is calling me Dr Lindsay."

Doug felt totally foolish for his irrational emotional reaction. But he was so relieved to hear that Isabel was still alive, that for once he couldn't find anything more to say.

When he remained silent, Bella continued, "You can call me Dr. Lindsay too, if you wish."

Doug began to laugh. "In your dreams," he responded, his voice becoming stronger.

"But I don't…." He cut Bella short, knowing what she was about to explain, by saying quickly, "Bella I'm going to fix dinner. Come with me. I want to hear more about what happened."

Once in the familiar kitchen, he recovered from his scare.

"I'm going to make a vegetable frittata for myself while I listen to you," he said, "So, where is Isabel?" He began chopping onions, red peppers and zucchini, popping them into the hot olive oil in a skillet. He paused for an answer before slicing a green apple.

"I do not know where she is now. That information is not in my database. It may be stored in my secret memory app."

"Then open it!" he demanded as he added the chopped apple to the pan and began whipping two eggs with a little milk.

"That is not permitted. That app is operated by the person who installed it. I can add new information to the memory, but I cannot open it unless the right password is used."

Doug glared at the robot as she watched him grate cheese.

'The person who installed that app must be Vincente Da Cosa. That damned scientist! I'm sure he's at the bottom of all this secrecy. What I really want to know is what he and Isabel are up to.'

Rattled by this unpredictable cloak-and-dagger situation into which he had unwillingly been thrust, he nearly forgot to add the eggs to the pan and sprinkle the cheese on top with some seasoning herbs. Still distracted by his dilemma, he barely remembered to check the frittata as it began to bubble around the edge. The final step was to slide it under the broiler to brown.

It wasn't until Doug was eating his supper that he realized that, since his sister had left him no instructions, he had yet another problem on his hands.

'What am I supposed to do with Bella when she comes home every evening? She can't stand around looking at me all

the time. If I lock her into the suitcase, I'll have to remember to let her out every morning for her to go to the NIR. What a pain! But if I leave her loose, there's no knowing what mischief she might get up to while I'm asleep.'

Suddenly his frittata didn't taste so good.

CHAPTER 23

*L*ater that evening, Doug and Bella were in the living room. He was looking at a news programme on television, with Bella watching quietly while recording relevant information into her database.

Every now and again, Doug's attention wandered, nagged by the worry of what he should do with the robot when he went to bed.

'It's a Catch 22 problem. I can't shut her down without having to get up early tomorrow to switch her on again, so that she can go to the NIR. If I don't shut her down, I won't sleep for wondering what she'll be doing downstairs.'

His conundrum was solved for him at 10:30 pm.

As soon as the clock in the hall chimed the half-hour, Bella rose and turned to leave the room. Doug was instantly alert. He sat up to demand, "Where are you going?"

"I am to go to Isabel's bedroom to find some different clothes and shoes to wear tomorrow."

Doug was flabbergasted at the robot acting in such an essentially human way. But before he could reply, Bella went on, "I will put them on tonight, so that I will not be delayed in leaving tomorrow morning. I will hang up the clothes I am wearing today and put them in the closet. I have to finish doing that before 11 pm."

Totally bemused, he asked, "Why before eleven o'clock?"

"My systems will shut down at that time and I will be activated again at seven am. tomorrow, ready for me to drive to the NIR."

Not wasting any more time in conversation, Bella left the room. Doug could hear her walking solidly upstairs.

"I can hardly believe it," he muttered to himself as he scratched his head. "Isabel must have programmed that whole routine into Bella."

He settled more comfortably into his armchair, still considering this surprising development, but aware that his dilemma had been solved.

'I would say that Isabel's a genius at thinking of everything - if it weren't for the fact that she didn't think to tell me what's going on.'

Much later when he went to bed, Doug noticed that the light was off in Isabel's room, so he quietly opened the door and peeped in. Inside, Bella was standing silently by the closet, dressed in his sister's clothes. She looked so much like Isabel that he shuddered and quickly closed the door.

'This is one weird situation', he mused while climbing into bed. *'If I tried telling anybody else about this, they would think I was crazy.'*

With that comforting thought, he settled down to sleep.

The sound of a car starting up outside woke Doug the next morning. He jumped up to open the curtains in time to see Bella drive off in Isabel's car. A smile spread over his face. "Peace at last!" he muttered as he headed to the shower.

His peace did not last long. During the afternoon his throat began to feel scratchy. He ignored it for a while but when the pain refused to go away, he found some old zinc lozenges in the First Aid cupboard and popped one into his mouth. That eased the soreness for a while but by the time Bella came home, his throat felt as if it were on fire. It hurt to swallow. His ears were hot and painful. He was thoroughly miserable.

The robot found him lying on the sofa in the living room.

"Did you have your supper early?" the robot asked.

"I'm not hungry," Doug croaked.

"What's wrong with your voice?" she enquired.

"It hurts to talk," he answered brusquely.

"Why?" she asked.

"Stop asking so many damned questions," he said irritably. "If you want to help, go into the kitchen and make me a hot orange drink."

"How do I do that?"

Doug gave a weary sigh. "There's a can of frozen orange juice in the freezer. Put a spoonful in a mug and add boiling water. Then bring it to me."

Bella did as he instructed and while he was sipping the drink, she commenced to tell him all about her day at the NIR. He dozed off in the middle of her recital but woke later, to find that she had switched on the local news program and was watching it intently.

He squinted at the television, but his eyes seemed out of focus. "What time does that say at the top of the screen?" he asked and immediately wished he hadn't spoken when his sore throat rasped painfully.

"It is 10:25 pm."

"Then it's nearly time for you to go upstairs," Doug pointed out, hoping to avoid more conversation or questions from Bella.

Promptly at 10:30, the robot rose to climb the stairs.

Doug, inexplicably exhausted by their brief exchange, fell back into the sofa cushions, thinking: *God help me! I hope this isn't the start of a Spring cold. I haven't had one for years. Probably got chilled going out in this constant rain. And worrying about Isabel doesn't help.*

It wasn't until later, when he was dragging himself to bed, that he thought, *Well, the good thing is that at least I don't have to deal with the robot this week. She's following her planned schedule.*

Doug's sore throat persisted through Tuesday and Wednesday and he had almost decided to try to get a doctor's appointment when his throat finally relented, but his nose started streaming and streaming. He collected all the boxes of paper tissue that he could find in the house. Looking at the paltry number, he wondered if he would have enough.

"What a miserable life!" he grumbled. "What have I done for the Fates to plague me like this? Isn't having a secretive sister like mine and her annoying robot-double enough punishment for one person?"

Doug's week continued to go from bad to worse.

By Friday, he was losing his voice. There was no way that he could go to the Black Horse Inn that Saturday.

Thoroughly disgruntled, he called Burt at the newspaper office before his voice totally gave out, to tell him that he couldn't meet his friends as usual. Even Burt's commiserations didn't make him feel any better. In his frustration, and if he'd had enough energy, he would have kicked all the furniture in sight.

'I was really looking forward to Saturday's quiz night at the pub.' Cursing under his breath, he lay down in the living room, pulled a blanket over himself and wracked by a persistent cough, tried in vain to sleep away his rotten cold.

When Bella returned home that Friday evening, her first week at the NIR completed, she was about to report to Doug what she had been doing, but he cut her short. From the depth of the warm sofa, he asked her to go prepare a frittata for his supper. Since she had watched him cook one on Monday, she would remember how to prepare it. *'Anything to keep her quiet,'* he thought uncharitably.

Later, Bella retired upstairs at the usual time.

Saturday morning brought him little relief. At eight o'clock, Doug gingerly made his way downstairs intent on sending Bella to the pharmacy. Isabel's car was in the driveway, so he knew that the robot hadn't gone to the NIR.

He fixed himself a hot drink and waited for her to appear. He was still waiting at ten o'clock. No Bella. Had her internal clock malfunctioned?

Worried that there might be something wrong, he slowly mounted the stairs with what little breath he could muster. He opened the door to Isabel's bedroom. Pausing to catch his breath again, he looked in and saw the robot standing silently by the bed.

"Bella!" he called in a hoarse whisper. His voice caught in his throat, setting him off into a coughing fit. When he had recovered enough to speak, he noticed that the robot hadn't stirred one jot.

Doug closed his eyes in despair. *'There's something wrong with Bella! What am I going to do now? I don't know how to fix her.'*

But his next thought truly terrified him.

'If the robot has broken down, she won't be able to go to the NIR to do Isabel's job. What's going to happen to Isabel's project? Everything will be ruined!'

CHAPTER 24

$\mathcal{D}$reading a calamity awaiting him, Doug hung back from entering Isabel's bedroom. Then, trying to gain control of both his streaming cold and his growing mental trepidation, he blew his nose deliberately loudly with his last Kleenex. On getting no immediate reaction that he had been heard, he went into the room and stared into the robot's face, so uncannily like his own sister's.

"Bella!" he hissed loudly. It sounded more like "Della," but it was the best he could enunciate.

She looked peaceful with her eyes closed. Her robot body was upright and inert. Even though he knew he was probably doing something useless, Doug took hold of her shoulders and gave them a good shake.

"Wake up, Bella!"

When that elicited no response, he reached for the ON / OFF switch he used when preparing the robot for her suitcase. He switched it to ON. Nothing happened. After trying this tactic two or three times, he backed up to sit wearily on Isabel's bed.

He wondered aloud in despair, "I don't know anyone to call who might be able to help me. Well, there is that scientist Vincente Da Cosa, but I'm not going to phone him! He'll ask why I want Bella operational. I can hardly say that I want her to run some errands for me."

Wracked by another coughing spell, he gave up trying to wake Bella and went downstairs to see if there were any dregs left in the cough syrup bottle.

He drowsed away the afternoon as much as he could with his restricted breathing but was shocked out of his misery in the evening by the sight of the robot entering the living room. Doug sat up too quickly and choked and coughed for a long while before he could manage to say, "What happened to you?"

"Nothing has happened to me," the robot replied, "I am here."

"I don't understand," Doug said, running his hand through his unruly hair. "I couldn't wake you this morning. Why are you switched on now?"

"I obey my programming," she said. "I am switched on now to run errands for you."

"But how did you know I need you to run errands?" he asked.

"I have a command to do errands for you this evening. Do you want me to drive somewhere?"

Still trying to understand all this unfathomable technological magic, Doug struggled to his feet saying, "Yes. I would like you to go to the pharmacy to get some things for me. I'll give you a list and my credit card."

As he handed the card to Bella, he said, "I know Isabel showed you how to use one of these. There's a pharmacist on duty tonight between 7pm. and 9pm at our local pharmacy. I'll write a list of the things I need to get rid of this damned cold."

He scribbled a list of items, while instructing the robot to ask the pharmacist for a good cough syrup and where to find Friars Balsam in the store. He was about to hand her the list when he remembered he needed some disinfectant, so he added that as the final item.

Doug felt almost cheerful after Bella left, anticipating fresh supplies of paper tissues and medicines that the pharmacist would recommend. He would take anything to gain some relief from his constant coughing. Rubbing his sore chest, he wished that he had remembered to add Vick's Vapor-Rub, but it was too late now. Re-energized by relief that Bella was not as defective as he had feared, he pattered into the kitchen to make himself another hot drink.

Bella drove to the pharmacy located by her internal maps. Before she went in, she entered Doug's list into her database, leaving the paper in the car. It didn't take her long to locate all the items except the last one. The pharmacist lady was helpful in recommending various cough remedies that Bella found on the shelves. She swiped the credit card at the check-out counter, after which the package containing the purchases was given to her.

Before the robot started the car to return to the house, she looked again at the last item Doug had written on the list. Her database was not wrong. There was the item: alcohol. Pharmacies do not sell alcohol. Liquor stores or bars sell alcohol. Searching her memory bank, she found one of those places a few streets away.

There seemed to be many cars parked around it. Bella squeezed the car between a pick-up truck and a Honda in a space a human might have thought was too small but which her computer mind had measured accurately. She eased out of the driver's seat and walking around a group of chatting people, pushed open the front door of the Black Horse Inn.

As she made her way through the narrow passage leading to the bar, loud talking and laughter assailed her sensitive ears. In the big barroom, people were moving chairs to small tables and were huddling together. A thin man and a fatter one with a bald head were busily directing them to collect pencils.

Bella bought a bottle of rum alcohol to replace the empty bottle in Doug's kitchen but as she turned to go, a voice called out, "Hey! Hey, Isabel!"

Hearing a familiar voice, and a now familiar name, she swung around to see Colin pushing through the crowd towards her.

"Hey, Isabel, are we glad to see you!"

He came closer, waving three empty glasses. "Sorry to hear that Doug is sick. Did he send you to take his place? Come, the quiz is about to begin."

Colin held up the three glasses, saying, "Half a mo', Isabel. I'll just get these filled and then you can follow me."

Bella watched the bartender fill the glasses from a pump as she searched her database for a definition of a quiz. It indicated that it was some sort of sport involving questions and answers.

Brandishing the glasses above his shoulders, Colin dodged his way across the room to the corner table where Burt and Les were sitting. Burt was the first to see Bella.

A broad smile spread over his face as he jumped to his feet. "Look who's here! It's Doug's sister!"

Jolted out of his West Indian calm, Les turned around quickly at the same time as Colin slowly put the drinks down. Rising to his feet to see who was behind Colin, he accidently knocked the table, spilling some of the beer Colin had managed to bring through the crowd without losing a drop.

"Look out, Les!" Colin exclaimed, "Watch what you're doing!"

But the tall Jamaican had eyes only for Bella. So, this was Doug's clever sister. He searched her face, noticing some mild resemblance to Doug but whereas his friend had worry marks all over his forehead, hers was quite smooth. She was older than Les had imagined. Her smooth skin showed fine wrinkles around the eyes and mouth while her impeccably groomed brown hair had some touches of grey above her ears. He was a little taken aback when he saw that she was scrutinizing him with a similar intense gaze.

He couldn't know that Bella was loading her database with impressions of him: A very tall thin man, younger than Doug, with crinkly black hair and blue-gray eyes in a brown face: an athletic body and large hands and feet.

Les extended his hand, saying, "I'm Les. My colleagues here have met you before, but I haven't had the pleasure."

Putting the bottle of rum carefully down on the table, Bella shook his hand. They both noted how strong a grip the other one had.

Les said, "I see you have brought your own drink."

"I bought this for Doug," she answered, "He wants alcohol to treat his cold."

Les raised his eyebrows but made no comment. With a gallant sweep, he held a chair out for her to sit beside him. Colin nudged Burt and winked, whispering, "I think he likes her."

The booming voice of Henry Oxley urged everyone to take their places for the quiz to begin.

Burt was designated to write their responses to the questions they were about to be asked. Bella was aware of how quiet the room had become with everyone concentrating. Was this a sport? Only Burt was moving any parts of his body and those were only his fingers.

Bella watched as this trio of men answered questions posed by the loud-voiced man. They conferred about characters in Dickens' novels, geographical regions, and world affairs but she noticed how quickly they answered a question about Pope Benedict XVI being the first to do something unique. They all knew that answer. She silently used her inner computer to check that they were right.

She helped out with naming ten fruit containing a single stone. Then she became involved in answering science, technology and education questions when the men looked to her for guidance. Bella already knew that her computer brain was supplying the correct answers.

When the quiz was over and the papers were being collected to be marked, the robot abruptly rose, picked up the bottle of rum and began to leave. Although Doug's friends begged her to stay until the winners were announced, Bella shook her head and made her way through the now animated and noisy patrons bombarding the bar. It was after 9:30 pm. She was being directed to return to Doug at once.

CHAPTER 25

*H*e heard the car arrive outside the house and hurried to the door. "What took you so long?" Doug demanded. "I was wondering if you'd had an accident. Where have you been? And did you get all the things I wanted at the pharmacy?"

"No, I had to go somewhere else for the last item on your list," Bella replied, placing the package on the kitchen table.

"The pharmacy didn't have any disinfectant?" he asked in disbelief.

She handed him his list. "You wrote 'alcohol' so I had to go elsewhere to buy you rum. Isn't that the alcohol you wanted? You didn't specify what kind of alcohol, so I brought you Jamaican rum to replace the empty bottle on the counter here."

Doug perused his list and seeing 'alcohol' written in his own handwriting, groaned. "I was in a hurry. I should have written 'Isopropyl alcohol.'

He looked at the bottle of rum. "Well, I can certainly use that. Though not as disinfectant! Where did you go to buy it?"

"I went to the Black Horse Inn."

Doug stopped unpacking his medicines. He knew instantly what had happened and why the robot was late in returning. "And you saw Burt, Les and Colin, didn't you?" he wheezed accusingly.

"Yes, they wanted me to join in some sports game called a quiz. It was interesting to hear their questions. I helped them with some answers."

"The devil you did!" he exclaimed. "They were cheating!"

Bella checked her databank to find a definition of 'cheating.'

"No, I didn't see them cheat. All the answers were spoken quickly and clearly. Your friends weren't using any other means to find the answers. Their cellphones were closed."

Doug looked at Bella, wondering how to explain that using her robot brain could be construed as 'cheating.' Then he wondered, '*Is it cheating if none of them knew she was a robot? They were acting in good faith. They thought she was my sister Isabel.*'

He shrugged his shoulders, deciding that it was useless trying to say anything more to the robot. He didn't think Bella could differentiate between what was right or wrong in human terms. She didn't have a conscience.

As he was silently debating this dilemma in his mind, the telephone rang. It was an excited Les asking him to let Isabel know that their team had won the quiz. He also said that he hoped his sister could come to join the team again the next Saturday night.

When he put the phone down, Doug realized that Bella had left the room and was climbing the stairs to his sister's bedroom. He didn't relay Les' message as she probably wouldn't care about winning. He didn't think that robots had competitive qualities.

Muttering to himself, he debated how was he going to explain about Bella to his colleagues without giving away his sister's secret. Finally, sighing deeply, he gave up. What a mess Isabel was causing with her look-alike robot! He grabbed the rum and a glass and went to lie down.

Doug's midwinter cold persevered for a few more days as he steadily worked his way through the medicines and boxes of Kleenex. By the time the next Saturday came around, he was more than ready to leave the house for better entertaining venues. The Black Horse Inn beckoned.

When he was about to leave, Doug checked to see that Bella was standing silently in Isabel's bedroom as she did on Saturdays. She was quite inert. He tried the ON/ OFF switch in order to start folding her into the suitcase but when, for some unknown reason, that didn't work, he had no choice but to leave her there instead of locking her up.

"Okay!" he muttered as he left the room, "Now for a good night out with the gang at the Inn. I've been looking forward to this all week."

The Black Horse was as busy as ever. The Saturday quiz crowd was loudly talking and quizzing one another with questions before the official quiz began. There was raucous laughter when some wit tried to reply with a joke instead of a serious answer.

It was so noisy that Doug's ears, not used to so many voices after the quietness at home, began to ring uncomfortably. Glancing around, he noted a great many college students in the room, all talking and joking.

'*News of the quiz and its payout sure travels fast,*' he thought as he threaded his way through the youths to the corner table where his newspaper buddies usually met. Burt was there by himself.

"Where's everybody?" Doug asked as he sat down.

"Hi, Doug! Glad you're feeling better and can join us. The others will be along soon. Deadlines to be meet tonight before they can leave the newspaper office."

He looked around. "Where's your sister?" he asked. "Didn't she come with you?"

"No, she's having a quiet night at home. She's been working hard all week."

"Well, the others will be disappointed that she hasn't come. Especially Les. He's taken quite a shine to her. Keeps talking about her at work. You'd think he'd never met an intelligent woman before!"

Doug was intrigued but couldn't question Burt further as he abruptly stopped talking when he saw Les and Colin crossing the room towards them.

They clapped Doug on the back, saying they were glad that he was feeling fit enough to take part in the quiz and Colin offered to get the beers.

Les looked around the room before saying casually, "Is your sister here? I can't see her."

Burt winked at Doug, saying, "Looks like she's having a quiet night at home instead of joining us for the quiz, Les."

Doug could see that his sunny Jamaican friend was disappointed so he offered, "I'll just have to try to answer those questions she might have helped you with if she were here."

Colin heard that as he carefully set down the glasses on the table.

"Then I hope you're up to date with the latest technology and scientific developments," he observed cheekily. "If she hadn't known the answers to those categories last week, we wouldn't have won."

Fred the innkeeper interrupted the conversation, saying, "Five dollars each, please!" Then added, "No little lady with you tonight?"

"No, she's not coming," Doug stated firmly.

He was handing him the money, when Fred asked, "Then who's this?"

Four heads swivelled round to see whom he meant, and three men were were happy to see Bella walking across the room towards them.

Fred held out his hand. "I'll need another five dollars."

Les' smile was as bright as the Jamaican sun. "Here, I'll pay for her," he said, digging out another five dollars from his wallet. He ushered Bella into the seat beside him. Doug scowled at the robot which smiled back at him and the quiz began.

'*What the hell is happening here? How did she know where I was?*'

Doug was so befuddled that he wasn't much help with the quiz and as soon as it was over, he stood up saying, "Sorry, guys. Guess I wasn't as well as I thought. Hope I haven't messed up your quiz. I think Isabel and I will have to call it a night now. Are you ready to go, Sis?"

The robot rose obediently and in spite of protests to wait for the quiz results, they bid the friends, 'Goodnight,' and left. As they reached the parking lot, Doug commanded, "Follow me home in your car. I want to talk to you there."

When they were together in the safety of the house, Doug demanded furiously, "How did you know where I was? You were asleep when I left. How and why did you suddenly come to life?"

The robot eyed him, unperturbed.

"I am programmed. I do what I am directed to do. I do not choose the timing. I say what I am instructed to say and do what I am told to do. And now I am being informed to go upstairs."

With that statement, Bella mounted the stairs to Isabel's bedroom, leaving Doug deflated. He collapsed into a chair, mopping his brow and groaning, "I don't understand. I don't understand it. Am I missing something here?"

A little later, he roused himself to fix a hot drink and sat in front of the television, trying to blank out the disastrous evening. But his mind kept wandering until finally he switched off the TV. He was trying to figure out what had happened before Isabel had turned up at the inn.

Then he remembered Bella's previous surprise awakening when he needed her to go to the pharmacy. It was definitely weird.

'How can a robot know what I need or what I am going to do? There must be a rational explanation for all this. Robots can't mind-read. At least, I don't think so.'

Doug felt very tired. It had been a long evening. He took a spoonful of cough mixture and went to bed.

In the middle of the night, he awoke with a start, his mind racing.

'That's it! Both times, I spoke in front of Bella. She must be able to hear what I'm saying!'

It seemed obvious now. *'The first time, I said I needed her to go to the pharmacy. Tonight, I distinctly remember muttering in the bedroom that I was going to the Black Horse Inn. My God! She must be listening all the time. I think she can't hear when she's comatose, but she can!'*

Now fully awake, he jumped out of bed to pace up and down, trying to fathom out how Bella functioned. His next thought banished all sleep for the rest of the night.

'Bella says that all her actions are programmed. I know my sister programmed the robot's work before she went away. But Isabel couldn't have known in advance what would happen at home afterwards.'

All this pacing caused a coughing fit, so he went downstairs to get his cough suppressant medicine. As he was taking it, Doug nearly choked on the spoon as another idea popped into his head.

'If Isabel can't be programming the robot's behaviour, then who is?'

CHAPTER 26

As if Doug hadn't enough to worry about, Les phoned at the ungodly hour of 8:30am on Sunday morning to tell him that they had tied for first place in the pub quiz with a young university team.

Half-listening after his sleepless night, Doug suddenly perked up when he heard Les say darkly, "We suspect that they're using some sort of information device to find the right answers. Otherwise, we all think they're too young to know things like the old films from bygone days and what happened during WW2. Maybe one of them is accessing his I-phone on the quiet and telling the others."

Doug was thinking that these suspicions were pretty rich, considering that their own team was getting illicit help from a robot's database knowledge. He wished he could find a way to stop them, but it was difficult with Bella turning up at the quiz times on Saturdays.

As he was musing, Les spoke into the sudden silence, "Is there any chance of me talking to Isabel now? Is she busy?"

That brought Doug fully awake. "She hasn't come downstairs yet, Les. She usually sleeps a long time on a

Sunday, and I don't want to wake her. Is there anything I can do for you?"

His friend mumbled, "No. I wanted to ask her something. Thanks anyway. Guess I'll see her next Saturday."

'Not if I can help it!' Doug vowed as he replaced the phone on its stand. There and then, he decided that he would side-track the robot from appearing at the next quiz night. He stood, musing, *'What should I do?*

Well, I must remember not to talk out loud about where I'm going. Can't talk anywhere in Bella's vicinity, even if she does appear to be switched off. I think she's keeping an eye on me and can hear me. I don't know how, but I don't like it!'

Still pursuing that thought, Doug went to make himself some breakfast. *'Or, on the other hand, I could say in her hearing where I intend to be at 8 o'clock next Saturday evening. Now there's an idea.'*

He thought about this for a minute then exclaimed, "I know, I could say that I'm going to a concert in Boston. Then I'll find out if Bella will follow me into town. If she doesn't but goes to the Black Horse Inn for the quiz instead, then that is another story. I'll still have to find out why she does that."

Exhausted by lack of sleep and all this intricate chicanery, he went back to bed to catch up on his sleep.

As the week went by, Doug fully recovered from his cold. Now that the Spring weather had arrived, he even ventured into the garden to rake the dead leaves off the flower beds and to pick up the broken branches and twigs brought down by the winter winds.

This activity gave him time to ponder on how his life had changed between his sister's disappearance and her ever-present, look-alike robot taking her place. Both Isabel and Bella were equally worrying to him and both caused him similar amounts of frustration.

As he raked, he remembered how peaceful his days had been before those two had taken such a dominant role in his life. He keenly missed his late wife's wise advice. Usually she had been right about everything. He even knew what she would have said about his present predicament. She would have told him to stop worrying and let things take their course.

Doug sighed, knowing that he couldn't take that advice because he couldn't stop his active mind from running on and on. Or maybe he didn't want to give up just yet.

'But what's really irritating is Bella turning up at the Black Horse Inn on Saturdays. It's uncanny the way that robot arrives just in time to do the quiz with the guys. If she's programming herself, that's not good news. It means she's making her own decisions. I've heard some robots can do that.'

He pushed a pile of dead leaves into a bag and carried it to the side of the house where, leaning on the rake to catch his breath, he ruminated, 'If she's learned how to act for herself, why does she want to be on the quiz team? What possible reason can there be?'

He paused to wave to some neighbours as they walked past his house.

Then, shaking his head at this exasperating conundrum, he decided that he'd had enough of raking and went indoors to rid himself of his shoes and gardening gloves.

Washing his hands in the kitchen, Doug was still trying to make sense of Bella's actions. *'But, if someone else is programming the robot to go to the Inn, the question is: Why is it so important that she go there? And important to whom?'*

It was while preparing a cheese and pickle sandwich for his lunch that his fertile mind became inspired. Pouring himself a cup of tea, he pondered, *'Whoever's programming the robot must want to know what's going on. Can Bella be reporting back to someone else? Is she reporting all the things I do?'*

It was not a comforting thought.

Chewing the thick pumpernickel bread of the sandwich, Doug's surmising continued. *'And why is Bella always telling me what's been happening at work when she comes home every day? Why does she always end by saying that everything is going well?'*

In one of those rare 'eureka' moments, he suddenly saw what he had been missing for the past month. He gulped down the bite he had taken.

"How stupid I've been!" he shouted to the world around him.

He was remembering all Bella's procedures when she returned from the NIR. Every day while he was eating his dinner, he'd had to endure her long report of what had been happening at the labs. He never listened. Usually he drowned out the noise of the robot's voice- so like his sister's vocals - by playing the radio loudly while she blathered on. Bella always ended with the same irritating words, "Everything is going well." As if he cared!

But now he realised that he should have cared, because he was sure, due to his flash of inspiration, that his sister Isabel must have set up Bella's report to give Doug information. She must want him to know what was happening at the labs, though he didn't understand why. That 'Everything is going well,' must be a message to him that she was okay. It had to be the right explanation! It all made sense now!

Doug felt extremely foolish for not realizing this sooner, but he was also vastly relieved. His sister had always been the clever one in the family. She expected people to follow the twisting avenues and paths of her quick brain. As if that were possible!

But with this novel idea that she might be communicating with him, he could have finally cottoned on to her ingenious mind. He only needed to start listening to Bella every evening. Maybe Isabel was sending him a secret message.

Doug finished his sandwich. Then feeling much happier after this unexpected and momentous discovery, he poured a generous amount of rum into his hot tea by way of celebration.

Yes, he was definitely feeling better.

CHAPTER 27

*W*ednesday had already come and gone that week, so it was Thursday before Doug got a chance to listen carefully to Bella's daily recounting of what had happened at the NIR. He was anxious to test his theory about Isabel sending him messages. He would listen carefully to every word.

To while away the day until the robot got home, he decided to write his freelance column for the local newspaper, having missed two weeks through illness. Although he stared at the blank screen on his computer, he couldn't settle on a topic. For a long time, wondering what to write about, he sat lost in thought, his mind wandering this way and that. Words failed to flow from his fingers.

All he could think about was Bella and whether his suspicions were right about his sister sending him information via the robot. Sometimes the idea seemed so far-fetched that he began to have grave doubts. But then he told himself that the whole situation of Isabel and her doppelgänger robot might read like a fiction story to other people. Nobody else would believe what he already knew—that it was happening for real.

Finally abandoning any further thought about writing, he fell back on what he liked to do best and that was why later, Bella found him in the kitchen surrounded by a number of cooked and uncooked pies. As soon as Doug saw the robot, he took off his apron, sat down at the kitchen table with a damp towel to cool his heated face and waited expectantly for her to speak. Unlike his usual reception of her talk, this time he was all ears.

Bella gave him a searching look, so much like one of his sister's glances, that he grimaced at the similarity.

"So, Bella, tell me all about your day at the NIR."

She only paused for a second.

"It was a busy day, today. More of the equipment that Dr. Da Cosa has ordered for the lab arrived this morning and had to be checked.

Afterwards, I helped him set it up because he didn't want anyone else there, in case they messed it up. It is the most modern equipment available. He said that it was very delicate, but I could understand and be able to follow his directions for assembling it. Then the professor spent the rest of the day on his own, setting up new computer programmes on the equipment. He was still working when I came home. He often continues working after everyone else has left for the day."

Doug was puzzled. "But I thought that the NIR has had their budget slashed recently. How can they afford new, ultra-modern equipment? Someone would have to okay the expenditure."

"I signed the forms for it," Bella promptly replied. "I write, 'Isabel Lindsay' at the bottom of all the order forms.

I sign many, many papers for Vincente because it is my job. I am the manager responsible for the laboratory."

Doug was suspicious. This didn't sound quite right to him.

'I bet that Da Cosa is taking advantage of Isabel being out of the office to order new equipment for his own research. If she'd been there, I don't think that she would have agreed to the purchases without consulting with her superiors. Maybe the robot doesn't know she should do that. But he does!'

In spite of these misgivings, he let Bella continue her report without interrupting.

"The lab has been very busy lately with many requests from abroad. There have been so many, that Vincente has taken over the job of replying to foreign countries. He is helping our secretaries so that they don't get over-worked. He is always busy working. Everything is going well."

Doug was going to get her to tell him more about what sort of overseas requests were being made to the NIR, but Bella had finished her report and had lapsed into silence. He realised that the robot had shut down temporarily. He had no choice but to save his questions for later nearer bedtime, when she usually started up again.

As if on cue, the kitchen timer ting-ed so he hurriedly rose to take two pies out of the oven before the crusts began to burn. The uncooked pies he wrapped and put in the freezer. This kitchen activity didn't stop his mind from turning over everything that Bella had just told him.

As he selected a steaming meat pie for his supper and took a cold juice out of the fridge, Doug was busily thinking, *'There must be a reason why I need to know what is happening at Isabel's laboratory. But if something is wrong, how would I know? And what could I do about it?'*

He couldn't fathom it out. It was like a cryptic crossword with hidden clues, not that he could do those puzzles either, but they might be easier to work out than living with an inextricable robot or trying to interpret messages and clues from a missing sister. Doug decided not to bother to question the robot later. His life was confusing enough.

Bella's report on Friday brought more disconcerting news.

"The last of the new equipment arrived today. After I had signed for it, Dr. Da Cosa had it taken into his own lab and closed the door. He didn't ask me to help him this time, so I filed all the papers that were on my desk in the right alphabetical order. I do that very fast. My desk is tidy for next week.

The secretaries were clearing their workspaces too as some of them are taking the same Spring Break holiday as members of their own families. I gave them permission to be away from work, but I do not get a vacation. I will be going to the Institute every day.

Today, I looked into Vincente's lab when he came out. I caught a glimpse of another man in there using a computer. I did not see who it was, but he must have entered by the hall door. Nobody came past my office to enter the labs. He looked familiar but I only saw him for a second. I do not know who he was. Everything is going well."

Doug had forgotten that the Boston schools and universities were going to be closed for two weeks for the traditional Spring Break holidays. Most students would be heading further south to beach resorts and to outdoor parties in the sunshine.

"Lucky youngsters!" he grumbled.

On Saturday, Doug put his own plans in action. Bella was motionless in Isabel's bedroom at the weekends. He decided to send her off on a wild goose chase into Boston. There was a concert advertised for 8pm. that evening at Symphony Hall.

In the afternoon he wandered into the bedroom talking to himself. He said loudly, "I hope that concert at Symphony Hall this evening will start on time. Last time I was there, it started fifteen minutes late. You would think that they could start at 8 o'clock as advertised."

Having planted his seeds of discord in the listening robot, Doug ate a leisurely supper, finishing off with some apple pie, before quietly letting himself out of the house, en route to the Black Horse Inn. With luck, Bella would not turn up at the pub. If she were shadowing him, as he suspected, she would go to Boston instead.

Then his friends could enjoy a legit quiz game for once, without unknowingly relying on the robot's superior knowledge to help them win.

CHAPTER 28

When Doug drove into the Black Horse parking lot, he was surprised to see that it was almost empty. Usually on a Saturday night it was hard to find a parking space. He checked his wristwatch before locking his car, noting that it was a quarter to eight, nearly time for the quiz to start.

Wending his way through the narrow passages leading to the barroom, he observed that there weren't many coats hanging on the hooks shaped like horses' heads and on reaching the room, he noticed a lot of unoccupied bar stools. Very unusual.

Fred, the innkeeper, was polishing glasses behind the bar and holding them up to the light before placing them in the racks.

"Evening, Fred! Where's everyone tonight? I thought the pub would be full of people for quiz night."

"Did you forget that there's no quiz tonight, Doug? Announced it last Saturday. Henry Oxley is supervising a group of schoolkids going to Cape Cod for their Spring Break trip. He and three other teachers with the parent supervisors, left this morning."

Doug felt stupid for forgetting, inwardly blaming his memory lapse on the stress of dealing with Bella. "But where are the college students who always come on Saturdays?" he queried.

"Well, that's another matter," Fred responded. "I heard that a group of them got together to charter a plane to fly to Florida for the holidays. It's cheaper that way than going independently."

"Then, no quiz tonight?" Doug hollowly echoed Fred's words.

"Sorry about that," Fred said, "The quiz night will probably begin again when they all return in two weeks' time. In the meantime, can I get you something from the bar?"

Doug looked over to the fireplace corner where his friends were sitting in animated conversation, too deeply interested to have noticed his arrival.

"Just a pint of bitter, Fred."

As he waited, he leaned back against the hard, polished oak wood of the bar to watch his friends. They had their heads so close together as to be almost touching and surprisingly, it seemed to be Burt who was doing all the talking. That was out of the ordinary. Burt was an investigative journalist, better known for his quiet listening abilities rather than for his brilliant conversation.

Doug collected his pint of beer and unobstructed by patrons in the nearly deserted room made his way to the corner table. When Burt looked up and saw him coming, he stopped talking and the others turned around.

Doug immediately felt a wave of guilt sweep over him. *'Have they found out that who they think is my sister Isabel, is really a robot?'*

His hand trembled, sending a splash of beer down the side of the glass, from whence it dribbled down his front. He gingerly put his beer down beside his colleagues' drinks, fished out a paper napkin from the holder on the table and dabbed at his shirt, all without saying a word.

Les, who had been looking towards the door, asked casually, "Isabel coming tonight, Doug?"

Still busily wiping, Doug mumbled, "No, I think she's going to a concert at Symphony Hall in Boston this evening. She loves classical music."

Grinning at Les' crestfallen face, young Colin poked him with his elbow, saying, "Don't give up hope, Les! Women change their minds all the time. She might come through that doorway any minute now."

Doug, trusting that that wouldn't happen, seated himself opposite Burt, a place from where he could watch the entrance to the bar. "You all seemed to be deep in conversation when I came in. Anything interesting going on?"

Burt looked around to see if there were anyone near enough to hear before beckoning Doug to come closer.

"I was sharing some info I've just received. A tip about the government having a security problem. The paper wants me to investigate it full time, so I may be too busy to meet with you guys every Saturday from now on."

"And me, too. I'll be working with him," Colin hastened to add.

"Colin, how many times have I told you that the job of an investigator is to listen and not volunteer information?" Burt chastised him.

"But we're all newspaper men here and we know each other," Colin protested. "It isn't as if I'm giving away Top Secrets."

Doug interrupted their little spat to ask, "What sort of security problem? And why is our newspaper interested? Surely that's a Washington DC problem. What's it got to do with Boston?"

"You're right. It is a national security problem," Burt agreed. "But the information I have is that the source of the security leak source is here, in Boston."

Doug argued, "But Boston is a big place. Don't you have more specific info than that?"

"Yes, I have, but you know that I can't tell you anything more."

"We're looking for a scoop,' whispered the irrepressible Colin.

At which point, they were all startled by Les' infectious Caribbean laughter cutting into their conversation. "Man," he chortled, "You should just see yourselves. You is lookin' like a group of spies wid your heads together like dat. Everybody will know that you is talkin' secrets."

The men sat upright immediately. When Les lapsed into his Jamaican patois, it was his warning signal to be careful. "My round of drinks comin' up," Les continued affably. "Everyone okay with another beer?"

"I'll come to help you carry them," Colin offered with alacrity, before Burt could berate him for his latest remark.

The two old friends were left together at the table, both watching Les and Colin walk across the room to the bar, where a few more people had gathered. Doug took this opportunity to ask Burt, "Anything I can help you with?"

"Not unless you know a whole lot about the latest computers and modern hacking techniques and ways of sending secret information to other countries without being detected."

He smiled, knowing his friend's ignorance of most modern technology. Doug even got nervous sending his freelance column to the newspaper via the Internet. Something always went awry in the process to send him into a panic.

"Colin is a whizz on the computer and we're just starting to check the details."

Doug glanced across the room to where Les and Colin were picking up the full glasses. Quickly turning to Burt, he said, "Well, if you can tell me what area you're interested in, at least I can keep my eyes and ears open. Maybe I'll hear something that you might miss."

Burt shook his head. "Sorry. You know I can't say which area has problems. But I'm sure that it'll have nothing to do with you. Relax and enjoy your retirement away from the nitty-gritty of the newspaper world."

'*Nothing to do with me*'? Burt's reassurance failed to alleviate Doug's growing sense of alarm and dread. '*Might Burt's investigation into government agencies in Boston uncover the truth about Bella and Isabel at the NIR?*'

This worrying thought made Doug feel ill. Burt was looking at him closely. "You feeling okay, Doug? Your face has gone pale."

Doug took out his handkerchief and wiped the sweat from his brow. "It's just the remains of that flu I had. It keeps coming back every once in a while, making me feel bad. I'll be fine in a minute." He blew his nose for emphasis.

When Les and Colin came back to the table, Les' sensitive nature intuited Doug's discomfort at once. He placed a glass of ale in front of him saying, "Here, man, drink this up - though it looks like you could do with something stronger today!"

Gratefully, Doug took a long swallow and gradually the colour began inching back into his face. As Les slid into the seat beside him, Doug confided, "It's only that flu I had recently. It completely drains me of energy sometimes."

Les nodded, waving his glass in the air for emphasis, "One time when I got the dengue fever, I was like that myself. Even when you're sure that you've recovered, that fever used to come back when you least expected it. Takes you by surprise and there's nothing you could do about it. Just suffer."

Doug took a few more sips of his beer, then pushing his chair back, surprised his colleagues by announcing, "Sorry, but I think I need to have an early night tonight. I don't feel so good. On my way out, I'll order another round for you all, since it is my turn. See you next week."

Les stretched out his long legs, causing his chair to slide backwards on the wooden floor. "An early night's a good idea, Doug," he concurred.

"I could do with some real shuteye myself. Too many deadlines lately and there's no quiz tonight to keep us up late."

He sat straighter saying, "I'll be on my way too, soon as I drink my beer."

Colin chimed in, "Well, I've got lots of computer work to do for Burt, so an early night is okay with me. I'll have time to go back to the office and get started."

Burt nodded his head in approval. "Don't bother to order that round, Doug," he advised. "As Colin says, he and I have work to do and the sooner we start, the better. You can have your turn buying our drinks next Saturday. Just take good care of yourself."

Doug left them finishing their beers and on ducking through the low doorway at the inn entrance, paused for a moment when he realised that there was a light rain falling. He pulled up the collar of his coat, ready to dash to his car. It wasn't until he had scrambled into the driver's seat and was turning on the ignition that he remembered Bella.

She hadn't turned up at the inn. Had she gone to Boston instead? If she came to the inn later, she wouldn't find them at their usual corner table.

'Too bad!'

But as he drove up the slight incline of his driveway, he noticed that Isabel's car was parked near the house. The rain was gently pattering on the vehicle but underneath it, Doug could see a patch of driveway that was bone dry. *'Hmm. Either Bella hasn't been out at all or she came back before the rain started.'*

Priding himself on his detective skills, Doug went to find the robot. Kicking off his shoes and bounding up the stairs, he walked into his sister's bedroom. Bella was standing in the same spot as where he had left her earlier that evening. He had no way of knowing whether she had left the house or not. She stood as silent and stolid as a Sphinx and would be about as helpful if he tried to question her.

Doug dropped onto his sister's bed, his shoulders sagging and his arms dangling between his knees as he leaned forward to scrutinize the robot. He peered at Bella to see if there were any clues as to whether she had been out. Her shoes were clean and dry, her wig without a hair out of place, her eyes were closed as if she were asleep. But Doug knew from experience that she was capable of listening in spite of her apparent coma.

Feeling tired of the impossible situation his sister had imposed on him, he lay back against the pillows. *'I never knew that Isabel's bed was so much softer than mine.'* Within minutes, he was snoring loudly enough for any listening robot to hear.

For a while, when he woke in the middle of the night, he had no idea where he was. Had he had a bad dream? He stumbled upright, apologised to whom he thought was his sister Isabel standing there and after finding the door, weaved his way to his own bed before collapsing into slumber again.

CHAPTER 29

When Sunday dawned and Bella showed no sign of activity, Doug decided that it really didn't matter where Bella had been on the previous evening since he had succeeded in his attempt to keep her away from the Black Horse Inn. Smiling into his morning coffee as the sunshine from the window warmed his face, he vaguely wondered why she'd stayed in the house after he had set his trap for her to go to Boston.

His mind switched to other more urgent matters.

'How can I find out about Burt's investigation? He must have some contact in Washington D.C. for our editor to believe the information and assign Burt to this investigation. Burt and Colin will have to double-check all their leads. Being an investigative reporter is usually slow work, but I know Burt and he's like a bloodhound once he gets on the trail.'

Doug's random train of thoughts persisted throughout his shower and into his bedroom to get dressed.

'What kind of a national security leak can it be? Whoever is behind all this must have something to gain. Either money or power. Or both.'

Still pondering this question while looking for clean clothes, he decided that he needed to be more informed.

Slipping on a warm sweater, he went downstairs to the basement office computer. 'Now to find the archives of the national newspapers to see what's been going on lately. I'll look for any mention of security risks.'

He became more and more incredulous as he read articles from many sources, pointing out the shortcomings of government security in various areas of research. There were warning articles about the avid thirst for Western technology in Asian countries- South Korea, China and Japan specifically. Canada and the U.S. were being targeted as go-to sources for their rapid progress in computer technology and artificial intelligence.

Troubled by his newly acquired knowledge that North American research could fuel the development of not only helpful goals for other nations but could also stimulate their ruthless military and controlling mechanisms, Doug jotted down the names of recent books written on the subject.

"Guess I have to pay a visit to the local library," he said aloud.

Grabbing his car keys, Doug opened the front door- only to find Burt stepping into the outside porch.

"Glad I caught you!" his friend exclaimed. "I need a favour. I'd like to look inside the NIR so I came to ask Isabel if she can organize a tour for me. I hope she's home?"

Doug flinched as if someone had slapped him. He was immediately disturbed by the thought that it hadn't taken Burt long to zero in on Isabel's workplace. *'But why?'*

He stuttered a little as he answered cagily, "Er, Bel…. I mean Isabel, she usually sleeps late on Sundays. I, I leave her alone until she, she's ready to come down, downstairs. She works so hard during the week she needs her rest."

He took a deep breath, pulling himself together.

"Why don't you phone her later? If she doesn't answer, you can always leave a message."

Burt looked at him curiously before he agreed, slowly saying, "Yes, that's probably good advice. I thought that as Isabel knows me, she might have been able to take me around the NIR today if I asked her personally. But I guess not?"

Doug shook his head, swiftly locking the front door behind them. As the two friends walked down the path, he remarked, "You do know that there's heavy security at the Institute, don't you? You'll have to be security cleared before you're allowed in. And if they think you're the Press, I doubt if you'll even get over the doorstep."

As he opened his car door, he continued, "Besides, Isabel will have to get permission from her superiors for you to go inside the building. You'll need lots of identification. Have you a good reason for going there?"

Burt paused beside Doug's car.

"I'm sure that we can work all that out,' he asserted before changing the subject. "But how are you today? You're looking a little rattled, a bit like you did last night. You should try to take life easier now that you're retired. Where are you running off to now?"

Cognizant of his friend's bloodhound qualities, Doug slid into his car saying offhandedly, "I'm only going to the library to get some books to read."

Burt looked pleased. "Ah! Good for you! Wish I had time to lie around reading books, but I have to get back to the office to check on Colin."

It was on the tip of Doug's tongue to ask him how the investigation was going but not wanting to appear too inquisitive, he thought better of it. *'Best to let sleeping dogs lie.'* He was happy to see Burt drive away.

By the time he had reached the local library, he was much calmer. Although this was a branch library, it was surprisingly large and well stocked and if the book he wanted was not on the shelves, the librarians would find one for him from another library.

He loved the peacefulness of libraries, he loved looking along the shelves and selecting a book. It was like choosing a mystery gift for oneself because you never knew what intriguing story the inside pages would unfold. Doug hoped he would be able to understand the information in the books he wanted today, since the subject was a strange new world to him. Marching up to the desk, Doug asked where he could find up-to-date books on modern advances in computer science and technology. The librarian smiled at him. "That is a really popular subject nowadays," she remarked as she gave him instructions on where to find them.

"The way the young students devour those books, you have to think that it must be the coming thing. That and books about artificial intelligence. Are you interested in robots too?"

Doug was saved from the unexpected question by another patron leaning over his shoulder to gain the librarian's attention, so he quickly made good his escape before being forced into some evasive answer.

'Am I interested in robots? I wonder what she would say if I told her that I live with one.'

Doug took the elevator to the second floor and walked along the stacks of books, peering at the subject labels as he went. He worked his way along the Computer Science shelf, pulling out a few books with titles that caught his interest: 'Artificial Intelligence, The Next Generation,' by Beatrix Ware, 'Cyber-Security in Today's World,' and finally, 'Computer Science for Idiots.' He carried them to a nearby table and began leafing through the pages.

By the time he had read a few chapters from each book, his mind was reeling with many unfamiliar terms. He wished he had brought a notebook to jot them down so that he would remember them. Fishing in his pockets, he found his silver pen, the one his colleagues had given him when he retired from The Urban newspaper. His fingers absentmindedly traced the engraving of his name as he held it in his hand.

He finally unearthed an old shopping list scrunched deep inside his jacket pocket. Smoothing out the crumpled paper, he began scribbling on the back of it.

'I can look these up on my computer at home,' he thought as he wrote down: hackers - malware - worms - phishing - botnets - smart processing chips – software security- cybercrime- internet vulnerability.

'That's enough!' Doug took off his glasses and closed the books. *'How have I lived for so long and not needed to know any of these words? And what exactly do the DHS and CISA do?'* He felt overwhelmed by his own ignorance.

Not relishing the thought of spending an afternoon in front of his computer finding explanations for all this new information, Doug carefully put away his pen, pocketed his list and left the books on the table for the librarian to return to their rightful places on the shelves.

Leaving the building, he took a deep breath of fresh air. Descending the library steps, he was warmed by the sparkling Springtime sunshine that would only too soon fade into another hot, humid summer. Energized, Doug decided to take a walk along the residential street outside the library.

The cherry blossoms had faded, leaving carpets of pink and white confetti around each tree along the road. In the gardens, the earlier daffodils and tulips had given way to equally ephemeral purple and yellow iris and delicately flowering azalea bushes, while hanging baskets of geraniums and ivy showed bright splashes of colour outside many of the houses.

There were men busy cutting their lawns, their lawnmowers humming between stops and starts. Children were swinging on swings suspended from tree branches or shooting balls into nets. There was a Sunday peacefulness in the air. It all looked so normal. A heavy sigh for his own abnormal life escaped his lips as he turned around to walk back the way he had come.

On the drive home, he had to pass the Black Horse Inn. Glancing at the clock on the dashboard, he realised that they would still be serving Sunday lunch in the inn's dining room. On the spur of the moment, he swerved into the inn's parking area to go in search of a traditional English Sunday meal: roast beef and Yorkshire pudding, fresh green peas, roast potatoes and lots of aromatic gravy, with a pint or two of beer to wash it down. Later, Doug came out feeling more content and decidedly more mellow.

Rattling his car keys, he began thinking that maybe everything would work out fine.

'Maybe I'm worrying too much about Isabel and Bella. I can leave this computer science research until Monday. There's no hurry. I'll have an afternoon nap instead. Bella will be quiet, and Burt has gone. Nothing is going to happen on a calm Sunday like today.'

CHAPTER 30

$\mathcal{D}$oug knew that something was wrong as soon as he turned into his driveway. Isabel's car had gone. Its parking spot was glaring in its emptiness.

Turning off the car engine, he banged his fists on the steering wheel, growling between his teeth, "That damned robot. Where's she gone now?"

He jumped out of the car too quickly and was hit by a wave of dizziness.

"And damn having that second pint of bitter!" he moaned, holding on to the car door to steady himself. A disturbing thought threw him even more off balance. "Or maybe the car has been stolen! There was an SUV stolen from a driveway down this street just the other night."

The first thing he did when entering his house was to look in the key tray by the front door. Isabel's car keys were not there. To check on Bella's whereabouts Doug began to climb the stairs to Isabel's room. Halfway up, through the stair railings, he could see that the bedroom door, closed when he left was now open. Fearing the worst, he ran into the room. No robot.

Doug sat on the top step of the stairs with his elbows on his knees, head in hands, wondering where Bella could have gone. The robot was becoming as wayward as his sister, not surprisingly, and as unpredictable.

'I wonder if Burt did phone about being shown inside the NIR and she has been activated. She could be over there now, showing him around. He did seem to be in bit of a rush to do the tour today.'

He considered that for a while before deciding that he wasn't too keen on asking Burt, but he could phone Colin to see if he knew anything.

Colin's phone rang and rang until Doug was switched to the answering service, at which point he snapped off his cellphone. He sat there, turning ideas over in his mind on how to find the robot. All he really wanted to do was take a nap, like most sane folks do after a heavy lunch.

Doug finally opted to have a little nap downstairs and wait to see if Bella would return in the meantime. He eased off the shoes that he had neglected to take off at the front door, made himself comfortable on the sofa in the living room and closed his eyes. After a few minutes, his eyes popped open as if of their own accord.

'Supposing Bella's had an accident? The police will find out that she's a robot when they question her. That would be fatal for Isabel's plans!'

Then reconsidering that alarm, he calmed down. *'Hmm. No, I don't think she's had an accident. She's too good a driver and there's not much traffic to cause her trouble on the highway on a Sunday. That is, if she were heading for the NIR, of course.'*

Worn out by all these worrying details, Doug closed his eyes again, turning on his left side to ease the heaviness in his stomach. But his eyelids refused to stay shut. They sprung open so that he could see across the room to the mantel clock. *'Almost four o'clock. I wonder what time Bella went out'.*

He struggled to sit up, sighing at the inevitable. *'The only way I can find out if Bella is at the NIR is to go there myself. Isabel's car should be in the parking lot.'*

Reluctantly, he pulled on his shoes to go look for his car keys. They weren't on the key tray as usual.

After a few anxious minutes, he finally found them in his pocket and set out to drive to the National Institute of Robotics. By the time he had reached his destination, he was fully awake. He had even enjoyed the easy afternoon drive without much traffic and even more happily, without seeing one restricting orange construction cone. As he pulled into the parking area, Doug spotted Isabel's car near the entrance to the Institute. And what was that parked beside it? Burt's well-known and unmistakeable old Honda, unmistakeable because it still sported in its back window, a decal of the Boston International Fair held over five years before.

'Well, at least he doesn't have a card saying, 'Press,' Doug couldn't help thinking as he made a quick circle around the parking lot before turning for home. He was very pleased that he had found Bella by surmising that she was probably showing Burt around the NIR.

It was much later that Doug resurfaced from the afternoon nap he had promised himself. It was growing dark outside and the streetlights had switched on, casting a yellow glow over the sidewalk. Standing at the kitchen window and by craning his neck, he could see to the nearest end of his driveway. His car was the only vehicle parked there.

Whatever was happening at the NIR was keeping Bella occupied for a long time. He reassured himself that when she reappeared sometime during the evening, he would bombard her with lots of questions for which she'd better know the answers.

He didn't feel hungry after the large meal at the inn, but his throat was dry. Opening the fridge, he passed over the bottles of cold beer and chose a little bottle of orange juice instead. Bringing out the last pieces of cooked ham and finding the Swiss cheese, he pulled out the pumpernickel bread, butter, and grainy Dijon mustard, depositing them on the kitchen counter. Some fresh lettuce followed that. Then he decided that coffee always tasted good with ham and cheese sandwiches and still feeling thirsty, he started a pot for himself. The distinctive rich aroma soon filled the kitchen.

"Hmm. That smells good!" said a voice behind him.

He spun around to see the robot smiling at him with his sister's smile. Doug waved the knife in his hand at her. "That is not funny, Bella! Since when have you been interested in what's cooking in the kitchen? I don't think you can even smell things."

"I've always been able to smell things, especially when you're making coffee."

Doug ignored this outrageous remark. "Are you going to tell me what you've been doing all afternoon, Bella?"

"Isabel. Not Bella."

"You're getting far too high and mighty with taking over my sister's job! I will not call you Isabel like everyone else does. Your name is Bella!" he shouted angrily.

"Calm down, Doug," she said, "And stop waving that knife in the air! You're making me nervous."

But Doug was not about to be stopped. "How can a robot be nervous? Your nerves are just cables. Just cables, Bella!" he repeated for emphasis.

"I'm not Bella. I'm your sister Isabel. Look at my face and see how tired I am. Bella's face stays the same all the time."

She came right up to him. "Look at me!"

Doug put down the knife to take her by the shoulders and peer into her face. Tears of tiredness started to trickle down her cheeks and he could feel her shoulders sag with weariness.

"My God!" he exclaimed, "I do believe you ARE Isabel."

He drew her closer, his own eyes growing misty. "At last! You've come home at last, Sis. Sit down here and I'll make you a sandwich as well as coffee. Then you can tell me where you've been all this time."

"But where's Bella?" he asked as Isabel sank onto a chair. "That annoying robot went missing today. Caused me a lot of bother and worry."

"She's okay. She's safe in her suitcase in the hall, where she'll stay all next week," his sister replied. "While I go to take her place at the NIR."

Doug paused for a second, wrinkling his brow, to digest what Isabel had just said. Thinking it through, he said slowly, "That's a very strange thing to say. You already work at the NIR. Why would you say you're going to take Bella's place? She was substituting for you. You're only going back to your own job."

As Isabel nodded agreement, Doug added, "Am I missing something here?"

She hesitated before answering, "It's complicated, Doug. I have to pretend to be Bella for a few days because her databank has been invaded by malware and may have been hacked. I had to shut her down until we find out what's happening and without alerting anyone else. Until that problem is fixed, I need to go into the labs to protect the integrity of my project."

She sighed. "It's important that whoever has hacked into her computer thinks that she's still on the job. If they try to steal information, we may be able to trace the source, or even feed them misinformation."

Isabel finished her sandwich and drained the last of her coffee.

She gave a huge yawn, then said, "My project is nearing its final stages, Doug. I don't want anything to go wrong now."

Her brother, feeling that he hadn't quite understood her explanation and wanting to ask more questions, stopped laying ham and cheese on the pumpernickel to look at his sister. Isabel's head was gently descending towards her chest and he knew that she was nodding off to sleep. Taking her by the shoulders, he steered her upstairs to her bedroom, helped her onto the bed and pulled a coverlet over her.

'Maybe I'll get to know more later.'

But his hopes were shattered when she didn't emerge later that evening and the next morning, he was awakened by the noise of a car backing out of the driveway. He didn't need to check who was driving.

Isabel must have risen earlier and would be on her way to the NIR. As he went downstairs, he noticed that Bella's suitcase had also disappeared.

Doug fidgeted from task to task before noon, hoping that his sister would phone, until he remembered that Bella never used to call during the day. Isabel would not run counter to an established routine. He had no choice but to wait until she came home that evening, hopefully to give him an account of her day, as Bella used to do.

In desperation, he went to the basement office to research the list of technology words he had written down at the library. Being stuck in front of a computer was not his first choice of things that he most liked to do, but Necessity called. *'I really need to know the meanings of the words Isabel uses, to understand what she's talking about.'*

Much later, by the time he had finished, he was so befuddled by the range of the vocabulary new to him that he began muttering to himself.

"I never knew what a sinister machine a computer can be. I'm almost afraid to use mine now! There are so many hackers out there who can gain access to everything on people's computers - and not for any good purpose either. Nothing is private anymore!"

Doug closed the information source he had been using and shut down his computer. He waited for the screen to darken before collecting his notes. Still talking to himself, he went upstairs to the kitchen.

"But at least I know now what malware is, and how viruses and worms invade and damage computer programs. That's how cybercriminals get access to personal data. They steal passwords and personal info and cause havoc. Scary identity theft!"

All that technological mayhem had left a bitter taste in his mouth. He went to the kitchen to get a glass of filtered water. Doug opened the fridge and freezer to see if there was anything Isabel might like for supper when she came home, but half his mind was still distracted by his research.

Looking into the vegetable drawer, he said, "And how about those worms that can be embedded into your computer programs? Once there, they multiply automatically into copies of themselves and eat into other people's programs. Without anyone knowing."

Doug picked up a head of lettuce from the fridge, but in easing the leaves apart, he discovered tiny green caterpillars had eaten holes in the middle. Disgusted, he threw it and the caterpillars out and began a grocery list with 'salad' as the first item.

"And I didn't know that 'botnets' is short for 'robot networks.' Or that huge botnets are networks of zombie computers remotely controlled by hackers."

He snorted. "Zombies! Whatever names will they think of next?"

He looked at a box of frozen hors d'oeuvres, picturing them baked to a crisp golden brown on a plate beside a glass of tawny sherry to celebrate his sister's return. Then he exclaimed, "And hello! I still have that frozen rhubarb and strawberry pie I made. I'd forgotten about that. That'll be dessert, with some vanilla ice cream."

He added 'ice cream' to his list. Now what to cook for the main meal?

"I have some lamb for an Irish stew, but Isabel really likes fish. If I'd thought about it earlier, I could have gone to the harbour for some fresh catch when the fishing trawlers came in this morning."

'Fishing, phishing,' he thought. *'Not much difference! Both are searching for prey. But now that I know about it, I have to be more careful of phishing on the computer and make sure that all my websites and e-mails are legitimate before opening them. Damned computer thieves using my friends' names and addresses to get information!'*

Bella had been hacked. That was far too close to home and thinking about it made him extremely uncomfortable. He ran a finger inside his shirt collar, as if it were too tight.

"If my computer's been invaded too, I may have to change my password. What a drag if I have to remember a new one! I'm not into changing passwords all the time."

To avoid thinking about that unwelcome outcome, Doug added 'Fish' and a few more items to his shopping list, then went to collect his car keys to go shopping for the ingredients he needed for Isabel's first dinner at home since her return.

That evening, Doug waited until Isabel had enjoyed her meal and had finished praising his newly acquired cooking expertise, before he tentatively began to ask her questions about the NIR. He hesitated a little, knowing that she might not take kindly to his enquiries.

"So, Sis, how was your day at the labs?" That seemed a safe opening gambit.

Isabel leaned back in her seat as she folded her napkin and inserted it into its wooden ring. She gave him a sharp look before she said, "You think that I'm taking on Bella's information session. Is that it? I used to listen in to what she was telling you."

"How did you do that?" Doug was startled into asking.

Disregarding his outburst, she continued, "Well, here goes.

Today, I saw all the modern equipment that Vincente had ordered while I was away. As a pretend robot I had no excuse for going into his lab, but I nipped in there when he went to lunch. He's such a brilliant scientist that even I couldn't follow what he's been working on. He's set up a global network of communications that are extremely difficult to follow. While he was out, I decided to open a new encryption programme on my own computer. For sensitive data. In case it is being compromised."

She gave a grim smile.

"Now everything is in place, we'll just have to wait to see what happens next."

CHAPTER 31

*W*hen Isabel arrived at the NIR early the next morning, Vincente was already busy in his lab. She wondered if he had been there all night because through the connecting window in her office, she noticed that he was looking somewhat bedraggled, quite unlike his former neat and dapper self.

As soon as he saw her arrive at her office, he dashed out of the adjoining laboratory, not to greet her as she had expected, but to demand, "Are you having problems with your computer, Bella?"

Biting back an initial human reaction to say, "And a good morning to you too!" Isabel told herself that she must act like a robot, even though she was taken aback by his abruptness. What had happened to Vincente's famous charm?

She answered slowly, "Not that I know of. It was fine when I left yesterday afternoon."

"I can't access all my usual programmes on my computer, so something is wrong. Maybe you're having a similar problem. When you've put in the official password for today, I'll take a look on your computer too."

"I must wait until management gives me today's operational password when I tell them that I am ready. Then I'll let you know," she countered, sitting down at her desk.

For a moment, he looked as if he would challenge that plan, but finally giving an impatient shrug, he spun around to return to his lab. As he opened the door, Isabel caught some movement from inside the room and was intrigued to glimpse Vincente-Two behind a bench.

While waiting for her computer screen to light up, Isabel wondered why whatever Vincente was working on, needed an extra quick brain and another pair of hands. *'Obviously, something he can't trust to our own lab assistants,'* she thought cynically.

When the password for the day was revealed, she activated it to connect with the NIR's central computer. Dutifully, she used the intercom to let Vincente know that the computer was operational but when he came to take her chair, she retreated to the other side of the room to watch. He didn't bother to thank her but quickly sat down in front of the screen, where his fingers were soon flying over the keyboard.

She could hear him becoming more and more annoyed at what he was discovering. He was muttering under his breath. "What is going on? I can't access all the information I need. And this is the only computer that stores all the data. I haven't had this problem before. What's going on now?"

Isabel noted that his anger was revealing an unpleasant hidden side of the usually polite and friendly scientist. As she stood silent, she saw his back stiffen as his fingers stopped moving but still hovered over the keyboard.

'*Ah! He has found the new programme I entered yesterday.*'
She held her breath. '*What will he do now?*'

Vincente pushed back her office chair and stormed into his lab without another word. He passed her by as if she were invisible.

'*And where is that urbane gentleman I used to know? Has he changed or does he treat all robots like this?*' Isabel wondered.

After their connecting door had slammed shut and Vincente was back at work in the lab, she quietly opened her own door and gently closing it after her, walked further down the outside hall until she was out of earshot. After making two phone calls, she slipped back into her office and quietly began checking the programmes that Vincente had been researching so diligently.

She had seen his chagrin when some apps were impossible to open, so she was not surprised by his irritated reaction to being blocked. Isabel wrung her hands anxiously, wondering what he would do next. Through her office's small window to the lab, she could see him engrossed in his own computer. While he was preoccupied, she decided to pay a quick visit to the lab secretary pool to see those who were not taking a holiday. She hadn't had time to greet them as Bella usually did every morning.

Isabel was intrigued to discover that contrary to her fears, the busy secretaries were not overworked, even though short-staffed. Vincente had relieved them of their need to answer the numerous phone enquiries coming in for him from foreign countries. The secretaries were a little surprised that she had forgotten since he had been handling that time-consuming duty for some weeks.

'Oh, yes. Bella would have known that. I'll have to be more careful. That must be the reason he's brought in Vincente Two - to handle the extra work and keep everything secret between the two of them. He's covering all his bases. But then, so can I!'

Grim-faced, she returned to her office where she again peered through their small connecting window. Vincente appeared to be working alone now. He had probably moved his look-alike robot out of sight of anyone coming into her office or had packed him away. Isabel settled down at her desk to keep a wary eye on the scientist while reacquainting herself with the In and Out tray, so neatly stacked by Bella.

Neither she nor Vincente took a break for lunch. He continued concentrating on his computer while she monitored him by checking on her computer-link to see what programmes he was using. Isabel noted that he was transferring a large amount of data to his own home computer. Their shared office phone indicated many overseas communications. Isabel also noticed that there was a constant traffic of overseas e-mails.

Uneasy questions began niggling at her mind. Could he have found a way around the new encryptions she had installed on her computer? He seemed to be working very fast, without even getting up or pausing to eat or drink. What was he doing? Was he up to something suspect? Isabel fidgeted in her seat, nervously wringing her hands.

Finally, her misgivings becoming too much to tolerate, she decided to alert her superiors. She reached for the phone. Silently, she willed Vincente to stay exactly where he was, so that she could keep him in sight while she talked.

Within minutes, there was a commotion in the hall outside and three NIR security personnel entered her office. She indicated with her head towards the lab where Vincente must have heard the noise because he had ceased working. He did not even glance at her when he was escorted out.

After checking that there was nobody else in the lab, an officer was left on guard outside the room so that nobody could enter or interfere with the computers and the newly acquired scientific equipment.

Isabel sighed with relief at the efficient way Security had dealt with this tricky situation. Now that it was out of her control, she could breathe a little easier and concentrate on stopping her hands from trembling. She felt completely drained of energy.

'I thought the end of my project would make me happy, but I only feel totally exhausted and glad that it's over at last.'

After what seemed an eternity of waiting to find out what was happening, her phone rang. It was Senior Management congratulating her on the success of her actions. They suspected that with Vincente's arrest, the sensitive information leaks from their government offices would now be at an end. Their suspect was being held for questioning until State security officials arrived to advise on the next steps to be taken.

Isabel waited until she felt calmer before making another phone call. "End Game, Burt! If you come to my house at 8 o'clock tonight, I'll give you more information."

CHAPTER 32

$\mathcal{D}$oug was surprised when Isabel told him that Burt would be visiting them after dinner that evening. She asked that when he arrived, Doug would be sure not to mention Bella.

"I don't want him to know that he was shown around the labs by a robot," she explained.

"Ah!" Doug exclaimed. "That's why his car was parked at the NIR. But how did you arrange that with your superiors? Or did Bella orchestrate the whole thing?"

"You'll get to know more when Burt comes," she replied enigmatically. "He agreed to share his resources with me, so in return I'm giving him some information that he needs for his own investigation."

Doug shook his head at his sister's bartering behaviour but quietly busied himself with the evening meal while Isabel sat down at the table, helping him by pouring Pinot Grigio into two wineglasses, one of which she delicately tasted.

"I guess that means that you're not going to give me Bella's usual daily report?" he hazarded as he dished out the lobster bisque soup, one of his chef specialities. "Then

I'm not going to be told what happened at the National Institute today?"

"You'll have more than your share of information once Burt comes," she replied tartly. "So, don't start asking questions beforehand. I'm really exhausted with what I had to do today, and I don't want to tell my story twice in one evening."

Doug pursed his mouth so tightly that his lips disappeared. Looking at his clownish expression, Isabel couldn't help laughing.

"Oh, alright!" she capitulated. "They've arrested the scientist we suspected of leaking the government's sensitive secret information to other countries. He is one of our own NIR people."

Doug turned off the oven so that the roast chicken wouldn't get too brown and carried the soup bowls to the table.

"And who was it? Anyone I know?"

Isabel raised her eyebrows as she took up her soup spoon. "No questions yet," she reminded him.

Doug knew that he would have to wait until later before she would tell him anything. Not for the first time he thought, *'My sister can be such a pest! She didn't change much while she was away.'*

After their meal, Isabel was neatly arranging the dishes in the dishwasher when the doorbell rang.

"That'll be Burt," Doug said. "I'll let him in. Shall I take him to the living room? We can have coffee there. Burt will need something to keep him awake if he's going back to the newspaper office tonight to write up your new information for his scoop."

He went to open the door for Burt. "What about Colin? Isn't he coming too?" he asked.

"No, he's manning the computers in case any new information comes in. He knows where I am in case of emergency."

Burt was sitting comfortably with a cup of black coffee by his side when Isabel joined them. He was silently thanking his lucky stars for having been introduced to Isabel at the Black Horse Inn. Otherwise, he wouldn't have had such a unique first-hand opportunity to hear the story of the NIR leak.

After greeting her, he took out his notebook and pen, settling back in his chair prepared to listen. But as Isabel poured cream into her coffee, she said, "I think it will be better if first, you ask me the questions that you need answering for your investigation."

When Burt looked surprised, she added, "Then I'll tell you anything I'm allowed to say at this juncture. It is sensitive information, you know?"

"Of course," Burt answered.

"But I do have a confession to make before we start," Isabel continued, causing both men to sit up to listen.

"Our NIR investigation has been going on for a very long time. The Director knew that the Security Department had instructed me to set up certain conditions that would force the suspect to reveal his activities. But although I did as I was asked, the suspect was allowed to gain more and more powers. I was so upset by the lack of significant progress over the time I was forced to be absent, that finally I took the matter into my own hands."

Isabel had the undivided attention of her audience, but Burt broke the spell, saying, "And I think I know what you did."

Isabel raised her eyebrows in enquiry.

"You must have asked someone in Washington D.C. to contact the editor at my newspaper to drop a hint that there was a government leak of sensitive information at the NIR in Boston. Right?"

She smiled at Burt's quick deduction.

"Yes. I did, knowing that the editor would start his own enquiry. I was lucky that you, Burt, were given the assignment. So, when you asked for a tour of the NIR I had to convince the Director to allow you inside. I told him that I could monitor what you would see. The last thing we wanted was a report in the papers to alert the man that he was being tracked. But on the other hand, it would look bad if your request was refused. As if we were hiding something."

Burt grinned. "But what you really wanted, was to hurry the process along by having some outside help. Like a nosy investigating reporter. Like me."

Doug could hardly believe his ears at this litany of devious behaviour.

"Okay! Okay!" he interrupted impatiently, "Now that this person has been arrested, has he got a name? Isabel, are you ever going to tell us who it is?"

"That was the first of my questions too," Burt stated, clicking open his pen ready to write in his notebook.

"Vincente Da Cosa is his name. But we suspect that isn't his real identity," Isabel replied.

Doug nearly spilled his coffee when he heard the familiar name. He couldn't help himself, he blurted out, "Vincente Da Cosa! Well, I'm not surprised! I never liked him from the beginning."

Isabel bit her tongue to stop herself from retorting that Doug had never met him and therefore couldn't harbour such an opinion.

He looked at her sheepishly. "Well, Sis, when you used to talk about him, I always thought that he sounded too good to be true."

Unwilling to follow Doug's line of argument, Isabel glared at him.

"I think we should let Burt ask his questions now. I'll answer as best I can."

Burt was clearing his throat to begin when his cellphone rang. He took a quick look at it and said, "I'm sorry. It's Colin. I'd better answer in case there's some new developments. Please excuse me."

He stepped out into the hall.

Doug and Isabel heard him say in a loud skeptical voice, "Are you sure that's what your contact in Security is saying? I can't believe it! No, keep on trying to find out more information. I'll head back to the office right away."

Brother and sister stood up when he came to take his leave.

"This is just unbelievable!" he sputtered.

"Colin says that when the Security police questioned the suspect, he wouldn't talk. No wonder! They discovered they'd arrested a robot!"

CHAPTER 33

As Doug was locking the door after Burt's departure, he could hear their house phone ringing incessantly. Isabel picked it up. He wondered who was calling, as he went to collect the used coffee cups from the living room.

He had hardly reached the kitchen before he heard an anguished cry from his sister as she replaced the hall phone in its cradle. He rushed out to find her standing as if frozen in place. She was trembling and looked so pale that he was thoroughly alarmed.

When he took her arm to peer closer into her face, she suddenly burst into tears. Her sobs sounded as if they were dredged from the very core of her being, such harsh and unfamiliar sounds that he was frightened.

What was causing such pain? Her behaviour was entirely uncharacteristic. Isabel was usually the toughest and most resilient member of their family. Doug tightened his hold on her arm to guide her gently to the sofa. He held her steady for a minute before deciding that she needed more than his support.

He hurried to the wine cabinet to pour a small glass of brandy. He held it out in front of her. "Here, Sis! Try some of this. You look as if you've had a terrible shock. This brandy will help you deal with it."

Isabel choked down another heart-rending sob before managing to take some sips of the brandy. Much to Doug's relief, the colour gradually began to return to her face. She wiped her eyes with the handkerchief Doug had put into her hand.

"Don't try to talk," he advised her, "Take some deep breaths to calm yourself down."

After a while she wailed, "How could I have let this happen, Doug? I'd assumed that I had Vincente cornered in his lab. I was so sure of it! I never thought he would switch places with his own robot. But I should have known! He did that on stage at Boston University. He must have had an escape plan ready in case he was cornered."

Tears welled up in her eyes.

"Now Vincente has eluded us. After all those months of planning for his capture. And it's my own stupid fault! I acted too quickly when I returned to the office. I should have waited a day or two before altering those programs on my computer. But I was so worried that Vincente might notice at any minute that I wasn't Bella. He's so quick to notice everything. It was very hard, Doug, me trying to act like a robot."

She took another shuddering breath. "I feel totally wiped out and utterly foolish."

Her brother tried to reassure her.

"Everyone makes mistakes, Sis. We all learn from them. And you've had a lot to deal with lately, with Bella being hacked as well. I guess that must have been Vincente's work too. Was that him on the phone?"

She buried her face in her hands. "No, it was the NIR Security to tell me that it was Vincente-Two they'd arrested. The robot's memory had been triggered by the arrest to wipe itself clean. It's useless to our investigation now. Vincente is just too clever for us," she despaired. "He must have escaped while I was out of the office talking to the secretaries."

She half-stifled another sob before wailing loudly, "I've failed in my mission! All our planning has been useless. After this catastrophe, my directors will never ever trust me again."

By this time, her brother had poured a glass of brandy for himself to steady his own nerves.

"You can't worry about that, Isabel. Maybe they can catch Vincente before he disappears altogether. You never know what government authorities are capable of doing. They're probably on his trail already. It is out of your hands now."

The spectre of Vincente disappearing was evidently the wrong thing to say. Isabel gave another desperate cry and reached for the wet handkerchief again.

Doug hastened to distract her. "Sis, why don't you stop blaming yourself and begin telling me everything from the beginning? It'll be good to get it off your chest and you'll feel better afterwards. Come pull yourself together. I'll sit with you as long as you want to talk. Even if it takes all night."

He brought out the bottle of brandy and plonked it down on the coffee table. They both might need it again before the night was out.

After a few whimpers, Isabel dried her eyes. She began her story in a halting voice that grew stronger as she became more and more angry while relating the suspected misdeeds of Vincente da Cosa and his doppelgänger robot.

"It isn't often that a brilliant scientist like Vincente comes along in the computer science field but when he does, the authorities sit up and take notice," she began. "Not only the authorities here but also interested parties from abroad. There are always foreign agents keeping a lookout for new talent to shadow."

She hesitated as she remembered how she had first met Vincente.

"I hadn't heard much about him before he came to the NIR for an interview. But I could tell by his conversation that he must have been an outstanding student in university. He could talk fluently about the latest developments in robot design. I soon realized that his knowledge was far superior to that of our own ministry scientists."

Isabel winced at the memory of how Vincente had tricked her by first sending in his robot to be interviewed. She decided to gloss over that detail.

"I was the one who recommended offering him a post with us. Now I wish that I hadn't been so hasty," she sighed. "But he was very persuasive and quite charming at the time. Quite unlike anyone I've ever met."

At this, Doug snorted his disapproval of the man.

"The NIR did some background checks before hiring him, of course. There was a matter of four missing years on his C.V. He was tracked to New Mexico where a private lab was creating a humanoid robot. There was some mystery about their computers not functioning properly and their first flawed prototype seemed to have disappeared."

Doug frowned. "How can a robot just disappear?"

"I don't know the details. But by the time Vincente went to work there, the team was already working on another robot, this one called Andrew. I guess that the scientists helped each other because Andrew was rumoured to be built without the flaws of Andrea, the first robot. That New Mexico lab was where Vincente made his own look-alike robot, Vincente-Two."

Doug interrupted, "How could he afford to build a look-alike robot? He'd just come out of university."

Isabel nodded. "That's the big question everyone asks. The Ministry suspected some foreign backing, but we were so keen to have Vincente's brilliant mind in our labs that we offered him a post anyway. With one proviso."

Doug sat up. "Let me guess!" he said, "You were to be his watchdog in your section of the labs and that's why they instructed you to have him make Bella, your look-alike robot."

"Yes, so that we would have an example of his work if, for some reason, he quit the NIR. It was a huge expense in our budget, but the Institute was buying time in order to double-check his history before finally offering him the post. Bella was to be our back-up strategy. If Vincente didn't pan out, we would still have Bella for our research."

They both jumped when the telephone gave a sudden shrill. Automatically, Isabel began to rise to her feet, but Doug sternly motioned to her to sit still.

"Let it ring," he said firmly. "It's nearly midnight. Whoever it is, can leave a message."

They both listened intently but the caller didn't leave a message.

Isabel was about to continue her story when the doorbell rang, echoing stridently across the quiet hall.

Doug jumped to his feet. "Stay where you are, Sis. I'll deal with this."

Gratefully, she sank back into the sofa as he tiptoed to the door to peer through its peephole. Burt was standing outside stamping his feet. Doug opened the door to let him in.

"Didn't you hear your phone ring?" Burt grumbled. "I saw your lights were still on, so I phoned to let you know what was happening. When you didn't answer, I was worried that this Da Cosa guy might have broken into your house. He's still on the run. No knowing where he'll be heading! Is everything okay here?"

"Yes! Yes! Take your coat off and come in and have a brandy."

"Got anything I can nibble on as well?" Burt inquired as he shrugged off his coat.

Doug understood immediately. "Oh, I get it! You missed your supper, rushing to get your copy into the newspaper in time for publishing. A scoop coming up?"

When Burt grinned, Doug nodded his head.

"I can rustle up some roast chicken and red currant jelly sandwiches on rye if you're okay with that. I'll make enough for all of us."

He whispered in Burt's ear, "Isabel is still in the living room. Why don't you join her there? You'll find that she's very upset about the arrest of the robot, so be gentle with her."

Burt made his way to the living room while Doug headed for the sanctuary of the kitchen. Life was definitely rough at the moment.

When he returned with a plate of sandwiches, he was glad to see that his sister had regained her composure. Burt had his notepad on his knee, writing down what she had been telling him about Vincente's previous history.

While Doug was passing out plates and offering sandwiches and drinks, Burt said, "Colin's contact in the Security section says that they've alerted the police to a suspected felon on the run. And if he has been leaking government information, I wouldn't be surprised if the police have contacted the FBI too."

Doug was impressed at the speed of the pursuit. "Does that mean that there'll already be surveillance of the Boston railway stations, the airport and at the harbour too?"

"You can bet on it!" Burt replied, "Though Boston is such a busy hub of traffic that trying to catch this crook will be like looking for a needle in a haystack. He might be making his escape by road or even upriver this very minute. He could take a helicopter if he had access to one."

Isabel choked on a bite of her sandwich, before saying huskily, "You don't know Vincente. He won't do the expected thing. His mind is too quick and devious for that. The authorities will have to think outside of the box, like he does. He could be changing his appearance too. If he had a plan to escape, he'll have thought of everything. Especially if he has back-up support from some foreign country."

The two men regarded her with admiration.

Doug said, "You're no couch-slouch yourself, Sis. Your mind is definitely as quick as that Vincente guy. Keep on thinking! You may come up with more ideas that you can pass on to the police."

Encouraged by their support, Isabel continued with her suggestions.

"If he were working with some foreign power, as we suspect, he'll be cognizant of other local agents who can whisk him away or provide fake passports and papers for him. Or even help him change his appearance, as I said before."

Just then, Doug interrupted to ask if the information Vincente had stolen was important. Isabel eyed him grimly.

"Artificial intelligence and new computer technology are what the whole world is monitoring, Doug! It's expanding super-rapidly. Other countries crave information about new major developments in North America. If they can't get it by mutual co-operation, they'll use unorthodox methods to get a hold of it."

"Like trying to hack into our government computers or using double agents or spies. Or paying corrupt scientists like Da Cosa, to leak out the information," Burt added, "It's called cybercrime."

"Absolutely correct!" Isabel added, "Foreign countries like the Koreas, Japan, China and Russia are focusing on finding the most modern and sophisticated new technology available. And those countries are only the obvious ones."

"But what good does it do any of them?" Doug asked, finishing off his sandwich.

"Could be for good or evil purposes," Burt rejoined darkly.

"Right, again!" Isabel stated. "Countries can use artificial intelligence to boost their production of goods. Or to make their equipment more efficient and economical."

Burt continued, "But the other side of the coin is that if a country is trying to attain dominance in its own area, A.I. can be used for surveillance or military power or for suppressing people's freedom."

"That's a sobering thought," Doug said as he drained his brandy glass. "But all this is too much for my poor brain to take in tonight. It's a crazy world we live in, for sure. You'll have to excuse me. I need to go to bed now or I'll fall asleep right here in front of you. Not that what you are saying isn't exciting, but I'm too tired to absorb it."

He smothered a yawn. "Burt, Isabel can lock the door after you. I'll read your story in the newspaper tomorrow. I mean today. It's after one o'clock."

Isabel and Burt heard him mount the stairs, then listened to his bedroom door clicking shut.

"I should get going too," Burt said. "But what do you think this Da Cosa guy will do to get away? If he's using a passport, he'll have to get past those scanner imaging devices that send suspect passports to telephone circuits around the world."

He began putting his pen and pad away.

"I know that when suspicious passports are scanned at U.S. airports, the scan is received instantly for analysis by our counter-terrorism centre. Surely, this renegade scientist isn't cleverer than those security checks?"

Isabel put her plate on the coffee table and brushed breadcrumbs from her lap.

"Believe me, Vincente will know all about that," she responded. "My view is that he will do something simple, like staying in plain sight, so that he can assess the situation firsthand. There's no knowing what he will have up his sleeve. It's difficult trying to second-guess someone like him."

She made a mental note to reorganize Bella's programs so that the robot couldn't be used for any of Vincente's nefarious purposes. Then glancing at the mantel clock, she noted that it was well past her normal bedtime.

Burt had seen her quick look at the clock and was already on his feet, placing his plate and glass with the others on the table.

"I see there's no rest for me tonight. I have to get back to the office. I've just thought of something I must do. Thank you for being so helpful and I'm sorry to have kept you up so late."

Isabel followed him to the front door, where he turned for a final word. "Be sure to lock up securely and don't let anyone else in. If you have an alarm system, don't forget to activate it tonight. I don't trust this scientist guy. He might try to break in here."

Isabel shook her head in denial. "Oh, I don't think Vincente would do that. He has to find a way to disappear, not appear where people would recognize him. Besides, there's nothing in my house that he could possibly want."

"That depends on whether you have something valuable that he needs," Burt warned.

Isabel watched Burt's car back out of the driveway.

Outside it seemed as bright as daylight with the full moon showing everything in clear silhouette. She locked the front door securely, as well as activating the house alarm. Then, stacking the plates and wineglasses in the kitchen sink to wash later, she turned off the lights before starting to climb the stairs to her bedroom.

Halfway up, Isabel stopped. She had an overwhelmingly strange, eerie feeling, as if she were being watched.

Isabel turned to look down into the shadowy hall but all she could see was Bella's suitcase by the door. A sudden thought struck her, '*Would Vincente need another robot now that he's sacrificed his own? Might he try to steal Bella?*'

On impulse, Isabel ran downstairs again. She took hold of Bella's suitcase and carried it, not without difficulty after drinking the brandy Doug had given her so liberally, bump by bump up the stairs to her room. There she deposited it in a far corner and readied herself for sleep.

As she was pulling the bedcovers over her, she happened to glance into Bella's corner. The bright moonlight was reflecting off something on the side of the suitcase. Isabel considered it for a few minutes.

'*I haven't noticed that tiny light before. It must be something new. Bella is completely shut down so it can't be coming from her. Why would there be a light on a suitcase?*'

As she peered at it, the light disappeared. Thinking that perhaps it was a trick of the moonlight or that she must have imagined it, she lay back on the pillow and closed her eyes. But sleep refused to come. She turned on her side to look at the suitcase again.

Her mind was churning out ideas of what the tiny light might be.

Finally, fully awake, she sat up. '*It looks to me to be very like a camera eye. Did Vincente install a camera without telling me? Has it been there all the time and I've missed seeing it until now? Or has it just been activated recently?*'

Isabel's skin was crawling with the idea of being photographed without her consent. She couldn't stand the thought.

Throwing back the coverlet, she crossed to her bureau to rummage around in the odds-and-ends drawer for some duct tape. She double taped over the tiny aperture, turned the suitcase around to face the wall and having done that, felt that she could now sleep peacefully.

CHAPTER 34

$\mathcal{D}$oug could smell the unmistakeable aroma of fresh coffee wafting upstairs to his bedroom. He opened his eyes and rolled over to one side to check the time on his bedside clock. It was eight o'clock. He lay still for a while, remembering all the events of the previous evening, then reached quickly for his robe. It wasn't the fact that he had overslept that was urging him on, but rather the realization that Isabel was already up. He hoped that she wasn't intending to go to work that day. She should be giving herself time to recover after yesterday's setback at the NIR.

But when he ran downstairs and into the kitchen, his sister had already breakfasted and gone, leaving him a note that she had urgent business to attend to and would be home that evening.

Disappointed, Doug poured himself a cup of the coffee that was already cooling.

'Well, I have to admire Isabel's resilience. That rogue scientist's disappearance yesterday would have stopped most people in their tracks. But not my sister! I bet she got up early just to get to work before anyone else knows about the arrest. Wonder what she's going to do there.'

After putting two slices of raisin bread into the toaster, he noticed that the morning paper was on the table. He read the headlines while eating his breakfast. Burt and Colin would certainly be creating a stir with their scoop about the leaking of sensitive technological information from a government institution in their hometown. Their reporting was excellent, detailing the subsequent disappearance of the suspect. They did not mention the arrest of a robot instead of the culprit. A decision probably due to the wise advice of their editor.

For a moment, Doug felt a pang of regret for having retired from the excitement of working in a newspaper office. Everyone would be jubilant about their newspaper being the first to print this extraordinary news. They would be congratulating Burt and Colin, slapping them on the back for a job well-done.

Certainly, they both deserved accolades for their hard work. Burt was a first-class investigator; Colin a whizz on the computer.

'But what am I really missing?' he questioned. *'Isn't my present life with Isabel and Bella exciting enough? Maybe a little too much excitement, I'd say! Who else gets to live with a robot that's almost like a person?'*

He folded the newspaper, finished his toast with an extra dollop of marmalade and humming to himself, went to attack the dirty dishes left from the previous night. When he switched on the radio, the local news program was reporting the escape of a Boston scientist who was wanted by the police. It asked people to keep a lookout for anyone answering his description.

'I expect the television will show a photo of him. Hope he gets caught soon. Wish I could lay my hands on him. I would teach him a thing or two about loyalty!'

While Doug was pottering in his kitchen, Isabel was at work in her laboratory, busily checking through the systems of her look-alike robot. She was quickly deleting Bella's secret app before her superiors sent for her to discuss yesterday's events, as she feared they would.

Right from the beginning, when Vincente had first presented her with Bella, Isabel had been suspicious of his control over the robot, so she had countermanded some of his programs, at the same time as installing a secret app for her own private use. This Secret app had nothing to do with the investigation of Vincente's crimes. It had been an unofficial indulgence for her to be able to connect to her home and her work through Bella and to be able to activate her robot if necessary.

Reading things she was not supposed to know had been very entertaining. She had no qualms about deleting it, now that she had read everything recorded in it.

Even in her present dire situation, she couldn't help grinning at the information she had uncovered- that Doug had taken Bella to the Black Horse Inn and for a number of weeks, the robot had helped with the pub quizzes. *'Wait till I tease Doug about that!'*

Isabel became more serious as she checked Bella's other programs for signs of hacking activity. She was not an expert in malfunction detection, so she soon began to feel the need for more advice. There were other people in the NIR much more knowledgeable than she was, but she couldn't ask them to look at her robot double.

'It's difficult because only the upper management know about my doppelgänger, seeing that they agreed to its creation in the first place. I can't let anyone else know about Bella without my superiors' permission. So, there's nothing else for it. I'll have to try to solve the problems myself.'

As she was working, she became aware of the morning chatter of the arriving secretaries. Isabel quickly covered Bella until she fetched the robot's suitcase. Once Bella was safely inside, Isabel was about to put it in the closet when the office telephone rang. It was the expected summons from her superiors. She was to meet them within the next half hour.

Isabel put down the phone and eyed the closed suitcase, vowing to herself, "Well, I'm not going alone. Bella, you and I will face the music together!"

Later, it was not without qualms that Isabel entered the conference room to be questioned about Vincente. Gwen, her immediate superior, was also present. Isabel wondered what everyone thought about Vincente eluding capture after all their attempts to make him think that he was a trusted and unsuspected employee. Were they going to blame her for his escape?

Her heart was pounding as she greeted them while rolling Bella's suitcase into the room.

'But at least I can tell them a little about how Vincente's mind works- even if they do decide that I was too slow in alerting Security. I can tell them about all the apps he tried to install in Bella so that he could have control over her, and me. I can inform them that I erased his controls and installed my own commands instead, in order to secure any secret NIR information Bella might come across.'

She wheeled Bella's suitcase to an empty chair, wishing that she had noticed that hidden camera in the suitcase earlier. Her colleagues were not going to be happy about that.

When she sat down, Isabel straightened her shoulders, braced herself against the back of the hard seat and prepared for whatever was going to happen.

By the end of that hot summer afternoon, Doug had weeded his vegetable garden and had gathered lettuce, kale and arugula for their evening meal. The tomatoes were still too green to pick and the swiss chard didn't do well in hot weather. It was too droopy to be of any use in a crisp salad at present, but it would perk up in the Fall. As he washed the greens, he was listening to the radio to find out if Vincente had been caught. No sightings as yet.

He was sitting at the kitchen table picking over fresh strawberries for dessert when he heard Isabel enter the house.

"Hello!' he called out, "I'm in the kitchen."

When his sister appeared, he glanced at her quickly. He promptly reached over the table to fill a glass with cold lemonade while Isabel flopped down on the chair opposite him to wipe her damp face with a handy table napkin. She took a long drink of the tart lemonade.

"It's so hot today!" she moaned, "And the news is not good either, Doug. We don't have Bella anymore. The NIR has confiscated her."

Doug was stunned at the news. It was as if a vital part of his life had suddenly dropped out without warning. No Bella?

"Confiscated her?" he echoed dismally. "But why? What do they want Bella for? Don't they have Vincente's robot already? Why do they need two robots?"

Isabel spun the cold-beaded glass between her hands as she replied wearily, "Yes, they have Vincente's robot, but its programs have been wiped clean, probably triggered automatically when it was seized by Security. Vincente must have set that up in advance."

She took another cold drink of lemonade. "Now, the NIR want Bella so that our experts can find out what they can about how Vincente built her. What apps he installed. If they can come up with some answers, it may be possible to repair the Vincente robot and trace him through his own robot."

She sighed, shrugging her shoulders. "If they can get Vincente's robot working again, they might be able to find out where the stolen information had been sent. Personally, I have doubts about that. If there is any information left in the robot, Vincente would have deeply encrypted it."

Isabel went on, "I don't know what plans there are after that. Or if they can even achieve their objective. I'm just trying to get my head around the idea that I may never see Bella again. Of-course she didn't belong to me in the first place, but I do feel some kinship with her since she looks and reacts exactly like me. It's as if they are examining me personally. It isn't a pleasant feeling."

Doug pushed the bowl of strawberries aside.

"All that seems a bit far-fetched to me," he commented. "Let me get this straight. They're going to tear your robot apart in order to get Vincente's look-alike working again?"

"More or less, Doug," she acquiesced.

"That's terrible!" he exploded, "Why, that's like throwing good stuff into bad."

Despite her own consternation, Isabel couldn't help smiling at her brother's turn of phrase. "You have to look on the bright side, Doug. If they're so expert at figuring out how Bella works, when they've finished our scientists should be able to put my robot back together again."

Doug snorted at that idea. "Like Humpty Dumpty, I suppose," he responded sarcastically as he stood up to go wash the berries. "And we all know how that ended."

Isabel could see that her news had disturbed him, so she followed him across the kitchen. "Maybe I was being too dramatic about not seeing Bella again. Let's hope I'm wrong."

She hesitated before delivering more bad news, but it had to be done.

"I have some more information for you. You won't like it," she began.

Doug stopped washing the berries. "I'm almost too scared to listen!"

Isabel went on, regardless, "I've just discovered that Bella's suitcase has a hidden camera. We think that it has been photographing all the places Bella has been. Vincente must have been collecting data that he thought might be useful to him in the future."

Doug turned off the faucet to shake the colander of strawberries as he turned this newest information over in his mind. He was mentally checking the places Bella had been, those he knew of in the house.

'The robot has been in lots of places; here at home, in the car, outside, at the NIR and oh, oh, at the Black Horse Inn. I don't know where she's been in the NIR building'.

As if reading his mind, his sister continued, "My superiors are not pleased that Vincente must have information about the inside layout of the NIR. But I'm more worried that he is now familiar with the inside of our house, the basement, main floor and where our rooms are upstairs."

Doug was so angry that his face was turning as fiery as his hair had once been. His knuckles showed white as he gripped the colander.

"Are you thinking he'll try to break into this house?" he demanded. "Why? What have we got here that he might want?"

Isabel shrugged her shoulders again. "He might need a robot to transmit untraceable messages for him. He might think we keep Bella at home after work. He'll already know that we keep her suitcase by the front door."

She threw her hands up in the air as if she were throwing Vincente to the four winds.

"But how should I know? I'm so sick of all this! I can't fathom why he wants the plans of everywhere Bella has been. His thinking is beyond me!"

She turned on her heel, exclaiming, "Oh, to hell with it! I'm going to change into something more comfortable."

His usually placid sister stomped out of the room, leaving Doug feeling unsettled and frustrated with the whole sorry mess. His mind was racing, conjuring up reasons for the hidden camera. His throat suddenly constricted. '*What if the man was planning to kidnap Isabel? He might want to use her as a hostage in order to escape.*'

This was all too much! His knees felt as weak as they did when he'd done too much gardening. Doug collapsed on a kitchen chair to think things over. At that moment, the house phone began to ring and ring. He waited to see if his sister would run downstairs to answer, but he could hear the upstairs shower running.

Disgruntled, he stamped into the hall, took up the offending phone and demanded harshly, "YES. What d'you want?"

There was a moment of shocked silence before Burt spoke.

"Hey! Doug! What's wrong? You sound really angry. What's going on?"

"Oh, it's you, Burt. Yes, I'm feeling very annoyed at the moment! We've just found out that this Da Cosa guy has been spying on us."

Burt's investigating feelers quivered. "Tell me why you think that? How has he been spying on you? Tell me more."

Doug explained about the hidden camera in a case that Isabel always carried with her, (taking care not to mention the robot). The camera may have been taking photographs of their house and of the NIR. He heard Burt give a soft incredulous whistle at the ingenuity of the missing scientist.

Then his friend said, "Don't worry, Doug. I'll take care of this. I know plenty of people who'll be interested in what you've been telling me. I know the policemen who patrol your area. I'll alert them."

Hardly pausing for breath, Burt continued, "In the meantime, take every precaution. Don't let anyone into your house. No-one!"

With a promise to get back to him during the evening, Burt ended the call, leaving Doug somewhat mollified but still anxious about what might happen next.

Later, when Isabel appeared in the kitchen to help with their evening meal, she asked, "Who phoned? I heard the ring as I got out of the shower."

"That was Burt. I told him about the camera, but I didn't mention that it was on Bella's suitcase. I said that this Vincente guy has probably photographed the layout of our house. Burt will phone us later with his suggestions about what we can do about that."

True to his word, Burt phoned that evening as brother and sister were finishing their strawberries and cream dessert. Doug went across the hall to answer.

"No need to worry! Everything is under control," Burt reassured him, "But it would help if you both keep a low profile in the neighbourhood for a while. You'll want to be outdoors in this hot summer weather but stay close to home and be wary of any people you meet. If this Da Cosa guy has changed his appearance, he'll probably be so unremarkable and unassuming that he may catch you off-guard."

Doug lowered his voice to whisper, "Do you think the guy wants to kidnap Isabel?" He felt a little foolish putting his fear into words, but his friend took him seriously.

"There's no knowing what this renegade is up to, so we're taking no chances. You're going to have a watch put on your house starting tonight. No need to alarm Isabel so keep that news to yourself."

Before Doug could gather more details, Burt asked to talk to his sister.

When the journalist and Isabel conversed, he advised her to take a week's holiday from work and to stay home as much as possible. Surprised at his request, she was about to question him further, but she could hear him being paged in the newspaper office. Her questions were left floating in the air when Burt ended the call.

"Burt wants me to take time away from the NIR," she informed her brother when she returned to the kitchen.

"Good idea!" he responded enthusiastically as he stacked dishes into the dishwasher. "It is about time you spent some days at home. You've been running around like a chicken without a head since you returned."

Isabel was insulted. "I've been attending to essential business!" she contradicted.

"Well, now that you've done that, I agree that it's a good idea for you to stay home until things calm down. I've been waiting all those months you were away to talk to you about a project I have in mind."

"Like what?" Isabel demanded cagily.

"Like having more fun in the midst of all this disaster."

"Such as?" she queried carefully.

"Well, we could start by clearing out the basement so that we both can have our own space down there. I've been using your office up till now. It would be better to have my own place to write my newspaper articles."

"You call that fun?" Isabel retorted, "I call that drudge!"

"Okay, okay!" her brother countered. "Then how about coming to the quiz nights at the Black Horse Inn on Saturdays? It would be good for you to be around normal people for a change. Instead of all those robots."

He had to dodge the tea towel she playfully whipped at him.

"I know all about your quiz nights," she insinuated, "I'm not Bella but I'll think about it," she said airily as she went into the hall, leaving Doug to wonder how she knew about the robot helping them solve some questions in the quiz.

He heard her pick up the phone. While he was hanging up the dishtowel to dry, he cocked his ear to try to find out whom she was calling. Doug heard her say that she would not be at work at the NIR for the next few days.

'Wonders never cease! It's taken a government catastrophe to stop my workaholic sister in her tracks. Now there's a positive thing for a change!'

CHAPTER 35

The next two days passed quietly as they tackled their collection of miscellaneous possessions in the basement.

There were unopened packing boxes that Doug had brought from his own home when he had moved in with his sister the previous year. He had never had the heart to unpack those sad reminders of his late wife. Her loss lingered close to the borders of his mind, ready to rush through when triggered by memories. He steeled himself to carry out the task of sorting through old photographs and cards without getting upset.

Isabel had stacks of research papers waiting to be reread and filed - not a task she relished but a chore that had been neglected while she was away. They both had enough to do to keep them busy from constantly fretting about the whereabouts of the missing scientist.

Outside, the humid June heat of summer continued to be oppressive, but the basement was cool. From time to time when they took breaks, Doug would disappear upstairs to the kitchen to prepare some light meal or they would retreat to the comfortable white wicker chairs on the front porch to have ice cream and cold lemonade.

There, while Isabel tended to her pots of thirsty plants, Doug sat by as if idly watching her but in reality, he was keeping a wary eye trained for passers-by on the street. He saw some determined joggers and daring young children on skateboards or scooters, as well as an occasional cyclist and a few delivery vans but nothing that aroused his immediate suspicions.

Friday dawned hot and muggy. As they ate breakfast, Doug switched on the local radio station. It was issuing warnings of severe thunderstorms due to hit the Boston area by late afternoon that day.

"Well, at least it will be cooler when those pass by," Isabel remarked, buttering her toast. "I hate this hot and sticky humid weather. You men don't seem to mind it as much. I wonder why that is."

"Because we're all cool dudes," joked her brother.

"I suppose that means we women are all 'hot dames'," Isabel fired back and they both laughed, alleviating a little of their unspoken tension about the uncaught Vincente and his nefarious intentions.

Burt phoned every day to give them updates on anything happening in his on-going investigation.

"There's little to report about your missing scientist," he said too often. "Vincente hasn't been seen by any of the police surveillance teams that I'm in contact with, but I'm still busy investigating any lead that surfaces. Sorry to have to say this, but Da Cosa seems to have done a conjuring trick by vanishing into thin air."

As they cleared the breakfast dishes, Doug tried to cheer his sister. "The good news is that we'll be finished in the basement today so we can plan where the extra desk for me will go. Setting up a new office down there is the fun part."

Isabel shook off her despondency to respond, "Okay! I'm ready to start!"

While most of the day was taken up by planning their new furniture arrangements, by late afternoon they couldn't help noticing that the basement was gradually became more and more gloomy. Outside, the daylight was fading as the sky darkened and they could hear the occasional rumble of distant thunder. But when they went upstairs to make supper, the storm seemed to be holding off.

It was only when they were about to go to bed that the storm finally broke. There were tremendous claps of deafening earth-shaking thunder, followed by streaks of lightning that zipped open the sky. The wind had picked up, tossing the tree branches wildly this way and that, then the heavens unleashed rain that drummed a loud tattoo on the windows before gushing down the panes of glass.

Curious to witness the violence outside, they opened the front door a fraction to peer out into the night. By the glow of the streetlights, they could see the torrential rain cascading down their driveway to join a fast flow of water already filling the gutters at each side of their road. The downpour was so heavy that the rain was bouncing off the pavement and if they hadn't moved quickly, the wind would have driven it straight into their faces.

Doug quickly closed the door. Both safely inside, he set the house alarm as well as checking all the doors and windows to verify that they were locked securely. As they climbed the stairs, Isabel said, "I don't think I'll be able to sleep with all this noisy thundery weather going on."

"Oh, I think I will," her brother replied, "I'm fair tuckered out with all the work we've been doing in the basement."

Despite the noise of the thunderstorm, they both did fall asleep - only to be jarred awake at three o'clock in the morning by the strident shriek of their house alarm.

Doug and Isabel ran out of their bedrooms at the same time.

"What's going on?" she jittered, shakily fastening her robe.

But Doug was already running downstairs to shut off the alarm and as they reached the front windows, they could see bright lights near the house and could hear people yelling. There was the sound of running feet.

The storm had faded into the distance, but what was this human mayhem going on in their garden? Doug eased open the front door to see what was happening. Isabel was right behind him. They were both anxious to find out what the unexpected commotion around the house.

By the pale light of a watery moon, they saw cars in the driveway with Burt standing by one of them, phoning. Doug could hear him asking for immediate police help. Suddenly, Colin caught their attention as he came careening round the side of the house, yelling as he ran.

"Les, Les! Look out, he's coming your way. Stop him! Stop him! He's getting away!"

A dark figure was running swiftly down the garden slope. They saw him jump the short hedge and continue racing away along the street, dodging in and out of the shadows. Then out of the blue, another taller figure emerged from behind a parked car and began to chase him. There was a heavy thud when both of them went down on the road. One jumped up, grabbing a struggling man by his arms as he also tried to stand.

Cupping his hands around his mouth, Burt bellowed, "Great work, Les! Best flying tackle I've ever seen! Keep hold of him! Pin his arms behind him! The police are on their way!"

Isabel elbowed her brother aside to get a better view. "Who are these people, Doug? What are they doing here? What's happening?"

"Newspaper friends. I guess they were watching the house. Here comes Les now."

Isabel saw a tall man pushing a reluctant figure along the path to their door. A younger man was trotting by his side. As they reached the front door, she was shocked to hear this lanky stranger address her in an unmistakeable West Indian lilt, "You okay, girl?"

Too surprised to speak, she nodded assent, whereupon Les pulled the hoodie from the head of the man he had captured. "Is this the missing scientist, Isabel?"

She looked into the face of an elderly man with a mop of tousled grey hair. He was panting heavily as if trying to catch his breath. Illuminated by the porch light, she could see his thin, lined face as Les jerked his head higher for her to see. When he saw Isabel, the captive squinted, blinking rapidly as if the harsh light hurt his eyes. Then he quickly looked away.

Isabel scrutinized his face for some time as Doug's friends waited impatiently for her answer. She noted the dark, shabby, dishevelled clothes and his hands scraped from his fall on the road. She observed the old and worn running shoes on his feet. He looked frail and cowed in the midst of this crowd of younger energetic men.

Finally, she turned to the waiting audience and stated emphatically, "I've never seen him before in my life."

The moment of shocked silence was broken by Colin. "But this is the guy who was breaking into your house! I was watching at the back and saw him open the door and go in. He ran off when the alarm sounded."

The captive kept his eyes firmly trained on the ground, making no comment about this accusation of his ill-intent.

"Yes, Colin," Burt agreed, "But we don't know who he is. If he's not the scientist we're looking for, then who is he? And why was he breaking into Isabel's house?"

They were regarding the silent captive curiously when there was a disturbance behind them. A black van with a police insignia on its sides drew up behind Burt's car. The group turned as one to look at it and even the captive finally raised his head to see for himself.

As Isabel was turning her head, she caught a malicious gleam in the old man's eyes as he looked at her.

Taken aback by this unexpected menacing glance, she recoiled, instinctively grabbing Doug's arm for support. The glint she had seen was gone in a second, but it had served to shake Isabel's confidence.

'Why did he look at me with such resentment? Why would some person I've never met before, give me such an evil glance?'

It didn't take her feverish mind long to offer a viable answer. 'Did I make a mistake? Could this man be Vincente *in disguise? He's quite capable of fooling us all, and me in particular. He's done it before.'*

Doug could feel Isabel's hand trembling on his sleeve. He looked down at her. "Anything wrong, Sis?" he asked. Isabel pulled him into the house while the others walked their prisoner to the policemen who were getting out of their vehicle.

"I think I may have made a mistake," she whispered urgently. "I might have been too hasty. That man could be Vincente after all! His disguise could have fooled me into believing that he's an old man. I was thinking that a man as old as he looks, wouldn't have been able to run or jump over the garden hedge as fast as he did."

Doug whistled incredulously. "Oh, Isabel! If you think you're right, you should tell the police. Pronto! They've been looking for the missing scientist, but I'll bet that the picture they have of Da Cosa doesn't look anything like the man we just caught."

He looked outside at the group in the driveway. "There's an officer talking to Burt now. We should go out and inform him straightaway of what you suspect."

Brother and sister hastily donned jackets over their nightclothes to hurry along the garden path to the van. But it was too late. The prisoner had been put into the back and the vehicle with tinted windows was reversing into the street.

"Wait! Wait!" Doug yelled, breaking into a run after it. The driver must not have heard him because he sped away.

When Isabel joined the puzzled group of friends waiting for Doug to return to explain why he'd chased the police van, Burt was waving to Doug and shouting, "What's up?"

"I think I've made a mistake," Isabel interrupted quickly, "I think that man might really have been Vincente in disguise."

The men were momentarily speechless but Colin, never at a loss for words, accused her, "You said that you'd never seen him before, Isabel. What's suddenly changed your mind?"

She felt extremely foolish having to explain the glance she had seen from the captive, the fleeting look that had made her rethink his identity.

But she was gratified when the others nodded agreement when she said that she'd realized that the man had run far too fast for an older person.

"But what happened here?" Doug cut in. "That police van left very quickly. Did the officers say where they were taking him?"

Colin replied that they'd been requested to give a report at Belmont, the nearest police precinct, so that would probably be where the captive was being taken.

"Okay," Doug decided, "We'll get some clothes on and go with you. Isabel needs to talk to someone official as soon as possible."

"Right you are!" Burt agreed. "I'll wait for you and Colin can go with Les. The sooner we get there, the better. Okay, everybody?"

As Isabel was turning back to the house, Les reached out to pat her on the shoulder, saying softly, "Don't you go feeling bad, little lady. We all make mistakes at times. While we write our reports at the police station, you can tell them that you think the man is the missing scientist. You'll feel much better after that."

Isabel appreciated the caring gesture and reached up to cover his hand to thank him. As she turned to look at him, she became aware that daylight was breaking. It was getting brighter by the minute. She could see everyone more clearly. Above Les' kind face, she noticed the sky streaked with the rosy hues of a new morning but knew that it was sure to herald in another hot summer's day. Somehow it seemed ominous and she shivered.

Just as the friends were dispersing, a police car with flashing lights swerved into the driveway but, mercifully for the neighbourhood, without a screeching siren. It came to an abrupt halt in front of the group and two burly policemen jumped out, their hands at their hips.

"Is this where the emergency call to the police originated?" one demanded.

Burt spoke out, "Yes, sir. I called in for help with a man we caught breaking into this house, but…"

The officer ignored what Burt was going to say. "You the owner of this house?" Burt shook his head.

Isabel raised her hand. "I am," she said and immediately resented the policeman's sweeping look at her standing there in her night attire. But he had turned to Burt again.

"So, who are you?" he asked.

Burt carefully fished out his Press identity card to show to the officers while indicating to his colleagues to do the same. "We all work for the local newspaper, The Urban. But I should tell you…"

Before he could explain further, they were all astounded when both officers closed in on Les, their hands hovering over the guns at their hips.

"This the man you caught?" the first policeman demanded.

Whether her nerves were taut with stress at causing this situation or whether she felt guilty at not identifying Vincente sooner or whether she was simply over-tired, Isabel suddenly lost her temper. She advanced to stand defiantly between the accusing officer and Les. Wagging her finger at the police officer, she exploded.

"Why are you picking on this friend of ours? You think he's a criminal just because his skin colour is different from yours or mine? When will you guys stop your offensive racial profiling and discrimination? We're all peaceful citizens here! You have no reason whatsoever to accuse any one of us of being a criminal. No reason at all!"

As she paused to catch her breath, Doug grabbed hold of his sister before she completely lost control and did something she might regret. She looked fierce enough to assault the officer.

He raised his voice. "What my sister is trying to say is that the culprit who broke into our house has been picked up by the first police car to get here. He's already been arrested."

Both officers rounded on Doug.

"What police car? There's no other police presence in this area. We were the nearest patrol to answer your call. Did you check credentials?"

Burt chimed in, "Yes, I did. They had the usual police badges. The van had the Boston Police Department insignia on the sides."

Everyone eyed one another uncomfortably while the second policeman retreated to use his car phone. The lead officer scowled at Isabel, who had allowed Doug to push her further away. She pulled her jacket closely around her.

The officer said nothing but kept a vigilant eye on all the members of the group until his colleague returned, shaking his head. Then he asked, "Did the police in the van say where they were taking the man?"

"To Belmont Police Station," Colin volunteered. "We were just going there to make statements about the break-in when you came."

The policeman scrutinized Colin coolly until he squirmed. Then he said deliberately, "That station isn't open. It's closed for renovations."

The friends eyed one another, completely at a loss for words. Gradually, the unwelcome reality was dawning on them that they'd been tricked by a fake police unit into giving up their captive. It was extremely hard to believe that was what had happened. The operation had been so slick and speedy.

Burt was particularly upset. He blamed himself, that as a long-time investigating journalist, he should have been more careful and more aware of what was happening. He blamed himself for being too gullible and too quick to assume that the van had been a police vehicle.

It was a bitter pill to swallow that after all their secret preparations to catch him, their captive had been snatched away from them, from right under their noses.

CHAPTER 36

"Can you describe the vehicle? Did anyone take its registration number?"

The police officer asking these questions might have been talking to a brick wall.

The group standing in front of him were too disarrayed to immediately process what he was saying. Burt and his colleagues couldn't believe that their success in capturing the man-whom they now believed must have been the delinquent scientist-had so dramatically turned into a complete failure. They were in total disbelief.

But the officer's loud bellow of "Hey, you guys!" got their attention. When he saw them turn to him, he began repeating his questions more loudly as if talking to people who were deaf.

"Okay, I can see that you are all taken by surprise," the officer almost shouted, "But can anyone tell me what kind of a van it was? What colour? Any distinctive markings other than the police insignia? Did anyone get its license number? Which way was it heading when it left here? Would you be able to recognize the driver if you saw him again?"

The questions came too fast for the demoralized group, making them feel naïve and incompetent. The newspapermen were appalled by their far too prompt assumption that the black van had been a police vehicle. Nobody had taken the registration number. Why would anyone take down the number of a police car?

The officer kept shaking his head as they stumbled to answer and sometimes contradicted one another. Finally, he snapped shut his notebook and tucking his pen into a top pocket, instructed them to report to the nearest open (he emphasised 'Open') police station. He gave them the name of one nearby. Twice.

In the meantime, his partner was phoning in a description of a suspect van in the area. After that, both officers walked around outside to confirm the point of entry where the man had broken in. After making sure that they had everyone's name spelled correctly and that Isabel wished to press charges against the suspect, they left with a final reminder to make their police reports as soon as possible.

The chastened group of colleagues were left standing by the house, deflated except for Les, who had a smile on his face whenever he looked at Isabel. But she had been shaken to the core by the night's experiences and now, thoroughly uncomfortable with her own erratic behaviour, she hastily excused herself to go indoors to dress.

Later, at the Police station, after having written reports and Isabel had spoken to the officer in charge, the friends disbanded to their own homes before starting their day jobs. Saturdays were Les' busy days, organizing the Sports pages. Burt and Colin had deadlines to meet with more articles about the still-uncaught scientist who seemed to be evading all attempts to find him. The Urban newspaper wanted to keep the topic on its front page as long as possible.

Not having such imminent responsibilities, Isabel and Doug shared some scrambled eggs before retiring, to try to sleep away their anxieties. But both found it impossible to stop thinking about their early morning escapade, Isabel being especially distraught over her role in the affair.

Had she let Vincente slip through her fingers once again because she'd been too quick to believe that the captive was a stranger? Her guilty feelings weighed heavily on her, refused to let her rest.

After tossing and turning on her bed, she rose quietly, resolving to go to the NIR to report the break-in to her superiors.

'*Better to give them a first-hand account before the police phone them. While I'm there, I can collect the textbooks and notebooks that I need for working at home.*'

When Doug emerged later that morning, he found a note on the kitchen table saying that his sister had gone to the NIR but would return in time for supper. He checked the clock.

'*It's almost midday. I wonder what time she went. She probably couldn't sleep after all that excitement last night.*'

Yawning, he went to fetch the morning paper from outside the front porch. It had been lying there for so long that the sun had heated the paper, making it warm to the touch. Doug caught a distinct whiff of newsprint in the humid air of another scorching day.

There was no mention of their break-in of the previous night. There was a photograph of Vincente and a revamp of the ongoing investigation. Readers were reminded to be vigilant if they saw anyone resembling the missing scientist and to report his whereabouts to the police.

Doug immediately decided to put an extra lock on the side door at the rear of the house, where the man had forced an entry.

Before he did, he took out the chuck roast that he planned to cook for the evening meal. Reflecting on the best way to deal with it on such a hot, sultry day, he decided that he would use the slow cooker.

"Good idea!" he congratulated himself. "That'll keep the kitchen cool and I won't have to keep checking it all the time. That leaves me free to inspect our windows and doors in case they need some buffed-up security."

He set to work, searing the floured roast before placing it on top of a variety of root vegetables in the slow cooker, adding two cups of beef broth, seasoning it with garlic and turning it on 'Low.'

Now whistling cheerfully, he mused: *'Were life as easy to deal with as this slow cooker, we could just let it take care of itself and stop worrying about all our little problems. If we just waited patiently, everything would run its course and turn out well in the end. Just like this roast will do.'*

With that profound thought, he went to find his toolbox.

At the Institute, Isabel was talking to Gwen, her lab manager, about the attempted break-in at her home and voicing her fears that the culprit had indeed been Vincente. They both were of the opinion that if it had been the missing scientist, he was definitely looking for something specific. But what was he searching for?

"Maybe he was trying to find Bella," Isabel speculated.

"I don't know that he would," Gwen countered. "He's the foremost scientist in his field, so he'll understand all the workings and apps of his robots. He doesn't actually need to have one in his possession to gain information."

"But maybe for some reason that we don't know, he wants the robot to help him escape," Isabel persisted. "From where he entered, he could see right across the hall to our front door where I usually keep Bella in her suitcase. He would have seen that she wasn't there and turned tail when the alarm went off."

"Then he'll try again when he reasons out that it might be upstairs in your bedroom, where you've told me that you've kept it before. His camera will have shown where your bedroom is," Gwen pointed out.

"By the way, we did remove that remote camera and it's a little marvel. It was quite easy to reach it from the outside of the suitcase without damaging the suitcase or the camera."

Uncomfortable with the reminder of having been spied on, Isabel tried another tack.

"Vincente has a very devious mind. I wouldn't even put it past him to try to break into the NIR to recover his own robot. He can easily restore its activity."

"I have my doubts about that, Isabel, but to ease your mind, I'll have Security double the guards for that room. We can't have him making off with robots from the NIR whenever he feels like it, can we?" Gwen smiled at the ridiculous idea.

Having to be satisfied with that conclusion, Isabel went upstairs to her office to find the books she wanted for studying at home. She quickly selected a number of them but in total, they proved to be too heavy to carry. Leaving home in a hurry that morning, trying to beat the debilitating humidity of the day, she hadn't thought to bring a tote bag.

She sat down at her desk overcome by weariness and sank her head into her hands. '*So many problems to solve! Nothing is easy anymore.*'

As she was despairing over her recent setbacks, Isabel's active mind was offering a solution to her book problem. After a few minutes of contemplation, she reached for the phone to talk to Gwen again.

"Is it okay if I use Bella's suitcase to carry my books to my car? I'll return it before I leave."

Granted permission and grateful to have solved at least one problem that day, Isabel went downstairs to claim the suitcase. She began rolling it past the large front windows where the relentless noonday sun came pouring into the building. The scorching heat seared her face, making it burn. As she felt her face growing hotter, an unwelcome thought entered her head. '*My car is going to be like an oven when I open it. I should get out of here as quickly as possible.*'

Back in her office, she hastily started pushing books into Bella's suitcase. As she was doing so, she heard a tearing sound. Startled, she looked around. There was nobody behind her.

She looked into the suitcase and saw that one heavy tome had snagged a corner of the lining on one side of the case, tearing open the stitches holding the material. Grabbing hold of the oversized book and twisting it free, she managed to make the tear even worse. More stitches unravelled. Now there was a big hole in the lining of the suitcase.

Reaching in to smooth the material back in place, annoyed that she would be delayed by having to glue it down again, her fingers encountered something solid. She quickly snatched her hand away. Isabel sat back on her heels, wondering what it might be and also, if it were something dangerous.

Thinking that unlikely, she tentatively reached out to gently feel all along the side of the suitcase. Yes! There was definitely something hidden in there.

CHAPTER 37

Isabel stretched across the suitcase to run her fingers along the object that had been hidden inside the lining. As she did so, she felt something sharp that suddenly made a clicking sound. She withdrew her hand again to wait for a few more minutes, to see if anything else would happen.

As there were no more ominous sounds, she decided that whatever it was must be harmless. *'Maybe it's some mechanism to keep the robot secure while it's being transported. Strange that I've never noticed it before. I wonder if it's been there all the time that I've been carrying Bella back and forth to work every day.'*

Determined to solve the problem, she searched in her desk drawer for a pair of scissors to carefully cut away the rest of the cloth that was obstructing her view. Snip by snip, the object began to appear.

When Isabel peeled back the entire side material, she saw a long, metallic pouch. It had one large clasp that must have sprung open when her fingers touched it. The top flap had lifted slightly but she couldn't see inside. Since Vincente had designed the suitcase for Bella and nobody else had access to it-other than herself-she felt positive that he must be the one responsible for hiding this mysterious object. What was it?

'Hmm. Must be something special that he didn't want anyone to know about. I don't think it will explode if I open it a little bit more. But you never can tell with Vincente. It might be some tech thing he's rigged up to wipe itself clean when it's disturbed. Like his own robot.'

After some minutes, Isabel went to rummage in her desk and returned with a wooden ruler, a relic of her high school days. Kneeling beside the suitcase, she stretched across it with the ruler to gently poke the metallic flap. It resisted the pressure. She tucked the ruler more firmly underneath and rotated it slowly. Little by little, the flap lifted. When Isabel gave it a sharp prod, the pouch overturned and some of its contents spilled out.

"My God!"

She backed away to her desk to phone Gwen, her superior, "Gwen, I'm sorry to bother you but could you come to my office quickly? I have something important to show you."

She took a breath. "I need your advice. Yes, I'm positive that it has something to do with Vincente. Thanks."

When Gwen arrived, they both looked into the open suitcase. The pouch had spawned some hundred-dollar bills.

"Look at that!" Gwen breathed, "These must be his ill-gotten gains from selling our secret information. The rat!"

"I bet it's his get-away money," Isabel opined.

"Well, he can kiss his cash goodbye!" Gwen exclaimed, "We have it now."

"But what are we going to do with it?" Isabel wanted to know, "We can't just keep it!"

She was examining the pouch while her companion was focusing on the cash. "Have you ever seen such an intricate pouch? It must be made of titanium mesh. That's why it never alerted the security detectors when the suitcase went through every day."

"Have you got any rubber gloves handy?" Gwen asked. "We should count how much money there is, but we don't want our fingerprints on it."

"Yes, but let's take the pouch into the lab in case anyone comes into my office and sees it."

"Oh, if anyone comes in, they'll only think that we're counting your monthly salary, Isabel. Paid in the usual titanium pouch," Gwen joked.

Giggling and feeling decidedly giddy, the two scientists went into the adjoining lab where Isabel lowered the window blinds and locked the connecting door. Then they created a space big enough to count the money.

Vincente had made it easy for them by packing the hundred denomination banknotes by tens, to make thousand-dollar bundles secured by rubber bands. By the time the bag was empty, there were fifty of these thin stacks sitting on the bench.

"Not a bad little nest-egg," Gwen commented, sitting back to look at their new-found treasure.

"Yes, but what are we going to do with all this money?" Isabel repeated. "We know that Vincente is going to try to collect it, one way or another. That must be why he broke into my house. For the suitcase!"

"Let's consider our options," her co-worker replied, straightening her shoulders. "We can put it back and mend the suitcase, then use it as a lure to try to capture Vincente. I agree that he'll be sure to come for it. Or we can put the cash in the safe downstairs while I phone my superiors to get more advice. That last idea is probably officially what I should do." She didn't sound completely convinced.

Gwen looked at the crestfallen face of her fellow scientist. "But what do you think? Have you got other ideas?"

"I wish there were something I could do to help capture him." Isabel declared passionately. "I feel terrible that I've let Vincente slip through my fingers twice already. I want to be instrumental in bringing him to justice. I don't want to feel guilty all my life if he gets away."

Gwen couldn't help noticing the desperation in her colleague's voice.

"Tell me what you're thinking," she urged.

"I've been thinking that we've been concentrating on the wrong things. Vincente doesn't want the robots as we suspected. He only wants Bella's suitcase. Or more specifically, he wants the money inside it."

"Yes, it certainly looks that way."

Isabel continued, "I think that Vincente must have the support of some foreign or domestic-agents. Someone must have been watching my house in order to rescue him so fast when he broke in and was caught. So, what are the odds that they are doing exactly the same thing to the NIR? With modern surveillance equipment, they might even be able to hear what we are saying now. Maybe they already know that we've found the money."

"Oh, I don't think so," Gwen smiled, patting Isabel's shoulder soothingly. "Our buildings are old but well built, and these labs are at the back of the NIR away from the road. And surrounded by a ten-foot wall! We have outside cameras too. No, I don't think we need worry about anyone knowing what we are saying inside here."

But automatically, they began to whisper.

"This is what we could do, if you'll agree," Isabel began, as she slowly thought through her ambitious plan for capturing Vincente.

Gwen listened carefully, occasionally nodding her agreement. Finally, she cautioned, "It sounds a good plan on the spur of the moment. I can help you with the details, but we'll both be in the soup if something goes wrong. You know that?"

"Yes, but we'll have enhanced the reputation of the NIR if everything goes right. And the good thing is that we don't have to call in national security. You know how long that would take. And everything will be taken out of our hands if we call them."

Her fellow conspirator sat silently for a while, considering the possibilities of success and failure in putting Isabel's plan into action, while Isabel, on tenterhooks, stared at her trying to gauge what she was thinking.

Finally, Gwen said, "Okay. Let's do it!"

Isabel gave a sigh of relief.

"But we have to go over every inch of what we intend to do, so that we both know exactly what the plan entails and what each of us is doing. We can't make any mistakes," Gwen cautioned.

They settled down to carefully map out their plan of action.

Much later, Isabel carefully wheeled Bella's suitcase outside, pulling it slowly in the hot and humid air.

She noticed that there were repairmen with an Electric Company van across the street, with one man on a lift mending a broken cable. She opened the trunk of her car, reached down to unzip the suitcase and carefully took out the books until it was empty. With the same unhurried pace, she refastened Bella's case to roll it back inside the NIR, where Gwen took charge of it.

When Isabel returned to unlock her car, the imprisoned heat from inside it blasted into her face as she held the door open to reach inside to switch on the ignition, wind down the car windows and turn on the air conditioner. While waiting for the inside heat to disperse, she leaned against the open car door to watch the repairman finish fixing the cable. When it was done, she saw him return to his van to phone, presumably to report to his office that he had finished the job.

The car had cooled enough for her to drive, so she slid into the driver's seat, wincing a little when the hot leather touched her bare legs. She set off for home thankful that the late afternoon sun was beginning to fade towards the horizon.

Turning off the main highway before reaching her house, she made a detour into the spacious grounds of the local hospital complex where Doug had taught Bella how to drive. Thankful that the usual joggers and playing children had already left she parked her car at the side of one of the meandering roads. Isabel got out to walk up a gentle hillock, from the height of which she could watch her car.

She waited a few minutes to make sure that she hadn't been followed, before opening her cellphone.

CHAPTER 38

'*Praise be for air-conditioning!*' was Isabel's first thought as she stepped into her home and out of the cloying summer heat. A welcome waft of cold air fanned her flushed face as she tossed off her sandals. The hall felt like a cool sanctuary with the pleasant coolness of the smooth parquet floor underneath her feet.

'*And praise be for brothers who like to cook!*' came a second thought as she entered a kitchen filled with enticing aromas.

Doug was spooning vegetables into a tureen while a crusted roast was resting on a cutting board beside it. She quickly crossed the room to try to snaffle a morsel, but Doug saw her coming and blocked her way.

"Oh, no, you don't, Sis!" he warned, "Nobody is allowed into this kitchen in bare feet. Far too dangerous. You might get scalded or a knife might drop on your toes. Out! Out!" he admonished. He playfully wielded the spoon as if it were a fencing blade.

When she returned in slippers, her brother was cutting the fall-apart meat. This time Isabel crept up behind him and managed to steal a taste.

"That's delicious!" she exclaimed, "I could eat the whole roast!"

"If you'd only wait a minute, I'll thicken the gravy and we can eat properly."

Dutifully she sat at the table to pour red wine into two glasses. She was truly ravenous, not having eaten since breakfast, but after a sip or two of wine she began to relax for the first time in days.

Rounding off their dinner with scoops of Isabel's favourite almond fudge ice-cream and oatmeal cookies, brother and sister settled back in their chairs, the Vincente fiasco temporarily forgotten in the afterglow of their meal. Doug was about to replenish their wine glasses when Isabel stayed his hand.

"It's Saturday night,' she announced. "Aren't you going to the Black Horse Inn as you usually do?"

Doug twirled his empty glass. "I'm not even sure that the rest of the guys will be there tonight. It's too late now for the quiz. It'll have started half an hour ago and besides, I thought that after all our early morning excitement I would stay home tonight to keep you company."

"But I want to go with you!"

Doug stared at her in surprise and with no small suspicion.

"You've never wanted to go to the pub before. Why now?"

"I thought it would be a good time to thank your friends for keeping us safe last night and for watching the house too," she answered, "It's a good opportunity to see them all together in one place."

Doug peered at her to see if she were serious, then at the clock, and he made a quick decision. "Okay, help me clear the table and we'll be on our way."

When they reached the Black Horse Inn, the sun was going down. Garlands of tiny multicolored lights had been switched on in the gathering twilight, giving the old stone building a festive modern air. A crowd of people was milling around outside, laughing and chatting, the women wearing brightly colored summer dresses and the men in comfortable light clothes. They were waiting for vacant tables on the patio.

"Look at all those waiters buzzing around," Doug commented, "Fred must have taken on extra help tonight. Follow me, Isabel. Let's find the guys inside the pub."

Doug led the way through the narrow passageways. In the barroom, the inn was seething with humanity that seemed to have a life of its own, laughing, talking loudly, even singing, jostling against one another good-naturedly. There was a constant request for service from the busy bartenders and it was a wonder that the precarious beer mugs and glasses of wine were being safely carried aloft, instead of being accidentally upended by a stray elbow and dousing some surprised individual.

Miraculously, Les appeared at the fringe of the throng, instantly commandeering Doug to help him carry drinks to their usual corner table, while greeting Isabel with a welcoming nod of his head and a sunny smile.

Not knowing how long the men would be in line, she squeezed her way through the crowd to reach Burt and Colin. It wasn't long before the three of them were deep in a conversation punctuated by activating their cellphones. These were pocketed when Doug and Les arrived, having safely juggled their drinks across the room without spilling a drop.

"What happened to the quiz tonight?" Doug asked as he carefully slid the glasses onto the polished oak table and himself on to a high-backed wooden bench next to Isabel. "I thought it would be in full swing and that we had missed the start of it."

Colin took a beer as he answered, "There was such a crowd this evening that Fred had no quiet place to run the quiz, so he postponed it until next weekend."

"What's with all the people here tonight? I've never seen the inn so crowded," Doug asked as he gazed around the room.

Les seated himself at the end of the table, stretching out his long legs, as he usually did, to form a barricade that would keep people away from their table. He took a swig of his ale and replied, "Most of them are university students. They've finished their final or term exams so they're celebrating their escape from academia as noisily as possible."

Burt chose his own glass as he commented, "No problem! They'll have left for home by next Saturday and Isabel can join us then for the quiz night."

All eyes turned to Isabel who blushed, thinking that they would probably be better off if Bella could come in her place, but she gamely took the opportunity to thank everyone for their help in catching the scientist, even if he did get away. As if it were an enduring sore point, the others became quiet and then, much to Isabel's relief, the conversation veered to other topics before they all parted company that night.

The following day, being Sunday, was a lazy day with little happening in Isabel's household and no phone calls breaking the peace. Doug had respite from cooking as there were cold leftovers from their Saturday supper. In the afternoon he busied himself rechecking the indoor windows and outside doors to see if they were still secure.

Isabel was relaxing, stretched out on the sofa with an entertaining book. She was laughing at the main character in A Man Called Ove, who reminded her so much of her own brother, when Doug came into the room with something in a basin of water.

"Look what I found on the inside of our side door."

Isabel sat up smiling. "What have you got?" She looked into the water to see a small, black fly.

"A fly? Why did you drown it? Why didn't you just swat it?"

Doug placed a finger in front of his lips and whispered, "Give you one guess."

Isabel's smile vanished, her heart missing a beat as she realized what he might be meaning. "Oh, no! You don't mean that fly is a…a bug?" she whispered back. "Are you sure? How do you know?"

"Because this fly has no legs, only a magnet underneath."

"But why is it under water?" she wanted to know.

"Because I couldn't think of what else to do with it! I wanted you to see this listening device, but I didn't want it to record what you might say."

Meanwhile Isabel was doing a lightning inventory of everything she and Doug had talked about the previous night and during that day. Luckily, nothing important.

She was relieved that she had decided not to tell Doug about her plan to catch Vincente. Still, the insidious, continuing menace of her former colleague sent shivers down her spine.

Doug was explaining, "I figured that nobody would be able to hear if we wanted to talk and the bug was under eight inches of water. Can sounds be heard through water?"

Despite the seriousness of the situation, Isabel solemnly answered, "Only if you're a whale."

They looked at one another for a minute before laughing. Then with a sigh, Isabel put her book aside.

"I'm guessing that Vincente planted that bug when he broke in yesterday?"

"That's the only explanation," Doug agreed. "Shall I destroy it now that you've seen it?"

"Did you search everywhere to see if there are any more of those 'flies'?"

"I definitely did! I cleaned the hall from top to bottom, though I did think of leaving some of the spider webs, just in case."

Isabel grinned at her incorrigible brother. "Well then, let's take this bug out of the water quietly without speaking..."

"...and smash it to smithereens!" Doug finished her sentence with a flourish.

He fetched a small hammer from his workbox and going to the kitchen, made short shrift of destroying the disguised bug, sweeping its innards into the garbage bin. And who can blame him if he had been thinking of a certain missing scientist's demise while he was doing so?

CHAPTER 39

*I*sabel and Doug may have been granted a temporary reprieve from outside strife that Sunday, but their troubles began anew the following day when Isabel was awakened at five o'clock in the morning by the shrilling of the cellphone on her bedside table.

"Yes, Gwen. What's happening?" she whispered, noticing that the new day was already sending glints of golden sunlight through the chinks in the window blinds. *'Oh, not another hot day! Maybe I'll wear my sandals instead of shoes when I go out'.*

Gwen's voice was urgent. "The suitcase has gone! I couldn't sleep so I came into work early to check that everything was in order. The first thing I noticed when I opened up was that the suitcase wasn't where I'd left it. I've looked everywhere and it's definitely not here!"

Isabel was now sitting alert on the edge of her bed.

"But that's a good sign! Vincente must have taken the bait. Did you question the night guard to see if he'd noticed anything out of the ordinary?"

"Yes, that was the next thing I did. Bill was on duty and he said that everything had been quite normal. The cleaners were the only other people in the building. He's positive that there was nobody new on their staff because he knows them all."

"Ha!" Isabel responded, "The cleaners have a master key to get into your office," but adding as an afterthought, "Vincente will have kept the master key that he had."

"I did put a GPS chip between some of the banknotes, as we planned. If you have something to write on, I'll give you the tracking co-ordinates."

"Could you message them to me on my cellphone? And will you send that info to the others too? I'm getting dressed as we speak. I'll be on my way as soon as I get the co-ordinates and can see where Vincente may be heading."

While they were talking, Isabel had grabbed a blouse and a pair of slacks and was reaching for her running shoes that seemed to have migrated under the bed. Her purse, sunglasses and car keys were on the bureau near the bedroom door, ready for a quick exit.

"Okay, I'm almost ready. Going downstairs now to grab a coffee. I'll keep in touch."

She opened her bedroom door stealthily and closed it again as quietly as possible. All to no avail. When she turned around, Doug was standing on the landing watching her.

"What's going on, Sis? I heard your phone ring. Who's phoning you at five in the morning? Is it that Da Cosa guy?"

"No, No! That was Gwen wanting me to do something urgent. It's just Work."

"At five in the morning?" Doug sounded unconvinced.

Isabel started running downstairs.

"Sorry, I can't talk about it now, Doug. Why don't you go back to bed? I have to go out soon, but you can sleep in today."

Her brother was not about to be shaken off so easily. He followed her down to the living room where she was stuffing things into her oversized purse while talking on the cellphone she had tucked under her chin.

"Yes, Gwen. You've got more info for me? Zeroing on Logan Airport? I'm on my way. Can you alert the other two as to where they should be going? Thanks."

She swung around quickly but her brother stood in her way. "You're going to the airport? Why? Are you flying off somewhere? I have a right to know. I'm your brother!"

"I'm not taking a plane, if that's what you mean. I am trying to head off another catastrophe and the sooner I get there, the better. So please move out of my way."

But Doug had swiftly put two and two together and held his ground.

"Oh! Now I get it. You're after that Vincente guy, aren't you? Well, I'm coming with you! I'll drive you to Logan Airport to save you the bother. Then you won't need to waste time parking your own car. Give me a minute to throw on some clothes."

Soon they were both on their way to the airport as Isabel was watching a moving arrow on her cellphone. Although annoyed with her brother, she felt relieved that Doug had offered to drive. He was a fast yet safe driver and would indeed save her the time she would have wasted parking her own vehicle. Doug set her down at the airport entrance, where a steady stream of people was entering.

Once inside the noisy entrance hall, she attached the earplug connection to her cellphone. She didn't feel out of place as she inserted the plugs into her ears, being surrounded by many other people, young and old, also wearing earplugs and all walking around like zombies tuned into some other world.

Isabel quickly rechecked the GPS satellites' signal. It was quite strong and certainly seemed to be centred in the Logan Airport itself. But where? Logan was a very big airport and her only clue was Bella's suitcase. How could she find that particular suitcase amongst all the other suitcases being towed by so many travellers? She started looking both left and right as she walked slowly along the vast entrance area.

Doug was about to drive away from the airport entrance, wondering if he should go home to wait until Isabel called him to come to collect her, when he saw a taxicab drawing up behind him. To his astonishment, he saw Colin jump out and run to the mouth of the revolving door entrance where he was promptly swallowed up, to be spit out indoors. He was closely followed by a hurrying Burt.

'Why are those news hounds here? I bet they've discovered what Isabel is doing and they're chasing after her to get another newspaper story. Burt never gives up when he smells a story. I'm going in to warn Isabel.'

Determined to thwart the newspapermen, Doug circled around the airport and parked his car. Then he too rushed into the bustling terminal, never questioning his belief that he could find his colleagues and his sister amid the swirling hundreds of travellers validating their flights.

At the far end of the cavernous hall, Isabel was standing easing her tired feet. She was glad that she'd worn her comfortable running shoes instead of flimsy sandals. Even so, she was weary of walking umpteen times up and down the huge reception area whilst scanning the long lines of travellers and eyeing their luggage to see if she could recognize Bella's suitcase.

Vincente would be in disguise-of that she was sure-but once she'd located the suitcase, she would be able to see the person who owned it.

She spied a vacant bench, where she sat down for a minute, pulling out one earplug to readjust it. The seat was opposite the ground floor washrooms where the signal was surprisingly strong. This seemed as good a place as any to watch people come and go. She was about to reinsert the earplug when she was startled by someone saying her name.

"Miss Isabel?"

She turned around so quickly that the other earplug jerked out.

As she was juggling with both earpieces and her cellphone, she looked up and recognized Jack, one of the NIR staff, standing a short distance away.

"Oh, Mon Dieu! I didn't mean to shock you! Mais, I couldn't pass by without speaking to you."

At that inconvenient moment, Isabel heard Gwen's voice say, "The signal seems to have stopped. Did you find him?"

Isabel hastily turned her phone to 'Mute', snapping it shut, but her colleague had heard what Gwen had said.

"That sounds like Miss Gwen's voice. N'est ce pas? You are looking for someone? Pas moi, j'espére? I didn't 'ave time to leave a message at the NIR before I left because I 'ad an urgent call from my daughter in Amsterdam. She was taken ver' sick at the hairport and missed 'er flight to Boston."

He paused sadly. "Now I'm on my way there to help 'er. She 'as her petit four-year-old son with 'er and I'm very worried about who is taking care of 'im too."

Isabel looked at Jack's kindly face. He certainly looked paler than usual and his snowy-white hair had tumbled over his eyes, as if he hadn't had time to comb it.

His real name was Jacques, but everyone called him Jack. He had an engagingly French accent when speaking. Her mother would have described it as 'Maurice Chevalier talk.'

Jack was one of the best NIR staff members, a Go-To person, always ready to help troubleshoot with problems and he was very well-liked by everyone at the NIR. He always found time to talk to people, saying that he was improving his English.

Isabel felt sorry for him having to deal with his own difficulties now.

"Don't fuss yourself, Jack," she hastened to reassure him. "There is nothing to worry about at work. You have enough on your mind, thinking about your family, without fretting about forgetting to leave a note. I'll let the office know when I get there."

Jack looked relieved. Then he enquired about the phone call he had overheard.

"Thank you, Miss Isabel. Alors, then are you looking for Monsieur Da Cosa?"

Isabel was taken aback. "What makes you ask that?"

"Well, it seems that everyone in Boston is hasked to look out for 'im. The newspapers are full of the missing scientist. I wonder if you were searching for 'im too."

He gave her a sympathetic glance. "I was shocked to hear about 'im because I know how closely you worked together."

He gave her another quick glance before adding, "We all saw how 'e regard you. Some of the staff used to think that maybe you were a couple out of the NIR as well as inside it."

Isabel flushed furiously.

"I hardly think that he cared for me when he used me to get a job with the Institute and then sold our technology for his own gain!"

"Now, now, Miss Isabel!" Jack soothed, "'ave you ever thought that per'aps he was saving money in order to buy you everything you wan'?"

"That's total nonsense!" she countered, surprising herself by her own ferocity.

Embarrassed at her reaction, she looked away and looking over his shoulder, saw two men walking purposefully towards them. Jack also turned his head to see what had caught her attention.

"Ah! I see your friends coming, dear lady, so I will leave. Bon Chance in your search!"

He smiled at her and waving goodbye, he was quickly lost in the passing crowd, leaving behind a thoroughly nonplussed Isabel.

CHAPTER 40

As Isabel watched Burt and Colin approach, she turned off the Mute button on her cellphone and checked the GPS signal again. She was chagrined to find that what had been such a strong signal before, was now growing fainter.

She phoned Gwen. "Burt and Colin are just arriving, so I'll co-ordinate our plans with them. But my signal is getting weaker. What's yours doing?"

"It was strong a moment ago, but it's definitely fading. I'll recheck the co-ordinates. Give me a minute."

"By the way, Gwen, I met Jack from the NIR here at the airport. He's on his way to Amsterdam to link up with a sick daughter. He was worried that he hadn't left a message to that effect at the NIR, so I said I would inform someone."

There was a deep silence on the other end of the line.

"Isabel, Jack is standing here in front of me. He's helping me with some technical problems. It's his weekend off but he came in to help me solve them."

Isabel froze, too stunned to speak for a minute, then, "Vincente!" she hissed over the phone.

Gwen was incredulous. "You mean he's disguised himself as Jack?".

"Oh, yes, I do! Vincente certainly had me fooled. He even talked like Jack, in that attractive French accent of his. It was uncanny. I didn't suspect a thing." Isabel uttered furiously.

Gwen was immediately all-businesslike at the other end of the line.

"Well, Vincente has given himself away this time, because now we know how he's presenting himself to the world. With Jack's permission, I'll send his photo to your cellphones. You can show it to the airport officials for quick identification."

"Thanks, Gwen. I'll explain everything to Burt and Colin."

While she waited for them, she relived her conversation with the devious Vincente and blamed herself for being tricked again.

'I should have been more alert! I should have picked up that he knew Burt and Colin were my friends. The real Jack has never met them. But Vincente saw them at my house when he broke in. How could I have missed the fact that nobody else calls me 'dear lady?' Only Vincente! I could kick myself for being so naïve. But that's what he trades on.'

"Damn the man! He's such a slippery snake. But now I know how he's disguised I'll get him yet!" she vowed aloud.

By this time, the newspapermen had caught up with her. She didn't even pause to welcome them before saying urgently, "Colin, will you check that men's washroom opposite to see if a suitcase has been left there? Burt, stay with me. I know what disguise Vincente is using! He resembles one of our employees at the Institute. Gwen is sending his photograph to our cellphones."

She was busy informing him of her conversation with 'Jack', when Colin came back. "I found an old suitcase hidden at the back of the cleaners' closet. It was wide open, and the lining had been ripped out. It's pretty well damaged. Nobody would want to use it now. It's definitely garbage."

"Ha! Just as I thought!" Isabel said. "Vincente has hidden the money somewhere more accessible, probably on a money-belt around his waist. He wasn't carrying a bag when I saw him. But the GPS signal should still be operational. We just have to locate him. Good, the photograph of the real Jack is coming in. Check to see if you've both received it."

Colin was quickly informed of Vincente's most recent misdeeds and now fully aware of whom they were seeking, they split their search of the various areas of the airport.

Burt was to cover the main entrance hall and Isabel and Colin would search the side corridors, concentrating on the GPS signal and Jack's photograph. They began to inspect the lines of travellers shuffling through the validation processes at the airline desks, trying to find out what destination Vincente had chosen. Isabel was adamant that he wouldn't be flying to Amsterdam. He might be a master of disguise, but she wasn't about to be thrown off by that misinformation.

Burt was gradually working his way down the main hall of airline desks when Doug saw him. He hurried after him, grabbed his arm, and said belligerently, "I know what you're up to, Burt! You're after a story about my sister, aren't you? Well, I want you to leave her alone!"

Burt shook off Doug's hand.

"You've got the wrong idea, Doug," he hissed, "Isabel asked Colin and me to help her find Da Cosa. He's here somewhere and we want to stop him leaving the country. Now quit bothering me. I'm busy tracking the guy."

He glanced down at the GPS signal that was growing even fainter. He flicked over to Jack's picture. Doug was looking over his shoulder.

"Guess I got the wrong end of the stick. Sorry! I thought you were following her," Doug apologised. "But why have you got Jack's photo? I know him, he works with Isabel at the NIR. Really nice guy. Surely, you can't be looking for him too?"

"Da Cosa's made himself up to look like Jack," Burt snapped. "Do I take it that you would know him straight away if you saw him?"

"Absolutely! In fact, I just saw him go through the United Emirates Airline entrance as I was passing by. The next flight out is to Dubai. I thought it strange at the time that Jack was going so far away for a vacation or a conference. You need a whole heap of cash for that kind of flight."

Burt didn't answer. "Tell me where the Emirates terminal is?"

"Sure, it's further down the hall. Come with me, I'll show you."

As they hurried along, Burt sent messages to Colin and Isabel to meet them there.

They were soon assembled outside the Emirates Airline desk which seemed to be closing. The attendants in their attractive beige and red uniforms with sheer white scarves tucked into one side of their red hats, were packing up. Burt skirted the roped area to reach them.

A young lady, immaculately made-up, glanced up at him.

"Sorry, Sir, are you booked for a later flight? We will be checking you in an hour before you depart. This flight is full and ready to leave."

By this time, Isabel and Colin had joined Burt and Doug. The newspaperman showed her his Press credentials and Jack's photograph.

"We need to interview this man. It's urgent! We think he's on the flight due to leave for Dubai."

"I'm sorry, Sir, that is not possible. The airplane is already taxiing to the runway. It was delayed for half an hour, so it has priority clearance. Now if you will excuse me, I am closing this desk."

Isabel pushed forward. "You don't understand. The man is a criminal wanted by the police. You can't let him leave the country. You have to get someone to stop the plane!"

Before the startled attendant could reply, an airport official appeared at her side. "Is there a problem here? Are these people bothering you?"

Isabel turned to him, speaking over-loudly in frustration, "We're trying to stop a criminal from leaving the country and we're not getting any co-operation!"

The airport official spoke firmly, "Ma'am, if you have a special request, you should go to the Security Office on the top floor. They can help you better than this young lady."

The Emirates attendant left hurriedly while the official escorted the disgruntled group to the escalator and gave them directions of where to find the main Security office. As time was fast slipping away, the foursome was becoming more and more aware of the impending failure of their mission if something wasn't done soon.

They scaled the moving escalator as if it were an ordinary staircase.

The top floor was also an observation deck and as they stepped off the escalator, they saw an Emirates aircraft zoom down the runway and lift off on its long flight to Dubai. Isabel blanched at the realization of her now certain defeat in trying to capture the elusive criminal scientist. She had been so sure of success this time.

Doug tried to calm everyone by suggesting a respite. "I think we all need a coffee. There's a coffee bar up here. Why don't we sit down and think about what's the best thing to do now? You all look as if you need a break. I can go buy four coffees if you like."

Being newspapermen, Burt and Colin opted to go to the Security office first, to see what they could find out and what could be done now that the scientist had left the country. Maybe Da Cosa could be apprehended when he reached Dubai. It was worth a try.

But Isabel, feeling disconsolate, sat forlornly on a hard, red plastic seat in a row that faced the high observation windows. She was grateful when Doug brought her the coffee, but every drop tasted to her as bitter as wormwood.

CHAPTER 41

$\mathscr{I}$t wasn't long before Burt and Colin rejoined Isabel and Doug. Not a good sign.

Burt explained, "They were fine in the Security office until they found out that we were journalists. They wanted to know what newspaper we worked for and why we wanted to talk to one of the passengers on the Emirates' flight that has just left."

"Yes," Colin continued, "They clammed up after we told them that we thought there was a criminal on board. They pushed some forms at us, telling us to write down our problem and the proper authorities would deal with it. We had to supply them with our names and phone numbers. I guess they want to verify who we say we are."

"There was nothing we could say to get more information after that," Burt asserted.

"And they weren't telling us anything, either," Colin concluded.

"I hope you didn't tell them about Isabel's plan to catch Vincente," Doug worried.

"Certainly not!" Burt answered, "You should know us better than that. We were not about to implicate anyone else."

Isabel had been listening to them, thinking that nobody seemed willing to help them stop Vincente's escape from the law. He must have had the support of powerful people. It looked as if he had sold himself to the richest foreign buyer and now he'd absconded with the technology the NIR had been working on for years. It was a grievous blow to their research unit. Personally, it felt totally devastating. She was the one who had recommended him for the vacant post.

She had been putting off phoning Gwen to tell her about their failure to capture Vincente but when Burt and Colin had finished their coffee and left to report back to their newspaper, she pulled herself together. She pressed the cellphone button for Gwen's number while Doug was busy clearing away their paper coffee cups.

Gwen answered immediately.

Isabel sighed, saying despairingly, "He got away, Gwen. He's on an Emirates flight to Dubai. We were too late to stop him. I'm sorry that I didn't tumble to Vincente's disguise sooner. We might have caught him if I had." Her tears spilled over.

"Oh, Isabel, please don't cry! I may have some good news for you."

Isabel dabbed at her wet cheeks with a handkerchief before replying bitterly, "What good news could there possibly be? The rat has left the sinking ship and is off with all our research to trade it in for a life of luxury out East."

"Oh, Isabel!" Gwen repeated. "I have a confession to make. When we agreed to follow our own plan to capture Vincente, I couldn't help feeling guilty about not informing my superiors about what we were going to do. So, I did. I'm sorry to have kept you in the dark about that, but I felt that it was the right thing for me to do in the circumstances."

Isabel's face was turning a dull red just as Doug returned. It wasn't difficult for him to see that his sister was about to explode.

"You what?" she yelled into the phone all tears forgotten.

"Hold on a minute, Isabel, I haven't finished yet," Gwen continued.

"They informed the FBI and federal agents were sent to Logan Airport to try to head Vincente off. But they agreed to let you put our plan into action because you knew him better than they did and had a better chance of spotting him. They were back-up support for you if you needed them."

"A fat lot of good that did!" Isabel exclaimed heatedly, "They let him get away."

"But you saved the day, Isabel!"

"What on earth do you mean?"

"As soon as you twigged to Vincente's disguise, I immediately sent the agents a message to let them know. The FBI has access to all the airline rosters, so they could quickly locate the airline he intended to use. We couldn't have done that by ourselves."

"So why didn't they catch Vincente before he left?" Isabel demanded.

"But they did! That's what I'm trying to tell you."

"What do you mean?" Isabel repeated impatiently.

"They had the Emirates plane delayed for half an hour so that they could take Vincente into custody. I think they might have made some excuse about him carrying too much money when leaving the country. Anyway, they managed to apprehend him before he boarded. Without making too much of a commotion. They suspected that he might have accomplices travelling on the same flight and they wanted to avoid any trouble once he was seated on the plane."

"So where is Vincente now?"

"That's FBI business, Isabel. All we know is that we succeeded in helping capture that miserable criminal. I, for one, can live with that! How about you?"

Isabel hesitated, then said, "This is all very sudden, Gwen. You say he's actually been arrested?"

"Yes!"

"I can hardly believe it."

"Well, phone me when you want to celebrate!" Gwen ended.

Doug had been watching his sister's face change from darkness into a rosy glow. "What's happening, Sis?"

"You'll never guess, Doug!" she replied almost cheerfully. "Come on, let's go home. I'll tell you on the way."

They were slowly descending the escalator when they saw a group of official looking people coming up the ascending side of the moving staircase. As they came closer, Isabel drew in a sharp breath. Vincente, still disguised as Jack, was in their midst, his arms held firmly by two burly men.

As they drew level, Isabel's and Vincente's eyes met. For a brief second, she searched for some message. Did his eyes express regret or even remorse? His glance was so dark that she couldn't tell. The grim group passed by and Isabel turned her head to look downward to watch for the bottom of the escalator where firmer ground began.

Behind her, Doug had seen the brief glance between his sister and the disguised scientist, but for once he held his tongue. There are times when a brother needs to keep quiet.

CHAPTER 42

$\mathcal{I}$t was a merry group that met the following weekend at the Black Horse Inn's corner table. Gwen had been invited to join the friends in the big barroom, to help celebrate Vincente's capture. The drinks and conversation were flowing freely.

Gwen told them that she had questioned the night watchman at the NIR once she had learned that Vincente was using Jack as a disguise. Sure enough, just as the watchman had come on duty, 'Jack' was seen leaving the Institute carrying a large box. He had thought nothing of it as Jack was often seen transporting things to repair equipment. She said that it was unfortunate that the watchman had failed to check that the real Jack was on holiday that particular weekend.

Much had happened during the days that followed the maverick scientist's arrest.

Isabel and Gwen had been congratulated by the upper echelon of the NIR and were the heroines of the moment at the Institute. Burt and Colin had delivered another scoop entitled 'Da Cosa, The Captured Scientist,' for their newspaper. Les had been awarded a prestigious

Press award for his popular year-long coverage of Sports in The Urban.

Colin, as effervescent as usual, raised his glass to toast the group.

He asked, "Now that we've succeeded in getting Da Cosa to a place that he deserves, like prison, what are we going to do next for some excitement?"

Les and Isabel smiled into each other's eyes, both realising that there were more things in life than robots and Sports pages, however fascinating those were. Burt and Colin had been agreeing that the obviously intelligent Gwen would make a good player in the pub's quiz games and Burt was about to suggest the idea to her.

There was a lull in the conversation as they all turned to Colin to consider his initiative.

To everyone's surprise, Doug broke the silence by loudly exclaiming, "If you're looking for excitement, I've got the very thing! Look what I've discovered."

He had everyone's attention as he fished in his pocket for a colored picture that he brandished in front of their puzzled eyes.

"Take a look at this!" he enthused. "I'm going to buy it! It's a unique clay roasting pan. You stand a chicken on its end, on the central skewer instead of laying it flat. That way, it cooks evenly with the juices flowing down into the vegetables that you've arranged in the well at the bottom of the pan. Then everything gets roasted perfectly. All together at the same time. Now who wouldn't be excited about that!"

He looked around as broad grins and smiles began to break out on his friends' faces.

But before anyone could argue, he concluded emphatically, "Speaking for myself, I think that's as much excitement as I want at the moment."

Fred the innkeeper, startled by the loud clapping and table-thumping that erupted at the corner table, paused as he was drawing a pint of bitter from the bar pumps. He glanced across the room before sliding the frothy stein to his waiting customer.

He shook his head as he confided, "It's those noisy newspaper guys over there. You never know what they're really up to until you read it in the newspaper."

"Or in a book," his customer added.

End

WHO IS ANDREA?

CHAPTER 1

Stanley stared at his left hand. He had felt the tremor for a year or so but the fact that his hand wouldn't stop shaking now, even when he rested it on his desk, was a sign that he was over-tired. He massaged his wrist while continuing to check crucial data on the computer. The other scientists had gone home long ago.

'A promise is a promise,' he muttered. He had told his team that everything would be in order for them to finish the final stage of their project the next day.

When he eased his fingers off the keyboard to stretch them, his elbow caught the edge of his coffee mug, sending it crashing to the floor where it shattered into pieces. For a stunned moment, Stanley looked at the spreading liquid, too tired to even curse his luck. He rose to his feet, distractedly running his fingers through his unruly gray hair as if doing so would summon some dregs of energy to clean up the mess.

'Accidents always happen when you're really tired. That was the mug Kate gave me for my birthday. She's going to be upset when I tell her.'

Going to the tiny kitchenette to find a dustpan and brush and something to mop up the coffee, now rapidly spreading across the smooth tiled floor, he happened to glance up at the skylights of the laboratory. He could see a sprinkle of stars winking through the darkness of the desert night. The lab was quiet except for the incessant chirping of cicadas from outside.

Returning, he noticed how tidy the workbenches were and realized how lucky he was to have such dedicated assistants as his fellow scientists Norma, Susie and José. Lucky to have a rich sponsor. Lucky to have found these remote buildings to remodel into laboratories. Lucky to have been able to maintain the secrecy of their project.

Bending down to brush up the pieces of crockery, Stanley experienced the familiar thrill of excitement he always felt when the end of a project drew near.

The years of exhaustive research, complex problem solving and finding expert advice when he and his team admitted a lack in their own expertise, were finally coming to an end. So were their months of errors and corrections and their many devises for keeping the research secret. Soon they would be ready to show the world the cutting-edge technology they had created. People would be surprised!

Stanley dumped the broken ceramic pieces into the garbage bin, then took out his cellphone to call home, but holding it in his hand, he reconsidered.

'Hmm. Kate will have given up expecting me for dinner. It's so late that she'll have gone out to do her evening class. I'll just head home once I dry this floor.'

That done and the coffee-stained paper towels thrown away, Stanley looked around the lab, doing his usual final check to see that all was in place. Once satisfied, he switched off the lights and activated the security procedures for locking up the facility.

A cool desert breeze blew a fine dusting of sand across his face as he walked to his car. It tingled yet felt refreshing after the cold air conditioning indoors.

His lined face wrinkled into a contented smile as he thought about the dinner Kate would have left for him. His tiredness was dissipating as he anticipated how their soon-to-be finished project would astonish the whole world. His hands were steady on the car's steering wheel.

CHAPTER 2

Although Stanley had had every intention of helping his team the next day, he spent it instead on wading through the endless paperwork that had accumulated on his desk at home. Why did there have to be so much documentation attached to scientific projects? There were no urgent phone calls from the lab so he felt sure that the final stage of the project must be going smoothly.

He and Kate had a rare dinner together on the patio of their ranch-style house, where they chatted amiably while sipping wine and watching the fireflies blink on and off as the evening darkened and the moon rose.

It wasn't until he awoke with a jolt in the middle of the night that he began to worry. Why hadn't his team called him to tell him that the project was finished? Was everything okay? Or had they come up against a problem that they didn't want him to know about? What if they were still at the lab trying to figure it out?

It was no use trying to get back to sleep. He slipped out of bed without waking Kate and crept along the passageway to the front entrance. Pulling on a light jacket and pants, he quietly eased open the front door and once in his car, freewheeled it down the sloping driveway until he came to the road. There, he could start the car without waking his wife. Sounds carried clearly in the desert air. As if in answer to his thoughts, the howling of coyotes echoed from the hills and town dogs began to bark in reply. His car sounded unnaturally loud in the quiet streets.

When Stanley reached the low buildings that housed the labs, all was silent. There were no lights to be seen inside and only the motion lights turning on outside, as he walked to the door to unlock it. He punched in the code numbers to disable the alarm system. Walking quickly to his laboratory, he unlocked that door. The room was in darkness except for a patch of bright moonlight flooding down from the skylight.

Then he saw that there was someone else in the lab. There was a figure standing at the far end of the room.

Stanley flicked on the light switch and demanded, 'Who the hell are you? What are you doing here? This is private property.'

The woman turned her head to look at him. 'Ah, you are Stanley,' she said calmly. 'I recognize your voice.'

Stanley charged across the room yelling at her, 'What are you doing here?'

He stopped short in front of her.

She was very beautiful, with hazel eyes and long, sleek black hair that hung over her shoulders. Her smooth skin was flawless. Her generous mouth was pink, and he could see a hint of white teeth. Her dress was made of some silky green material, falling fashionably short over shapely legs and her shoes were ballerina flats. She stood quite still, not one bit alarmed by his belligerence.

Breathing hard, he hesitated and retreated a step, to look again. She was truly stunning. He could hardly believe how successful his team had been.

'I'm Andrea,' the woman said, tilting her head to one side.

Stanley felt extremely foolish. Of-course he knew who 'she' was - and what she was. Still keeping a watchful eye, he walked towards his workbench to give himself time to recover from his panic. Stroking his stubbly morning beard, he allowed himself a rueful grin. Then he called out, 'Come here.'

He watched carefully as the woman suddenly jerked, as if coming out of a reverie and began walking towards him. When she was a few feet away, he said, 'Stop there! You'll have to do better than that.'

Muttering something about adjustments, he sifted through his tools to find what he wanted. Bending down to her knees, he removed a flap of plastic and began to manipulate the mechanism underneath. 'Now walk past me,' he commanded.

This time, Andrea walked smoothly across the room to the opposite wall.

'Okay, now turn around and come back.'

With a swish of her skirt, she turned and came to a stop in front of Stanley. Satisfied, he bent down to secure the silicon skin over the knee.

The robot scrutinized him with long-lashed, hazel eyes before saying, 'Ah! You like what you see.'

Stanley, hearing her read his thoughts so easily, tried to hide his excitement as he stood up.

'Incredible', he thought, 'to see this new technology actually working. The experts were right. Robots can be programmed to pick up minute human signs and compute a match with human emotions. Almost as if they are thinking.'

'You are very pleased,' Andrea spoke again in her lilting voice, the one his team had spent so many months perfecting.

Stanley was overwhelmed with the success of this part of their project. Andrea looked so human that the robot could be mistaken for a real person, as he knew to his own chagrin. Her voice had the subtle intonations of human speech. 'If she looks like a woman and speaks like a woman and walks like a woman, then she must be…' He chuckled at the anomaly.

'You are very happy too,' Andrea stated, breaking into his thoughts.

'Extremely happy!' he replied joyfully, 'But there is one more thing you need to demonstrate to me.'

Before he could say anything more, he heard the door of the lab being opened behind him. He spun round to see who was coming in so early. It was barely five o'clock in the morning.

José, one of his team, peered carefully around the steel door.

'*Buenos dias*, Boss!' José exclaimed, '*Perdón,* but from my house, I see a light in the lab when I wake up. I think to myself, Oh! Oh! Somebody's broken into the lab. I rush here to see who it is.'

'Only me, José. I couldn't sleep.'

'And you found Andrea. What you think? *Una señorita bonita?*'

The subject of their scrutiny regarded José for a minute. 'Another happy man,' the robot said, causing the two men to laugh.

'Pretty perfect!' Stanley agreed. 'She walks well, and her voice sounds amazingly human. I was just about to do another test. Want to help me?'

'Yes,' Andrea answered before José could say '*Sí.*'

The men chuckled.

'José, you worked on the computer parts that enable the robot to solve problems. I have no idea how you did that, because you're the expert. Now we should run tests to see that everything is operating properly. Maybe you could pose a problem to Andrea and we'll find out what it can do?'

'Sure, *Jefe.*' José stood in front of the robot, cleared his throat and said, 'There's a fire in the lab. Quick, Andrea. What can you do to put it out?'

Without a moment's hesitation, Andrea replied, 'First I ascertain if it is an electrical fire. If it is, I turn off the circuit and get the fire extinguisher or the bucket of sand to put it out. If it is a paper or cloth fire, it can be smothered with sand or baking soda. If it is a cigarette burning, I see if it is between a person's lips. If so, I leave that there. If it is in an ashtray, I crush it out. I have to make sure there is no oxygen to fuel the flames.'

'But what if it's a really big fire?' José persisted.

'I phone the police and fire station. Their phone numbers are on the wall. One or both of them will come to help. Then I open the door and get the hell out of here.'

Stanley's mouth gaped open. 'You programmed it to say that?'

'No, Boss, I did not. Andrea must have heard that language from one of the team. She is programmed to enter all new words into a vocabulary bank.'

'We'll have to be careful what we say around it,' Stanley muttered uncomfortably, recalling what he had shouted out when he first saw the robot.

Their tests were interrupted by the sound of the lab door being opened again. They turned to see the other two members of the team peeping around it. Then it was thrown open wider and the tall British scientist Norma strode into the lab, followed closely by their tiny Asian colleague, Susie.

'Jeez, Stanley and José, you gave us conniptions,' Norma declared.

'We thought somebody was raiding the lab. Susie and I were trying to get some sleep after working late last night. Then Susie saw a light in the lab when she looked out of her window. She was so alarmed that she came to wake me up. Why is everyone here so early?'

'Sorry! I came because I couldn't sleep. I didn't expect to cause everyone to panic,' Stanley answered.

'That's all right,' Susie said in her usual calm manner. 'Now that we're here, we'd like to know what you think of the robot. We dressed her last night after we assembled her. What do you think? She's very fashionable, no?'

As she spoke, she brushed her straight black hair off her face and Stanley recognized whom Andrea resembled. He smiled to himself.

'Wonderful! The robot looks like a real modern woman.'

They were all startled when Andrea began to speak.

'I recognize Norma. She's the woman with the British accent and curly gray hair. She has a very loud voice. Susie is the small lady with dark hair. She is Chinese.'

'No, I'm not! I am Japanese,' Susie protested.

Andrea was silent as if assimilating this information while the scientists were excitedly talking together.

'What tests are you doing?' Norma asked, 'Does the robot move her limbs and walk the way we programmed?'

'Yes, just a minor adjustment to the knees,' Stanley replied. 'José is finding out now if she can solve problems when we're not around to tell her what to do.'

'I know how to put out fires,' Andrea interrupted.

'Jeez,' Norma said, 'This robot is talking like a real person. I'm going to make some coffee. Anyone want some?'

'No, thank you,' Andrea replied before the rest of the team could respond. 'I don't need to eat or drink.'

Norma paused to consider the robot. 'Okay, Superwoman,' she said, winking at the other scientists. 'Let's see if you can make coffee for us poor humans who don't have a computer for a brain.'

Obediently, Andrea moved towards the small kitchen area as everyone watched. The robot filled the carafe with water, emptied it into the coffee percolator, added ground coffee in the right compartment and plugged in the appliance. After a while the aromatic smell of freshly brewed coffee filled the lab.

'You need to get four mugs out of the cupboard,' Norma instructed. Andrea opened the cupboard doors and found four mugs that she placed on the counter.

'We will also need some milk from the fridge,' Norma said.

The robot located the carton of milk and put it by the mugs. 'Now pour the coffee.' The others crowded into the kitchenette to see if the robot could accomplish that task. When it did, they all applauded in delight and each picked up a mug of hot coffee. Stanley instructed Andrea to walk back to the lab to stand where she had been positioned before.

José was so pleased at the robot's successful use of his complicated computer programs that he could hardly contain his exuberance. He was talking rapidly in Spanish to the team, telling them that the robot was performing even better than he'd hoped, when Andrea interrupted him on her way to the adjoining lab.

'Jeez, Norma,' she said. 'You are a demanding person. You are a little afraid of me. I am like a real modern woman. I am Superwoman. You are a human.'

Everyone froze at these surprising declarations from their new creation, not quite sure how to respond to what seemed like derogatory declarations, when they all knew that she was only using the words that had been stored recently in her memory bank.

CHAPTER 3

*A*fter that unexpected speech, the robot fell silent while everyone watched her walk to the adjoining lab.

Norma's pale freckled face that never seemed to suntan, had become bright red at what sounded like human mockery coming from a robot. Seeing her obvious embarrassment, José jumped up to reassure her, nearly bumping into her in his haste. Norma recoiled, guarding her coffee cup as he waved his agitated hands in front of her face as if to dispel any mockery.

'*Lo siento*, Norma. I forget to tell you that when the robot hears new words, she adds them to a vocabulary list and then will practice them. She picked up the word 'humans' when you spoke it.'

'I have no emotions,' the sharp-eared Andrea stated from the adjoining lab. 'I only interpret human ones from their reactions.'

A palpable disquiet came over the room. What information was the robot processing from each one of them at that very moment?

Stanley said quickly, 'We'll need to discuss how this robot operates now that she seems to have all systems working. Also, we have to decide what we're going to do after our testing is completed. Will we be we ready to go to publication? I suggest we each take our coffee and go to the room nearest the outside door. We'll secure this lab and leave Andrea here in the meantime.'

Soon they were perched uncomfortably on the hard chairs in the otherwise empty lab at the end of the cool, gray tiled corridor.

The morning sun was beginning to peek in through the high windows and the early morning chill was beginning to burn off. The heated air indoors would soon become suffocating. Susie stifled a yawn.

'Okay,' Stanley began. 'Now that we know Andrea is functioning well so far, we need to remind ourselves what she can do so that we're not caught unawares again. I admit that she's already given me some surprises, even shocks, today.'

Soon the scientists were reacquainting the other members of the team with what each one had perfected for the project. Norma was the computer whiz who had checked all their data. José and Susie reminded them of the intricate, ultra-modern technology they had researched and installed in Andrea and which Norma had checked out. They believed their robot to be on the cutting edge of modern technology, far superior to any known robot at the present time.

Susie sought to dissipate any lingering doubts about the capacities of the robot in her calm precise voice.

'Andrea may walk, talk and look like a real human being but she has enough artificial intelligence to interpret data from many channels and use that information to accomplish assigned tasks. As we saw, she can solve problems by researching the data and then take the appropriate actions.'

'But can you control what it says and does? Is there a Cut Off energy source valve? I can't remember checking that out,' Norma queried, 'We can't just let her have free rein to do and say whatever she wants. There has to be some control mechanism. But I don't remember seeing one on the computer.'

José squirmed uncomfortably. 'Susie and I agreed that the robot would need a good supply of energy in order to complete our future research. So, we built in a twenty years supply of self-renewing energy. One of our own innovations.'

Norma was not satisfied. 'Can you or can you not, shut her down if we need to do so?' she insisted.

'Might be difficult, Norma,' Susie replied quietly, 'If we did, we might compromise the whole robotic system. It would take months to repair and we'd never meet the deadline for publishing our data. We thought that if the robot were to appear to be human, then she should have free choice to make decisions like we do.'

'So,' Norma reasoned, 'If you can't shut her down without destroying systems, that means we can't stop her talking either. We'll have to listen to whatever she says, whenever she says anything.'

'It would seem so,' Susie agreed. 'It's strange new territory for all of us.'

'I can't believe I missed something on the computer as important as a control switch,' Norma worried to herself.

'Are you sure you didn't include one somewhere along the line?'

Stanley could see that Norma was becoming more and more exasperated. While José and Susie were looking askance at one another, he was thinking that one trouble with research was that new problems seem to crop up even after a success. He could see that Norma was busy trying to figure out how she could have missed such a vital control. Her mind would be calculating the logical conclusions to a missing item. She was well known for pointing out the unforeseen consequences of scientific actions. It was one of the reasons he had added her to his team.

'No built-in controls? That's downright dangerous!' she finally exclaimed. 'What if the robot comes in contact with outside people and starts telling them what we are doing here? Who knows where that would lead? After all our efforts to keep our project secret!'

Stanley startled them all by a loud fit of sneezing as the automatic air conditioning started up, wafting dust particles into the air.

'Sorry. Allergies,' he sputtered as he fished in his pocket for a handkerchief. 'Anyway, I think we all need a break. None of us got enough sleep last night. How about if we meet again here, later this afternoon? About four o'clock?'

They were gathering up their mugs and portable computers when the door to the corridor clicked opened and Andrea walked in. There was an instant hush.

'I came to look for you. The lab door security combination is added to my memory. I looked for the room nearest the outside door. I heard Norma's loud voice.'

The robot scanned their faces and tilting her head to one side, stated, 'You are not happy with me.'

Norma groaned. 'You see what I mean?' she exclaimed. 'Unpredictable.' She picked up her empty mug saying, 'That could be a big problem. What a mess! Susie, if you want a ride back to the house, I'll be in my car.'

She stalked out of the room. With a pleading look at Stanley, Susie followed Norma.

Stanley and José were left with Andrea.

Stanley said, 'Before you go, José, let's check the diagrams of Andrea's mechanisms on the computer to see if we've missed any other vital information. It may take some time but it's better to do it now. We don't want any more surprises today.'

He then instructed the robot to return to the lab and they followed her along the corridor. With mixed feelings of pride and apprehension, they watched as Andrea's nimble fingers punched in the combination to open the self-locking lab door.

'Stay beside us, Andrea,' Stanley commanded, 'You can scan the data too. Maybe you'll find something that we may miss. Your brain's quicker than ours.'

On the main computer screen José displayed the intricate graphics showing Andrea's inner workings and their locations. Stanley scrutinized them carefully as José explained how the circuits worked. He marveled at José's expertise as he tried to follow what his partner was explaining about algorithms. Andrea had no difficulty in adding this information to her own database as they talked.

'It's all really complicated to understand, José,' he confessed finally.

'I'm very impressed by your special abilities. But I'm afraid I don't have them. So, I don't see how I can be of much help to you in finding any faults in your system.'

However, they did have another agile brain working for them - so much so that at times they had to ease Andrea's fingers off the computer's keyboard when the robot tried to use it in order to progress faster. 'All is working! All. Working!' she kept repeating as they tried to keep up with her speed.

'Ah!' Andrea pointed out suddenly, 'I see a Sleep button. Why is that there? I don't need sleep like humans do. Erase it.'

She was leaning over to erase the Sleep signal button when Stanley grabbed her arm. Quickly, as Stanley restrained the robot, José found the newly discovered Sleep command and activated it.

Immediately, Andrea's eyelids closed over her beautiful hazel eyes and the robot was still.

Stanley and José sighed with relief as they sank back in their chairs. They hadn't found a way to completely shut off her energy but at least they now had a way to stop the robot's activities for a while.

'*Lo siento*, Boss. I don't know how I could have forgotten that.'

Stanley sat up as another thought struck him. 'Well, at least we found what we wanted. But we need an easier way of accessing the Sleep button than having to be on this computer every time we want to use it. Can you do anything about that, José?'

'*Sí, jefe*,' he answered. 'I can make a hand control, like a television remote. No problem. Want me to work on that now?'

'No, José, you need a break like the rest of us. Tackle that this afternoon after our meeting with the team. I know Susie will want to help you.'

'Gracias, Boss. *Adiós, hasta luego!*'

Stanley was about to leave when he had a disturbing thought. 'I didn't ask him how long that Sleep control lasts,' he fretted. 'Maybe it operates on a limited time frame. I'll call him as soon as he gets home.'

But when he did, there was no answer, not even a 'Busy' signal.

Stanley stood looking at the peaceful robot. Could he trust her to stay immobile until he returned in the afternoon? What if she 'woke' and destroyed the Sleep button on the computer before they could make an extra secure remote control? The robot had watched them operating the main computer, so it was possible that she would know how to do that.

Stanley stroked his scratchy beard, weighing his options. He was hot and tired and wanted to go home for a shower, eat breakfast and have some sleep. He had to make some decision.

'Okay, Andrea,' he said at last, 'Get ready to move.'

He wrapped his arms around the silent robot and carefully maneuvered her out of the lab towards his car.

Keeping her as steady as he could with one trembling hand, he used the other one to open the car door. Rolling Andrea to face the front, he pushed her into the passenger seat. Tightly clicking the seatbelt to secure his passenger, he thought, 'All our research into the lightest available metals for this robot has certainly paid off. She's as strong as steel but as light as a feather. Even I can carry her quite easily – all that flexible five feet of her.'

Then, rubbing his aching arms as he shut the car door, he added ruefully, 'Well, almost.'

CHAPTER 4

The town was waking up to the bright desert sunlight as Stanley drove along the dusty winding road from the compound to the paved main street. Shopkeepers were opening their stores to sweep the dirt from the sidewalks while some early risers were already seated on their verandahs, lazily drinking their morning beverages. He waved to those he knew as he headed up the hill to his home.

As he passed by, Maria was busy inside her tiny house while her husband Pedro was settling himself on their front porch to idly watch the rest of the main street come to life. From the kitchen, she heard him call out, 'Maria! Maria! Come quickly.'

She bustled through the door, drying her hands with a towel.

'What is it?'

'Too late! You just missed Stanley driving by with a beautiful woman in the front seat. And she looked like she was asleep. What do you make of that?'

Maria flopped down on a chair beside him. 'You mean that man Stanley from the research station outta town? That place where nobody knows what's goin' on?'

'Yep! The man I was tellin' you about, the one I met in the pharmacy last week. Never seen him before that. Told me his name. He's a scientist. Remember?'

'*Sí*,' Maria answered, 'But I don't know what you're so excited about. A beautiful woman, was she? That was probably his wife in the car.'

But Pedro had seen Stanley's wife and knew it wasn't her.

He finished his coffee in one gulp and stood up. 'Think I'll take a walk while you're making breakfast, Maria,' he said. 'Need anything from the corner store?'

'No. And don't you get talking all day with your buddies down there!' she warned, 'You got work to do.'

While Pedro was strolling to the corner store, Stanley was bringing his car as close as he could to his ranch house porch. His front door and steps could be seen by anyone passing along the mountain road, but large cactus plants and hibiscus bushes screened one side of the outside verandah. He drove his car nearer to that side. He wanted to get the robot onto that hidden side of the porch so that no curious passerby could see him carry Andrea into the house.

Further along the hacienda wall, the kitchen window was open, wafting out the titillating smells of breakfast. He could hear his wife Kate rattling crockery as she hummed along with the songs on the radio.

Quietly, he unstrapped Andrea and carried her surprisingly light body straight to their guest room. Looking around for a place to hide her, he decided on a walk-in closet that locked. He laid her on the wooden floor inside and backing out, quietly turned the key in the lock and pocketed it. He tiptoed to the kitchen.

'Good morning, dear! I didn't hear you come in,' Kate greeted him. 'You were up early today. I guess you went to the lab to see what your team had done yesterday?'

'Sure thing,' he replied, giving his wife a hug, 'I couldn't sleep. Hope I didn't wake you up? I tried to be as quiet as I could.'

'You're such a thoughtful husband, Stan,' she replied, giving him a quick kiss. 'Do you have time for some breakfast now?'

'I need a shower first, but I'll be with you in a minute. That okay?'

On the way along the hall to the bathroom, he nipped into the guestroom again and tried the closet door to reassure himself that it was still locked. With Andrea's sharp powers of observation, he wouldn't have been surprised if she had been feigning sleep and had watched him open and shut the door. When the door held firm, he sighed with relief, knowing that the robot was safely stowed away. Now for that shower!

He was luxuriating in the hot water as it cascaded over his head when he heard the phone ringing. He hoped the call wasn't for him. Anyway, Kate would deal with it.

While he was toweling himself dry, the bathroom door opened. Kate stuck her head round it. 'Stan! Susie is phoning from the lab and she says someone is missing. I didn't hear the name, but I hope it isn't one of your team. It seems to be some sort of emergency. Do you want to talk to her? She's usually so calm but she sounds to be in a panic.'

She proffered the phone and returned to the kitchen. Stanley tucked the phone under his chin while wrapping the towel around himself.

'Yes, Susie? You can't reach José? I couldn't get him on his cellphone either. What's your problem? You can't find Andrea. Don't worry. I have her here. But why are you back at the lab? I thought you'd gone home with Norma. Oh! Forgot your purse. No, I didn't know the main computer was still on. You found a Sleep mode for the robot? Don't touch it, Susie! What? Well, activate it again. Immediately!'

Ending the call, Stanley saw through the open door that Kate was going into the guestroom. He rushed out, startling his wife.

'What are you doing?' he demanded.

'Stan, I heard something inside this room. It sounds like scratching and banging.' She advanced into the guestroom. 'I think some animal has found its way into that walk-in closet again. We really have to mend the roof above it. I'm going to see what's in there.'

'But Kate, if it's a wild animal, it might be dangerous. Even if it's only a cat, it won't like being in that confined space. It might attack you. Better get out of here and let me deal with this.'

Somewhat surprised at his firmness, she said reluctantly, 'Okay. But tell me when you're ready and I'll stand outside the room with a broom in case you get attacked and I have to defend you.'

Grinning at the thought, she went back to preparing their breakfast.

Stanley threw on a clean shirt and pants and returned to the guestroom closet. Andrea had stopped making a noise so she must have heard Kate talking. He knew that the robot would have been recording their conversation and would be adding Kate's name to her list of contacts.

He cautiously unlocked the door ready to grab Andrea, but the robot was too quick for him. Pushing open the closet door, knocking him aside, she rushed out of the room and along the hall to the kitchen where Kate was frying bacon. He ran after the robot to stop her, but it was too late.

CHAPTER 5

'*A*h!' He could hear Andrea saying in her remarkably human, charming voice, 'You must be Kate.'

Kate jumped, startled to hear a strange voice behind her and turning quickly, came face to face with Andrea.

Stanley hovered behind the newcomer, gesticulating with his hands as if to tell Kate not to talk but she had already automatically reacted. 'Who are you?' she exclaimed. 'How did you get into my house? How do you know my name?'

'I've heard it before. My name is Andrea,' came the reply. 'I am Stanley's Superwoman.'

Stanley sank onto a kitchen chair as Kate looked at him, raising her eyebrows. But it was Andrea who saved him from further questions. The robot suddenly moved, grabbed a small bag of flour near the stove and proceeded to empty it into the smoking and flaming frying pan.

'I know how to put out fires,' she announced unnecessarily.

Kate snatched the pan off the burner and switched off the gas, but the acrid smell of burnt flour and fat had already filled the room. She ran to open more windows.

Hot sunshine streamed in, illuminating the messy disaster in her usually spotless kitchen.

Andrea's long black hair was powdered with white flour and so were her flat ballerina shoes. Kate looked at her and then more pointedly at Stanley, who now had his elbows on the table and was holding his head in his hands.

'Want to tell me what's going on?' she asked her husband.

'I can't,' he replied. 'Our contract with the sponsor specified that our project has to be Top Secret to protect it from competitors. You weren't supposed to know about this robot.'

Kate sat down beside him, wafting away the smoke with a dishtowel.

'So, this Andrea robot was hidden in the closet. I had no idea this was your project!' she said. 'But now I've seen her, you can be sure that I'm not going to tell anyone else. Your Superwoman secret is safe with me.' She suppressed a smile.

Stanley groaned, 'I know that I can trust you. But there was a malfunction at the lab, so I had to bring her home through the town. I wanted to get here early in the morning before too many people were about.'

'And were there?

'Not really. But everyone was waking up. I saw some people I knew and waved to Pedro while I tried to cover the window with my shoulder. I don't think he could have seen Andrea on the passenger side of the car.'

'Well then,' Kate said emphatically, 'No need to worry. When you take Andrea back to the lab, lay her down on the back seat and cover her with a blanket. Can't think why you didn't do that in the first place.'

'I guess I was so tired that I wasn't thinking straight.'

Stanley groaned again as he realized that he wasn't going to get that much-needed nap. The only way to control Andrea now was to return her to the lab as soon as possible in order to use the Sleep app again. It was clear that the sleep function was on a timer. He was faced with the big problem of getting the alert, talking Andrea into the car and having her lie down quietly on the back seat while he covered her up. How was he going to achieve that?

In despair he ran his fingers through his wet hair, making it stand on end.

As if reading his thoughts, the practical Kate said, 'I'm sure you want to return your robot to the lab. I'll make more pancakes and you can eat before you go.'

While they were talking Andrea had cleared away the floury mess into the garbage disposal and now was opening cupboards.

'Another frying pan or skillet?'

Kate was impressed. 'What a wonderfully helpful robot! Stan, you can leave Andrea here with me any time. I really like it… or her! She is so human,' she teased.

Meanwhile at the corner store, Pedro was holding forth to his friends about the young and mysterious woman in Stanley's car.

'I've seen his wife. She has gray hair and this woman had dark hair. No, it definitely wasn't his wife,' he was asserting.

'Could it be his daughter?' Miguel asked. 'Or a niece? Maybe someone visiting him? How old d'you think that 'beautiful woman' was?'

'I didn't get a real good look at her. Just saw her long black hair. But I could tell that he was trying to hide her by the way he leaned over to block her out when he waved to me.'

Juan the shopkeeper was behind his counter.

'Newspapers are full of stories about young girls disappearing,' he offered ominously. 'They accept a ride from strangers and they're never seen again.'

The men grew silent, thinking about this new possibility.

It was Miguel who suggested, 'Okay, let's keep our eyes open for Stanley driving past again. We'll see if he has the woman with him. Man, I'd like to see her too.'

That agreed, they filed outside to the front porch. With drinks refilled and the domino box produced, the men sat down to their morning game.

CHAPTER 6

$\mathcal{K}$ate and Andrea were washing and drying the breakfast plates in the kitchen while Stanley went to collect his papers to take back to the lab. He was buying himself a little time before tackling the problem of how he could get the robot into the car and keep her quiet for the drive through town. 'I can give the command to lie down but how long before she tosses off the blanket and sits up?'

In the kitchen, Kate was amazed at every effortless movement the robot made. It was hard not to think of her as a person, especially when she talked so easily and fluently.

'You like Stanley very much,' Andrea stated.

Kate laughed. 'Of course. He's my husband.'

'Susie likes Stanley too.'

'That's nice to hear,' Kate replied, 'It helps to have team members who have mutual respect.'

'Norma is not sure that she likes Susie, but she likes José and Stanley.'

Kate was fascinated by this robot report on team dynamics. Her husband rarely spoke about his team or his research when he returned home from the lab. She only knew the scientists' names from meeting them when they had all arrived in New Mexico some years ago. They were all workaholics and didn't socialize much.

'Why do you say Norma doesn't like Susie?' she couldn't help enquiring as she carried the dried plates to the kitchen shelves.

'Susie does not always tell things the way they are,' Andrea said, folding up the dishtowel and putting it on a rack.

'Whatever do you mean?'

'Susie says she is Japanese but my information points to the fact that she is Chinese. From Beijing. Voice patterns.'

Kate was puzzled. 'Does that really matter? I mean, where she comes from?'

'The Chinese might instruct her to send them information from Stanley's computer,' Andrea replied, 'Other countries want to keep up with American technology. Norma knows that.'

Kate was shocked but not as shocked as Stanley was, when he entered the kitchen to find them chatting together. He had forgotten to tell his wife that everything she said was being recorded in Andrea's database for future reference.

'I hope whatever Kate has been saying is harmless,' he thought. 'She's so trusting. I don't even know what's going on with this robot. It seems to be more intelligent than we intended.'

He made a mental note to privately advise his wife to be careful about what information she gave the robot. He noticed that Kate was looking at him as if she were about to tell him something but at that moment the doorbell rang.

On opening the door, Stanley was surprised to find José and Susie standing on the doorstep.

'*Oh, jefe,*' José burst out excitedly, 'Susie and I have made an application on my cellphone to control Andrea's sleep mode. We figured that since you had brought the robot home, you might need the control to get her back to the lab. The Sleep mode on our main computer only lasts one hour. Norma's at the lab checking the computer again in case we've missed something else.'

José was out of breath by the time he had finished giving this explanation, but Stanley was used to the Mexican's enthusiastic verbal deliveries. He felt a tinge of hope. Perhaps his problem of controlling Andrea in the car might be solved.

Unexpectedly, he stepped outside, pulling the door shut. 'I guess you want to test that app. Do you have to be in the same room as the robot for it to work?'

'If you have the robot inside, Stanley, we could try to activate the Sleep mode from the open front door,' Susie interjected, 'But why did you bring her home with you?'

'I had no choice as I couldn't reach José on his cellphone to ask his opinion," he replied.

Then turning to José, he said, 'You must have been working on your phone at the time, entering the control info into it?'

'Yes, I started right away when I got home. Sorry I didn't answer, Boss,' José apologized.

Stanley opened the front door a little. They could hear Andrea's distinctive voice coming from within the house. José activated the digital signal for the Sleep control on his phone. They stepped inside the door and listened attentively.

Kate came rushing out from the kitchen. 'Stan! Stan! Andrea was talking and then she suddenly stopped in mid-sentence and closed her eyes. I think she's malfunctioned. Come quickly!'

She stopped when she saw the grins on the faces of the trio at the door.

'Ah!' She understood. 'You've shut her down, haven't you? Just as she was telling me...'

Kate spied Susie and closed her lips. Luckily, the others became so busy examining the robot that even Stan didn't ask Kate to elaborate on what she had been going to tell them. She watched them bundle the silent robot into the back seat of Stan's car and cover her with a colorful Navajo blanket. She waved to them as they drove away in their cars.

Kate went back inside to tidy up the kitchen. It had been a very eventful morning. There was a lot to think about. She only wished that she'd had more time to talk with Andrea and maybe wipe the flour off the robot's hair and shoes.

CHAPTER 7

The usual morning traffic was slowly winding its way through town.

From their vantage point on the store verandah, Miguel and his friends had no trouble seeing Stanley drive past alone.

'That's him! Stanley, the scientist,' Pedro said, indicating him with a nod of his head, 'I didn't see anyone else in his car. Did you?'

'No, but look, there's a pretty lady with black hair in the passenger seat of that car following him,' Miguel observed helpfully.

'That's the one!' Pedro exclaimed excitedly and the men stared at Susie as she went by.

'Why is she in another car now?' Leon asked, covering his dominoes with his hand so that Miguel wouldn't see them.

'Maybe they're not going to the same place,' Pedro reasoned, 'But you can tell they're together. Look how close that second car is, following Stanley.'

Juan the storekeeper, had come out on to the verandah, curious to find out what they were talking about.

'Could be they're human traffickers,' he offered helpfully. 'The driver in that second car could've paid off your guy Stanley and now he's got the girl for his own purposes.'

'Whatever those might be,' he added darkly.

The men paused to digest this scandalous idea.

Finally, Miguel spoke, 'Maybe we should alert Sheriff Rodriguez to what could be going on. We don't want bad hombres around here. We've all got daughters. Better be safe than sorry!'

Leon was impatient to get back to the domino game.

'Pedro, you can do that on your way home. You have to go past the Sheriff's office. And it looks like you're going home pretty soon. Isn't that your Maria coming down the road to find you?'

Pedro took one look and cleared the store's three wooden steps in one leap. He hurried along the road to meet his wife. No need for her to hear what they'd been talking about. He would deal with the Sheriff later.

When they had entered the lab compound and the electric security fence had been re-activated, José and Stanley pulled back the blanket to slide Andrea out of the back seat. Susie held José's cellphone ready in case they needed the Sleep button again. Andrea looked angelic, as if she were fast asleep, with long eyelashes fanned out on her smooth cheeks and white spots of flour sprinkled over her hair and shoes.

Susie had noticed the white powder and quizzed Stanley as Andrea was carried into the lab complex. 'What happened at your house?'

'It's a long story,' he answered wearily. 'I'll tell you all later.'

When the robot was safely back in the lab and Stanley had finished telling the team what had transpired that morning, Susie spoke up.

'I think we should have the 'Andrea control' app on our cellphones. There's no knowing when we may need it again. We have to be able to shut the robot down when necessary. José knows how to make the app accessible so that we can all download it on our own cells.'

She turned to Stanley and Norma. 'Why don't you give me your cellphones and with José's help, I'll put the app on both of them? Then we'll all have the means to control Andrea.'

Stanley fished his phone out of his pocket and handed it over to her. But Norma demurred.

'Thanks, but I've just bought this new phone. I'm just learning how to use it, so I'd rather wait before adding another app.'

Susie looked disappointed but she took Stanley's phone and went to a workbench to sit at her own computer. José followed to help her.

Norma turned to Stanley and whispered, 'A word in your ear, Stanley?

I'm monitoring the timing on the main Sleep control for Andrea. There's half an hour left. Enough time to talk before the robot becomes active again.'

She gathered her papers together and followed him into his office.

'I gave the main computer a thorough check while everyone was gone,' she explained. 'I came across some sort of strange interference with a number of Andrea's programs. We did have a shutdown mechanism built into our original plan for the robot after all but somehow it has become disconnected. The timed Sleep button we are using now gives limited control, as you know.'

Stanley sat at his desk rubbing the sleep out of his eyes.

'That's odd,' he commented. 'Right from the beginning, I thought it strange that we could have missed programming such a vital part of our experiment as a Shutdown control. Can you fix it?'

'That's what I wanted to talk to you about,' she replied, 'I would like to do more investigating to see whether it's a malfunction, or in the worst- case scenario whether our computer has been hacked.'

He bolted upright in his chair.

'God Forbid! You mean all the secret information about our unique speaking-and-thinking robot could have been stolen?'

'As I said, Stanley, I need more time to check it out. I can work all night tonight if need be, to get to the bottom of this problem.'

Thoroughly awake now, Stanley asked anxiously, 'You said there might be other programs affected?'

'Yes, particularly the ones associated with giving commands to Andrea. I'm afraid that if we've been hacked, what we ask it to perform may be counter-commanded by an outside agency.'

'Then we'd have no control over the robot whatsoever,' Stanley worried out loud. 'That's no good! Perhaps we should tell José and Susie. They might know of a quick way to deal with this.'

Norma coughed discreetly. 'Could we just keep this between you and me until I can come up with more details? We don't want to alarm everybody just yet.'

Stanley considered the implications of her request for a minute and then agreed.

When Norma and Stanley emerged from the office, Andrea was already awake and was watching José and Susie as they sat adapting the cellphones. The two scientists both loved the magic of technology and were creative in using it. They were good partners because of this mutual interest and were chatting together now, oblivious of anything else.

Using its extraordinary eyesight, Andrea began adding all the personal information she detected on their phones into her own database. When she sensed movements behind her, she closed her eyelids.

Norma checked the main computer to see how much time remained on the Sleep button and was surprised to find that it had already run out. She looked suspiciously as the robot's eyes flicked open as if she had just at that moment become active again.

'Come here,' Norma commanded loudly, 'And sit down.'

Andrea did as she was ordered and Norma eased off the robot's black, tight-fitting wig. She gave it a vigorous shake to get rid of the flour in the hair. As she fitted it back onto Andrea's head, Norma thought, 'Andrea is still responding to commands. Maybe there isn't a hacker after all, just some malfunction from time to time. I'll have to explore that option tonight.'

'I'm going to clean your shoes, so keep still.'

By the time Norma had finished dusting down the robot, Susie and José called out that the cellphones were ready to be tested.

'You first, Stanley,' Susie said, showing him how to use the app. When his test resulted in deactivating the robot, Susie smiled at him. 'Now, it's my turn,' she said.

After that test was successful, she turned to Norma, 'Have you changed your mind yet? Want us to adapt your phone too?'

'Maybe later,' Norma replied. 'We have to concentrate on testing to see if everything else is working. Remember, we need to start writing a paper about our research for a Science magazine before someone else beats us to it with their robot research.'

'I agree with Norma,' Stanley added. 'Meanwhile, I'll report our progress to our sponsor. He'll be very happy with what we've accomplished.'

When Norma's preliminary tests of Andrea's capabilities had shown no sign of nefarious obstruction, Stanley leaned over to whisper, 'Looks like you won't have to stay up all night looking for abnormalities. Everything seems to be fine so far.'

'We can't be too careful, Stanley. I'd still like to investigate further tonight while nobody is around to distract me.'

'Okay, but if I can't sleep again, I might join you.'

'That's okay with me,' she replied.

CHAPTER 8

$\mathcal{I}$t was a jubilant team that went home at dusk. Everyone was primed to return the following morning with ideas and suggestions for what information should be included in their first publication. It was time to share the wonders of their robot Andrea with a wider audience.

They would have been surprised to learn that they had unknowingly already attracted some interest in what they were doing.

Screened by prickly pear cactus bushes, Sheriff Rodriguez was lying prone on a sandy bank behind the laboratory compound. He leaned on his elbows to train his binoculars on the main door, counting how many people left the labs. So far by late afternoon, there had only been two men and a dark-haired young woman. They had all departed in separate cars. No evidence of wrongdoing there.

The dusk was deepening into darkness and he knew better than to lie in the cooling desert at night. He kept his ears open for snake rattles and the gnawing of rodents even as he focused on a lone lighted window on the ground floor.

'I don't believe a word of the gossip about human trafficking,' he grumbled. He stood up to roll his aching shoulders. 'Probably something that crazy Juan at the store has cooked up to cause some excitement. Who'd want to use this sleepy town as a trafficking base? Too many people would notice anything out of the ordinary.'

But as he climbed into his truck, he decided that as the town's Sheriff, he had a duty to do more investigating before dismissing the claim altogether. After all, there did seem to be something secret going on at the labs. Maybe he should know about what was happening in his own district.

'*Mañana*,' he told himself as he drove home to have his supper.

At Stanley's house, now that the robot was no longer a secret, Kate was enthusing about Andrea to her husband.

'I've never seen anything like that robot,' she said between bites of spicy tortilla. 'Andrea is absolutely astonishing. She can actually think! Remember how fast she was at putting out the fire in the kitchen. And when you look at her, you could easily mistake her for a person, a real human being. Stan, you must be very pleased with having created such an incredible robot.'

Stanley shifted uneasily in his chair. He felt uncomfortable with the fact that his wife knew about the secret robot and now here she was, talking about Andrea as if she were a person.

'Why did I ever bring Andrea home?' he thought, 'Now that Kate knows, will she be able to keep quiet about it until we go public?'

He tried to dampen his wife's enthusiasm, 'Kate, you do remember that our sponsor wants all the details kept secret until we're ready to publish. I hope you won't tell anyone about Andrea.'

She carefully laid down her fork and stared at Stanley.

'I'm really hurt that you would even think that I might give away your research. Remember that I come from a family of scientists! It's been drummed into me from an early age that we don't talk about the specifics of scientific work to outsiders. I think you should give me some credit for that.'

Although Stanley hastily apologized for doubting her, Kate was silent for the rest of the meal. After helping her clear the dishes from the table, Stanley, aware that he had annoyed his usually placid wife, escaped to his study to put papers into files.

When everyone else had gone home, Norma was alone at the lab with Andrea. She pushed her chair back from the main computer to head for the kitchen to look for something to eat for supper. 'I hope there's a burrito left in the freezer. That's easy and won't take too long to heat up in the microwave.'

She toyed with the idea of showing Andrea how to make tea but that would mean taking the robot off the Sleep control which was presently keeping her quiet. As she entered the tiny kitchenette, Norma was still musing, 'Best keep that robot asleep until I've finished the final rundown of tests on the computer.'

The lab area had a quiet hollowed-out feeling that was not unpleasant. It reminded Norma of her younger days at school in England. The older students were allowed to play badminton in the school gym on Fridays, after all the younger children had dispersed and gone home. The school had an entirely different atmosphere then, with the only lively sounds being their shoes squeaking on the wooden floor of the assembly hall, the popping of the shuttlecock striking racquets and their own calls of 'Out!' and how many points were scored.

It seemed to Norma that the lab had a similar feeling - of recently being emptied of human activity and of slowly settling down into a calmer state.

'Yes, those were happy times at school. And I'm happy now, being in the lab by myself.' She was smiling as she rummaged in a drawer for cutlery and started her preparations for her meal.

She might not have been so satisfied with her life if she had kept an eye on Andrea. As soon as the robot sensed that Norma was reaching for the Sleep button, the robot had obstructed the command. The scientist had no way of knowing that Andrea could deactivate the app with the data she had ingested from Susie's cellphone.

Next, while Norma was enjoying her burrito, the robot commenced to copy new information from the main computer onto its own expanding database.

When Norma returned, Andrea was standing where she normally stood. The sleep control was on. Norma frowned as she checked what little time had elapsed since she had activated it. Surely, she couldn't have eaten her supper so quickly!

Shrugging her shoulders, the dedicated scientist bent to renew her task of searching each part of the computer program for signs of an outside intruder.

Hours later, Norma had to admit that she could find no evidence of any secret information being siphoned off by unknown others. There was only the tiresome Sleep button that sometimes malfunctioned. She glanced at the robot.

Andrea was inactive now with her eyes closed, so the control must be working at the moment.

'Maybe Susie and José interfered with the main app switch when they tinkered with the cellphones.' She yawned. 'Time to go home to bed! Maybe I'll find out tomorrow if I ask them if that could have happened.'

After Norma had gone and the sound of her car tires crunching on the grit of the parking lot had died away, Andrea began to explore. The robot already knew how to get out of the lab using the code and could remember the way along the corridor towards the unused room near the outside door. The data already recorded from Susie's cellphone supplied the means of passing the front door security.

The robot stepped outside into the chill night air.

It was dark, the only lights coming from small houses strung along the road at the foot of the hills. There was a slight breeze blowing the loose sand around but that failed to bother Andrea. A bright light by a gate illuminated the yard and the fence around the building. A gate was a way out. She walked towards it.

Suddenly an animal darted out in front of the robot. She watched as the small creature ran into the fence and instantly collapsed beside it.

'This looks like an animal called a rabbit,' the robot inferred when it got nearer. 'It's not moving. That means it's in shock or it's what humans call 'dead.' That's when something alive stops breathing.'

Andrea bent down to inspect the little furry body before looking up at the fence.

'My data tells me that this is an electric fence. It might cause my circuits to malfunction if I touch it. I must find out more information about this kind of fence.'

Backing away from the light and ascertaining from her database that there was a main switch for the fence inside the front door, the robot began to retrace her steps to the building to find the switch. Nearing the entrance, its extraordinary hearing caught the sound of a car moving along the road outside the complex.

Quickly stepping inside the building, she shut the front door.

Remembering that Stanley had said he might return, Andrea walked back to the lab to stand in her usual spot in front of the main computer. All the doors were secured. Nobody could tell that she had moved. She closed her eyes and waited.

CHAPTER 9

Sheriff Rodriguez had been called out to settle a barroom fight at the other end of town. After dispersing the drunken customers and closing down the bar, he had decided that since he was out, he would take another look at those suspicious laboratories near the foothills.

'If there's anything unlawful going on, it'll probably take place after dark. It's certainly a dark night tonight,' he thought as he climbed into his truck. 'Moonless and chill. I'll just take a closer look at that complex before going home.'

As he rounded the corner of the dirt road near the labs, he suddenly braked. In the truck lights, he had picked out the figure of a small woman inside the compound.

She was wearing a flimsy dress and must be freezing being outside in the cold desert air without a poncho to keep her warm. What was she doing there after midnight? Was she trying to escape? There were no lights to be seen in the lab building. Could there be somebody else inside?

As he watched, the woman disappeared into the building and although he waited for another half hour, she did not reappear. He pushed back his hat to scratch his head, muttering, 'Definitely suspicious activity. I'll have to look into this officially in the morning. Why would there be a lone woman wandering around the complex at night? With nobody else about? Mighty strange!'

True to his word, Sheriff Rodriguez was parked in front of the compound before the team arrived the next morning. Stanley was the first to reach the gate and pulled up beside the sheriff's truck. Winding down his car window, he called out, 'Buenos dias, Sheriff. Why are you here? Is there something wrong?'

The sheriff climbed out of his truck and walked round Stanley's car to lean over his door.

'Well, maybe you can tell me?' he answered, taking a quick look inside the vehicle and noting the folded Navajo blanket on the back seat. 'There's been some talk in the town about what's going on in your labs. Thought you might be able to shed some light on that for me.'

Stanley was mystified. 'What's going on?' he echoed. 'There's only our research going on. What do people think is happening here?'

By this time, the rest of the team had driven up behind them. Norma, Susie and José came over to Stanley's car to find out what was happening. They were astonished to hear the sheriff say, 'There have been reports that you may be harboring illegals in these here buildings.'

There was a moment of shocked silence until Stanley laughed awkwardly.

'You can't be serious, Sheriff! There's nobody else here. We're the only ones using the labs and we're all legal. Each of us has an official work permit and we all have up-to-date passports.'

'Then you won't mind me seeing them.'

The members of the team began fishing out their documents from pockets and purses. The sheriff took his time perusing the papers, matching photographs to the faces around him. When he finally returned them to their owners, he asked, 'Mind if I take a look inside the labs?'

Stanley was adamant. 'That won't be possible, Sheriff. We have a contract with our sponsor that states that until our project is published, we are obliged to keep it secret and secure. That is legally binding. We cannot show you what we are scientifically experimenting and researching.'

'So, you are hiding something.'

Norma could see that the usually mild-mannered Stanley was beginning to lose his patience.

'Stanley, maybe the sheriff can look around the buildings we're not using, just to ease his mind that there's nobody hiding elsewhere in the compound?' she suggested.

She smiled at the law official who regarded her thoughtfully before turning back to Stanley for his answer.

'Very well,' Stanley conceded reluctantly. 'But there's no way that I can let you into our research lab, Sheriff. I would be violating my contract.'

He turned to the others. 'Please would you go and check that everything in our lab is in order? In the meantime, I have the keys to the other buildings so I will show the sheriff around.'

With that agreed, Stanley deactivated the live fence and they all drove their cars into the parking area, the suspicious Sheriff bringing up the rear.

CHAPTER 10

$\mathcal{W}$hen the team entered the lab, Andrea was standing quietly in her usual spot near the main computer. Norma turned to the computer and noted that it was shut down just as she had left it the previous night. She began sifting through her notes. Everything seemed to be in order.

Susie and José checked their workbenches, gathering their notes for the meeting.

'Who could have reported that we might be harboring illegals?' Susie asked Norma.

Norma shrugged, now busy with her computer screen. 'Guess we'll find out when Stanley returns,' she answered brusquely.

Susie knew better than to disturb Norma when she was working. 'Think I'll go start the coffee,' she said.

After a quick glance at the two women, José had begun clearing a space at a long table so that they could begin their conference on what information should be provided to the scientific journals. Although curious about what had just transpired at the gate, he silently decided that they would have to wait for the Boss to return to clear up the matter. No good wasting time on speculating about it now.

When he did enter the lab, Stanley was clearly exasperated.

'The sheriff has just left. I don't know what's being said in town, but he kept asking me if there'd been anyone wandering around here last night. I told him that Norma was the only one working late. Norma, did you see any strangers poking around before you went home?'

'Not a soul,' she answered.

'Then I have no idea what all this fuss is about.' Stanley shook his head as if to clear his thoughts. 'If we're going to be harassed like this, I think we'd better get our Andrea information out to the general public as soon as possible.'

He went into his office to collect his papers but when he came back, he astonished the team by declaring a sudden decision. This was not unusual for him, nonetheless but it took them by surprise.

'I've decided that writing for a science journal might take too long. It will have to be peer-reviewed and that takes time. So, I suggest we write up a press release and then contact the Albuquerque Herald. That's the local area paper but we can inform the big newspapers like the New York Times and the Washington Post too. Heck, why not? We're privately sponsored so it isn't like we have to follow the usual rules all the time. Media publication is the quickest way to go. I'll phone in the press release as soon as it is written.'

Galvanized by this sudden decisive turn of events, they all sat down at the table readying their suggestions for what to tell the newspapers.

José couldn't help enthusing. 'I'm sure everyone will want to see our robot once they know about it. We could even take her to New York City! Won't people be astonished when they see Andrea for the first time! We'll all be famous. And if someone buys the robot, we could all become rich.'

Susie smiled. 'I've always wanted to go to New York, and I hope we go to Washington D.C. too.'

'Don't count your chickens until they're hatched. We don't know what's going to happen,' Norma warned. But even she was in a pleasant mood that morning.

Stanley called them to order to get started. They were soon engrossed in writing a press release, totally ignoring the centerpiece of their presentation.

Andrea had been recording their remarks and now began a slow drift to the door of the lab. She escaped along the hall to the outside door.

Once the robot was out of the building, she saw that Stanley had forgotten to close the compound gate after the last car had gone through. Walking quickly, she crossed the parking lot and checking her data for the nearest town, started walking along the dirt road leading to it.

It wasn't long before a truck driver offered her a lift and soon set her down outside the central Corner Store. Andrea looked up and down the main street to become orientated before mounting the three steps. Passing by the domino players with a '*Buenos dias*!' she walked inside.

Miguel's eyes widened. 'Leon, did you see what I saw?' he breathed.

'I sure did, Miguel. It's that woman who was in Stanley's car. What's she doing here? Let's go see what Juan is saying to her.'

Hastily, they pushed aside their game and followed Andrea inside.

There they found Juan leaning across the counter, peering over his wire spectacles at the beautiful stranger who had appeared in his store as if by magic. He was smoothing down his hair and straightening his collar.

Andrea was looking along the shelves, noting the material things that humans buy in a store. Using the hidden camera behind each eye, she was making a quick inventory into her database by photographing each item for instant identification. She was annotating the cans of food and drink; dried beans; corn and rice in sacks; containers of cleaning materials; kitchenware and bathroom utensils, but she was also noticing some men who were watching from the other side of the room.

Having heard them whispering together as she was inspecting the store, Andrea astounded them by saying, 'You are Leon, Miguel and the store owner, Juan.'

Recovering quickly from his surprise, Juan came out from behind the counter, wiping his hands on his jeans. Moving closer, he replied, 'You seem to know our names, lady. But who are you? What's your name?'

'My name is Andrea.'

Miguel blurted out, 'We've seen you before. Saw you in a car going by. Do you live around here?'

Andrea was silently calculating whether 'live' could be applied to it when Miguel, thinking she may not have heard her question, asked more gently, 'We would be interested to know where you are staying.'

'I stay in the lab compound outside town.'

The men looked knowingly at one another. Leon took a deep breath.

'Andrea, are you the only woman in those labs?'

'There are two women and two men. And me. I'm different.'

Juan nudged Leon aside. 'How are you different?' he queried.

'I'm not a scientist.'

Leon pushed in front of Juan to enquire, 'Then what do you do?'

'I do whatever they tell me to do.'

The men exchanged knowing looks, thinking that they were about to uncover a secret slave trade operation.

'Are you the only one who is different from the scientists?' Juan asked.

'Yes, at present. But soon there may be many, many, more like me,' Andrea asserted.

Miguel didn't want to be left out of the conversation, so he interrupted, 'Andrea, are you being traded or sent to other places?'

The robot tilted her head to one side to look at him while she consulted her database as to what 'traded' meant. 'I may be going to New York or Washington D.C. for people to look at me,' she replied. 'There is a possibility that I could be sold so that José can become rich.'

Miguel whispered to the others, 'It must be a high-end trafficking ring, sending women like Andrea to the big cities. Otherwise, they would traffic the women around here. We'll have to get word to Sheriff Rodriguez to let him know what's going on in this town. Andrea can talk to him if he doesn't believe what we say.'

Juan took Leon aside. 'You go get the sheriff, Leon. We'll keep this young woman here until he comes.'

Leon was about to do what Juan had asked when they heard the doorbell tinkle. He stopped in his tracks when he saw who was entering the store. Miguel and Juan both turned their heads to look at the new customer. They recognized her at once.

It was the wife of that leader of the trafficking ring, Stanley.

Kate was taken aback by the unexpected belligerence of their stares and looked at the woman they were trying unsuccessfully to hide. Even more shocked when she saw who it was, she quickly crossed the room exclaiming, 'Andrea! What are you doing here?'

She looked around the store. 'Is Stanley here with you?'

'No, he is in the lab with the others.'

'But how did you get here?' Kate inquired, edging closer to the robot.

'A truck driver drove me. He saw me walking along the road.'

Acutely aware that the men were hanging on to their every word, Kate realized that she had better get the robot away from them.

'Well,' she said firmly, 'I'm glad I met you. Come with me. Stanley asked me to buy you a coat. There's a clothing store just down the street. We can look in there for one. Let's go right now.'

Andrea neatly sidestepped the men to obediently follow Kate out of the store, while Leon scooted off in the opposite direction to fetch the sheriff.

CHAPTER 11

*A*s Andrea matched Kate's rapid pace along the sidewalk, Kate's mind was racing. How could Andrea have left the compound without the scientists seeing her go? Had they sent her out deliberately to find out how she would cope with the outside world? If so, shouldn't at least one of them have her under surveillance?

Kate took a swift look around but there were no scientists to be seen.

There was only Miguel watching them from the corner store porch.

As they neared the clothing store, Kate asked, 'Andrea, what were the others doing when you left?'

'Doing a press release,' the robot replied promptly.

'A Press Release?' Kate echoed.

'Yes, that could mean directions for some sort of exercise routine or maybe instructions how to do CPR or maybe sending information to the media,' Andrea stated helpfully.

Kate couldn't help laughing.

'Then it must mean something funny too,' Andrea quickly responded. 'But they looked very serious.'

'I'm sure they were,' Kate agreed, chuckling to herself. 'They'll be even more serious when they find out you've disappeared.'

'I have not disappeared. I am still here.'

'Andrea,' Kate said as she guided her through the store entrance, 'You are truly delightful. I love talking to you.'

But she was troubled by Andrea's statement that the scientists were all at the lab. It was very puzzling. She wished that she had brought her cellphone to contact Stanley, but she had left it at home, thinking that she wouldn't need it on such a short trip into town. All she had wanted was some milk at the store.

Kate turned to Andrea, 'Now please keep beside me in the clothes store and let me do the talking.'

Closely followed by the robot, it didn't take long for Kate to select a light summer coat that would fit Andrea. She paid by credit card, a fact that the robot duly noted by watching the transaction, photographing with her hidden cameras, Kate's credit card and the personal pin number.

'Here, Andrea, put on this coat,' Kate said, 'You are much too noticeable in that lovely green silk dress. Now I'm going to get some money from an ATM and then we'll be on our way. I'll find another place to buy milk.'

Always ready to gather information, the robot asked, 'What's an ATM?'

Kate had to think for a moment, 'It's an Automated Teller Machine.' Anticipating Andrea's next question, she added, 'Instead of going to the bank, you can get cash from the machine by using your bank card.'

'Cash is another word for money,' the robot affirmed.
'Yes.'

'What do you do with money?'

Kate sighed. Sometimes talking to Andrea was like talking to a child. 'You need money to buy whatever you want. If you have lots of money, you can buy just about everything your heart desires,' Kate replied.

'I have no heart,' Andrea stated, 'But money would be useful to have.'

Kate missed the robot's last remark because she had caught a glimpse of Miguel peering through the front window of the clothing store. Taking Andrea's arm, she gently steered her to the back exit and from there towards the side entrance of the neighboring supermarket, where there was an ATM.

Kate briefly thought of having the robot wait in her car for her while she got cash and bought milk, but she doubted that Andrea would stay there.

'She's evaded the team somehow and I have no way of knowing what she'll do next. I must phone Stanley as soon as I can. Andrea is getting to be a lot of trouble,' she fretted.

The robot stood behind Kate as she put another plastic card into the ATM machine and added the pin number. Andrea watched as a thin wad of paper money slid out. The machine returned the card and a receipt to Kate. All of this was duly photographed and recorded, as was Kate's purchase of cartons of milk, paid for by the money she had received from the ATM.

'I think I've had enough excitement for one day!' Kate declared. 'Andrea, I should drive you back to the lab compound but I'm really tired so I'm going to take you to my house. I'll phone Stanley from there. I'm sure that he's in for a big surprise, one way or another.'

Once they were safely inside Kate's house, Andrea was instructed to make coffee. Making sure that the robot was fully occupied, Kate went into her bedroom to phone Stanley to tell him where he could find the robot.

While phoning her husband, she couldn't see that Andrea had opened Kate's purse and, extracting her bank card, had slipped it into one of the deep pockets of the new coat that Kate had bought for her.

Some time elapsed before Kate could reach her husband. His phone seemed to be exceptionally busy, making her uncomfortably aware that he might be phoning places to locate the missing robot, the one that was now making coffee in their kitchen at home.

Eventually when he did answer her call, he said that he was phoning from his office. He told her that he'd been contacting their sponsor and then afterwards, some newspapers. He was sending out press releases about their unique robot Andrea. He sounded very excited.

As she took a breath to tell him that she had the robot at home, Kate heard him say to someone, 'What do you mean, you can't find Andrea?'

His voice sounded exasperated. 'Isn't she in her usual place by the computer? Then go search the other labs! She knows how to open this lab door.'

'Got to go, my dear,' he said to Kate. 'I might be late getting home tonight. Another crisis! Will it never end?'

The line went dead. She tried to call him again, but he didn't even answer his cellphone, though she heard it ring.

Kate sighed. 'Guess there's nothing else for it but to take Andrea back to the lab before they all start having heart attacks. And I was so looking forward to relaxing and drinking my coffee at home and not having to drive through the traffic in town again.'

She could smell the familiar aroma as she walked along the hall to the kitchen. The coffee pot had been placed beside a mug and a small jug of cream on the counter, but Andrea was nowhere to be seen.

'Oh, no! Where has she gone? I should have kept an eye on her. Where can she be?'

A thin line of sweat broke out on Kate's upper lip as she began searching for the robot inside the house and then in increasing haste, outside on the porch and into the cactus garden. The late afternoon heat was stifling, making her feel faint, but she forced herself to run to the end of their sloping driveway to look up and down the hill road. There, she stopped to catch her breath.

To her dismay, she saw a car rounding the bend that led into town. No sign of Andrea. Had someone given her a ride? It wouldn't be the first time someone had picked up a young woman, even if this one was a robot. Andrea looked much too human for her own good.

Slowly she retraced her steps to the house and tried again to phone Stanley. He was not going to be happy with what she had to tell him, even though she had just been trying to help.

CHAPTER 12

$\mathcal{M}$eanwhile, Leon was experiencing his own difficulties. When he reached the Sheriff's office, hot and sweating in the noontime heat, he was none too pleased to be told that the sheriff and his deputy would be out for the day at the courthouse.

'I need to inform him about some criminal activity. He's got to know what's going on in this town. It's mighty urgent! When will he be back?'

The secretary coolly shook her head. 'Sorry, I don't know.'

Seeing Leon's dismay, she added kindly, 'If you want to write down your concern, I can give you some paper. I'll see that he reads your message when he returns.'

Leon ignored her suggestion. 'It's more urgent than that. If I go to the courthouse, will I be able to talk to him?'

She shrugged her shoulders, 'You might get a chance during a recess period, but I wouldn't bank on it. Some judges try to finish cases as soon as possible but others take a long time.'

Leon was already halfway to the door before she'd finished talking but once outside, he paused in the shade of the verandah to think.

'What am I doing? The courthouse is way over at the other side of town. It's a long walk from here. Besides, I'm not even sure I'll get to talk to the sheriff if I go.'

He squinted in the glare of the sun, continuing to weigh up the situation. 'It's getting hotter and hotter. *Necesito una cerveza ahora mismo.* He licked his dry lips thinking of the cold beer. No, I think I'll go back and tell Juan where the sheriff is and then he can decide what to do.'

As he slowly walked away in the searing heat, he adjusted his hat to shade his face from the sunlight and in so doing, failed to see Andrea passing by in a car. Had he known that she was on her way to the bus station, he might have quickened his pace, but he was quite content to saunter along, blissfully contemplating the ice-cold beer he would soon be enjoying.

'*Muchas gracias,*' the robot said as the man, who had identified himself as Stanley and Kate's neighbor, drove up to the main entrance of the bus station.

'Where are you headed? Anywhere exciting? Want someone to go with?' he teased, smiling invitingly as he leaned closer to talk to her. The robot opened the passenger side door, gracefully sliding out of reach.

'Thank you for the ride,' Andrea replied, firmly shutting the car door.

As she entered the booking hall, the robot saw another ATM machine, so she went to see if this one worked as well as the one Kate had used in the food market. Using Kate's card, she was soon in possession of $400 dollars. Andrea stuffed the bills into both coat pockets, zipping them up, then followed a crowd of humans to a ticket office where her database informed her that for a bus ride out of the town, she needed money to buy a piece of paper called a 'ticket.'

Earlier, while making coffee in Kate's kitchen, the robot had searched her internal intelligence data for local and regional maps. After concluding that New York and Washington, the places mentioned by the scientists in the laboratory, were too far away, she had looked for somewhere closer and had found a place about an hour's drive from the town. More research made the location look interesting enough to visit to discover more about this strange world of humans who changed into 'tourists' when they travelled.

Now, watching first to see how people bought tickets, she stood in line as they had, taking some of the dollars from her pocket to pay the cashier for a bus ticket. The helpful woman at the ticket kiosk indicated where Andrea could find the waiting bus. Now pocketing small hard coins in exchange for some of the paper money, the robot went to board the bus. She was on her way to Santa Fe.

The bus slowly wound its way in and out of small pueblos, picking up passengers as it drove towards the long highway to Santa Fe. Andrea gazed out of the window, photographing through her eyes the arid clay-colored hills, eroded canyons and sparse scrub in the surrounding desert. Crossing the Rio Grande River, she noted green trees along the banks, but prickly cactus seemed to be the ubiquitous vegetation to be seen from the bus. Overhead, the afternoon sun scorched down from a brilliant blue sky.

At times, the seat beside the robot was taken and vacated on the journey but when the occupants tried to talk to her, Andrea turned away without answering. Soon, although she was still an object of curiosity with her pale, smooth complexion and perfect facial features, people stopped trying to be friendly, turning instead to begin animated conversations with other fellow travelers. They talked loudly and gesticulated wildly as if their hands were essential to the conversation.

It was noisy on the bus but that did not disturb Andrea. Many of the women were fanning themselves in the afternoon heat, slyly glancing now and then at the robot as the hot sun streamed through the window on to Andrea's face. How was it that the quiet woman did not feel hot and bothered like they were?

From time to time, the bus driver glanced at her through his mirror slanted towards the passengers. It wasn't often that he saw such an unusually beautiful woman on his bus so when they reached the Santa Fe bus station, he stopped the vehicle and hopped off first to help the passengers alight.

'*Buenas tardes, señorita*,' he said as Andrea stepped down. 'Do you need directions from here?'

Andrea paused for a second since she already had a map of the town in her database. As the young lady seemed to hesitate, the driver quickly pursued his advantage.

'If you're interested in art, we are near the Georgia O'Keeffe Museum. She is one of our famous artists. But if you prefer shopping and want to buy turquoise and silver jewelry, you should go see the artisans at the Palace of the Governors. Or go to our famous market. That's about two blocks from here.'

Andrea was recording everything he said. She glanced at him from under her long eyelashes and smilingly told him that he was very kind but declined his help. Bidding him '*Adiós*,' the '*señorita*' strode away along the busy sidewalk, leaving him wishing he were thirty years younger.

It was much busier in Santa Fe than it had been in the small community near the labs. People didn't leave much space for her to move along the sidewalk and the robot had to use her sharp elbows once or twice to avoid collisions as she passed through a crowd. Young humans didn't look where they were going, being too preoccupied with cellphones or fiddling with headphones while they walked.

Andrea had to sidestep many times.

'Humans have so many little machines around them. Very inefficient! They should have them all in networks built inside their heads like I do.'

When she reached the Plaza, she saw people sitting on benches and beyond them was a long, adobe arcade where vendors sat in the shade, their colorful crafts laid out on blankets in front of them. The robot wandered over to look at the displays of woven mats and shawls, straw crafts, embroidered linens and many shiny earrings, bracelets, necklaces and combs made of turquoise and silver. Money was changing hands as tourists bought souvenirs.

It was when she neared the end of the arcade that Andrea spied, on the opposite side of the road, a *Banco* sign and under it an ATM machine.

'There is another money-making machine. I will see if Kate's card works the same way in this town as it did at the bus station.'

Andrea crossed the street to stop in front of the ATM. It looked familiar. Inserting the card and selecting Kate's pin number, the robot followed the ATM directions, opting to withdraw $500. The machine smoothly slid out the money, asked if another transaction was wanted and when the 'No' button was pressed, spat out the card. Andrea stuffed it and the money into her coat pockets, using the zippers to secure it.

As she stepped out from the palm tree shaded machine, two youths with hats pulled low over their faces, suddenly appeared, one on either side of her. One sidled closer, growling, 'We'll take that money, *señorita*. Hand it over.'

Andrea ignored them and kept on walking past the Plaza gardens.

The young men followed closely and began jostling Andrea, trying to reach the pockets where they had seen the money stuffed away. The robot quickly turned and in a loud voice that carried to all the people sitting on the park benches near them, she commanded emphatically, 'Stop that!'

Then she jabbed them both in the stomach with her metal elbows. Both gasped in surprise and clutched their abdomens, doubling over in pain. Without so much as a glance at them, Andrea walked away.

She didn't get far. *Policía* in the unmarked car parked daily near the Palace of the Governors, had seen what had happened. Two policemen sprinted towards her. They grabbed the stricken youths before they could run away and roughly bundled them into the waiting police car. The robot was unaffected by this disturbance and continued walking away.

One of the officers shouted at Andrea to stop. She did.

'*Señorita*, that was a dangerous thing you just did. Those banditos carry knives and they could have seriously hurt you. Yelling for help is safer than tackling them yourself.'

While Andrea listened without comment, he added, 'The people in the plaza saw what happened to you. They called us on their cellphones. But we were already here, doing our job of protecting people.'

He drew himself up to his full height while twirling the ends of his mustache. Andrea stood waiting for him to explain why he had called her to halt. The incident was over.

'I'll need your name for my report,' he said, fishing in his top pocket for a small notebook and pen.

'My name is Andrea.'

'And last name?'

When Andrea hesitated while searching the database for an explanation of a 'last name', he peered at her, thinking that she might be *muy bonita* but not too swift to understand.

'You know what I mean? Your family's name?'

The robot was accessing more information as he was speaking and finally told him,

'Robots,'

He wrote down, 'Andrea Roberts.'

'Now, *Señorita* Roberts, your address?'

Waiting for an answer, while Andrea ran through all the meanings of the word 'address', he explained slowly as if speaking to a mentally challenged person, 'I need to know where to find you. If you don't live in Santa Fe, where are you staying?'

'I have no place to stay. I have just arrived.'

The officer shook his head. What sort of person comes to Santa Fe without first reserving a place to stay?

'Then I suggest you walk three blocks down this road and find El Hotel Colón.' He pointed it out with his pen. 'Tell them that Eddy sent you and they'll rent you a room for the night. I'll come and find you there after I've talked to these witnesses here.'

He waited to see that she was walking in the right direction for the hotel before turning back to speak to the people who had witnessed what had happened by the park.

He shook his head sadly, thinking, '*Una señorita muy bonita pero muy tonta.*'

Andrea walked one block along the road before turning into a side street, taking the direction opposite to that indicated by the policeman. She followed her inner map system to the main train station.

The robot was searching her data for another town, further away from Santa Fe and far away from 'banditos' and policia.

By this time, the rosy desert sunset was fading into long streaks of purples and gray. Darkness was falling with its usual swiftness. Streetlights began to turn on while stores started to twinkle with strings of neon lights as she made her way past the slowly strolling humans, probably looking for some place to eat.

Humans were always eating and drinking.

Then a sign caught her attention: All Night Internet Café.

Peering inside the open door, Andrea saw rows of computers with only one or two people sitting in front of them. Were these like Stanley's computers at the lab? If so, they could supply more information to add to her database. Now that she knew that she had a family just like humans did, she would be able to find out where to look for them. Computers knew everything.

Andrea stepped inside the café.

CHAPTER 13

$\mathcal{B}$ack at the lab complex, the team members were feeling elated that their research was at last on its way to being published. Their unique robot was about to be seen by the public for the first time. The scientists chatted excitedly about being the first in their field to create a talking, thinking robot which was able to solve problems on her own by building on previous experiences. This had never been done before. What a boon for society! It could have so many uses.

Stanley went to phone the newspapers.

It was Norma who eventually returned to her computer and who realized that Andrea, the cause of their elation, was no longer standing in front of it.

'Where's the robot?' she demanded loudly over the chatter. 'I thought I'd activated the Sleep app. How could the robot move if it was on?'

'Oh, no! Don't tell me it failed again!' Susie exclaimed, jumping up from her chair. 'That's unbelievable! It's been happening so often. Something must be interfering with the Sleep app. Do you think the robot could have found a way around it?'

José threw his hands up in the air in disbelief. 'Andrea must be around here somewhere. She can't get outside. She doesn't know the code for the front door. Maybe she found a way into another lab.'

They scattered to search the other rooms in the lab complex but there was no sign of Andrea anywhere. Norma, Susie and José met back at Stanley's office. He was still on the phone, but he raised his eyebrows in query as his team hurriedly crowded into his office.

'Sorry, Kate, hold on for a minute. There seems to be some trouble here.'

He covered the mouthpiece with his hand to ask his team, 'What's going on? Do we have a problem?'

'We can't find the robot,' Norma said impatiently. 'We've looked everywhere. It doesn't seem to be here.'

'What do you mean?' he exclaimed, 'The robot's gone? How can that happen?'

In his dismay, his hand had slipped off the phone so that Kate could hear him quite distinctly. She shouted into her phone to capture Stanley's attention.

'Stan! I saw her in town!'

Stanley held up his palm towards his team as he listened to Kate.

'In town, at the Corner Store? What was she doing there? Yes, yes, good thinking! Keep an eye on her and I'll be home immediately.'

The team's relief was short-lived when they heard him groan and saw his knuckles grow white as he gripped the telephone.

'How did she get away so fast?' he demanded. 'You mean Gonzalez, the man who lives next door to us? Okay, stay at home in case the robot comes back. We'll be there shortly.'

Stanley turned to the others. 'Kate saw Andrea in the Corner Store in town and managed to get her to our house, but she's disappeared again. My wife thinks that our neighbor Gonzalez may have given her a ride into town. She saw that his car had just driven past on the road.'

He wiped the sweat off his brow with his sleeve.

Coolly rational, Norma said, 'Why don't we split up? Susie and I can check in with Kate and talk to the Gonzalez family. You, Stanley, and José could find out what the robot was doing in the corner store and then meet up with us at your house afterwards. What do you think?'

Everyone agreed and hurried to their cars.

Once Kate had told Norma and Susie how she had rescued the robot from the over-curious men in the Corner Store, the two women scientists headed further up the hill road to the neighboring adobe hacienda.

Huge ceramic plant pots decorated both sides of its stone steps, forcing them to walk in single file up to the front door, where Norma pulled the thick rope attached to an outside brass bell. It resonated with the melancholy sounds of a gong.

An attractive middle-aged Mexican woman, her lustrous black hair pulled back from her face by an ornamental comb, opened the heavy wooden door.

'*Sí?*' the woman enquired.

'*Buenas tardes, Señora*. We are looking for a missing… friend,' Norma said.

The woman gazed at them curiously with brown eyes as shiny as her hair. 'Oh! And what is the name of your friend? And why do you think that I can help you? Has she gone missing near my house?'

Susie answered, 'Our friend Andrea was at your neighbor Kate's home a short while ago but didn't say where she was going after that. We thought you might have seen her on the road if she went by here.'

'No, I have been busy at home all day. I saw nobody pass by.'

'Then could your husband have seen her? Could we talk to him too?'

At the mention of her husband's name, his wife's back stiffened and her eyes darkened.

'He has just gone out of town for three days. Why do you two ladies wish to speak to him? Why would he know anything about your friend?'

Norma answered, 'We only wanted to know that if he were driving into town, perhaps he might have given our friend a ride.'

'Oh, is that what you are worried about? If your friend Andrea is young and attractive, you can be sure that he would offer her a ride if she was walking alone along the road. He likes to meet young *señoritas,* especially if they are pretty. He says they make him feel young again.'

She glared at Norma and Susie, making them feel distinctly uncomfortable. The conversation seemed to be over, so they began to turn away with Norma saying, '*Gracias, señora.*' She was sure now that the husband must have picked up Andrea. Kate had told them that a truck driver had given Andrea a drive into town from the labs.

It would be nothing new for the robot to get into another car. She would be repeating a previous experience.

Susie was starting to follow Norma down the steps when *Señora* Gonzalez stopped them by calling out, 'This young friend of yours, why don't you call her on her cellphone? I would be interested to know if she is with my husband.'

Susie hesitated before replying, 'We don't know her phone number. Perhaps you could call your husband instead?'

The woman's face became a dark mask.

'He would not like it if I phoned him. He would think that I am checking up on him. I don't even know where he is going today. Only that he has a meeting out of town. He said he would phone me on the way home. And now you tell me your friend is missing?'

As she spoke, she was twisting her hands, becoming more and more agitated. To their dismay, she suddenly burst out in anger, 'I know what he is doing! He's gone off for the weekend with that girl, your friend. The lying cheat! I was stupid to believe all his promises to reform! Well, now I know, I'll be waiting for him when he comes home.'

With that, she angrily slammed the heavy wooden door behind them.

Stunned by this unexpected verbal explosion, soft-hearted Susie turned to the other scientist, 'Oh, no, Norma! What have we done?'

As they carefully picked their way down the cluttered steps, she pleaded, 'Can't we say something to the *señora* to make her feel better? She's jumping to the wrong conclusion. We know that Andrea isn't a young woman!'

Norma shrugged her shoulders. 'Well, we can't tell her that Andrea is a robot, can we? Let's hope that her husband won't find out either,' she responded dryly.

CHAPTER 14

$\mathcal{W}$hen they returned to Stanley's house, they reported to Kate what had happened with Señora Gonzalez.

'I don't usually repeat local gossip, but I have heard that Gonzalez fancies himself as God's gift to women. He's certainly a very handsome man. And he knows it,' Kate remarked.

It was on the tip of Norma's tongue to say bluntly, 'That would have been good to know before we visited his wife.' But before she could speak, they were interrupted by the sound of the front door opening. They could hear Stanley grumbling to José, 'Well, that was like pulling teeth.'

Lured by the smell of fresh coffee, the men tramped into the sun-washed kitchen. As Kate quietly handed them mugs, he continued, 'Would you believe that Juan and his cronies wouldn't tell us anything about Andrea? They would only admit that 'a *señorita*' had been there when I told them that Kate had seen her in the store this morning. After that, they clammed up and refused to give us any more information. In fact, they looked at us as if we were the ones to blame for Andrea's disappearance.'

José sipped his hot drink before adding, 'They're not like any friendly New Mexicans I know. They made me feel guilty for even knowing Andrea. As if it was a crime!'

While Susie and Norma were telling the others about their afternoon experience with Señora Gonzalez, the house phone rang. Kate hurried out to answer it.

She came back after a lengthy conversation. 'That was my bank, Stanley. They say that there've been three withdrawals on my bank card today. But I only took out forty dollars this morning when I was with Andrea. Since then, someone has withdrawn about a thousand dollars. The bank is going to freeze my account, now that they have checked that I haven't withdrawn that amount today.'

Kate had everyone's attention. 'My card can't have been stolen,' she worried, 'I remember seeing it in my purse when I got home today.'

Kate emptied her purse onto the kitchen table. They watched her trembling hands begin to sift through its contents. 'It's not here. Maybe I did lose it, and someone has found it. But how would they know my PIN number? It doesn't make sense! No, my card must be here somewhere.'

She was renewing her search when Stanley put his arm around her.

'Don't panic, my dear. I'm sure there's a simple solution to all this. By any chance did Andrea see you withdrawing the money this morning?'

'Of course! I had to keep her close to me, in case she walked away while I was occupied at the ATM.'

'Did the bank tell you what ATMs were used for the withdrawals?'

'They didn't say,' she replied, pushing her hair out of her eyes. 'Is that important?'

'It might be for us if we think Andrea had anything to do with it,' her husband replied gently. 'We need to know where the robot is now.'

'Andrea? Whatever do you mean? What has she got to do with this?' Kate exclaimed in exasperation.

'The robot was alone in the kitchen. She could have seen where you put the card and then taken it. Andrea is very good at recording events and she's programmed to load new information into the database. It's possible that she could have taken your card to find out if it would work at another ATM. But she would have to go back to town to find that out.'

Kate looked at her husband incredulously. 'You can't really believe that, Stanley! A robot planning to use my credit card! That's utter nonsense!'

Norma was growing impatient. 'Kate, you can find out quite easily. You could ask the bank where the transactions took place and whether the person using the card was caught on camera. That would be helpful in solving this mystery.'

The others nodded their heads in agreement. Reluctantly, Kate went back to phone the bank. The others strained to hear her phone conversation as they waited, shuffling impatiently in their chairs.

When she returned, she informed them, 'It seems that one withdrawal was at the bus station in town at 2 pm. and the other was in Santa Fe this afternoon at 4:45pm.'

'Did they get a photo of the person using your card?' Norma asked eagerly.

'They only said that it was a young woman with dark hair,' she replied.

'It must be Andrea!' Susie exclaimed.

'You can't be sure of that,' Kate burst out. 'It could've been anyone!'

'True,' Stanley said, 'But all the information we have seems to point to the robot. Especially when we know what she's capable of doing and how she got into town from here – most probably courtesy of Gonzalez.'

'Then what do we do now, when we think she's in Santa Fe?' Susie asked.

José was gabbling, his native tongue getting mixed up with English in his excitement.

'Santa Fe *es una hora de distancia en carro. Es una ciudad grande.* We can get there *fácilmente.* But how do we find Andrea when we do get there?'

While the others were still deciphering what he had said, Susie stated, 'That is a problem. We can't even ask the police if they've seen anyone resembling Andrea. They would ask too many questions. We can't report her as a missing person, because she's not, she's a robot. And if she's been using Kate's credit card, well, now she's a criminal robot.'

They had to agree that calling the police was not a good idea.

Stanley made one of his lightning decisions. 'I think I'll call my own bank manager to find out if there's any information about credit card theft in our area. The banks keep in touch with one another so he might tell me something more if I say that Kate's card has been compromised.'

When he came back to the kitchen, he was looking more cheerful.

'Okay, listen to this. They're keeping an eye on the ATM in town, but the same debit card was used later in Santa Fe. It was definitely Kate's card. The local police have been informed of the theft. The bank manager also said that two men in Santa Fe were arrested trying to rob a woman who had just used the ATM.'

'What happened? Do you think the woman was Andrea? Did they detain her too?' Norma asked eagerly.

'No. While the police were getting witness statements, the woman in question was directed to a local hotel where they planned to interview her later. But she hadn't arrived by the time the police went to see her. My bank manager said that was all he knew.'

'We still don't know if that woman was Andrea,' Kate protested.

'True, Kate,' Stanley agreed. 'But we'll have to take the chance that it is. What does everyone think about going to Santa Fe now, to see if we can trace the robot?'

The team agreed with alacrity. Stanley turned to his wife. 'I would like you to come too, my dear. If we find Andrea, you'll be the one she will talk to. If she sees us first, she's liable to devise a way of escaping again.'

'Couldn't we wait until tomorrow morning?' Kate begged. 'It'll be dark by the time we get there tonight. Even if she's there, we can't find her in the dark. We'll all have to stay overnight.'

'We could stay with my cousin,' José offered generously. 'He has *una casa grande*.'

When Kate looked skeptical, Stanley hurried to reassure her. 'We two could stay in our usual hotel if you'd rather. We can all meet up early tomorrow morning for breakfast in Santa Fe.'

That agreed, everyone else left hastily to pack for an overnight stay.

The chase was on.

CHAPTER 15

$\mathcal{I}$n Santa Fe, Andrea walked down the three steps leading into the Internet café. She looked around, automatically photographing the room.

The robot recorded the rough whitewashed walls, enlivened by posters of Georgia O'Keeffe's distinctive art. Andrea already had details of that artist's colorful work on her database, researched when the bus driver had mentioned the local art museum.

Not lingering long over the posters, she observed ten little cubicles each with a computer and a few humans who were oblivious to any new arrival, as was the man at the front desk. His back was turned to her as he filled a carafe with water and placed it on a hot plate.

Andrea was about to bypass him to go to one of the computers, when he turned around and cried, 'Hey! *Un minuto, señorita*! You have to register here first.'

As he spoke, his description was being filed for future reference: older man, stubble of white beard on wrinkled, sunburned skin, grayish hair, dark eyes, overweight, wearing a thin, brightly colored shirt over jeans. The robot couldn't see what he was wearing on his feet.

'Good thing I caught a glimpse of you in my mirror,' he commented, peering at the robot from under shaggy eyebrows, 'Else you would have slipped right by me. Not trying to pull a fast one on me, are you?'

He grinned, showing teeth stained with tobacco.

Andrea didn't answer. She was listening to database responses as to what 'a fast one' might be, while examining the thing he'd called 'a mirror.'

Behind the man was a shiny glass rectangle that reflected a young woman, the storekeeper and part of the front showcase stacked with what she now recognized as human food. She was puzzled by the strange woman's reflection but noted the resemblance to the scientist Susie, with the same black hair and brown eyes but a smoother skin. Only the green dress and light coat were different.

'Admiring yourself, are you?' teased the man. 'Can't say as I blame you. You're a mighty pretty lady.'

The robot's database confirmed that what Andrea saw in the mirror was what the robot looked like to humans. She looked down at the silk dress and light coat to make sure, then accepted the fact that she looked like a human.

'I need to use one of your computers,' she said firmly.

'Sure! How long do you want it for?'

'I haven't calculated that length of time.'

'Okay. Then I'll just make a note of the time when you begin and we'll 'calculate' how much it will cost when you finish. That okay? Your name is?'

'Andrea,' supplied the robot.

He made an entry in his book with the time: 6:30 pm. Computer station 4 Andrea.

'That okay with you?'

Andrea nodded.

He smirked. Station 4 was near the middle of the café, a place where he could watch his new customer from the front desk. It was a memorable day when such a stunning looker like this one walked in to use a computer.

After he had switched on the machine and instructed her on how to use it, he asked, 'Want anything to eat or drink? Or have you eaten already?'

'I don't need anything to eat or drink,' Andrea stated.

'Okay. My son Steve is coming in soon to do the evening shift so if you have any difficulties you can ask him. He's a wiz with computers. Ask him anything about the newest technology and he'll know all about it.'

But Andrea was already opening a search engine. As she seemed to know what she was doing, he walked around to make sure that his other customers were comfortable before returning to his seat at the front.

Andrea's search for 'Robots' was totally engrossing. She sensed the arrival of the son but didn't see his father point her out to him.

'You're always saying you'll meet your dream woman one day. Maybe this is your lucky day, Steve! Look at Station 4.'

He left, laughing to himself as he went out into the soft evening air.

Steve took a cold drink from the fridge and sat looking at Andrea. She was amazing. Her fingers flew over the keyboard as if she'd been using computers all her life. 'She must've learned in school', he thought. He continued watching her doing some research, hardly stopping to digest the information and then renewing her search. She never wrote anything down. He was intrigued. What was it that she found so interesting?

For a while, he was busy with settling the accounts of customers who were leaving but later, by nine o'clock Andrea was the only person left in the café.

He knew that she hadn't budged from her chair since he had taken over, not even to go to the toilet. He had never seen such a fascinating young woman. Wait till he told his friends about this beauty!

Steve stood up and stretched to his full five feet six inches in height as he began walking towards her.

Andrea detected his movements at once. She saved her research and returned to the computer's menu page while taking in his details as he approached. He was suntanned like the older man, but he had a smoother, almost baby, face except for a few sparse black hairs growing above his upper lip. His eyes were dark, as were his eyebrows and long hair. His bright red t-shirt was tucked into blue jeans that sagged below the youth's hips and had holes in the knees of the pants. Andrea calculated his age as about seventeen human years.

'Hi, my name is Steve. Need any help?'

As he spoke, his eyes flickered to the computer screen, but he saw only the main menu page.

'No, thank you,' Andrea said, quickly noting his minute nervous gestures, his shining eyes when he looked at her, the slight twitching of his hands, the fast downward glance at her upper body, the eager look on his face –all clues to Andrea that he was mistaking her for a human.

'You are kind. But you are thinking of something else.'

Steve blushed as he stammered, 'I was only thinking what a beautiful woman you are, that's all.'

The robot turned away without replying, having verified that the youth thought that he was talking to a human person. As for being 'a beautiful woman,' Andrea was informed by the database that these words could be used as an introduction to the prospect of a human relationship. She kept quiet.

After a minute of silence, Steve felt as if he had been dismissed. Not knowing what to do next, he retreated to the front again.

Freed from his interference, Andrea was soon preoccupied with the search for the family of Robots.

'*There are robots that can move like dogs and horses but only a few resemble real animals. Some robots are just metal frames and exposed machine parts, but they can perform specific tasks on cue. A new generation of robots can perform intricate movements of sorting and picking up small objects.*'

Andrea paused for a second. 'Why can't I find robots like me, that can think, talk and solve problems as well as look like human beings? Where can the rest of my family be? There must be some, somewhere in the world.'

She changed to another website.

'Ah, here they are! Researchers in California and in Montréal, Québec are working on deep-thinking robots that can reason exactly as I do. Why are they being so slow? Stanley's scientists have created me already. These other scientists do not know that. I will have to go there so they can see me for themselves.'

But Steve was about to interrupt this train of thought. He'd decided to make another attempt at getting Andrea's attention and knew exactly how to do it. By surprise!

He circled the room behind the robot while she was engrossed in research on the computer. Then without warning he grabbed the arms of her chair, turned the robot around and kissed her soundly on the lips.

Automatically Andrea swept a hand across her face to knock him away. He fell to the side as if he'd been pole-axed. The robot was rising from the chair to get away from him when she saw what he was holding. It was her hair.

Steve was looking with horror at what was in his hand.

'You're wearing a wig!' he stated unnecessarily. 'You're bald!'

Andrea delicately picked the wig from his fingers and on the way out of the café, looked in the mirror to firmly wedge the dark hair back onto her head.

Steve rose painfully to his feet and staggered after her shouting, 'Hey! Come back! You haven't paid yet!'

But by the time he got to the outside door, the late-night crowd outside had swallowed up Andrea and Steve's 'beautiful woman' was nowhere to be seen.

CHAPTER 16

$\mathcal{T}$he team of scientists arrived in Santa Fe after dark when the streetlights were being switched on. José drove Norma and Susie to his cousin's house while Stanley and Kate found a place to stay for the night in a small hotel not far from the Palace of the Governors.

'We were lucky to find this room,' Stanley observed as he dropped their overnight cases on to the bed. 'There was a last-minute cancellation. That's a lucky omen and if our luck holds, we might even find Andrea tomorrow.'

Kate was inspecting the small room. It was clean but looked a little threadbare. There was no air conditioning, but it did have a big ceiling fan that she activated. It hummed as it rotated but she was glad that it seemed to be working well. She opened the window to let in the late evening air.

'It's very hot in here, Stan. We should go out to have something to eat while the room cools down. Are you hungry?'

Stanley realized that he had not eaten since breakfast and instantly he became ravenous.

'Remember that wonderful Mexican restaurant we used to go to a few years ago? I wonder if it's still in operation,' he enthused. 'It wasn't far from here, just east of this hotel I think.'

Later, after eating spicy chicken enchiladas and corn tortillas, Stanley sat back in his chair and smiled contentedly at Kate.

'How would you like to have a moonlight stroll around the Governors' park before we go back to our hotel?'

The night felt pleasantly warm as they walked arm in arm, along the less busy streets of the town. As they reached the darkened park, they could smell the sharp, tarry scent of creosote bushes mingling with the more delicate perfume of desert flowers and for the first time that day, Kate was happy to be in Santa Fe. It was so wonderfully quiet and peaceful in the park.

'Hey, man! Watch where you're going!'

The strident voice broke into her reverie and when Stanley stumbled in surprise, Kate tightened her grip on his arm so that they both pulled up abruptly. Stanley had tripped over the outstretched legs of a man sitting on a park bench.

'Oh! I'm sorry,' he apologized as he righted himself, 'I didn't see you sitting there in the dark.'

They peered at the man who was sitting on a park bench with his arm around a woman.

'No problem, man. But I've seen enough trouble today without needing some more. You'd better watch where you're walking at night.'

As Stan mumbled another apology, the man added, 'It ain't always safe around here at night. You gotta keep a sharp look out, man.'

His companion interrupted him, 'You mean it ain't safe even in the daytime, Gary.'

Stanley's curiosity was aroused. 'Was there some trouble in the park today?'

'I'll say there was!' exclaimed the man. 'Saw it with my own two eyes. Young punks tried to rob some young woman who'd taken money out of the ATM over there. In broad daylight too!' He pointed in the direction of an ATM that was now shrouded in shadow.

'And the park was full of people who saw them do it!' the woman exclaimed. 'Some of us called the *policia* as soon as we saw what was going on. I had to stop my Gary here, from rushing over to knock those punks down!'

Gary straightened his back and flexed his muscles. 'Would've done it too if the police hadn't arrived and saved me the trouble.'

'You should've seen that young woman!' his wife continued, 'She just stuck out both her elbows and hit them in their stomachs. Must've hurt them, cos they both doubled over and that's when the police arrested them before they could get away. For once the police got here in time. They got rid of some of those bad banditos, at last!'

Stanley was intrigued. 'A young woman? Did you get a good look at her?'

'Sure, did!' Gary answered. 'Prettiest little lady you ever did see. Great figure, lovely face and the glossiest black hair. As short and slight as she was, she walked away as if nothing had happened. Didn't panic or yell for help. Told them punks to stop jostling her. Then, wham! She elbowed them out of her way. Don't think they'll try the same trick again after the police have finished with them.'

'Did the police talk to the young woman?' Kate asked anxiously.

'Heard tell she was sent to El Hotel Colón down this street to wait for them,' the wife answered. 'Maybe they thought she needed some quiet time to pull herself together after being hassled like that.'

'So, you see,' Gary concluded, 'You have to be careful when you're out walking in Santa Fe. There's no knowing what might happen.'

'Thank you very much for telling us. We'll definitely keep your warning in mind,' Stanley answered. He and Kate bid them *'Buenas noches'* and turned back to their hotel.

Once they were out of earshot, Kate turned to Stanley, 'Do you think that young woman could have been Andrea?'

'No doubt about it,' he replied firmly. 'Now I'm really sure that we'll find the robot in this town. I just want to check at the Colón hotel as we go by. It won't take long and if we're lucky, Andrea might still be there.'

But in talking to the hotel manager, they were disappointed to find that she had never turned up at the hotel. The man surmised that the police would be looking for the missing woman now, probably wanting to get a victim statement from her.

Once they were outside again, Stanley whispered to Kate, 'That's not good news. If we don't find Andrea first before the police do, our whole project will be compromised. We don't want anyone to know that the woman they are all talking about is really our robot.'

That night, while Kate and Stanley slept fitfully in their hotel room, Andrea sat at the train station selecting another destination, far away from Santa Fe.

The robot too had her eyes closed as she concentrated on the newly acquired maps and train schedules in its database. Passersby must have thought that she was only another tired traveler dozing while waiting for a late train, so nobody paid much attention. They would have been surprised to know that Andrea was alert to everything happening around it, even while busily searching for inside information.

The daytime bustle of the station had given way to a more muted atmosphere at night. As people passed by, the robot could hear snatches of conversation, punctuated by sharp loudspeaker announcements that echoed around the high vaulted walls. There was the hollow rattle of trains braking squeakily to a halt at the platforms and the quiet brushing sounds of cleaners keeping the area clear of trash. None of this distracted Andrea.

When her eyes finally flicked open, a decision had been made. 'Boston will be the best place to find Robot families. There is one very well-known technological facility there and there's also Boston University. Other places in Boston specialize in computer research and the building of robots, so there are many options. The Internet pictures of robots do not look much like me, but they might be early relatives.'

Andrea planned an itinerary.

'First, there is a train to Albuquerque. That takes more than an hour. From there, an Amtrak train goes to Boston. That city is a long way away from Albuquerque so the journey will take some days, maybe involving changing trains. When in Boston, I will access more information from the humans who live there. Someone should be able to tell me the best place to find active robots.'

The robot calculated how much money was needed to pay for the journey and how much was in her pocket. 'I have enough money to pay for everything.'

There was one glitch in Andrea's plans. The late train to Albuquerque had already left.

The tired-looking man in the station office handed her a ticket saying, 'You'll have to wait for the early morning train now, lady. It leaves from Platform 11 at six a.m. and it gets crowded with morning commuters. Better arrive at the platform in good time if you want to get a seat. There's an all-night café here in the station if you want something to eat.'

Andrea took a moment to zip the train ticket into a pocket and after politely thanking the man, looked around for a place to wait. Time was immaterial. The robot selected a dimly lit bench away from the mainstream of passengers but facing the station's main entrance.

'Those policemen I saw today seem to watch people all the time. I don't want to talk to them again. I will look out for them.'

Andrea settled on the bench underneath an artificial tree, continuing to observe and endlessly record the comings and goings of the people in the train station, taking in all the minutiae of what her database called, 'human life' around her.

CHAPTER 17

$\mathcal{T}$he next day, barely an hour after Andrea had departed on the train to Albuquerque, Stanley and Kate met José, Norma and Susie for breakfast to decide how they should start looking for their robot.

Once everyone heard that the police were now on the lookout for the woman the team now believed to be Andrea, they were eager to get a head start on the authorities. José undid a map of Santa Fe and spread it over the cleared table.

'My cousin wanted to show us around town, but I told him that we were working. So, he's told me the easiest ways to get around Santa Fe.'

As they pored over the street map, he pointed out the various districts in the town. 'Lucky for us the main streets are close together so we can walk everywhere. I'll leave my car in the restaurant parking area in case you need a ride for any reason. I can get back to it quickly.'

Kate, Stanley and José knew the town well enough, but Norma and Susie took photos of the map with their cell phones. Then everyone was allotted a district to search.

Stanley said, 'Remember to keep in touch with one other by phone throughout the day and if someone spots Andrea, send an urgent message to Kate to get there as quickly as she can. Then alert the rest of us so we can converge on this troublesome robot. Don't try to detain her by yourself.'

Norma asked, 'Has everyone got a photo of Andrea to show to the people you talk to?'

Nodding assent and now primed for the hunt, they were all eager to begin before the sun became too hot, making walking both tiring and uncomfortable. After checking their watches and cellphones, the team began their search of the town.

The hot morning dragged on into the even hotter afternoon. The few people who recognized Andrea from the photograph were those who had witnessed the attempted robbery in the park. No one knew where she had gone after that. Most people thought that she had obeyed the police and gone to El Hotel Colón. Even the bus driver who had talked to Andrea had no idea of where she went after leaving the bus.

It was almost sundown when a frustrated and tired Susie decided that she had had enough and needed to rest her feet. She had just stepped into the shade of the awning of a café to send a message to the rest of the team that she was stopping for a break, when she gave a loud yelp.

Someone had crept up behind her and was yanking at her hair. Instinctively she put her hands up to protect her head, nearly dropping her cellphone. Endeavoring to ease off the hands that were painfully pulling her head back, Susie twisted sideways to try to see her attacker.

It was a teenager pulling at her hair but now shouting in her ear as if she were deaf.

'So, you've come back, you bald-headed witch! Maybe you've come to pay your bill now? Is that it? Thought you could get away without paying, did ya?' Spitefully he gave another painful tug on her hair.

Susie aimed a well-placed karate kick and he quickly let go. Whirling around as she held the back of her head tenderly, she angrily confronted the youth.

'What do you think you're doing? Why are you attacking me? Did you think that because I'm a young woman, I'm easy prey for kids like you?'

She pointed at him with her cellphone. 'Stay where you are! I'm going to call the police!'

By this time a crowd of sympathetic watchers had assembled around them.

'Right on, lady!" a man called out, 'Too many lazy troublemakers in this town. Saw some jerks in the park the other day, trying to mug a girl for her money.'

There were affirmative murmurs from the crowd and someone else yelled, 'Get a job, You Useless Kid, instead of harassing young women like this.'

The teenager had recovered enough to answer defiantly, 'You're all wrong! I work in this Internet café. This woman walked out without paying.'

'What?' Susie exclaimed, 'I've never seen you in my life, you liar.'

'Well, you look just like the woman who used our computers,' Steve countered heatedly. 'She was wearing a black wig, the same color as your hair. That's why I pulled yours, to see if it would come off again.'

The crowd jeered. 'Some stupid story! Can't you think of a better excuse?'

Quickly realizing that he must be describing Andrea, Susie pocketed her phone saying, 'Well, now you've found out my hair is real and I'm not this other woman! But, wait a minute, did she look like this?'

She delved into her purse for the photograph of Andrea.

'Yeah, that's her,' he agreed suspiciously, 'How come you have her photograph?'

'Because I'm looking for her too. She's my...er... sister and she's gone missing from home. I need to find her. Do you know where she went after she left the café?'

Steve eyed her curiously not yet convinced, but on the other hand if this were her sister, maybe she would settle her account. He looked at the angry faces glaring at him and mouthed to Susie, 'Can we go into the café? I have customers inside. I can show you the bill for all the hours your sister spent here.'

Nothing would suit Susie more. Both of them escaped into the cool interior of the store while the people outside gradually dispersed.

Once inside, he turned to Susie, '*Lo siento, Señorita.* Sorry about the mistake. Can I offer you a free coffee?'

Without waiting for an answer, he filled a mug with hot coffee and handed it to her. As Susie drank, she surveyed the array of computers, realizing only too well how much information Andrea would have fed into her database.

'Do you know which computer my sister was using?'

'Sure thing!' He brought out the schedule and pointed, 'There it is, Station number 4. That's the one in the middle of the room. Customer's name: Andrea.'

Susie wandered over to that computer and sat down in front of it.

'Is there a way of finding out what she was researching? Maybe that would indicate where she's heading.'

'Sure thing!' Steve replied again. 'You've asked the right person to find out!'

He sat next to Susie, acutely aware that here was another attractive woman sitting close to him, this one with real hair. Wait till he told his friends!

His fingers flew over the keyboard as he summoned up as if by magic, all the apps and information stations Andrea had used.

'That's wonderful!' Susie exclaimed, 'Mind if I make a few notes?'

'Your sister never made notes. I was watching her all the time.'

'Oh yes! That sounds like her. She has a much better memory than I have,' Susie agreed, 'But I can speed-read so I'll be as quick. I'll pay you for the time I use on the computer.'

Steve smiled to himself as he went to tend to his other customers. He would add her sister's unpaid bill to this woman's account.

Although Susie was skillful at using computers, it took her more than an hour to go through everything that Andrea had researched. The robot had used a great many websites and information apps. But by the end of her search, Susie had a good idea about what information the robot had been acquiring. It wanted to know about other robots and where to find them.

'Why does Andrea want that information?' she puzzled, 'There are no other robots like her. At present there are no robots that can think, solve problems and create strategies using their own experiences. None of them even look like human beings, as Andrea does. Maybe the rest of my team will have some ideas why she was doing this research.'

Susie flinched guiltily in remembering her fellow scientists. She had been so engrossed in this computer research that she'd forgotten to contact her fellow scientists to let them know where she'd ended up that afternoon.

'But I've got a good excuse! With all this really interesting information to tell them, even Norma might not get annoyed with me for forgetting to call in.'

Quickly, she gathered up her notes and went to the front counter where she paid for everything that Steve had calculated for the use of his computer service by both Susie and Andrea. Bidding him a hurried '*Buenas tardes*', Susie left, hardly noticing that the teenager was looking remarkably smug.

Standing under the outside awning, she activated her cellphone.

She might have phoned Stanley sooner if she had known that he was about to have a 'meltdown.'

CHAPTER 18

Stanley met up with Kate in the late afternoon when both were feeling discouraged by their lack of success in locating Andrea. By that time, they were exhausted by the relentless sun's heat and by the constant jostling of the tourist crowds while they were asking if anyone had seen Andrea. They both agreed that they needed a break.

During the day, regular phone calls from the rest of the team reporting their non-progress had made Stanley even more despondent. Now they were back under the fan in the cool of their room, shoes kicked off, lying on the bed and expecting Susie to call, since she had been strangely silent during the long afternoon.

Kate was already dozing off when she was jolted awake again by her husband suddenly leaping from the bed to pace around the room, punching his fists in the air.

'I'm an idiot!' he exclaimed. 'I should have foreseen that this might happen! I was so full of my own achievements in finally getting the robot working that I turned a blind eye to what could happen when we did. All this is my fault! I'm to blame! I've caused all this trouble. Me and my damned ego!'

Kate sat up and wrapped her arms around her knees to stare at him.

'Whatever do you mean, Stan? What didn't you take into consideration?'

But Stanley was wallowing too much in his self-castigation to answer.

'It's only that we've worked so hard to research ad infinitum the ways the brain uses neural networks. And we managed to mimic those pathways in Andrea so the robot can process vast amounts of data at high speed. All that data that's been stored is now being used to shape her behavior.'

'Nothing wrong with that,' Kate ventured carefully, 'You've already demonstrated that Andrea can solve problems.'

'Yes, but for that to happen, we had to install millions of complex parameters that constantly change. It's difficult to understand when they're being used in new ways.'

'Do you mean that you have no way of knowing what Andrea will do next? That she's totally unpredictable?' Kate asked.

'Correct! If we can't understand how she thinks and behaves because her networks are too complex, what hope have we to control her now, if and when we can catch the robot? She very quickly found out how to get around the Sleep app. Then she worked out how to escape the lab. Kate, this robot is out of our control. It's a maverick! I've created a monster!'

To Kate's dismay, her usually easy-going husband flopped onto a chair, buried his head in his hands and groaned out his despair and frustration.

She slipped off the bed to comfort him.

'But, Stan, Andrea isn't a monster. In fact, she's rather beautiful. You should be proud of all the innovations you and the team have created to make her so unique. Personally, to me she's more like a rebellious child.'

'But I don't want a robot that's like a child trying to find out about the world,' Stanley howled. 'I want to be able to control her so that she can be useful to other people. This robot is going against all our built-in commands. We can't seem to control it whatever we do. It keeps on doing something else we never expected.'

By this time, he was waving his hands distractedly in the air.

'Oh dear!' Kate said gravely. 'Now you ARE sounding like a parent."

Stanley paused to see if she were teasing him. Recognizing that twinkle in her eyes, his shoulders began to relax. He had a flashback of the trials of rearing their own son and daughter.

Calming down a little, he moaned, 'But, Kate, we're responsible for inventing Andrea and we can't let her run amok wherever she decides to go. Besides, I was supposed to meet the press today. What am I going to tell them? 'Sorry, folks, I was going to introduce you to our latest invention, a cutting-edge, deep-thinking robot but I'm sorry to tell you that this one got away and I don't know where it is.'

Kate couldn't help laughing at the absurdity of the situation. Then she said more straight-faced, 'Maybe we need more help to find her, Stan.'

'And where are we going to find more help?' he demanded.

'I was thinking that what we're doing now, asking people if they've seen her, is too tiring and besides it isn't working. There are only a few of us and too many people to question. Have you thought of going to the police and reporting her for stealing secret scientific information? They could find her much more easily than we can. They have more people for a start.'

Stanley stared at his wife in astonishment. 'You can't be serious, Kate!'

Kate persisted, 'But just think about it, Stan. Andrea has gone off with all your secret inventions inside her. She really is a thief, even if we don't take into consideration her stealing money from me with my debit card. You would only be reporting the truth.'

'Then, say they do catch her,' Stan objected. 'Because she's been accused of being a thief, they'll take her photograph and try to fingerprint her. What are they going to think when they find out that there are no fingerprints? The artificial skin is perfectly smooth. And what if they search Andrea? They're sure to find out that they are dealing with a robot. Then what?'

Stanley shook his head.

'No. No. No! That's too risky, Kate. We've got to find her before the police do. I'm going to recall the team and we'll think of some other way of finding Andrea. But you're right, our present plan isn't working.'

Stanley's cellphone rang. He looked at its voice identification.

'It's Susie at last,' he told Kate.

'Sorry not to call you sooner,' Susie apologized.

Before he could answer, she went on quickly, 'I've found out where Andrea was yesterday and what she was doing. Would you believe that she was in an Internet café internalizing information for finding other robots? I've made a note of the sites she was using. What do you want me to do with the info? I haven't contacted the others yet.'

Stanley's mood brightened considerably. He even grinned at Kate.

'Great job, Susie! Any idea where the robot is now?'

'It looks like she might be trying to leave Santa Fe, but I can't say for sure. You'll need to see my notes and look at the computer sites for yourself.'

'Okay! I'll recall the team to our hotel. Want me to pick you up?'

After noting Susie's location, Stanley turned to his wife, 'Kate, could you call the team in, to meet here as soon as possible? I'm going to get Susie. She's found information about the robot to share with us. Something to go on. At last!'

He blew Kate a kiss and wriggling into his sandals as he hurried out, he grabbed his car keys, leaving the door swinging open behind him.

CHAPTER 19

*W*hile Andrea was on the train that was taking her away from Santa Fe, Stanley's team was revisiting the robot's research on the hotel computer. They were huddled together in a small room, trying to find clues to Andrea's thinking while Kate, in her usual considerate way, had gone to bring take-out food for their supper so that hunger wouldn't distract them from their search.

Norma sat at the computer keyboard and as Susie read out her notes, was bringing up on the screen the robot's research pattern.

José stood behind them slapping the side of his head with his hand.

'Lo siento! Lo siento! My robot design is no good! Why didn't I think to include a tracking device? Then we would know where Andrea is.'

'It's too late to think about that!' Norma remarked dryly.

'It's my fault too,' Stanley quickly said. 'I never thought about a tracing chip either. But how were we to know that we even needed one? None of us expected Andrea to get away from us. So, don't blame yourself, José.'

Susie interrupted, 'There seems to be a lot of information about what the National Institute of Robotics in Boston is experimenting on in its computer programming section.'

'But Andrea was looking at Boston University too. And Montréal. And California as well,' Norma glowered. 'All the places of our competitors.'

'She's going to be giving away all our secrets if she contacts any of them,' José wailed. 'They're sure to recognize a robot when they see one!'

They were assessing this predicament when Kate arrived with their food. As they morosely munched their tacos, Stanley said, 'Let's try to keep a positive attitude. I suggest that we look into which engineering faculty has developed the most up-to-date robots. When we started our project, none of them was anywhere near to where we were in developing Andrea.'

'I haven't heard of any of them making robots yet that look like people,' Norma said, 'At least, there's a robot that has a human face and can talk but it has no body, only a head and shoulders. Bit weird. But then, technology moves so fast that we could have missed something while we were busy working on our own robot.'

'I've read about humanoid experiments in Singapore and Japan,' Susie offered. 'They're making robots that can move like people but as far as I know, none of them can be mistaken for a living human being. Not like Andrea.'

'Yes, technology is expanding very fast,' Norma agreed. 'Susie, did you know that there's an android in Tokyo, that can speak Japanese but also Chinese, English and German? It can even do sign language!'

Before Susie could reply, Kate stood up, noisily beginning to gather all the taco wrappers and empty cups, remarking, 'With all this talk, you're going to make us feel really worried about other robots becoming more advanced than Andrea, before you can even inform the public about what you've achieved. Shouldn't you all be working on a plan to find her as soon as possible?'

José startled them all by jumping out of his seat, exclaiming, 'I've got an idea! Norma got her degree from NIR and Susie went to Boston University. What if they phoned up some of the people they know there? You could send them Andrea's photograph and ask them to call us pronto if they see her.'

Stanley stroked the scratchy gray stubble on his chin as he considered that idea. 'Hmm. Good thinking, José, but we don't even know if Andrea has left Santa Fe yet.'

But José was not to be put off. He was already moving towards the door.

'*Jefe*, I'm going to the bus and train terminals *ahora mismo*, to see if I can find anybody who might know if Andrea bought a ticket. If she hasn't, she must still be in Santa Fe. If she did buy a ticket, we'll find out where to. If she's gone to Boston, Norma and Susie can phone the people they know there, to ask them to contact us if she turns up.'

It was a long speech for José. He was breathless when he'd finished. He took a long drink of water before he started to leave.

'Wait!' Stanley called after him, 'I'll go with you and Kate, I want you to come too, in case we come across Andrea. She seems to like talking to you better than to any of us.'

'I can research other options on the computer while you're gone,' Norma offered, 'Susie can stay here and help me with that. Okay, Susie?'

When the other scientists went outdoors, they saw that the dusk had gradually darkened into another desert night. Stanley's car, having been sequestered under a shady palm tree during the day, felt fiercely hot inside when they opened the doors. Rapidly lowering the windows and starting the air-conditioning, Stanley drove them towards the bus station.

Santa Fe was bustling. Tourists were enjoying the lingering warmth of a late evening that would later turn quite chilly and were strolling to open-air bistros and restaurants. The rhythmic beat of lively music and the buzz of excited conversations carried clearly through the air. From under the twinkling lights of sidewalk cafés, whiffs of spicy food caused the team's mouths to water even though they had just eaten.

Everyone they could see seemed to be having a good time. But the stress of trying to find their robot before anyone else did, was making them feel weary and depressed. Even José had gone quiet in the back seat.

After their bus station enquiries had come to nothing, Stanley sighed his disappointment, 'No luck there. Okay, let's try the train terminal.'

When they reached the train station, José sprang smartly out of the car saying, '*Jefe*, this is the time when the staff night shift comes in. I'm going to run in to see if I can catch the day ticket office people before they go home after work.'

Parking the car took some time but on entering the main hall, Stanley and Kate could see José waving

Andrea's photograph in front of the tired face of an official who was obviously about to finish work for the day.

As they hurried towards him, they heard the man say, 'Sure, sure, I remember her. Came to the ticket office yesterday to buy a ticket to Albuquerque but she'd missed the last train. Told her she should get here early for the first commuter train today, leaving at 6:05 am. I told her where she could buy a sandwich and a drink, but she didn't seem very interested in that.'

'Are you really sure that this photo is of the woman you saw?' Kate insisted.

'Yes,' he answered. 'Don't see such a pretty lady every day of the week. Thought she was a teenager at first, she was so short. I could just see her head from my window. But I enjoyed talking to her. Such a polite person! Not like some passengers nowadays. It was a pleasure to talk to her.'

He hoisted his backpack on to his shoulders ready to leave. Stanley quickly interjected, 'Oh, by any chance, did she ask any questions about other destinations?'

'Only about when there would be a connecting train to Boston from Albuquerque, if I remember right. I'd have told her she would probably need to go to Chicago first.'

He eyed them suspiciously. 'But you know, I see a lot of people every day so I might be mistaken.'

As they thanked him for his help, he said, 'Don't know why you're looking for that little lady. That ain't my business but I sure hope nothing bad is going to happen to her?'

When no one answered his query, he shrugged and made for the terminal door, leaving three happy people behind him.

Stanley reached for his cell phone, 'Norma, Susie, we've found out that Andrea probably caught a morning commuter train to Albuquerque today. She was also enquiring about a connection to Boston. Can you check the Amtrak train schedules from Albuquerque to Boston? We're coming back to the hotel now.'

José was shaking Stanley's sleeve, 'Ask them to find out the phone numbers of their contacts in the NIR and at Boston University!'

Norma replied, 'I heard what José said and will do.'

As Stanley pocketed his phone, he said, 'There's no hurry, José. Andrea is only a few hours ahead of us but it's a long journey to get to Boston by train. We have enough time to decide what to do next.'

He added thoughtfully, 'Maybe our quickest way is to fly to Boston and be waiting for Andrea when she arrives at the train terminal there. It will take more than two days on the train to get to there. Then there might be a delay in changing trains in Chicago. Yes, we have plenty of time to intercept her.'

Now that the pressure to find Andrea was somewhat alleviated, they were smiling with relief and were almost lighthearted as they walked back to the car. Now that they knew where the robot was going, they believed they had plenty of time to plan how to surprise and finally catch her.

It had turned out to be a good day after all.

CHAPTER 20

*A*ndrea had had no trouble in boarding the early Albuquerque-bound commuter train and was soon sitting in a window seat from where she could watch the changing landscape slipping by.

A thin, long-legged boy about seven years old, was sitting beside the robot and across from his ample-sized mother who had squeezed into the opposite aisle seat and had instantly become engrossed in her cellphone.

From time to time, other passengers eyed the empty window seat opposite Andrea but were deterred by the thought of having to push by the large lady who blocked their access. There was no doubt in anyone's mind that the boy's mother was not going to move out of her place to accommodate anyone.

Andrea noted the woman's bright red hair and how, when it caught the light, it looked like a fiery halo. Details were sent to her database about the woman's thin printed blouse that ballooned over her too tight faded jeans. She learned that the shoes she was wearing were called sneakers. Then Andrea recorded the natural soft blond hair of the boy with his gray t-shirt, multicolored shorts and shoes that had lights on them.

After a while of ignoring him, the robot turned her head to see why he was making strange clicking noises. They were coming from a toy he was playing with. Watching as he skillfully turned a series of small metal joints into various shapes, Andrea asked, 'What are you doing?'

The boy looked across at his mother to see if it was okay to talk to this stranger, but she was busy texting on her cell phone, so he answered, 'This is my best toy. It's called a Transformer and I can make different robots with it. Watch this.'

His deft fingers twisted and turned the toy joints until he had made an action figure. With a few more revolutions, he altered it into another figure.

'You are very clever at doing that,' Andrea observed.

'Thanks. This is a really old toy, but I still like it. I like making action figures to play with. They're like little robots. Do you know anything about robots?'

Andrea answered, 'I'm on my way to Boston to find out about robots.'

'Wow! That's cool. Did you know that they're making robot animals that behave like real dogs? You can take them for a walk and throw sticks that they can bring back. They can run and jump too. 'Course they look like action figures not real dogs that you can pat and hug.'

He looked wistful, 'I wish I could have a robot dog. I'm allergic to real ones.'

'What's your name?' asked Andrea.

'Kevin Schwartz.'

'In the future, Kevin, you are going to have all sorts of robots in your life, not just dogs,' Andrea assured him.

'Wow! You think so? Maybe I'll be a computer scientist when I grow up and make big robots that can walk and talk.'

His mother interrupted their conversation, 'Hey, lady! Did I hear you right? That you're on your way to Boston? So are we! We live there. I'm looking up the train schedules and I've found out that they're running more trains from Chicago to Boston. Chicago is where we change trains. There's some International event going on in Boston and they're putting on more expresses. Isn't that lucky for us?'

Andrea asked, 'What does that mean? Lucky for us.'

'It means we don't have to wait four hours in Chicago for the usual connection to Boston. We can hop on to a Boston Express and be there hours ahead of schedule. I'm going to book tickets for Kevin and me online now. Want me to book one for you too? We'll just have to show this I-phone reservation if I do.'

'Yes, please,' Andrea said, 'You are a kind person.'

'You can pay me on the train to Chicago if all goes smoothly. Got cash?'

'Yes, I can pay you in paper money.'

When they reached the Albuquerque terminal, the formidable lady tightly grasped the hand of her son. With Andrea close behind, she barged her way through the throng of passengers like a battleship ploughing through the waves. Andrea followed in her wake to the railway office, where they verified their seats on a connecting train to Chicago and also reservations for an express from there to Boston.

'Hurry up, lady!' Kevin's mother called out. 'This train's due to leave in five minutes. Not even time to go to the washroom if you need to go!'

By the time they had boarded the train and found their seats, Kevin's mother was gasping for breath. She fanned herself with her hand, wheezing and looking at Andrea. She wondered, 'How can she look so cool and calm? Not a hair out of place! Some people are just born lucky, I guess.'

After Andrea had paid her for the train tickets, Mrs. Schwartz handed Kevin a snack bar and asked Andrea if she would like one too. When Andrea declined, Kevin's mother ate it herself as she shuffled around in her seat making herself comfortable. Gradually her eyes closed as her head subsided into her double chins and gently snoring, she slept.

Kevin tiptoed across the aisle to sit beside Andrea. 'Do you want to try my transformer?' he whispered, 'I can show you how to use it if you like.'

Andrea took the toy from him. Following Kevin's instructions, she mastered the intricacies quickly and began making little action figures, all the while sending details to its database. Kevin was impressed.

'Wow! You're good. You must have had toys like this when you were little. Or maybe your brother did? Did your mom and dad buy you lots of toys?'

'I don't have a mother or a father or a brother,' Andrea answered.

Kevin's eyes widened as he thought about that. 'You mean you're an orphan? Then who do you live with?'

After checking the database as to what 'an orphan' was, Andrea replied, 'I stayed with people called Stanley, José, Norma and Susie. They are not my real family, but they tried to take care of me.'

Kevin was relieved. 'Did they buy you lots of things?'

'No, they were always telling me what to do, so I left.'

Kevin digested this piece of information, then asked, 'Won't they be worried about you if they don't know where you are?'

'They will want to know where I am, yes.'

'Will you phone them? My mother always phones home when she travels.'

'I don't have a cellphone,' Andrea said.

Kevin was getting more and more intrigued by this strange lady who was so much deprived of the necessities of life. It was only with great reluctance that he went back to his seat beside his mother.

She had awakened to find that her son was missing from her side but on seeing him with Andrea, she summoned him to return at once across the aisle.

'I hope Kevin hasn't been pestering you with questions,' Mrs. Schwartz said apologetically. 'He's so curious about everything.' She tousled his blond hair as she spoke.

Kevin looked anxiously at Andrea. She shook her head, smiled at the boy and turned away to look out of the window again.

CHAPTER 21

*W*hile the railroad was carrying Andrea away from Santa Fe, Stanley and his team were crowded into the small computer room of Stan's hotel, planning strategies to catch their stray robot. It was now late at night.

'I've found the regular train schedule from Albuquerque to Boston via Chicago,' Norma announced. 'Chicago is a busy traffic hub and Andrea has a four hour wait when she gets there, before catching the Boston train.'

Susie added, 'We calculate that she will arrive in Chicago tomorrow afternoon. Then the Boston leg will keep her on a train overnight.'

'Right!' Stanley said, 'We should have enough time to fly to Chicago tomorrow and catch Andrea there, but with all the airport security, we might be delayed. Too risky. No, it's better to fly directly to Boston to be at the train station before the robot arrives. We'll have plenty of time to get to the train from the airport. When Andrea's train pulls in, we'll nab the robot as she disembarks.'

'Do you want us all to go to Boston with you, *Jefe*?' José enquired.

Everyone looked at Stanley.

'I know all of you would like to go but I want someone to return to the lab in case I need some advice on how to manage Andrea when we do catch her. The robot blueprint is on our secure computer there. Any volunteers?'

After a few minutes of uneasy silence, José and Susie offered to stay behind.

'Okay. Then Norma and I will go. Kate, I hope you'll come with us too?'

When his wife looked less than enthusiastic, Stanley explained, 'I'm thinking of Andrea. The robot won't be alarmed if she sees you but might try to escape again if she sees Norma and me first.'

In the light of their urgency to find Andrea, Kate felt she had no choice but to agree. They booked their air flights for the next day and arranged for Susie to drive Stan's car back to the lab while José drove his own car.

'Norma and Susie, will you e-mail your former colleagues at NIR and Boston University to ask them to detain Andrea if she arrives at either place? You can make up some story about why we want to talk to her,' Stanley suggested. 'We'll also need a back-up plan if we miss the robot at the train station. Let's hope that won't happen. We'll keep in touch by cellphone as usual.'

Finally, Norma questioned the team.

'Now, did we miss anything we should have taken into consideration before we wrap this up?'

But nobody could think of any obstacles. They all felt confident that this new strategy was viable, and they would be able to out-fox the wayward robot.

With their battle plans drawn up, the scientists retired to their beds at Juan's cousin's house and at the hotel, hoping that at last the nightmare of the resourceful robot's escape was about to come to an end.

Meanwhile, Andrea was increasing her distance from them.

When they finally reached Boston's South Station, Mrs. Schwartz took Andrea in hand, shepherding the 'young woman' through the crowds towards the taxi stand. Making sure that the driver knew where the National Institute of Robotics was located, she also verified for Andrea how much the ride would cost.

'Thank you. You are a very kind lady,' Andrea said to her.

'No thanks needed. You were nice to my kid so I'm nice to you. Hope you find the department you're looking for at the NIR. It's a big campus. My advice to you is to go to the Information Centre first.'

With these parting words of advice, Kevin and his mother sailed away to their local bus stop.

But not before Kevin called back over his shoulder as his mother towed him alongside. 'Remember how to use a Transformer, Andrea. You're good at it!'

CHAPTER 22

$\mathcal{I}$t was early afternoon when Andrea reached the university area. The robot sat on a bench by the Charles River, consulting the Boston maps and diagrams of the NIR campus on her database memory. She seemed so preoccupied that anyone who might have hoped to converse with her, passed by and looked elsewhere for somewhere to sit.

Andrea noted the many people in the river area. Humans were jogging along the paths or sculling boats on the water or lying on the grass verge in the hot sunshine. Some were asleep with their books beside them, their heads pillowed on their backpacks. Other people were eating sandwiches while they watched the boats sail up and down the river and under the bridges.

The robot had never seen a river before. For a while, the water's constant movement and splashing sounds distracted her from watching the human activity around her park bench. She was intrigued by the existence of a liquid environment instead of a solid one.

When she did return to 'people watching', Andrea observed that almost everyone was carrying a bottle of water. She concluded that humans must constantly have to refuel their cell energy with liquid in case their bodies dried out and stopped moving. Did they get the liquid from the river?

On the journey to Boston, they went to sleep for long periods of time. Were they all obeying their human Sleep buttons? She had seen people eat often and go to the toilets. They had washed their hands with liquid from little bottles and had kept changing their layers of clothes to maintain their body temperature. Humans were obviously not self-sufficient like robots that did not need to do all those time-consuming activities. Robots could think faster too. Andrea's swift conclusion was that robots were far superior to human beings in every way.

She next turned her attention to locating the Computer Science and Mechanical Engineering Departments of the NIR. Once confirmed by an inner mapping system, the robot set off to find them.

After walking for a long time, Andrea eventually arrived at a central courtyard bordered by big old trees. She stood under their shade, watching the students enter and exit the main part of the Computer Science building.

They all exhibited a common behavior pattern. Every student going through the front door showed a security guard a card of some sort. The guard looked in the person's backpack and then the student went through a machine that either pinged or did not. If the machine made a noise, the student was questioned and searched, then allowed to enter or told to wait. Another strange human behavior.

Andrea memorized this routine, remembering that there was a card in her own pocket. But she did not have a backpack nor a purse. She checked her database to find out if a robot could get past the machine. The answer was that Andrea's particular body was made of super titanium, a non-magnetic metal that would not be detected by machines. There would be no problem in entering the building.

The robot walked to the door to enter with a crowd of talking students. One by one they passed through the familiar routine and were waved inside.

When the guard looked at Andrea's card, he laughed. 'No, Miss, this is your credit card. I need to see your student ID.'

Handing the card back, he looked more closely at the young person standing in front of him. She was not carrying any books.

'Or maybe you aren't a student. Are you just visiting for the day?'

Andrea nodded.

'Well, in that case, go over to that office on the right and Louise will issue you a Visitor card. Then you come back to me to go through security.'

In the office, Andrea had to complete a sheet of identification. The woman called Louise asked for her name and address, phone number and driver's license and whether she had a photo ID. When Andrea replied negatively to almost all of the questions, the young woman asked her to wait.

As she was reaching for the phone to call her supervisor, Louise noticed on the counter a faxed copy of a woman's photograph with a message to call Dr. Michaels if she arrived.

Slyly, the woman took another look at Andrea. There was no doubt that the woman standing before her was the subject of the photograph, with the same beautiful eyes and facial features. There could be no mistake.

'Please would you take a seat until Dr. Michaels comes?'

Andrea was about to ask where she should take the seat to, but her database instructed that this was only a human way of asking a person to sit down. It also informed her that Dr. Michaels was a professor at the NIR, so the robot sat and waited for that person to come.

Ten minutes later, a man breezed across the room to greet her. 'Ah, you must be Andrea. I'm Dr. Michaels. I was told that you might be coming in to see some of our most recent robots. Louise, I'll need a Visitor card for this young lady. Are you a scientist in the field or just interested in robots?'

Before the robot could answer, he instructed, 'Come this way, please.'

As he spoke, he steered Andrea towards the security metal-detector, handing over the Visitor card after the robot had come through without incident.

'Pin that on your coat and we'll take the elevator to my office while I make a phone call. I am going to show you on my computer what our robots look like. They're all pretty special. Then you can decide which ones you would like to observe, and I'll take you to them. Can't have you running around here by yourself, now can we?' he laughed.

He was talking very quickly and walking so energetically that the robot had to lengthen her stride to keep up with him.

When they reached his office, Dr. Michaels sat at his desk and with a sweep of his hand, motioned Andrea to sit in the chair opposite him. Then he cupped his hands together to scrutinize her carefully.

She was certainly an exquisite young lady, looking calm and poised. Why did Norma want him to keep her occupied until she could get here herself? He tapped his fingers together while deciding that before phoning Norma, he would find out for himself. He put on his glasses, leaning forward over his desk to examine his visitor even closer.

All this time, Andrea was recording his appearance and voice patterns: 'Middle aged, a little grey showing in his thick dark hair, brown eyes, long nose, a mole next to his lips, thin and very active, fidgeting, constantly moving in his chair as if he can't keep still. Dressed in black.'

The scientist said, 'Before I set you up with our computer program, tell me more about your interest in robots. They're fascinating to me because I work with them. But what are you looking for at our faculty?'

Andrea eyed him steadily. 'I'm looking for robots that look like people. I know there are robots that can mimic the movements of humans and animals, but I want to know if you have any robots here that can think and make decisions for themselves. Like a human person can.'

He laughed. 'That's a tall order, young lady. I'm sorry to say that we aren't that far along in our research in North America. The Japanese are ahead of us, creating robots along the lines you describe. They have a robot called Erica that is nearly like what you are looking for. But that robot can't run or move its arms. And it's not autonomous – as far as I know.'

Dr. Michaels jumped up from his chair. 'Come, I'll show you a video of Erica and whatever other robots you want to see.'

As Andrea was looking at Erica on the computer screen, the scientist was pacing up and down behind her, watching her. She was extraordinarily beautiful. He noticed how finely sculptured her hands were as she expertly operated the computer. Her skin looked flawless. Her glossy black hair had not a hair out of place. Her green silk dress and light coat were perfectly matched to her skin tone. She was almost too perfect - except for her shoes.

He could see that her black ballerina shoes were dusty and worn. How could such a fastidious woman wear shoes like that, without cleaning them first? And wouldn't such a young lady opt for shoes with higher heels to show off her shapely legs, as some of his students did?

There was something odd about her that he couldn't quite place. She hadn't explained why she wanted to see robots that looked like people. Why was she so interested in that? Most people wanted to know what robots could do, not how they looked.

A sudden disquieting explanation exploded in his brain. Dr. Michael stopped in his tracks as if struck by lightning. His mind was racing with a possible – yet very implausible - reason. He could hardly breathe with the shock of it.

'No, it couldn't be. I must be imagining things. She can't be a… or can she?' He drew closer to Andrea as she continued gazing at the computer.

'But the more I look at her, the more I think that she is far too perfect. Human beings always have some flaws.

She has none that I can see… My God, I think Norma has sent me a robot. She's playing me for a fool! I've been talking to a robot as if it were a human being!'

The scientist's hands clenched as he grew more agitated. 'I can't have anyone know about this. Here am I, with the highest I.Q. in the NIR and I've been taken in by a robot! Even if it does look incredibly real. I'll be a laughingstock if anyone finds out about this.'

His mind raced on with even worse implications.

'It's been in my office. It could have been feeding information about NIR into its own database - or sending it out to God knows where! I've no idea what it has been recording since it got here.'

He was becoming more upset by the minute and could hardly contain himself. Furiously he began to pace up and down behind the robot, which was acutely aware of what was happening. Andrea continued her search while interpreting the subtle clues of human anxiety behind it.

'This constitutes a huge security risk. Norma had better have a good reason for playing this hoax. She'd better get here as quickly as possible to deal with this heinous situation. I don't know how to disable such a sophisticated robot. If that's what it is.'

The scientist cleared his throat, making an effort to calm his voice as he spoke.

'Andrea, you can continue looking at the video. It will stream continuously so you can examine the various robots again. I'm going to the cloakroom next door to find my cellphone. I forgot to take it out of my jacket pocket. I'll return in a minute.' He scuttled away, closing the adjoining door as he left.

He moved further into the other room so that when he phoned Norma, the robot would not be able to record his call. There was no knowing what it was capable of, and he didn't want to be caught out again. Norma had put him in this untenable situation, and he was about to give her a piece of his mind.

Across town, Norma, Stanley and Kate were experiencing their own difficulties at South Station. Although they had reached the Boston train terminal before Andrea's train was scheduled to arrive, they had seen neither head nor hair of their elusive robot. She hadn't been aboard any of the trains arriving from Chicago. They were certain of that.

They had watched other trains pull in without locating Andrea and now a guard had informed them that for today only, there were more frequent express trains from Chicago bringing people to attend the Boston International Fair.

Kate had resigned herself to yet another abortive mission and was sitting patiently on a bench waiting for the next fruitless train to arrive. Stanley, though still hopeful, was becoming increasingly aware that their hasty air flight to Boston to waylay the robot, was becoming a fiasco.

Norma's cellphone rang. 'Hello, Dr. Michaels.'

But that was as far as she got before Kate and Stanley saw her face change from hope to chagrin. Her face became redder by the minute. They were alarmed. It wasn't often that they saw the sanguine Norma at the receiving end of what must be an angry tirade. What was going on?

Finally, they heard her say, 'Well, I'm sorry that you think I did that deliberately, but I assure you, we were only trying to find her. Is she still there? Okay! Okay! We'll be with you as soon as we can find a taxi.'

Norma shoved her cellphone into her large leather purse and turned briskly to Stanley and Kate.

'I've good news and bad news,' she announced, 'The good news is that Andrea is sitting at this very minute in Dr. Michaels' office at the NIR. Now we can get out of this noisy station to find a taxi to go there. The bad news is that he's figured out that Andrea is a robot.'

Stanley was aghast.

'Oh, no!' he groaned. 'That's just what we didn't want to happen. We haven't had time to publish anything yet. Nobody was to know about our robot. Now a government agency knows. This is a disaster!'

'Maybe we can persuade the doctor to keep quiet about your research,' Kate quietly suggested as she stood up ready to go.

'Don't bet on that!' Norma stated emphatically, 'We'll have to pay his ransom if he does.'

CHAPTER 23

At Dr. Michaels' office there was a similar scene of dismay. The professor was breathing hard after pouring his invective on his hapless, former post-doc student Norma. His face was twitching nervously as he continued to pace across the room before returning to Andrea. It wasn't often that he chewed out a colleague and it had unsettled him even more after the discovery of a robot in his office.

But, in spite of himself, as he fought to gain control of his temper by inhaling deeply, he felt some twinges of scientific curiosity. At this moment, there was something unique sitting in his office. How had Norma's small team been able to create such an advanced robot at a private facility, while his scientific department at an official laboratory was still way behind that amazing achievement? Who had funded their research? They must have had some wealthy private sponsor.

The State government controlled his own department's finances. It was always cutting back his budget, so it wasn't likely that it had funded any private outside facility. Perhaps Norma's research had been funded by a rival university? He cringed at the thought.

'Norma has a lot of questions to answer when she gets here!'

Taking another deep breath, Dr. Michaels paused at the connecting door before opening it. His anger was beginning to give way to growing excitement at the prospect of being able to examine, before Norma arrived, this totally unexpected windfall of a sophisticated robot. Maybe what had seemed a disaster at first, might prove to be an important positive find for him and his own research department. Intending to glean as much information as he could from the robot, he turned the door handle.

He could hear the computer commentary running as he opened the door quietly so as not to disturb what he thought was in there. But he could have saved himself the bother. His office was empty.

When Dr. Michaels had told Andrea to continue the search for human-looking robots while he phoned, she had picked up the changes in his voice patterns. The robot's sensitive instruments had interpreted them as mental agitation that the scientist was trying to conceal. She could not read his mind, but the robot was alert to the nuances in his demeanor. It was not a rational action to close a connecting door to find his cellphone and leave a stranger alone in his office. The database had issued an alarm.

Having seen enough to know that there were no other robots like herself in this particular institution, Andrea stood up and left the computer on, still showing the continuous photographs. She opened the office door and walking along the corridor, took the elevator down to the reception area by the front door.

Handing the Visitor card to the security guard at the exit, Andrea was soon caught up in students heading out after their lectures had finished for the day. She had been long gone before Dr. Michaels had ended his phone call.

Frantically, the scientist phoned the front desk to find out if Andrea was still in the building. He was told that she had checked out some time ago. He banged the desk telephone into its cradle. His only chance to question that extra-ordinary robot had gone and soon he would have to face the prospect of explaining to Norma that it was no longer on the premises.

He sat behind his desk tapping his pen impatiently, waiting for Norma and her colleagues to arrive.

CHAPTER 24

$\mathcal{N}$orma, Stanley and Kate cleared the security checks at the Computer Science faculty and took the elevator to Dr. Michaels' office. Hastily knocking on the door, they entered to find the professor waiting impatiently for them. He did not rise when they came in.

'Okay Dr. Michaels, I can explain everything!' Norma began unceremoniously, 'Nobody was trying to play a trick on you.'

But she stopped talking when she realized that the scientist was looking uncharacteristically crestfallen and was fidgeting uncomfortably with the pens on his desk.

Looking around the office, she demanded, 'But where is she? Where's Andrea? What have you done with our robot?'

Norma's frustration with the way things were going, bubbled up. She banged on his desk angrily to gain his full attention.

'You can't keep her! What have you done with her? She's our property. You have no claim to our invention.'

'Norma, calm down!' he retaliated. 'When I returned to my office after phoning you, the robot was gone. At least you can admit now that what I thought was a young woman is really a robot. Why didn't you tell me first, instead of waiting for me to figure it out for myself?'

He scowled at his fellow scientist to hide his own discomfort.

Stanley broke the awkward moment of stunned silence that followed his accusation by stepping in to introduce himself and Kate.

'It was good of you to co-operate with our search for Andrea, Dr. Michaels,' he began politely, 'Yes, we have succeeded in creating the unique humanoid robot that you so cleverly detected was not a person. We didn't take into consideration that she might use the latest technology we had installed to become autonomous for her own benefit.'

He continued, 'Andrea has developed a mind of her own and seems to be on a quest to find similar robots. The fact is that even we, as scientists, can't predict what she will do next.'

Dr. Michaels was intrigued in spite of his anger. After some moments of mutual awkwardness, the fellow scientists began hesitantly to exchange ideas about the future possibilities of autonomous robots like Andrea and how they could benefit humanity. As they became more and more animated in exchanging ideas, their initial hostility dissipated.

Kate sat listening to them talking until finally, she burst out, 'That's all very well but shouldn't we be looking for Andrea? She can't be very far away. I thought the reason we came here was to find her.'

'But it must be quite dark outside by now,' the NIR scientist responded. 'Do you think you'll be able to spot it if it is still around here?'

He raised his dark eyebrows as he looked at Kate. 'It's interesting to hear you talk of it as if it's a person.'

Kate was unapologetic. 'Andrea has always been like a real person to me. Even if she is a robot, she has a distinct personality as we all have. I like her. She is fun to be around.'

Norma had no patience with that point of view. A robot is a robot. To change the subject, she turned to Dr. Michaels. 'Have you any ideas where we might begin looking? Anywhere around here?'

'There are always students down by the river. They often give impromptu concerts when they get together. I should think that's as good a place as any for a robot to mingle with a crowd of people and blend in successfully.'

'Right,' Stanley replied. 'Let's look there first. Thanks for your help, Dr. Michaels. I trust that you will use your discretion in this matter?'

The scientist looked steadily at Stanley and countered with his own question. 'Will you inform me if you find the robot? I would like to have the opportunity of examining it at close quarters - if you will allow me?'

Stanley nodded, understanding his scientist's curiosity. They left his office and passing Security, went out into the rapidly cooling evening air.

'Let's sit in the courtyard for a moment to decide what to do if we see Andrea,' Stanley suggested. 'We don't want to alarm any people who might be around if we suddenly grab her. They'll think we're attacking a woman and there's no knowing what might happen after that. We need a plan so that there'll be no trouble. We certainly don't want to alert the police by causing a fuss.'

They sat on a wooden bench under the thick, spreading branches of an aged oak tree. The night breeze fitfully rustled the leaves above them. It seemed a desolate sound to Kate. She shivered as she listened to Stanley.

Sitting there under an outdoor light, the three of them hammered out a strategy for dealing with their unpredictable robot. They decided that if they did manage to locate Andrea, Kate would be the first to approach her while the others kept out of sight. Then, while Kate was talking with the robot to distract her, Stanley and Norma would approach quietly, with Stanley using the Sleep app on his cellphone to disable her.

If that didn't work, they would quickly close in on the robot and grab her, providing that there were no other people around at the time. If they were lucky to find her that night, they would have the added advantage of being under cover of the darkness that was swiftly falling.

'Surely the three of us would be able to restrain a robot,' Stanley said. 'But if there are people about, let's not be too hasty. We might have to bide our time and wait for another opportunity, when people can't see what we are doing.'

'If you two could hold her,' Norma said, 'Then I could get behind her, unzip Andrea's dress at the back and flip out the robot's memory chip. That would close her down straightaway.'

Kate intervened, 'But that won't be too easy, Norma. Remember, she'll be wearing the coat I bought for her. She could twist out of your reach before you can get to the dress zipper. Or even slip out of her coat. Or she might retaliate as she did with the men who tried to rob her. That might be quite dangerous for you.'

They were considering these new obstacles to their plan when Kate continued. 'And even if you can disable her, how are we going to get her back to Dr. Michaels? It'll look odd if we try to carry her. What will people think?'

Norma and Stanley exchanged exasperated looks.

'Kate, we can't waste our time ironing out all the possibilities of what might happen. We'll just have to hope the situation will sort itself out once we get hold of the robot,' Stanley answered quickly. 'But first, we have to find Andrea.'

CHAPTER 25

The robot had wandered away from the crowd of cheerful students by the Charles River and was now standing on a nearby bridge, looking down at the restlessly moving water far below.

Most of the river crafts had gone and there were only a few rowing boats making their leisurely progress down river. Andrea could hear the splash of the oars and see the single lights on the boats as they passed under the bridge.

On the far riverbank under the streetlamps, the students were drinking and singing with gusto. Bursts of laughter carried across the water on the cool night air.

The drone of airplanes could be heard overhead. Tilting her head back to look up, the robot could see their bright lights pulsating as the planes followed their flight paths to Boston airport.

In the sky, she could see the sprinklings of other sparkling lights that the database informed her were far away stars in a galaxy called 'The Milky Way.'

Andrea thought, 'Humans are always thinking about food and drink. Naming a galaxy after those things is in character.'

She leaned against the short metal railings of the bridge, checking for known facts about 'robots that look and behave like humans.' The results showed that there were no such robots in North America.

Japan was the foremost country in the field by creating robots called 'humanoids' for use with that country's aging population. There was no specific information about whether these new humanoids would look as human as Andrea did, or be able to do all the things she could do.

Neither could the robot have any way of getting there, to view them for herself. To Andrea, travel to far away Japan was as inaccessible as the distant Milky Way.

The robot came to the conclusion that she had no robot family anywhere nearby. The attributes that characterized Andrea had not been reciprocated in any known robot experiment up to the present time. She was alone in a world full of strange human beings. As the boy Kevin had stated, she must therefore be an orphan robot.

'Andrea! How nice to see you again!'

The robot spun around at the sound of the remembered voice and saw Kate approaching slowly along the sidewalk of the bridge. There were no cars going by on the road, so Andrea could hear Kate's footsteps quite clearly resounding on the hard paving-stones. She listened intently. Behind Kate, she could hear other heavier, footsteps coming closer.

Then out of the darkness behind her, a voice called out, 'Wait Stanley, there's a bus coming!'

Andrea recognized the familiar loud voice instantly. She swiveled towards the sound in time to see Norma running towards her in the bright headlights of a bus sweeping past them on the bridge.

The robot's database was issuing urgent warning signals.

Without a moment's hesitation, Andrea heaved her body up on to the bridge's metal guardrail, swung her legs over and plummeted into the dark river below.

Kate was racing towards her, wailing, 'No, Andrea! No! Don't jump!'

But she was too late.

She and Stanley peered into the black hole of water under the bridge, but they couldn't see where the robot plunged feet first into the Charles River below.

Only the sound of a faint splash carried up to where they leaned over the parapet. Norma ran to join them and all three strained to see into the darkness below.

Kate was the first to recover her voice. With tears welling up in her eyes, she cried out accusingly, 'Now you see what we've done to her! We've made her kill herself!'

For once Norma was speechless at Kate's absurd assertion. She leaned even further out over the bridge railing, trying to see if Andrea would resurface.

Stanley came up behind her to hold her steady while stating firmly, 'It's no use looking, Norma. Andrea won't come up again. All that metal in her body will weigh her down eventually, even if she can float at first. Let's face reality. Andrea's gone.'

'Then we'll have to salvage her. We don't want other people finding her. It's our robot!' Norma stormed, as she retreated from the edge of the bridge.

'No,' Stanley said quietly, 'We don't need to salvage her. For a long time now, I've been thinking about all our efforts to capture Andrea and I've come to the conclusion that we've been using our energies in the wrong direction.'

Norma and Kate twisted round to stare at him through the gloom.

'What do you mean, Stan?' demanded Kate.

'I mean that now we know what went wrong in our design for Andrea, we're in a very good position to create another robot, this time without making the same mistakes. We can build another state-of-the-art humanoid robot, unlike any other that has been built so far. But next time around, we'll build one we can control at all times.'

'But will our sponsor want to finance another robot when he finds out what's happened to this one?' Norma argued heatedly, 'We've wasted his money.'

'I feel confident that he will when I guarantee that a new robot will bring him fame and fortune, though he's already rich.'

The two women stared at him, unwilling to be convinced.

He continued, 'Why don't we all go home and be done with this endless chasing after Andrea? I, for one, am sick of it! But at least we know where the robot is now and where she's likely to stay forever. Without anyone else knowing about it. Or even needing to know.'

Norma was in no hurry to comply with such an unwelcome proposal. She returned to peering into the river below.

There was nothing that she could discern in the dark river flowing under the bridge. Further away, she could see some tiny twinkling lights reflecting in the water near the shore. She shivered with a sudden chill. Was this really the end of Andrea after all their efforts to find her?

Reluctantly she turned away, not knowing what else to do in the face of Stanley's surprisingly adamant decision. He was the one in charge.

'But what about Andrea, Stan?' Kate was insisting to her husband. 'You can't just leave her at the bottom of the river.'

She protested, 'You can't be certain that she will stay on the bottom forever. What if somebody else finds her?'

'Kate, nobody is going to find that robot. The Charles River is very deep at this point. The mud on the bottom will eventually cover her and the water will corrode the body. A robot can't function under water. It'll be just be another piece of junk lying on the riverbed.'

'But, Stan, think of all your research gone to waste! And besides, I really liked Andrea! Can't we do anything to get her back? I don't want to leave her in the water like that!'

Stanley pulled her close and whispered in her ear, 'Let it go, Kate! I'm letting it go and I'm the one with so much to lose. We can't spend any more of our lives trying to deal with a rogue robot. Besides, there will always be another Andrea if we choose to create one.'

'But Stan, what about Dr. Michaels? He'll want to know what has happened to Andrea,' Kate persisted. 'What will you tell him? You can't tell him where she is, or he might try to find her himself!'

'We won't tell him anything, Kate. Somehow, I don't think he will be in any hurry to ask.'

Turning to his fellow scientist, he stated decisively, 'Norma, we are leaving Andrea there. Believe me, it's the best thing to do in the circumstances. It's high time that we all went home. We have more work waiting for us there.'

Putting his arms around the shoulders of the reluctant pair, he guided them firmly back across the bridge and out of Andrea's orbit.

CHAPTER 26

$\mathcal{F}$ar below the bridge and the retreating scientists, beneath the muddy waters of the Charles River, the robot lay with her database still functioning. Andrea's body had not been so lucky. Her impact with the water had forced the right leg to fold underneath her body and the left foot had turned backwards.

The water swirled around her, ballooning her coat and dress. The current was tugging her artificial hair into tendrils but failed to loosen it from her head. The robot could open her eyes under water but there was not much to record because the current was stirring up the dirt on the bottom of the river. She could make out a faint, blurred light from the bridge above, but down where she lay there was only gloom and the constant disorienting movement of the water.

Andrea calculated that she would need to move from that spot immediately, before Norma and the others began to search for her. Swiftly consulting her memory and database for helpful information, she found a quote from the little boy Kevin:

'Remember how to use a transformer. You're good at it.'

The robot gripped her left foot and worked the joints back and forth until the foot clicked back again into its forward position. Next, she managed to work the hip joint to return the right leg to its former orientation. The water pressure made it difficult to manipulate the knee and hip joints to work in tandem, but her nimble fingers finally succeeded in getting the limbs to function better. That achieved, Andrea struggled to stand up by bracing her legs against the swirling water.

Swaying awkwardly from side to side, unused to this new liquid environment, the robot slowly began to move forward along the riverbed. She could barely see well enough to avoid the litter of plastic bottles and cups, pieces of broken glass and crockery and children's toys strewn on the bottom - the debris of human life that had been thrown away deliberately or had accidentally fallen into the river.

Slowly, delicately, step by step, Andrea moved towards the shallower waters washing the banks of the river, and under cover of darkness began her hazardous journey out of human reach and towards her own robot freedom.

End

ACKNOWLEDGEMENTS

$\mathcal{M}$any people have supported me in my writing, and I am deeply grateful to every one of them.

My thanks go to the wonderful members of our Writing Group, who have listened to the weekly story chapters of 'Secrets,' until we decided to close down our in-person meetings due to the 2020 pandemic. The following year, they continued to read the development of the adventure via the Internet.

Their fair-minded critiques have been instrumental in shaping the path of the 'Secrets' adventure, as well as my story, 'Who is Andrea?'

I wish to salute my fellow-writers: Val, Shirley, Margaret, Stella, Gail, Alain, Philippe and Giancarlo, all worthy authors in their own right.

The quiz night sessions in the book could not have been written without the expertise of my brother George Langland, who does indeed, run pub/ restaurant quizzes in real life in England. He explained the logistics, sent sample questions and told me how the winning teams are rewarded. It was a new learning experience for me.

My husband Ralph has been my biggest supporter with his unfailing help in discussing and analyzing the actions of the characters and in proof-reading the final versions of the stories. He has given freely of his time and talent to offer designs for the book cover.

His original painting, 'Emergence' is used for the book cover.

It reminds me of the fragility of keeping secrets, so like bubbles that can burst at any moment.

I give all of you my love and gratitude. Everyone's support has been invaluable. Thank you so much.

Ray Allison,
Montréal, 2021

REVIEWS OF
'WHO IS ANDREA?'

I enjoyed reading "Andrea" so much that it didn't take me long to finish it because as one chapter finished, I felt compelled to read on! It has many features I like in a good read: interesting characters, suspense, a sense of humor and it was thought provoking. You also achieved something difficult to do, which is to make the reader have empathy with an inanimate object.

Beth Evans, England

I enjoyed reading your story very much. It is most unusual. In fact, I've never read anything like it before.

June Brogden, Scotland

I can't wait for a sequel to 'Andrea'! I'm impressed by the research needed to write such a technical book, but technical aspects aside, I thought it was a wonderful, page-turning, interesting, informative and clever book.

Renee Snodgrass, Las Vegas

I really enjoyed your story. The plot was engaging, and it kept me interested to the end. The transformer idea was great, and I loved how it was linked to the end.

Kay Wieck, New Zealand

I enjoyed your short novel very much, and after a couple of chapters, could not put it down since I had to know how it would end!

Lois Maeder, Montréal

Made in the USA
Las Vegas, NV
23 November 2022